TARGET AND DESTROY

Tom Marcus, former MI5, grew up on the streets in the north of England. He joined the Army at sixteen and went on to become the youngest member of the Armed Forces to pass the six-month selection process for Special Operations in Northern Ireland.

He was hand-picked from the Army into MI5 as a Surveillance Officer. He left the Security Service after a decade on the frontline protecting his country due to being diagnosed with PTSD.

An extraordinary battle and recovery took place which led Tom to write his first book, *Soldier Spy*, which has been vetted and cleared for publication by MI5. It's the first true ground-level account ever to be told and the first time in the Security Services' history a Surveillance Officer has told the real story of the fight on our streets. His debut book went straight to number one on the *Sunday Times* bestseller list.

Tom now consults on projects within TV and film including the TV dramatization of his book *Soldier Spy*. *Defend or Die* is his second novel, following on from *Capture or Kill*.

Due to the ongoing specific threat to Tom Marcus, MI5 insist he keep his identity hidden and he continues to work with the Security Service and other agencies to ensure he stays safe.

TARGET AND DESTROY

TOM MARCUS

PAN BOOKS

First published 2023 by Macmillan

This paperback edition first published 2023 by Pan Books
an imprint of Pan Macmillan
The Smithson, 6 Briset Street, London EC1M 5NR
EU representative: Macmillan Publishers Ireland Ltd, 1st Floor,
The Liffey Trust Centre, 117–126 Sheriff Street Upper,
Dublin 1, D01 YC43
Associated companies throughout the world
www.panmacmillan.com

ISBN 978-1-5290-6545-9

1 3 5 7 9 8 6 4 2

A CIP catalogue record for this book is available from the British Library.

Typeset in Janson by Palimpsest Book Production Limited,
Falkirk, Stirlingshire
Printed and bound by CPI Group (UK) Ltd, Croydon, CR0 4YY

Visit **www.panmacmillan.com** to read more about all our books
and to buy them. You will also find features, author interviews and
news of any author events, and you can sign up for e-newsletters
so that you're always first to hear about our new releases.

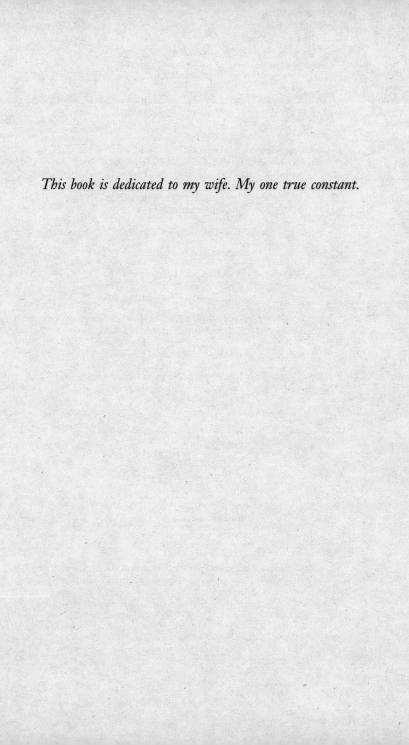

This book is dedicated to my wife. My one true constant.

TARGET
AND
DESTROY

1

Logan glanced at the clock on the top-of-the-range brushed-steel cooker and decided it was time for the evening performance. He got up from his stool at the black marble kitchen island, put his phone in his pocket and walked over to the floor-to-ceiling window overlooking the river. He stood there for a full minute, paying no attention at all to the stunning view.

'Here I am,' he said under his breath, 'if anyone's interested.'

Was there someone actually out there, checking to see if this luxurious penthouse flat was occupied? Logan's heart rate quickened fractionally as he imagined being in the cross hairs of a sniper's rifle. It was a peculiar feeling, trying to make himself as conspicuous as possible, when for all of his professional life he'd worked hard to be invisible, to go unnoticed: first as a surveillance officer for MI5, and then for Blindeye, the clandestine team of ex-intelligence operatives secretly tasked with doing the dirty jobs the official security services couldn't.

Still feeling uncomfortable at being so exposed, Logan

decided that was enough staring out of the window for one evening. Now it was time to move through the rest of the penthouse, opening and closing blinds, turning lights on and off, putting the integrated sound system through its paces or selecting a movie to play on the giant TV, all to make it clear to the watchers – if there were any – that someone was home. It was a shame that operating the cooker was beyond his competence, all that high-tech wizardry going to waste, but Logan wasn't going to risk pressing the wrong button and sending it all into meltdown for the sake of a fried-egg sandwich.

The clothes were another thing he didn't feel comfortable in. If anyone was having a proper look, not just content with clocking a silhouette, he had to look the part, which meant regular visits to the cavernous walk-in closet in the master bedroom, taking off his usual T-shirt, jeans and trainers and dressing up in something more suitable for a hedge-fund billionaire – or whatever the real owner of the penthouse was. It wasn't lost on Logan that some days that meant putting on another pair of jeans, another T-shirt and another pair of trainers, the only difference being that the new ensemble had cost several grand more than the one he'd just taken off. But maybe there was someone out there on the other end of a high-powered telescope who could spot the difference. As he knew from experience, it was all in the detail. And that was just as true whether you were trying to blend in with the wallpaper or make an exhibition of yourself.

All in all, though, despite the nightly game of charades, it wasn't a bad gig. The sleek minimalism of the place – no annoying clutter and every surface black, grey or some sort of muted off-white – made it feel more like a private hospital ward than someone's home, so Logan really never felt like an intruder – more like a nightwatchman in a cutting-edge tech company. Which was good. Logan wasn't ready to be somewhere that felt like a home yet – his own or anyone else's. It was more than a year since Sarah and Joseph had died, and the house they'd shared on the edge of the estate with the hills sloping up behind was the only place he ever wanted to think of as home. He'd never really had one as a kid himself, growing up mostly on the streets, and when Sarah and Joseph were taken from him, the idea of home went with them. Playing the part of someone who had a life and a place they called their own was as much as he could manage.

He went back to his stool at the kitchen island and picked up the scrap of paper lying next to his coffee cup, reading the numbers and letters of the licence plate over to himself again, even though he'd long ago memorized them. For the hundredth time, he thought about making the call, and for the hundredth time the same thing stopped him.

If he opened this door, there'd be no shutting it again, no matter what lay on the other side.

Instinctively he looked round, hoping to see Sarah perched on the stool next to him, brushing a strand of blonde hair from her face with a warm smile. Now, more than ever, he needed her to tell him what to do. But the stool remained unoccupied, as he half-knew it would be. The truth was, she hadn't appeared to him since he'd moved into the penthouse. Could it be something to do with the place itself? Was there something about it – too cold, too clinical? Did she just not like the decor? Was she afraid Joseph would get his muddy feet and sticky fingers all over the pristine surfaces?

He shook his head.

Don't be so fucking stupid. She's dead. She's not worried about the fucking furniture.

So why hadn't she appeared to him? For a moment he felt panic start to grip him. Had something happened to her? But what more *could* happen to dead people? Nothing worse than dying, surely.

'Oh, for fuck's sake,' he said aloud, his voice echoing off the bare walls.

Well, if Sarah wasn't going to come to the penthouse, he'd just have to go to her, to the one place he knew her spirit was always present.

The place where they'd buried her.

He looked at his watch. Not yet ten. He was supposed to stay in the apartment until eleven at least, showing his face at the windows, moving around, using all the facilities: the entertainment system, the gym, the sauna and jacuzzi, turn and turn about, making one-sided phone calls and having video conferences with non-existent people until it was time for bed. Sometimes he'd even put the TV on and sit in the big leather armchair with his eyes closed and noise-cancelling earbuds in for an hour.

But surely even reclusive billionaires went out sometimes. How much TV could they watch before going even crazier than they started out? And who the fuck was going to know anyway? Well, his employers were probably able to monitor the penthouse's electrical output, or had a direct connection to the computer that worked all the gizmos, so they could see exactly what he was doing.

But this was an emergency. He needed to go and see his dead wife. An hour there, less than an hour back at this time of night, and he'd put on an extra late show for the watchers when he got back, so no one could complain.

Can't say fairer than that, he thought.

Five minutes later, back in his normal clothes with a wind-breaker and a dark baseball cap, he was standing by the front door punching the various security codes into the keypad. He waited for the confirmation beep that told him he hadn't forgotten anything, opened the door and then shut it behind him with the pneumatic hiss of a giant freezer, feeling like one of the pyramid builders, sealing up the pharaoh's resting place behind him with a deadly curse upon would-be tomb robbers. Then he was padding down the empty corridor towards the lift that led directly down to the basement car park.

It was 11.05 when Logan drove slowly past the gates of the cemetery, his headlight beams picking out the heavy chain with its oversized padlock. He drove on for another fifty yards, then turned right down a badly lit lane hugging the cemetery wall, until he saw the twisted oak he'd noticed on his last visit. There weren't many houses here, where the cemetery wall blocked your sunlight and the view from the first-floor bedroom would be rows of depressing tombstones, but he knew there was a cluster of three houses a little further down the lane, hunkering down behind tall, thick hedges. He parked the car near enough to look like it belonged there, before walking back to the tree and standing for a moment to listen.

A little wind rustling the branches, the distant cry of an owl, a twig breaking on the other side of the wall as a fox or a badger nosed its way round. Nothing to suggest he wasn't alone. He turned the torch on his phone on for a few seconds to see where the hand and footholds were, then switched it off and put it back in his pocket. No problem. Three feet up, one of the bricks was broken and he wedged his right foot in the gap then braced himself against the trunk of the tree with his left foot and heaved himself up until his hand closed round a branch. Pulling himself upwards he swung a leg over the wall, careful to avoid the shards of broken glass decorating the top, then the other leg, then let go, landing softly on a leaf-covered bank on the other side.

He brushed himself off, making sure he hadn't snagged any of the glass and looked around, listening again for any sounds that didn't belong in a cemetery at night. Given how easy it was to scale the wall, he wouldn't have been surprised to bump into a few teenagers after the thrill of a quickie on top of a tombstone or just looking for somewhere to share a bottle of vodka and a smoke without getting hassled, but everything seemed to be quiet. He made a quick sweep with the phone torch to get his bearings. There was a neat row of marble gravestones in front of him, with a path a few yards to his right, winding between the plots. That, he knew, would take him to the main path that led from the entrance through the middle of the cemetery and from there he'd have his bearings. He turned off the torch and started walking.

Fifteen minutes later, after picking up the main path and then taking a branch off to the right when he came to a statue of a weeping angel leaning over a sarcophagus, he approached the section of newer graves where Sarah and Joseph had been laid to rest. He was ashamed to say that he'd been in no fit state to choose what kind of headstone he wanted for them. In the depths of his alcohol-numbed grief after the crazed knife attack that took them, it had seemed the most stupid, pointless question in the world. But Alex, bless her, had done the right thing, as usual, and the mottled-grey marble with the beloved names and the heart-breaking dates was just right. Here was someone, it seemed to say, who was much loved but didn't want any fuss, which was Sarah down to a tee.

He knelt down and brushed the dirt from the stone. The little spray of flowers he'd left on his last visit now looked more like a bunch of dried herbs. He would have liked to bring a fresh one, but he hadn't had time. He'd never been very good with flowers when she was alive, so he knew she'd understand now.

The important thing was to talk to her, to ask her what he should do.

He waited, listening to the muffled night sounds. Normally he didn't have to wait long. Sarah knew when he needed her; sometimes even when he didn't know it himself. She'd stopped him from topping himself when there seemed no point in going on, telling him he had a job to do, that he had lives to save, that they'd all be together as a family again one day, he just had to be patient. When he'd had blood on his hands, she'd shed tears with him, so he didn't feel so alone. So he didn't get swallowed up by the blackness.

So where was she now?

He shivered, but he knew it wasn't the cold. It was the feeling of being alone. Just being at the graveside, even when he couldn't see her, he'd always felt her presence somewhere nearby, as if she was playing grandmother's footsteps. But not now.

Minutes passed. With each one the place felt emptier.

He picked up the little bunch of dead flowers and squeezed it in his fist, letting the fragments drift away, then stood up slowly. He knew she wasn't going to come now, however long he waited.

And that, he suddenly realized, was her answer to his question.

He stood still, with his hands at his sides, looking into the darkness stretching out ahead of him.

Right, decision made, then, he thought. He took out his

phone and scrolled through his contacts until he found the name he was looking for.

The call was answered after two rings.

'Hello?'

'Ryan, mate, it's Logan. Sorry to be calling so late.'

'That's all right. Is something up? Are we back in business?'

Logan was pleased Ryan didn't use the word 'Blindeye'. 'Not as far as I know. This is personal. I need a favour.'

'Not a problem.'

'Top man.' Logan hesitated. 'Are we . . . ?'

'Snug as a bug in a rug,' Ryan assured him.

Good, the phone's secure. Logan took a deep breath. No turning back now. 'OK, I've got a licence plate I need you to run for me.'

It was dawn when Logan returned to the penthouse. Ryan had come back with the address while he was still driving, and he'd pulled into a lay-by to write it down, part of him wanting to drive straight there, and part of him wanting to tear the piece of paper into little pieces, chuck it out the window and forget he'd ever seen it. In the end he just sat there, as if staring dumbly at it would make it give up its secrets. As if he didn't have to go there and see for himself.

When he eventually pulled out onto the motorway again, he wasn't sure where he was going, back to the penthouse to get some rest and plan the thing properly (at the end of the day, he was a professional, and this was just another job) or just say fuck it and go directly to the address without any real idea what he was going to do when he got there. The first option was the smart one, of course. But was it also a cop-out?

In the end he just pointed the nose south and let the car take him wherever it wanted to go, and eventually found himself back in the penthouse's underground garage, the engine clicking softly as it cooled, like a whale relieved to be back with the rest of its pod after straying into unfamiliar waters.

He'd take his time, then. Think through the possibilities. Decide on a cover, if he needed one. A weapon? Would they be armed? Whoever 'they' were. Or would that just make things more dangerous? Perhaps there was an innocent explanation for everything.

'Don't be a twat, Logan,' he muttered to himself as the lift doors closed.

Once he'd successfully reassured the security system that papa was home, made a pot of strong coffee and laid out a single sheet of paper and a row of three sharpened pencils on the black marble worktop, he'd figured out a way to proceed without going round in circles and driving himself nuts. Imagine you're back in the Service. Just think of it as an op. Something you've been tasked to do. You don't have to understand the whys and wherefores, just do your job.

Bollocks, of course, but worth a try. He picked up a pencil and began to make a list.

Forty minutes later, his concentration started to go. He tried blinking away the fatigue and pressing on, but soon the words he'd already written stopped making sense and he decided there was no point. He thought about making more coffee, then about trying to get some sleep, and in the end settled on going for a run. If in doubt, pound the pavement until your lungs are busting and everything hurts and a good dose of pain wipes the slate clean. Switch the brain off, then on again, and just hope it powers back up.

He was tying the laces of his worn and still muddy running shoes (not what your average billionaire would be seen dead wearing, but fuck it, maybe he's an eccentric) when his phone buzzed. He was going to ignore it but a quick glance showed it was Ryan's number.

Shit. What now?

Reluctantly he took the call. 'What's up, mate? You got some more info for me?'

'No, sorry, that was all she wrote. This is about . . . business.'

'Ah.'

'Yeah. Looks like we're needed back at the office. There's a meeting at ten.'

Logan let out a breath he didn't realize he'd been holding. 'Right. I'll see you there.'

He ended the call and put the phone down. For a moment he couldn't think. He closed his eyes as a wave of emotion flooded through him.

He realized, with a stab of shame, that it was relief.

2

Logan got to the Clearwater Security building at 9.45. Although technically he, Alex, Ryan and Alan were all employees of the company, with the salaries, tax bills and national insurance contributions to prove it, the fact was that Clearwater Security had no clients and did no work. Since they supposedly dealt with top-end corporate entities who demanded the highest levels of discretion, it wasn't entirely surprising their balance sheet had plenty of numbers on it but no names. But the real reason was that Clearwater Security was an empty shell and the work they did in its sleek, well-appointed office was so far off the books that if the police, Special Branch or MI5 had had the faintest sniff of it, in a flash they would all have been enjoying a mug of slop in a cell rather than Mrs Allenby's best Darjeeling served in delicate bone-china cups.

Logan didn't give much of a fuck about fancy tea, and had to wrack his brains to remember if he was supposed to put the milk in before or after it had been poured, but Mrs Allenby was still his boss, even though the firm she nominally ran didn't exist, and he wasn't going to get on her bad side if he could help it. Which was why he'd turned up for the meeting in good time, and was now sipping politely while they waited for her to get them up to speed.

Mrs Allenby, dressed in a brown tweed skirt and jacket, her cream silk blouse adorned with a small amber brooch, looked more like a headmistress of a posh girls' school about to hand out end-of-term prizes than the leader of a renegade team of ex-intelligence officers tasked with neutralizing terror threats, but Logan had learned the hard way not to underestimate her. Her last job before her retirement, as PA to the Director General of MI5, had clearly involved more than just taking dictation and looking after his appointments diary, but none of them had yet managed to put the rest of the pieces of her career together.

Pushing her horn-rimmed spectacles down on her nose, she rested her steely gaze on him for a moment, and instinctively he tried to make his mind a blank. The rational part of his brain told him she couldn't read his thoughts, but there was no point taking unnecessary risks, was there? If he didn't know her story, there were things it was better she didn't know about him, too.

After a few moments, apparently satisfied with what she'd seen, she readjusted her glasses and looked down at the notepad in front of her.

'Well, here we are again.' She nodded briefly at Ryan, with his baggy black golf shirt, tinted glasses and slicked-back ponytail, seemingly ready for an all-night session in a Vegas casino; then Alan, looking pasty and overweight, as if he hadn't stirred out of doors since the last op, which Logan thought was entirely possible; and finally Alex, chameleon-like as ever, today presenting as a funky yoga instructor in sweatpants and flip-flops with a yin-yang T-shirt.

What was it Wellington had said while inspecting his troops before Waterloo? *I don't know what the enemy will make of them, but they scare the shit out of me.* That was the gist, anyway.

Mrs Allenby paused. Maybe she'd had the same thought. But last time they'd done all right – more than all right: innocent lives saved; bad guys . . . well, better not to think about what had happened to them. Some nights they formed a grisly queue waiting to take their place in Logan's nightmares, pale, bloodless corpses, pointing to their exit wounds and muttering unintelligible curses.

'Mr Logan, are you with us?'

He gave himself a little shake. 'Yeah, sure.'

'All right, then. First let me tell you all the good news. As far as I am aware there is no imminent threat requiring the deployment of Blindeye's . . . special talents.'

Meaning the fact that we operate outside of the law, Logan thought to himself.

'But there is something of a loose end still remaining from our previous operation against Paul Martindale and his so-called Tenth Crusade.'

She paused and Logan hoped to God she wasn't going to say, 'Namely, where *is* he?'

Instead, to his relief, she said: 'DCI John Tenniel. Rather

a considerable loose end, in fact. And you know how I can't abide those. But it's far more than just a question of neatness.'

She paused, frowning, as if she didn't want to have to say what came next.

'It's within the bounds of possibility that the man now heading up the UK's National Crime Agency is himself a criminal. At the moment, this is pure conjecture. Possibly even a fantasy. We have no hard evidence and not even a plausible theory that would explain the circumstantial evidence we *do* have. We've joined some of the dots. Now we need to join the rest. The question is: how?'

She looked around the table, as if waiting for someone to put their hand up and say, 'Please, Miss, I know!'

Which was fair enough, Logan thought. It wasn't as if they hadn't all been asking themselves exactly the same question while they'd been away from Blindeye waiting for the dust to settle.

'Let's review what we know,' Ryan said. 'Or at least what we think we know.'

Christ, Logan thought, shifting in his seat, *please don't start with all that unknown unknowns bollocks.*

'Tenniel's on the up. He's got a reputation as a thief-taker. But he's ambitious, wants the top job, heading up the NCA. And bringing down a high-profile gangster like Terry Mason is his big test. Plenty of people have tried and they've all come up empty-handed. Either Mason's got in with the Freemasons, or he's very, very smart. Too smart to get tripped up by a garden variety surveillance operation. So Tenniel knows he's got to up his game, bring something new to the party. He goes on a joint police-intelligence surveillance course, trying to expand his skillset, and that's when he has his light-bulb moment. What if he could get some of these spooks along with their hush-hush high-tech gizmos to work for him? He targets three of them that come top of the class, and—'

'But how?' Alex interjected. 'Why would they risk their careers? It couldn't have been money. We worked with them. We *knew* them,' she added with a catch in her voice. 'Craig and Claire, anyway. They joined Blindeye because they didn't care about all that shit. They just wanted to make a difference.'

'Maybe that was how he got to them,' Ryan said. 'He saw how dedicated they were. Maybe he laid it on with a trowel about how Mason was untouchable, that without their help he'd just carry on doing what he was doing, ruining lives. Maybe he had evidence, I don't know, pictures of young girls . . .'

He stopped mid-sentence. Nobody particularly wanted to finish it for him.

Mrs Allenby picked up the story. 'So, by whatever means, he secretly seconds them to his surveillance operation. Mason is convicted of multiple crimes on the basis of the evidence gathered. Tenniel gets his promotion.'

'Champagne all round,' Alex said, sourly.

'Except that in the following months all three officers die.

A road accident, a heart attack, falling under a tube train. In each case, no actual evidence of foul play, but—'

'A hell of a coincidence,' Alex said.

'Too much of one,' agreed Mrs Allenby. 'So who killed them and why?'

'The obvious answer's the wife,' Logan said with a shrug.

Alex gave him a look.

'No, I mean it. We don't know how involved she was, but Stephanie Mason was no shrinking violet, that's for sure. So she decides to take revenge on the people responsible for bringing down her husband's criminal empire. Why not?'

'Because,' Alex countered, 'she couldn't have known about the MI5 involvement – let alone the identities of the officers – unless someone tipped her off, and that someone could only have been Tenniel. Why would he do that?'

'To cover his tracks,' Logan said. 'He was using her. He probably told her he was under orders to bring her husband down. But he'd rather make deals than put people in jail. She must have thought with Tenniel on her side she could keep the family firm going. And then he puts a bomb under Stephanie Mason's car to close the loop.' He shrugged. 'He doesn't like loose ends, either.'

Alex folded her arms. 'The other hits were made to look like accidents. Why suddenly start blowing people up in broad daylight?'

'Time,' Logan said. 'He had to move quickly before someone else got to her and put the thumb-screws on.'

Mrs Allenby scribbled something on her notepad. 'Well,

in any event, if Stephanie Mason did orchestrate the murders, then the link died with her.'

'So we have to look at Tenniel,' Alex said.

Alan, who up to this point had looked half-asleep, suddenly came alive, appearing distinctly alarmed. Logan knew he was thinking through the logistics of putting electronic surveillance on the head of the National Crime Agency.

Mrs Allenby looked at him. 'Mr Woodburn?'

Alan chewed his lip. 'His office would be . . . I don't know . . .'

Logan knew Alan never liked to admit he couldn't think of a technical workaround, however well protected or sensitive the target was. Over the years, while in A5, Logan would be the first to admit he'd ruthlessly exploited Alan's pride in his technical ingenuity. But this was beyond even Alan's capabilities. They were just setting him up to fail.

'Fucking impossible? Suicide?' Logan suggested, finishing Alan's sentence for him.

Mrs Allenby gave Logan a sharp look, then turned back to Alan.

'I don't know the NCA's protocols, obviously,' Alan said, carefully. 'I'd assume regular electronic counter-surveillance sweeps throughout the building. The windows will be blast-proof glass, meaning you can forget a laser, even assuming you could find a location to set it up. That leaves transport. He'll have a driver, which means a different car every week, and they'll be regularly checked too.'

'What about his home?'

'I'd have to look at the location. But you'd assume his phone's routed through the system, and he'll have the same level of surveillance. I mean, with a bit more detail, maybe I could . . .'

Mrs Allenby decided to put him out of his misery. She looked at Logan and Alex. 'What about putting physical surveillance on him? Could the two of you manage that?'

Logan shrugged. 'We could give it a go. Seeing just how good the Met's drivers are at spotting a tail might be fun.'

Mrs Allenby narrowed her eyes. 'I sense a "but".'

'What would be the point?' Logan said. 'I mean, if there's one thing we know about him, it's that he's good at covering his tracks. He knows he can't afford any slip-ups. Not in his position. So what's he going to give us?'

Mrs Allenby didn't look pleased, but Logan could tell she didn't disagree. 'Which leaves us . . . ?'

Logan drummed his fingers on the table. 'The one thing we do know is that the hits were professional. Not just professional: top of the range. How many people would be capable of pulling off three in a row like that? And then having the balls to top their employer. Maybe just one guy. And if we can get to him, then we can find out who was really behind the whole thing.'

Mrs Allenby looked at him sceptically. 'That's all very well in theory, Mr Logan, but how would you propose going about it? How do we find this individual? I don't imagine he's in the Yellow Pages.'

'Or her,' Alex put in.

Mrs Allenby smiled. 'Indeed. Or *her*.'

Logan didn't reply for a moment. He was thinking back to his childhood, if you could call it that, and a moment when it almost came to an abrupt end in a rat-infested shooting gallery. He had a face; he just needed a name. And then, in a flash, it came to him.

'I think I might know a way,' he said.

3

'Bloody hell, Logan, you've landed on your feet.'

Alex had her nose pressed to the big window, with the sprawl of London all the way to the horizon below her. She narrowed her eyes.

'I think I can see my flat. Oh, no, it's just a bit of bird shit on the glass.'

'Very funny. Do you want a coffee or something?'

Alex turned. 'That coffee-maker looks fancy. Reckon you can do me a skinny decaf latte?'

Logan frowned. 'No. The kettle's the only thing in this place I can figure out. I got a jar of instant. Milk or sugar. That's the options.'

'I'll have a tea then.'

He grinned. 'That's my girl.'

Logan put teabags in a couple of mugs, added boiling water and a splash of milk, and set them down on the kitchen island.

'It gets boring after a while,' he said.

'What?'

'The view.'

'I'll take your word for it.' She turned, indicating the interior of the penthouse with a sweep of her hand. 'So what's the deal then?'

'You mean what's a low-class scumbag like me doing living in a place like this?'

She grinned. 'Exactly.'

He shrugged. 'Can't get my head round renting somewhere. Feels too permanent, if that makes any sense. But there's this agency, unofficial like, run by a bloke I used to know when we were squaddies. If you need someone to house-sit and you want someone who's ex-Army for extra peace of mind.'

She nodded. 'So you're getting paid to live a life of luxury? Fucking hell.'

'Actually I'm on double time. I'm supposed to make it look like the owner's in residence.'

She considered that for a moment. 'While he's off doing something he shouldn't? I'd like to know what.'

'Fuck knows what it's all about. I don't even know if it's for real. Got to go through the motions, though.'

Alex came and sat on a stool opposite him. 'So what's up? I know you didn't invite me round to show off your soft furnishings – lovely though they are.'

Logan looked away. He'd asked Alex to come to the flat so he could finally tell her what had happened on the bridge that night. She'd known he was keeping something from her right from the off. She had a nose for things like that. Part of the training or just a female thing? It didn't matter. The point was, she'd been there for him when he was at his lowest ebb, and he'd paid her back by not being honest with her. She deserved better, even though she probably wouldn't thank him when he did finally spill the beans, it was all such a fucking mess. But he knew if he shut her out much longer, he'd be in danger of losing her for good. Then he'd have lost all three women in his life: his wife, his best friend, and . . . he wasn't sure what to call the third one.

He looked up. Alex was watching him carefully. She could tell he had something he needed to get off his chest. If he clammed up now, she'd probably take a swing at him. He felt relieved and terrified at the same time. For a moment he considered telling her about what happened to Martindale instead, throwing her some juicy red meat to put her off the scent, but he knew it wouldn't be fair to burden her with that.

'You remember that time I left the office, went for a walk to clear my head? We were all so fucking knackered. I came back and I had a few bumps and bruises. I'd ripped my jacket. You asked if I'd been in a fight.'

Alex nodded. 'Yeah. You said something about a couple of kids trying it on.' She smiled. 'I thought it was all bollocks.'

He smiled grimly. 'Well, you were right.'

Logan picked up his tea, then put it down again.

'So? What really happened?'

'There was . . . this woman. She was on the bridge, about to jump off. I grabbed her just in time.'

Alex cupped her mug in both hands. She nodded slowly.

'OK. Being a good Samaritan and all that. Why didn't you tell me?'

Logan hesitated. 'I . . . gave her my number. I thought, you know, no point in just walking away and hoping she doesn't do it again. I said if she wanted to talk, I knew something about . . . feeling like that, being in that place.'

'More good Samaritan stuff. And did she call?'

'Yeah. Yeah, she did. We met for a coffee, and she told me about herself.'

Alex looked thoughtful. 'OK, that all sounds good. I don't see why – oh, wait a minute. She told you about herself, she was baring her soul, and you . . . you told her about—'

'Fuck's sake!' Logan snapped. 'Course I fucking didn't.'

Alex held her hands up. 'OK, OK, I'm just trying to figure out what happened that's so fucking terrible you couldn't tell me about it.'

'Sorry.'

'It's OK. So, what then?'

Logan slowly let out a breath. 'We met up again, in an all-night diner. I . . . liked her.'

Alex's expression softened. She reached out and put a hand on Logan's arm.

'Right. I get it now. Sorry, I was being a bit slow. You saved this woman from killing herself, but of course you couldn't then just walk away, and so you spent some time with her, and found you . . . had a connection, something more than just the fact that you'd both been in the same situation.'

'Yeah, something like that.'

'But of course, you felt guilty, because of Sarah – which is stupid – perfectly natural, but stupid, and so you kept it to yourself, kept your feelings bottled up inside like blokes do, hoping they'd just go away, but now you've finally come to your senses.' She smiled. 'How am I doing?'

Logan nodded, smiling himself now. 'Ten out of ten.'

'OK, then. So tell me about her.'

Alex saw a shadow fall across Logan's features.

'What?'

'What you just said . . . all that . . . yeah, that's all true. I was feeling . . . well, things I hadn't felt for a long time. And it was tearing me up inside. I didn't want Sarah to . . . know. But I knew she would.'

He quickly looked up to check Alex was still with him, now that he was talking about communicating with his dead wife, but she was nodding sympathetically. If she thought he was nuts, she was hiding it well.

'So you still feel guilty?' she said.

'No, that's not it. I mean, yes, I do, but that's not the problem.'

'Bloody hell. So what *is* the problem?'

'The last time we met, it was just before I went into lockdown with Martindale, at the church. I told her I had to go away. I couldn't tell her where and I didn't know when I'd be back. *If* I'd be back. I couldn't tell her anything. I felt like shit.'

'And how did she react?'

25

Logan felt his voice catch in his throat. 'I thought that would be it. She'd never want to see me again. I mean, why would she? She'd told me all her secrets and I couldn't tell her mine. She must have thought I . . . I don't know what she thought.'

'So she walked out.'

'No. No, she didn't. At least not at first. She took a deep breath and said OK, she'd live with that, seeing as she had no choice, as long as I promised to tell her everything when I came back.'

'So is *that* the problem? You don't want to start a relationship built on lies, but you can't tell her the truth because that would put her in danger. It would put *you* in danger.'

Logan laughed sourly. 'If only. If only *that's* all it was.'

Alex's eyes widened. 'Jesus, Logan. So what *did* happen?'

'Do you want another tea?'

'No, that one was horrible enough. Don't get distracted. Tell me what happened.'

'OK, but first I have to tell you a bit about her. She was married, couple of kids . . .'

'Wait. You haven't told me her name.'

'Lucy. Her name's Lucy. At least . . .'

'What?'

'Never mind. So they died – her husband and her kids – car smash. She was a teacher. And she's in the house now, on her own.'

'Right.'

'So she calls up, middle of the night, needs to talk. That's when we went to the diner. And that's when I told her I had to go away.'

'OK.'

'So there's a few tears, and then she gets up and leaves. Nothing more to say. But instead of sitting there, I get up and follow her. I don't know why, I just found myself doing it. There's plenty of people on the street, you know, it's Soho, so she doesn't clock me. Then this car pulls up, black Merc, top of the range, with three people in it. Smartly dressed, but not like they're having a night on the town, more like they were on, I don't know, official business. Two blokes and a woman. But the blokes, I could tell, they had the look: short hair, blank expressions. And the woman, ice-cold. Lucy gets in the back with her and there's not a flicker. And that's the last I saw of her.'

'You got the reg?'

Logan nodded.

Alex ran her finger round the rim of her mug while she tried to process it all.

'So she was the one telling lies,' she said finally.

4

After Alex had left, Logan finally went for a run. The pent-house, for all its light and space, had started to feel claustrophobic. Dark thoughts about Lucy made his head ache and his chest grow tight, so he felt he couldn't breathe. He started off along the canal, then dodged down a narrow alley and let his feet take him where they wanted.

Soon he was lost among the strange jumble of long-boarded-up two-up-two-downs and shuttered warehouses with broken windows, while the skeletons of half-constructed office buildings crouched over them like the Martians from *War of the Worlds*. The sinister red helter-skelter on the skyline suggested life and death, new and old, ends and beginnings, all mixed together like a nightmare where up was down and nothing was the way it was supposed to be.

A good place for ghosts, he thought. As his stride lengthened and his breathing settled into a steady rhythm, his mind started to wander along familiar pathways. Without thinking about it, he found himself checking out every boarded-up building he passed, looking for ways in, ways out, figuring out whether it would already be occupied by squatters or down-and-outs, addicts or just kids seeing if there was anything left to nick or smash up for a laugh, seeing if there were any overlooked corners that might be safe for a night or two.

Ghosts.

Suddenly he was a fifteen-year-old kid again himself, hungry, dirty, tired-out, every nerve in his body twitching as he scanned his environment for threats and opportunities.

'Where the fuck we going? This place is shit, man. There ain't even rats round here it's so shit.'

Jockey just laughed and grabbed his sleeve, pulling him along. 'Come on, man, I know where I'm going. Have a bit of faith, you know. When I show you this thing you going to thank me, I'm telling you.'

'You're so full of shit, man. If it's just some dead junkie whore you think you can fuck on account of her being dead, I ain't interested. She'll probably still tell you to fuck off out of it.'

'Dead junkie whore,' Jockey repeated in his sing-song voice. 'This is better than that, man. Twice as good! Three times!' He laughed again.

'It better be a hundred times as good or you're getting a smack.'

Jockey stopped in his tracks and looked at him seriously. 'What if it only like ninety-seven times? You going to smack me then?'

'Just fucking find the place,' he said, pushing Jockey along, 'I don't like moving around, this time of night. It's all right for you, no one can see you in the dark.'

'You a fucking racist, man!' Jockey said.

'If I'm a racist, how come I'm hanging round with you?' he said.

'Cos no one else want to be your friend. They all think you a psycho. Come on, crazy white boy.'

Jockey led him along a cobbled street, then down a set of crumbling concrete steps that led into a narrow courtyard. An acrid smell hit the back of his throat, like someone had been burning something and then the rain had put it out.

Jockey turned to him with a grin. 'What you think?'

He looked around him. Bare black walls on three sides reaching up into the darkness. His instincts told him it was a bad place to be. A rat trap.

'There's nothing here,' he said.

Jockey seemed delighted. 'That what it look like, man. Just a dead-end piece of crap nothing place, right?'

'Right.'

'Come on.' Jockey beckoned him further into the darkness. As they neared the other end of the courtyard he could see there was a pile of junk half-covered with a tarpaulin in the corner. Jockey walked over and pointed. 'You see?'

He squinted into the darkness. 'What? It's just a pile of . . .'

Then he saw it. A narrow gap at the angle of the walls. Jockey started pulling a plank of wood from under the tarpaulin. 'Come on.'

He grabbed one end of the tarpaulin and helped clear the junk away from the corner. 'You fucking joking, man. I ain't going in there. Not for any dead fucking junkie whore, anyway.'

Jockey grabbed him again. 'You won't get stuck or nothing. I already done it.' Jockey squeezed himself into the gap between the walls and started inching his way along. 'There's a spike or something sticks out in a little bit. Just watch out for that.'

'Fuck's sake,' he said, following.

After scraping and bumping his way along for a minute or two, he started to feel sick and dizzy. The walls seemed to be getting narrower. He could almost feel them squeezing together like something out of a horror movie. He was already terrified he wouldn't be able to get back.

'Jockey!' he called out hoarsely, twisting his head round as far as he could without braining himself. But Jockey had gone. He stopped, trying to steady his breathing, trying to work out whether it was better to keep going or try and retrace his footsteps. Where had the little fucker gone?

He decided to keep going, in case things got easier. Jockey must have gone somewhere. Then he saw it: at first just a change in the darkness in his peripheral vision, then what looked like a doorway, and then suddenly he was stumbling forwards, thrusting his hands out in front of him instinctively to break his fall. He heard the scrape of a match then saw Jockey's grin in its flickering light. 'Come on.'

Jockey led him up a flight of wooden stairs onto a landing, then beckoned him through a doorway into a wide, empty space with bare walls. 'You gotta watch the floorboards. A lot of them's rotten.' The roof was mostly gone, so there was enough light to see where they were going. Jockey started feeling along the wall to his left, then stopped. 'Here we go.' He pulled away a loose brick and started easing a Tesco shopping bag out of the hole. He put a hand inside and pulled out another bag, this time clear plastic.

Jockey turned with a grin. 'Ta da!'

He walked over. Even in the half-light, he could see it was packed full of white powder.

'When d'you find this?'

Jockey shrugged. 'Not long ago.'

'Have you tried it? I mean, it could be rat poison.'

Jockey clucked at him. 'Why you gonna hide rat poison so no one can find it, man?' He grinned. 'Better than some dead junkie whore, right?'

'I guess. What you planning to do with it?'

'Not stick it up my nose, that's for sure. I'm not a fool. I'm gonna sell it. We gonna make a lot of money. Get ourselves off the streets. Buy ourselves one of them penthouse flats they building and then it's party time, man.'

He shook his head. 'Off the street and into an early grave, you mean. What are you thinking, you dumb piece of shit? Somebody just left it here and forgot about it? You start trying to sell this stuff, they're gonna come and stab you in about one second.'

Jockey shook his head. 'Nah, man, we gonna be smart. I've got a plan. Listen . . .'

He stopped as they both heard it. Footsteps on the stairs. Two, maybe three. And not bothering to be quiet.

Suddenly there was a shadow in the doorway.

'Jockey, you thieving little cunt.'

Two more shadows joined him.

'I'm putting it back,' Jockey said, a tremor in his voice. 'I just found it, you know, just seeing what it was. I wasn't gonna take it or nothing.'

'Correction: thieving, lying little cunt,' the shadow said.

Jockey put the bag down on the floor, his eyes darting round the room, looking for a way out.

'You,' the shadow pointed at Logan, a blade glinting in the half-light. 'You can fuck off.' The two other shadows stepped aside, leaving the doorway open. Jockey flashed a glance at him, pleading, eyes wide with fear. The first shadow jerked the blade over his shoulder. 'Go on. Final offer.'

He looked at Jockey quickly, trying to communicate something with his eyes, but Jockey just stared back blankly. He turned and made his way to the doorway.

'Smart lad,' said the shadow.

He started walking down the stairs, feeling for each footstep in the dark, his brain going into overdrive. A weapon. He needed a weapon. There'd be something in that pile of junk, a bit of lead pipe or something, but that would take too long, they'd have carved Jockey up by then. He clattered his way down, making as much noise as possible, so they'd know he'd gone, all the time thinking, thinking.

He got to the bottom and went down on his hands and knees, searching in the dirt. Nothing. Some wire. A bit of wood, but it crumbled in his hands, rotten. Then the chink of glass and he'd found it. A bottle.

He started walking back up, willing his footsteps to be silent, trying to remember where the gaps between the boards were. He heard a high-pitched grunt, then a laugh and something heavy hitting the floor above with a thud like a sack of cement. He quick-ened his footsteps, hoping they were no longer paying attention.

When he got to the doorway, the first thing he saw was the flash of Jockey's white T-shirt as he lay curled up in a ball on the floor. He was making a moaning sound through gritted teeth and there was something dark dripping from his mouth. The shadow was standing over him, humming a tune he couldn't make out while circling the blade from side to side like a conductor with his baton, while the other two stood on either side, what looked like tyre irons hanging from their fists.

'I'd rather not be wasting my time on a useless cunt like you, Jockey, to be honest. But I'm afraid this has got to be done proper, so people get the right message. I'm thinking I might have to cut your head off, what do you reckon? Finish up with that, anyway. You know, big finale.'

He smelled the sour reek of urine as Jockey pissed himself. One of the shadows stepped back smartly. 'Dirty little fucker.'

He breathed in slowly. His heart was hammering so hard, he was sure they could hear it. He wanted to try and make himself calm but there wasn't time. He didn't have a plan: just go in hard and fast and keep going. He was aware he was about to do something he'd never done before. Could he do it? Strangely, yes, he knew he could.

So what was he waiting for?

'Right, let's be having you then,' said the shadow, switching his grip on the blade so he could stab downwards.

He smashed the bottle against the wall and they all turned as he launched himself forward. He saw an arm raised with a tyre iron, but instead of leaning away, he ducked under it and thrust upward, the jagged end of the bottle sinking in under the chin as the tyre iron swung down past him and clattered to the floor. He yanked the bottle out and pivoted, going low this time with a slash to the stomach that bought him enough time to look up and see *the next guy stepping backwards, trying to give himself some room. He heard a shuffle of feet: the big guy trying to get behind him. His body reacted before he could think, going after the other guy, feinting a jab to the face, then switching hands, going low with the now-empty hand and ramming the bottle end into his neck with the left, just as he felt a bright stab of pain in his back – swivelled again, just in time to parry a second blow, took a straight right to his nose, instantly filling his mouth with blood – keep your eyes open! – someone was twisting his wrist – too much pain – he had to drop the bottle – here comes the blade – he was shouting but no words were coming out – Jockey! – the blade sliced into his palm as he tried to grab the hand – jumped back, tripping over something hard. He leaned down and grabbed it – the tyre iron, slick with blood – he swung it blindly, heard a crack as it connected with bone, then a groan as the guy went down on one knee – last chance, nothing more in the tank, can't see any more, a blind swing and a crunch – most beautiful sound in the world – as he hit the back of the skull, just like cracking an egg – then one more, enough for one more, maybe one more –*

He dropped to his knees, heaving for breath, waiting for a stab in the guts, a crashing blow to the back of his head – but there was nothing, just someone jabbering away in a language he didn't understand, the odd word coming through – until, like magic, it turned into English, and someone was saying his name.

'Matty! Matty! You killed them, man! You fucking killed them!'

5

'Well, Jockey, I must say you've done all right for yourself.'

The house was at the end of a narrow lane leading off a quiet B-road on the Sussex–Hampshire border. Logan assumed there were other ways to approach the property, but judging by the ten-foot steel gate with cameras mounted on either side, there would no doubt be security fences around the perimeter, maybe sensors in the surrounding woods, too, to warn of unwanted intruders.

He walked up to the gate to let the cameras have a good look at him. He might have been able to find a sneaky way in if he'd really put his mind to it, but that wasn't his intention. He didn't want to spook Jockey into doing something rash. At least not yet.

Through the bars of the gate he could see a broad frontage of fresh white stucco, making the house look like a cake that had just been taken out of the oven, topped with red tiles that gave it a Mediterranean feel and startling aquamarine chimney pots like birthday candles. A gravel drive led to the solid oak double doors in front. If there were any vehicles, they were parked somewhere he couldn't see.

He waited patiently, hands held loosely at his sides, an amiable half-smile on his face, while whoever was looking at him sized him up. He was hoping if he stood there long enough someone would come out for a closer look. He'd give it five minutes, he decided, and if they carried on ignoring him, he'd get their attention some other way. There were no signs of life, no movements at the windows, nothing to suggest the place was occupied, but a slight fluttering in his chest told him there were eyes on him.

'Come on, don't make me drop me boxers and do a fucking cartwheel, you cunts,' he muttered to himself.

When someone finally emerged from the side of the house, he was surprised to see it was a woman. She was thirty-ish wearing a crisp navy suit and a white blouse, with her dark hair scraped back into a tight ponytail. She crunched across the gravel in an impressive pair of heels and stopped a yard from the gate.

'Can I help you?' Her voice was friendly but with a twinkle of steel in it. She had a slimline walkie-talkie in her hand.

'I've come to see Jockey.'

'Who?' Her bewilderment sounded genuine.

'Mr Cameron.'

She gave no sign that this name meant anything to her, either. 'I think you may have come to the wrong house.'

He smiled. 'I don't think so, darling.'

The 'darling' was to see if she could be riled, but it seemed to be water off a duck's back.

'I can give you directions back to the main road if you're lost,' she said without a flicker.

'Just tell . . . Mr Cameron, that his old pal Matty's come to see him.'

She looked sceptical. Maybe Jockey hadn't shared stories of his early days with the staff. He reached slowly into his windbreaker and he saw her start to raise the walkie-talkie, to call for assistance, then stop halfway when she saw what was resting in his palm. He reached forward.

'Give him this.'

For the first time she looked uncertain. She was curious, but there was no way she was going to put her hand through the bars of the gate.

He flicked the coin high in the air, and over the top of the gate. She was caught off guard for a moment, then recovered herself, took a half-step back and caught the coin deftly in her palm.

'Heads,' he said.

She looked down, then up, surprised.

'It's always heads,' he said with a grin.

Five minutes later she was back, this time accompanied by a young, heavy black guy in jeans, an oversized polo shirt, expensive-looking trainers and a blank expression. They both stood back while the gates slowly opened, then she gestured towards the house. 'After you.'

Inside, she ushered him down a broad hallway with chequerboard tiles towards a pair of French doors. Along the walls were photographs in black frames. They seemed to be close-ups of different body-parts or maybe piles of fruit. Logan couldn't tell. She opened the doors and walked through.

'*Matty*,' she announced, her tone putting the name in heavy quotes.

Logan followed her, the young guy keeping a couple of paces behind. The first things he noticed were the paintings, huge canvases, some of them a couple of metres square, all over the walls, riots of colour that didn't really look like anything, except possibly the results of a frenzied knife attack. Then he saw another guy, in a dark suit with a collarless burgundy shirt and shiny loafers. He was standing next to a green leather sofa where a dark-skinned man in a black silk dressing gown was sitting with a thoughtful expression on his face.

'Thank you, Lisa.'

The woman nodded and neatly turned on the spot. The two guys remained where they were.

Logan smiled. 'Hello, Jockey. Hell of a squat, mate.'

Jockey had definitely filled out since Logan had last seen him, his face less gaunt, though it was still marked by the scar under his left eye that made it seem to droop slightly. Even sitting down, he seemed to be taller, too, somehow.

'Derek's just going to pat you down.'

Logan raised his arms from his sides as the young black guy gave him a quick once-over, then ran some sort of electronic wand over his body. He must have passed the test, as Jockey nodded and Derek left the room.

'Do I need Tommy, too, do you think?' he asked, indicating the other guy standing by the sofa.

Logan shrugged. 'Depends on what he does.'

'He stops people from trying to kill me,' Jockey said.

'If I wanted to do that, I think I'd have planned it a bit better,' Logan said.

'Fair enough,' Jockey said. 'You were always good at improvising, though.'

Jockey's voice, along with his features, had undergone a subtle change. It was a still a little high-pitched, like he was about to burst into song at any moment, but slower, more deliberate, like he'd finally started thinking before speaking.

'How'd you know where to find me? I know I ain't in the phone book.'

Logan shrugged. 'You're not exactly living down a hole either. It's not that hard if you know what you're doing. Or you know someone who does.'

Jockey turned to Tommy. 'Off you go.' Tommy didn't look happy but Jockey held his gaze and eventually the guy moved towards the door, but not before giving Logan a hard stare. Logan nodded back civilly, one professional to another.

Once they were alone, Jockey opened his palm and looked at the coin. 'I can't believe you kept this. It almost got me my legs broken once, remember?'

'Happy days,' Logan said. 'It made us a few quid, too. Talking of which . . .' and he looked around the room '. . . this is all very nice. Cocaine business must be doing well.'

Jockey stiffened. 'Watch your mouth. I can get Derek and Tommy back here if you're going to be smart.'

Logan smiled. 'Come on, Jockey. Your best friend turns up out of the blue and you think he's come to kill you? If you're not a drug dealer, you're doing a bloody good impression of one. Unless you've branched out into pimping.'

Jockey allowed a half-smile to form on his lips. 'Not my style.' He sighed. 'OK, sit the fuck down and tell me why you're here. Not that it isn't a nice surprise, of course. You haven't changed a bit.' He looked Logan over. 'You might even be wearing the same threads, come to think of it. Do you want a drink or something?'

Logan sat down in an overstuffed leather armchair opposite Jockey. 'I'll have a cup of tea if the lovely Lisa's going to make it.'

Jockey scowled. 'Lisa don't make tea. She does other things.'

'I'll bet,' Logan said with a grin.

Jockey shook his head. 'You need to grow up, man.' He paused. 'So come on, what is it? You come here to chat about old times or you trying to shake me down?'

He was beginning to sound more like the Jockey Logan had known. His calm, in-control vibe, sitting back in his silk dressing gown with his flunkeys around him, was starting to crack – little twitches around the eyes, his fingers starting to drum on the arm of the sofa – gradually revealing the hyperactive tearaway underneath.

'What you looking at?' he asked, tetchily.

'The past,' Logan said. 'I'm looking at the Jockey I used to know.'

'He gone – crazy little fucker. It's Mr Cameron now.'

'Right,' Logan said, nodding. 'New Year, new you.'

'You do the best you can, right? So what about you? What you up to – no, don't tell me. I bet you went into the Army. SAS or some shit like that. Killing people – that was what you was good at. Even then.'

Logan didn't say anything. After a few moments Jockey looked away.

'Shit, man. I was joking.'

Logan was remembering.

After they'd made sure the drug dealer and his goons were really dead, they sat with their backs to the wall, trying to make a plan.

'First thing, you gotta get rid of them clothes,' Jockey said. 'You covered in blood, man. I'll get you a shirt, some jeans, shoes – then you put that stuff in a bag and we'll take it to the hospital.'

'I'm not going to a hospital. They'll call the cops as soon as they look at me.'

'No, man, you ain't going to no hospital. Ray's working night shifts at St Mary's. For a bit of blow he'll toss your clothes in the incinerator, no questions asked. Then you get the fuck out of here, far away as you can.'

Logan was feeling light-headed. He looked over at the bodies, sprawled in a darkened heap, and none of it seemed real. His mouth was very dry.

'What about you?'

'Don't worry 'bout me.'

Logan nodded, seeing stars.

'Come on, we need to get moving.'

Logan heaved himself up. Jockey put a hand on his shoulder.

'Listen, man. I owe you. I owe you big. I ain't gonna forget.'

Logan came back to the moment. 'You went back, didn't you?'

'What you talking about? Back where?'

'That night. After I got cleaned up, got rid of my clothes. You went back and took the stuff. You said you didn't want anything to do with it, seeing as it almost got you killed. But you were lying.'

Jockey didn't say anything. He seemed to be weighing things up. Eventually he said, 'I meant what I said. I was gonna leave it. But then I couldn't stop thinking about it, all that money just sitting there. Nobody except the rats getting high. What a fucking waste.'

'And you had a plan, didn't you?'

Jockey smiled. 'Turned out to be a good one, too.'

They were standing outside what Jockey referred to as the barn, but which looked to Logan more like a medium-sized aircraft hangar. Jockey had dressed in linen slacks and an expensive-looking white T-shirt for the tour. The rest of the house was off-limits, but he seemed keen to show off the extensive grounds: the tennis courts, swimming pool, the field with a couple of horses and another one covered with neat rows of vines.

'You making your own wine now, Jockey? I always had you down as more of a vodka and Red Bull type.'

'I don't drink the stuff.' Jockey shrugged. 'But they grow like fucking weeds. Climate change, you know? Every cloud has a silver lining. When you get an opportunity you gotta grab it. That's what I learned that night.'

Logan looked out over the field. He saw a quick flash of movement between the vines. A fox?

'The second thing I learned,' Jockey continued, 'was to get a good lawyer. Soon as I had some cash I bought a flat in one of them new high-rises by the river, some nice wheels – tinted windows so the fucking cops can't see there's a black face behind the wheel . . . oh, man, the smell of a new car, I'd never smelled that before, I swear it got me high – anyway, now I was looking the part, like someone serious, so I go out and get myself a proper brief.'

'Where?'

'You remember Jonjo? He's dead now. Anyway, one time his cousin got stopped with twenty grand's worth of gear in his car. Forty-eight hours later he's back on the street, free as a bird. I remembered the name of his lawyer, little weasel called Delancey, worked out of a shit-heap office on the Edgware Road. So I went and made him a proposition, kind of a profit-sharing scheme, if you know what I mean. He said you'll need an accountant, too, if you start making real money. Couldn't believe how sweet it all worked out. I'd found my – what do you call it? My *niche*.' He laughed. 'If I'd known where you were, I would have said come and work for me, you know? But you were gone, man, like, not a trace.'

'Bollocks,' Logan said, smiling.

Jockey shrugged, then pressed some buttons on a keypad and a door clicked open. Inside, the barn seemed even bigger, a cavernous space with a bare concrete floor and exposed brick walls. The door hissed shut.

'It looks basic, yeah?' Jockey said. 'But I tell you, it's got temperature control in here, humidity, everything.'

Logan was puzzled for a moment, then Jockey hit a bank of switches by the door, and an array of spotlights hanging from the roof buzzed into life. The walls were covered in canvases, some of them huge, bright explosions of colour that made Logan briefly put a hand to his eyes.

'Fuck, I could see you were into your paintings, but . . . bloody hell.'

Jockey was grinning like a maniac, so excited he was almost doing a dance on the spot.

'Beautiful, ain't they?'

'I don't know, they're . . .' Logan didn't have the words to describe what he was seeing.

'You're thinking, "What the fuck is that supposed to be? It don't look like nothing, except maybe a bomb went off in B&Q." OK, let me give you a lesson in art appreciation.'

Jockey put an arm round his shoulder and gently rotated him.

'What you looking at is . . . *money*.'

Logan looked around. The colours were blinding. He

could feel a headache coming on just looking at them. He squinted at a rectangular painting that looked like a time-lapse photograph of a particularly vicious dogfight. At least it was mostly grey and brown with only the odd splash of red.

'How much for that one?'

'You like that? You a connoisseur, man! You looking at seven-fifty.'

Logan whistled. 'And the whole lot?'

Jockey did a little twirl, looking around. 'I don't even know. A few mil.'

'Must cost a fortune to insure.'

Jockey shook his head. 'Nah. That's a mug's game. That's why I got Derek and Tommy and a few of them other boys. Lisa's handier than she looks, too. You want to steal from me you need to bring a fucking tank, man.'

'So what's it all for? What's the point? You come in here once a day to give yourself a hard-on?'

'You asking me what's the point of art, man. The big question!'

Logan scowled. 'Fucking hell, Jockey. When did you become such a ponce?'

Jockey sighed. 'I always had an eye, you know? I could see when things were, I don't know, *right*. I can't explain. Why is one of these paintings that don't look like nothing, that look like a child could have done it, why is it worth a million and this other one isn't worth a tenth of that?' He shrugged. 'Nobody can tell you that. But if you have a feel, if you can get in at the bottom, and you can afford to wait, make some mistakes, then you can make some serious cash out of this stuff.'

'So all this is an investment?'

Jockey steered him back towards the door. 'It's a little more complicated than that.'

He opened the door and they walked out into the sunshine. Logan took a breath of the cool air and he felt his headache begin to fade as they passed the tennis courts on the way back to the house.

'That painting you like . . .' Jockey resumed.

'I didn't say I liked it.'

'OK, whatever. But say you want to buy it. I say it gonna cost you seven-fifty. You say OK. Or maybe I say I got someone else who wants it: make me an offer. You end up paying eight-fifty. Or I say, you know what, that one's my special favourite, it's gonna cost you a mil.'

'What's your point?'

'The point is, we do the deal, and some nosy cunt looks at the paperwork, he can't prove you paid too much. Not in a court of law, anyway.'

'So it's a tax thing?'

'Nah, man, nothing to do with tax. You like ice cream?'

'Ice cream?'

'OK, one time they started putting air into ice cream. They got this machine pumps it in, kind of bulk it up, you know? So now it's like, I don't know, fifty per cent air. So they find out about this and some guy says to the people making the ice cream, "Now you're charging me a pound for a scoop of this stuff? It's a scam, 'cos I'm paying half of that for some air, which shouldn't cost nothing. You're charging me fifty pence for some fucking air." And you know what the ice cream guys say? They say, "No, the ice cream cost you a pound. You getting the air for free."'

'You've lost me.'

'The point is,' Jockey said, 'if I sell you one of them paintings for a million pound, and that seems like a little much, maybe you getting the painting for a million, but you getting something else for free.'

Logan thought for a moment. Then he got it. 'OK . . . and we're not talking about air, right?'

Jockey smiled. 'No, we not talking about air. You see what I mean? That's why you gotta get yourself a smart accountant, you want to make it in this business. You gotta find a way of moving stuff around, buying and selling, and still everything looks legit.'

'Sweet,' Logan said, nodding his appreciation. 'Sounds like you got everything figured out.'

'Well,' Jockey said, with a hint of sadness in his voice, 'I got a system that works. But you gotta keep things fresh, you know. Every once in a while you gotta wipe the slate clean.'

Logan nodded. 'People get greedy.'

'Exactly. And trust, as my grandma always used to say, is a perishable commodity. Come, let me make you that cup of tea you wantin'.'

'Fuck that, Jockey. But I'll have a beer.'

Jockey led the way up the gravel drive to the house. In his peripheral vision, Logan could see Derek and another man he hadn't seen before standing by the door to the barn, keeping an eye.

The kitchen was a disappointment – smaller and homelier than the one in Logan's penthouse, with an Aga and a battered-looking oak table. Jockey got a couple of cans of lager out of the fridge. Logan wondered if there was a wife, kids, somewhere about the place, but he didn't fancy wandering into that particular minefield.

Jockey handed Logan a can. They pulled the tabs and each took a good swallow.

'OK, Matty, I've been nice, I've given you the tour, told you all my secrets. Now your turn.'

'I already knew your secrets.'

Jockey's eyes widened. 'Ah, so that's it. You come here to my house to blackmail me. You do understand I could have you killed?'

Logan took a sip of his tea. 'That's what I was hoping you'd say.'

Jockey sat back in his chair. 'What? You still crazy, man.'

'When you were . . . wiping the slate clean. You didn't get Derek or Tommy or the other home help to do it, did you?'

Jockey didn't say anything.

'I mean, I'm sure they're steady lads, good at cracking heads and all that, but if you needed something done with no mess, no comeback, no loose ends, you wouldn't trust them to do it, would you?'

Jockey narrowed his eyes. 'Where you going with this?'

'You'd have paid to have it done right. You've got the money, after all. And you're smart, you can see three moves ahead. You know the important thing is not whether they can do the job, it's if the job stays done. You need someone who's so good at what he does, you can be sure he's not going to fuck up some job down the line and find himself in a cell giving you up to make a deal. I reckon you didn't just go to a pro, you insisted on the top man. The best of the best.'

'Ah. You want me to give you a name?'

Logan shook his head. 'I don't think you've got one. I think you went to a middleman. A broker, if you like. That way the guy's name doesn't get bandied around. You just pay your money, the broker takes his cut, and just like magic, one day your problem goes away. How am I doing?'

Jockey took his time before answering. 'OK, let's say that's the way things are. I still don't get what you want.'

'What I want, Jockey, is for you to give me an introduction to this broker. Tell him I'm a businessman, like you, with a problem he needs fixing and I want the top guy for the job. I need you to vouch for me, say I'm on the level, so he knows I'm not the law.'

'Are you?'

'You joking me? No, Jockey, I'm not the law. Just like you're not a fucking dealer in fine art.'

'And what are you planning to do if I introduce you to this man?'

'What do you care?'

'Trust, man. Like I say, it's a perishable commodity. If you do something funny, it's going to come back on me.'

'You don't have to worry, Jockey.'

'OK, now I'm really worried. And if I say no?'

'I'm not here to put the squeeze on you, Jockey. If you say no, you say no. What am I going to do? Go to the police and tell them how I killed three drug dealers when I was fifteen? I don't think so. I don't have any leverage on you.'

'So why should I risk my reputation to help you do whatever crazy shit you're trying to do?'

Logan took another sip then put his can down on the table. He looked at Jockey. Jockey tried to look away but couldn't.

'Because you owe me, Jockey. Remember?'

6

The rain was falling more steadily as the black saloon pulled up, making the low concrete building look even less inviting than usual. A man in a black suit with the epaulettes of a chief inspector got out and strode briskly up the ramp that led to the front doors, his driver hurrying after him.

Inside, he walked past the desk without acknowledging the duty officer and made for the double doors on the far side. He pushed his way through and turned left down the brightly lit corridor. He carried on until he reached a door with a sign saying 'Interview Room 2'. He grasped the handle and entered without knocking.

A uniformed sergeant was standing to the left of the door. He stiffened to attention as he recognized the senior officer. 'Sir.'

There was a plain wooden table in the middle of the room with two black plastic chairs on either side. A young man in a leather jacket with dark, greasy hair that fell over his eyes was sitting at the table. His hands were cuffed on his lap. His nose was slightly flattened, like a boxer's, and faint acne scars were visible through the stubble on his cheeks. He looked up at the man who had just entered without any expression.

Tenniel briefly met his gaze, then turned to the uniform and jerked his chin in the direction of the door. 'Thank you, Sergeant.'

'Sir.' The uniform left, closing the door behind him.

Tenniel took a chair on the other side of the table. He looked at his watch.

'You know who I am?'

The man nodded. 'Of course.'

'We have five minutes until your brief arrives.'

The man smiled, showing tobacco-stained teeth. 'We talk fast.'

Tenniel had built his reputation on knowing his enemy. As an ambitious young detective in the robbery squad, he'd run a successful string of confidential informants and he'd always known instinctively when their information was kosher and when they were trying to buy themselves time because their balls were in a vice. He knew because he knew them.

As Director General of the NCA, he wasn't running CIs any more, but he still liked to keep his hand in. He knew what happened if you started spending all your time looking at numbers and reading other people's reports. You lost touch. You didn't know who you were dealing with any more. You didn't know what they were thinking. And that meant you could make the wrong decisions.

So when he heard they'd arrested Selim Urcik for assault, no one thought it was odd that he wanted to run the rule over him himself before he was interviewed. Selim might be small fry, but as Tenniel was fond of pointing out, small fry could one day grow into big fish, and when they did, already having an insight into their personalities could make all the difference.

Sometimes when you're just making conversation, they get careless, let things slip. It might not seem like anything – the name of a girlfriend, the team they support back home – but if you're smart, you store it away. And then one day, maybe years later, you find yourself face to face in another interview room, when the stakes are a lot higher, and you might have an extra card to play.

And, of course, if you really want someone to open up, maybe get careless, it has to be one on one. No one can relax with a uniform standing there listening in. For a lot of them, the younger ones especially, having an audience just means they play to the gallery, showing how tough they are, spitting in your face.

Which is why no one thought it odd that Tenniel insisted on speaking to Urcik alone.

'It's Patterson, isn't it?' Tenniel said. 'He'll have you out of here in no time, slippery bastard.'

Urcik shrugged. 'It doesn't matter.'

Tough guy, Tenniel thought. Also: *poor bastard*. Urcik knew he was expendable. Putting on a front was all he could do.

'It matters that you pass on what I'm going to tell you to Mr Durgan as soon as possible. I don't want you stuck in a cell. So do what Mr Patterson says. No theatrics.'

Urcik squinted at him, not understanding.

'If you assault a police officer in here, even Patterson won't be able to get you out.'

Urcik scowled. 'Of course. I am not stupid.'

'Good. Don't let them provoke you. A detective called Erskine will be leading the interview. He likes to wind people up.'

Tenniel wanted to probe Urcik a little further. Maybe Durgan hadn't chosen him simply because he was expendable. Maybe he'd chosen him because he trusted him. Trusted him to tell him if Tenniel tried anything funny.

'What do you do for Mr Durgan?'

'Whatever he tells me.'

'Does that include killing people?'

Urcik looked at him. 'I am a driver.'

So, more than just a kid who wants to show me how tough he is, Tenniel thought. He looked at his watch again. Patterson was always on time.

'OK, Selim, I need to know if you have people in Wakefield.'

Urcik grinned. 'Everywhere.'

'Find out who's protecting Terry Mason.'

Urcik waited, expecting more. 'Just this?'

'For now.'

Urcik nodded. As Tenniel stood, there was a rap on the door. He'd left it too late. Outside in the corridor was a female PC and a small, slightly hunched man in a badly fitting pinstripe suit. He was clutching a battered leather briefcase to his chest. With his comb-over and thick glasses, he looked more like an accountant than one of the most feared defence barristers of his generation.

'Director General,' he said, nodding. 'I do hope you weren't having an inappropriate conversation with my client. I thought DI Erskine was doing the honours.'

'I was just getting to know Mr Urcik a little,' Tenniel said, ignoring the provocation.

'And how did you find him?' Patterson asked.

'Nasty little prick,' he said, brushing down his lapels. 'Like the lot of them,' he added.

'Tut-tut, I think that's what we call "unconscious bias" these days. You need to be more careful.'

'You'll need to be careful he doesn't slit your throat,' Tenniel replied. 'Once you've got him discharged, of course.'

'Let's not pre-judge the outcome, shall we,' Patterson said affably.

'Heaven forbid,' Tenniel said.

Their ritual sparring over, Tenniel turned and headed back down the corridor. He'd wanted to leave the building before Patterson made his appearance. Patterson knowing he'd been talking to Urcik made him nervous. But perhaps it was all for the best. If Patterson thought Tenniel had a hard-on for Urcik, that would only spur him on to spring him even quicker, just to show he could.

Tenniel smiled to himself. *If only you knew, you arrogant four-eyed little shit.*

His driver was waiting in the reception area. He stood up

as Tenniel approached. 'Back to the office, sir? You have that combined forces strategy meeting at eleven.'

Tenniel's heart sank. Another hour lost to pie charts and flow diagrams, another hour he'd never get back. What he needed was time to think. Time to plan his own strategy.

'Fine, Bolton. What's the traffic like? Let's see if you can beat your record without killing anyone.'

In the end they made it with minutes to spare. Bolton had used the siren and flashers on the home stretch, which was technically cheating, but the boy didn't like to come up short. You gave him a task, he was determined to execute, to over-perform if at all possible, even if he had to bend the rules to do it. And he didn't ask questions. Tenniel was beginning to think he had promise. As he pushed through the glass doors, he wondered if it was time to raise the bar a little. See just how far the boy would go. He'd need to be careful, though. There was always the possibility someone else was pulling his strings.

The meeting, in the end, was heavy on data but somewhat lighter on strategy. Terry Mason's downfall had changed the game, and now they needed to try and anticipate the moves of the other pieces left on the board. There were two obvious contenders: the Albanian sex-trafficking outfit, who had worked hand in glove with Mason right to the end; and the Turkish drug gang he'd fallen out with. Durgan's mob. There were some other players on the fringes, but they lacked the manpower to be anything other than scavengers, living off any scraps left over when the big boys had carved things up. So who was going to come out on top? Tenniel listened patiently to the competing theories, the pros and cons.

Barton from Serious Crimes pointed out that the Turks had cut out the middlemen and established a direct connection with the suppliers in Colombia, thereby simplifying the supply chain. With Mason out of the way, they could monopolize distribution as well.

Judith Dier from the Met countered that people-smuggling was going to get a whole lot easier with the chaos at the ports of entry – cue wry smiles around the table. Maybe with their increased profits, the Albanians would decide to invest in the cocaine business in a big way?

Tenniel let the discussion go back and forth, but after twenty minutes they were no nearer a definitive conclusion. The truth was, for all the impressive points-scoring, nobody knew.

Except him, of course.

He called a halt at 11.45, authorizing increased resources for confidential informants. 'We can analyse all the data until we're blue in the face,' he said. 'We need to have our ears to the ground, find out what's happening at street-level. One thing we can be sure of is that things will move fast.' And with that they closed their laptops, gathered up their files and made an orderly exit.

He waited until they were gone, then walked down the corridor to his office, closing the door behind him. Sitting at the desk, he picked up a glass paperweight and revolved it slowly through his fingers. How long had it taken him to get here? To be sitting in this chair, at this desk, in this office at the end of the corridor on the sixth floor?

But even though he had the keys to the kingdom now firmly in his grasp, part of him felt as if he'd just exchanged his freedom for a prison cell. As an up-and-coming detective trying to make his name, this office and the power it represented was what he'd dreamed of every single day. But with power came constant scrutiny. Every moment of his day was scheduled, organized, accounted for. He was where he wanted to be, at the centre of power, but that also meant he was exposed.

Not like the old days on the streets where he could be gone for hours – days, even – and as long as he got results, as long as the paperwork got done in the end, nobody cared. 'You're not going to catch any criminals sitting behind a desk,' he'd say smugly, if any of his more conservative colleagues challenged him, and if that wasn't enough for them, well, they only had to look at his stats at the end of the year. Not just arrests, but solid cases that went to court and then straight to the cells without passing 'Go'. He nailed the bad guys, they went down, and they stayed down.

And if that meant spending hours in seedy pubs and basement gambling dens, at dog tracks and snooker halls, instead of tapping away at a computer, filling in forms or sitting in meetings going 'yes sir, no sir' then that was what he'd do.

What he hadn't properly appreciated at the time, though,

was how rare that feeling was: knowing you were off the radar, invisible, untraceable. Sitting in a shady booth, or just walking the streets, and nobody knowing where you were. No one.

Whereas now? He was the spider in the middle of the web. Every strand responded to his touch. But he could never leave the web now, he could never be invisible again. He could never go to those places.

Those dark places.

His eyes moved to the photograph in the silver frame. A girl. Blonde hair in a ragged fringe. A shy smile showing a slight gap between her teeth. The sharp little chin that made her look like a pixie. She would have been fifteen when the photograph was taken.

The things he had lost.

To be where he was now.

He gently pushed the photograph away so she was no longer looking at him.

What was that quote?

The past is never dead. It's not even past.

Who'd told him that? It might even have been Elizabeth. In the days when they were still talking. He'd come home in the early hours and she'd still be up, her reading light on, deep in something from the pile on her bedside table. She wouldn't look at him. She'd keep her face stuck in her damn book as if it was the most fascinating thing in the world. Literally unputdownable. And then she'd start reading aloud to him.

Listen to this. What do you think of this? Who does this remind you of?

Did she really think he wanted to listen to a book at bedtime after the day – and sometimes the night – he'd just had? Did she really think he was even listening? Or was it just her way of saying, 'This is my life now. Sitting alone with a book while you're out doing God knows what. This is what you've reduced me to. And no, I'm not going to ask you where you've been, what you've been doing. Because I'm tired of the answers, the non-answers, the evasions, tired of the lies. I don't care any more. So I'm going to make you listen to my story, listen to what my life is like, alone with a book every night.'

And, he supposed, despite himself, he had been listening. To some of it, anyway. Otherwise he wouldn't have remembered. The bits and pieces, the phrases, the names, the places, real or imagined, that came back to him occasionally, when he least expected it. Glimpses of an alien world, full of unimaginable tragedies and impossible coincidences.

Left to his own devices, he'd never been much of a reader. Which was perhaps why some of this nonsense stuck in his mind.

'Who do you think killed her?' she'd say. 'The woman in the green coat, with her throat slashed, by the canal. Come on, you're the expert.'

Nobody killed her, she's not real, he found himself thinking, but instead he'd say, 'I'm tired. I'm going to bed,' and she'd purse her lips and make a sort of snorting sound, without looking at him, and carry on reading.

And then when he woke up in the morning she'd be gone. Perhaps, he sometimes wondered, she never slept at all.

God, how long had that gone on?

Sometimes it would be different, though. Sometimes she'd put her book down, and then she would look at him, while he was hanging his suit up or putting his shirt over the back of a chair, and she'd say, 'Do you want to know what Dora did today? Do you want to know what your daughter did?'

And he'd say, 'I'm tired. I can't think. Tell me tomorrow.'

But tomorrow would be too late. The window would have closed. Tomorrow she'd have her head back in one of her books, and all she'd talk about was another stupid story, as if she was making the point, in case he hadn't understood, that he'd missed his chance.

'I think the brother did it. He's definitely creepy. Or is that what I'm supposed to think? What do *you* think?'

What *did* he think?

He looked down and found his hands were clenched on the desk, his knuckles whitening.

What do I think?

The past is never dead.

It's not even past.

'I'll tell you what I think,' he said aloud. 'I think it's time to deal with Terry Mason.'

7

Logan had been waiting for two hours but there was still no sign of the car. There was no garage as far as he could see and plenty of space in the driveway, so where was it? Had Ryan got it wrong? Or was the address just a front? If this turned out to be a dead end, what was he going to do? He didn't have a Plan B. The name she'd given him, Lucy Jane Pargeter, had already come up blank. Strangely, that was the part that hurt the most: that she hadn't told him her real name. He still hoped somehow that at least the Lucy part was real.

'*My name's Lucy.*'

He could still hear her saying it.

'You're pathetic,' he told himself bitterly.

The sun was fully up now, the house bathed in warm light, and he was starting to feel exposed. The farm track fifty yards from the house had seemed perfect when he'd backed the car into it in the early hours: a narrow gap in the thick hedges that lined the road. It was hidden from passing traffic unless you were looking out for it, and it gave him a three-quarter view of the house. But now he realized that anyone looking out of the first-floor windows would have been able to spot him as the sun glinted off his paintwork.

'Getting lazy, Logan,' he chided himself.

He looked at the clock on the dashboard. He'd give it another thirty minutes. If she hadn't appeared by then, maybe he'd just walk up to the front door and ring the bell, see how she reacted, what her story was. At least if it turned out not to be her at all, he'd have saved himself a few more hours of sitting on his arse, waiting for something that wasn't going to happen.

Not much of a Plan B, but what else could he do?

He thought about getting out of the car and stretching his legs, more to see if it provoked a reaction from the occupant of the house than because he needed to, then realized his twitchiness was nothing to do with getting lazy or letting his professional standards slip. It was because it was personal. It was like he wanted to just rip the bandage off and see the wound beneath, however painful it turned out to be.

'Imagine it's a job. Just another job,' he told himself, knowing before the words were out of his mouth that it wouldn't work.

Twenty minutes later the car appeared and he was glad he'd stayed put. It swept past his hideaway and turned into the drive. As it came to a stop, the front door opened and a woman in a long camel-hair coat stepped out. Her hair was less severe than the last time Logan had seen her, and her skin didn't look as pale in daylight, but it was definitely the same woman.

He felt his chest tighten as the emotion flooded back, the sudden shock of seeing Lucy getting into the back seat of the car with her. He turned his attention to the driver as he got out to open the passenger door for her. Logan was pretty sure it was the same driver, too, with his buzz cut, pale moustache and goatee. The driver got back in the driver's seat and pulled away smoothly, heading back in the direction he'd come.

All Logan's doubts instantly vanished. *Now we're in business*, he thought, feeling a spur of adrenaline. He gave it ten seconds, then followed.

For the first mile or so he felt uncomfortably exposed. As the car wound its way past fields and woods, the only traffic was coming in the other direction, and Logan hung back as far as he dared without losing contact. The car slowed to twenty as it entered the next village, and Logan was resigned to losing it if it didn't pass straight through, but as he came out the other side he picked it up again, and even had to check his own speed to keep at a safe distance. Where were they heading? A junction with the A-road leading towards the motorway was a mile up ahead. That would make things a bit more challenging. Logan wished he'd accepted Alex's offer of help. Too late now. If today turned out to be a bust, he could always try again, assuming this was the regular route.

Up ahead the car slowed in the middle of a long, straight

stretch with woods on either side and for a moment Logan thought they were just going to stop. Had the driver clocked him? That would mean no chance of a repeat performance. He was fifty yards away, and preparing to overtake when the car slipped down a concealed turning into the trees and vanished from sight. Logan had to make a quick decision: if their destination was through those trees somewhere, then he needed to park up and follow on foot if he was going to avoid being exposed. But what if it was just a detour, and they ended up joining the main road again after a mile or two? Then he was fucked.

He should have prepped himself better, should have had the map in his head. Stop and follow or keep going? Heads or tails? He thought of Jockey's lucky penny.

It's always heads.

He carried on past, keeping his eyes peeled for somewhere out of sight to hide the car.

Hefting a small daypack, with the collar of his windbreaker pulled up and a black baseball cap low over his eyes, he followed the narrow tarmac road through the trees until he saw something up ahead shining dimly among the shadows. He slipped noiselessly into the damp undergrowth, then edged closer, trying not to mess up his clothes too much in case at some point he had to present himself as someone respectable.

Twenty yards away, he could finally see a series of steel rods projecting from the surface of the road, with two larger black metal posts on either side. The car must have had a device to deactivate the barrier before passing through.

Instinct made him scan the surrounding trees, and he knew if he hadn't been looking, he would have missed it: a tall metal pole, also painted black, with a discreet array of cameras at the top. He remained still, calculating whether the cameras could have picked him up before he left the road. No way of telling. Slowly, he backed deeper into the trees. Which way now? He wanted to keep away from the road, but there was no point just losing himself in the woods.

Did the road just carry on straight through? Or was the barrier also a turning point? Another coin toss. He decided to keep going at forty-five degrees to the road, then turn sharp right.

It was slow going, picking his way carefully through the undergrowth, stopping every few yards to check for more mounted camera points, but something told him he was on the right course. Eventually the bushes began to thin out and the trees became sparser. He slowed even further, resisting the impulse to plunge on and suddenly find himself out in the open. Then he saw something through a gap in the trees and stopped dead. He crept forward at a snail's pace, pushing brambles out of the way, until he could get a better view.

Off to his right the road emerged from the trees and turned into a broad drive, leading to a rectangular grey concrete building in the distance, looking out of place in this rural setting. Two smaller but equally hard-edged struc-tures stood off to the side, the squat cluster of buildings surrounded by gently rolling lawns all the way to the woods beyond, with a scattering of trees and what looked like a couple of large bronze sculptures.

There was no sign of the car.

Logan weighed up his options.

Once he'd stepped out into plain view he'd need a cover story, but even if it held up, it probably wouldn't get him into the main building. He didn't want to be escorted off the premises before he'd learned anything useful. He reached into his daypack and pulled out a pair of compact binoculars. He raised them to his eyes and focused on the main building. To the left of the entrance was a rough block of dark stone with a shiny plaque. He could just make out the words etched into the metal: *Mayview Clinic.*

He scanned the front of the building, then swept the binoculars slowly across the lawns. The whole place seemed deserted.

Then a figure emerged from behind a stand of cypresses. A man in a dark suit. He walked deliberately, arms held stiffly at his sides, eyes on the ground ahead of him, as if he was trying to figure out a problem. Logan thought his lips were moving, but at this distance he couldn't tell if he was actu-ally speaking.

Logan watched as another figure came into view: a man in fawn trousers, an open-necked blue shirt and a brown corduroy jacket. He was following behind the first man, but keeping his distance, slowing when the other man slowed, stopping when he briefly paused to examine something on the sleeve of his jacket, then resuming again, as if the two of them were playing grandmother's footsteps. At one point the first man looked round and the other man smiled broadly, arms loose, palms open, as if to show he wasn't a threat. The first man looked at him, as if weighing him up, then turned his back before starting off again.

Logan blinked, realizing he'd become so absorbed in the odd performance that he'd stopped paying attention to the rest of his surroundings. He looked quickly to his right and saw another figure heading in his direction across the grass from the direction of the main building.

He ducked sharply back into the trees, then picked his way carefully through the undergrowth until he found another vantage point with more cover from the overhanging branches. Moving forward, he parted some of the foliage and looked out again. The figure had changed direction to intercept the two men. The camel-hair coat was gone but it was definitely her. She walked up to the first man, smiling and nodding, then pulled back sharply as he made a sudden movement, reaching into the pocket of his trousers. The second man was behind him in a split second, his whole body tensed. The first man took his hand out of his pocket and held out an empty palm.

The woman nodded and smiled, then said something that sounded to Logan like, 'Oh, I see,' and the second man relaxed, taking a step back. The woman walked over and took him by the arm and they walked a few paces away, speaking quickly, with occasional glances back at the first man, who appeared to be frozen to the spot, gazing vacantly ahead of him. The second man nodded finally and the woman turned back to the buildings.

'Very good, Mr Herbert,' she said breezily as she walked past, but the first man showed no reaction, his eyes seemingly still fixed on something only he could see.

Logan leaned back against a tree and thought about his next move. Thanks to Ryan, he had now confirmed the mystery woman's identity: Dawn Redwood was the woman he'd seen with Lucy that night. And now he'd found out where she worked.

It made sense to see what he could find out about the Mayview Clinic, maybe talk it through with Alex, before figuring out what to do next. At this point, the most important thing was to make a clean exit and get back to the car without stumbling across any tripwires.

But something kept him rooted to the spot.

The two men had wandered off together now, leaving the lawns empty. Logan let the minutes tick by, wondering about the significance of the scene he had just witnessed. It was like a weird play. It would have helped if he had been able to hear more of the dialogue. Or perhaps not.

Still unwilling to go, he focused his binoculars on the nearest sculpture. It looked like . . . he couldn't think what it looked like. The result of a fight to the death between a lump of scrap metal and a blowtorch? It was probably worth millions, though.

Right up your alley, Jockey, he thought.

He lowered the binoculars and something flickered in his peripheral vision. The first man was back, this time alone. He was walking more purposefully now, as if he was actually going somewhere, not just wandering aimlessly, lost in thought. At one point he even looked at his watch.

The man came to a large cypress, stopped and looked towards the main building, then looked at his watch again. He seemed to take a deep breath, as if he was trying to calm himself, and clenched his hands at his sides.

After two minutes another figure appeared, a woman in a pale green trouser suit with long dark hair tied in a loose ponytail. She walked towards the man with an easy but slightly hesitant stride, as if she wasn't sure he'd be pleased to see her. She brushed a strand of hair away from her face with a little shake of the head and Logan instantly recognized the gesture.

Lucy.

His chest tightened as he watched her. She approached the man – Logan now thought of him as the Mad Professor – and said something Logan couldn't hear. The Professor cocked his head to one side as if giving her words proper consideration before replying. She put her hand on his arm and Logan could see him stiffen for a moment then slowly begin to nod.

'All right, Lucy,' he said in a surprisingly clear voice.

Logan found he'd taken a step forward without being

conscious of it, drawn to her as if by a magnet. He carefully pulled himself back into the undergrowth, still unable to take his eyes off her.

They were talking now, lots of smiling and nodding, some curious hand gestures on the Professor's part as if he was trying to solve an invisible Rubik's Cube. She touched his arm again, gently, and Logan tensed, shocked at the sudden stab of jealousy.

All of his plans went out the window in a heartbeat. He wanted to step out onto the grass, call out her name, make her . . . Make her what? He didn't know. And if she simply let him come to her, what then?

Would she throw her arms around him? Burst into tears? Say how sorry she was, how glad she was he'd found her, how she could explain everything?

But what if she didn't? What if she screamed? Ran? Or worse, showed no emotion at all?

He clenched his fists, frightened by the violent emotions he felt surging inside him.

'Can I help you?'

He whirled at the sound of a man's voice, polite but with an undercurrent of threat. How had he not seen him approach? He must have come out of the trees. He had cropped hair and a bodybuilder's physique under a closely fitting black suit and Logan recognized him immediately. The second man in the car.

'Bloody dog. Seems to have done a runner,' Logan said quickly in his best Home Counties drawl.

The man didn't reply.

'You haven't seen her, have you? Little terrier. More trouble than she's worth, but the wife would kill me if I lost her, stupid bitch.' He grinned. 'The dog I mean.'

He could see now the man had a discreet earpiece, and Logan wondered if he was listening for instructions. Logan risked a quick glance to his left. Lucy had her back to him. Had she seen him? There was no sign of the Mad Professor any more.

'Well, if she didn't come this way, she must be in the bloody woods somewhere.' He started to turn away, not sure if the man would try to stop him.

'This is private property,' the man said in the same flat voice.

Logan turned back. 'Thought I'd stumbled onto the golf course, to be honest.'

He squinted at the buildings as if seeing them for the first time. Lucy was gone.

'What is this place, then?'

'It's private property,' the man repeated, and Logan wondered whether that was all he was allowed to say or that was the only phrase he knew. For a second, he thought about getting the stupid bastard in a chokehold to find out, but he knew that was only because right now he just wanted to hurt somebody and this bloke was the only candidate within reach.

'Fair enough. I'll leave you to it, then, see if I can find the bloody dog. If I know anything, she'll be sitting by the car by now with a stupid grin on her face.'

He turned and started crashing noisily through the bushes, feeling the man's eyes on his back until he was swallowed up by the trees.

8

Terry Mason was lying on the bed, his hands folded over his stomach, making a 'to do' list in his head.

Item one: kill that cunt Tenniel.

No.

Item one: find out how he did it, *then* kill him.

No. Be smart. Do things in order.

Item one: reach out to Tenniel. Through Hopper, maybe? Lawyer to copper? No. Someone on Tenniel's team. Young enough and stupid enough to take a message, thinking he's going to get brownie points and not a slap.

Saying? *I've still got something to trade. Something you want. You think you've got it, but you haven't. There's more.*

Would Tenniel go for it? Or just think he was trying it on. Last desperate throw of the dice.

But even if you can get him to bite, or at least get him thinking, *maybe, maybe . . .*

Then what?

What's Tenniel got to trade?

He was still looking at fifteen years, minimum. Could Tenniel do anything about that? No, short answer.

There was one thing he could do, though. If Tenniel thought Mason still had what he wanted, he'd want to make sure Mason didn't have an accident. Until Tenniel got his hands on it.

And then . . . ?

How long could he string that out?

Not ten years, that's for fucking sure.

Mason closed his eyes and massaged the bridge of his nose. Another headache building.

Right. Start again.

Item one: kill that cunt Tenniel.

If anyone thought Terry Mason was finished, then they'd know better. Tenniel might have won the war, but he wouldn't get to enjoy the fruits of victory. Terry Mason could still reach out and put a hand round anyone's throat if he chose to.

Big ask though: Tenniel. That would take some thinking. And hard cash, plenty of it. Enough to be a problem.

Stephanie.

He didn't miss her. Let's be honest. The last few years had been brutal. Especially with all the grief about Kenny. But he needed her. Needed her brain.

Damn.

Item one: find out who ordered the hit on Stephanie. Make them pay. Kill their whole fucking family. Aunts, uncles, cousins, the old fucking grannies and grandpas still living in some one-horse shithole in the mountains. Kill the lot of them, and all their fucking sheep and goats and all. Burn the fucking village down while you're at it.

Not thinking it was locals, then, Terry? No, something in me waters tells me they weren't from Deptford.

He shook his head, annoyed with himself. A bright white lance of pain jabbed him between the eyes.

This isn't a movie. And you're not Tony Montana. Not any more.

How much power did he really have now? The firm had been put out of business. Investigations into various operations still ongoing. His crew scattering like rats in a cellar when a dog's been let loose. How many of them were hunkering down now, waiting it out? And how many had already decided that Terry Mason was as good as dead and gone?

Hopper had his ear to the ground. Hopper was in contact with people. Hopper said the infrastructure was still in place. You just had to adapt. Wait for things to blow over, then start pulling the strings again. But could Hopper be trusted? Or was he just bullshitting him, keeping him sweet until his bills got paid? Maybe he wasn't talking to anybody, or if he was, the word on the street was that with Terry in a cell and Stephanie dead, the firm was finished.

Item one: tell Hopper to sling his hook and get a lawyer with some new bloody ideas. *Yeah? Like what, for instance?* Ah, fuck it. They're all slimy bloodsuckers. Wouldn't trust a single one of them to tell you the time.

He put his hands to his temples. *Jesus H fucking Christ, what is this?*

Item one: get something to stop these fucking headaches.

And not from the infirmary. That pathetic alcoholic. Can't stop his hands shaking long enough to sign the chit. Not that you could blame him, his job. No. From outside. Get Carl's missus to bring them in. Just make sure you wash the packet before opening. *Ha ha.*

Don't trust any of the doctors in here. Don't trust anybody. Maybe the stuff they gave you is already rotting your guts. Poisoning you. Remember to flush the rest down the toilet and don't get any more.

Need something, though. Headaches are fucking killing me.

Item two: get another body put on this landing. Parker's fine. People are scared of Parker. But come at him mob-handed, two or three to keep Parker busy, and then what? He needed another pair of eyes, one in the back of his head. Someone handy. Not going to get anyone else like Parker, but someone with a decent rep. Who else was there? None of the old firm left. Had to sub-contract now. Someone's brother's cousin. Like that meant you could trust them, like they couldn't be got at, because they were family. *Right.*

Might as well just put an ad in the paper. *Bodyguard needed for high-status inmate in well-known maximum security prison in rural location. Bed and board included.* Ha ha. *High risk of getting a blade up your arse when you're not looking. But the wife and kiddies will get taken care of. Opportunities for training, if you like making toys for Romanian orphans. Where do you see yourself in five years' time? Sitting in front of the parole board, shitting myself.*

Seriously, though. Should he try and recruit that sicko on

D Wing? What could he offer him, though? If you gave him money, he'd probably eat it. Or stick it up his arse.

The idea of being anywhere near the cunt made him physically sick, but then it would everybody else, too. Who gives a fuck if you smell like shit, as long as it keeps everyone away, right?

Jesus. What are you thinking? These fucking headaches are fucking up your brain.

Item one: tell Kenny to fuck the hell off out of it. Don't even come and visit. Just get as far away as you can. Go to fucking San Francisco and marry that boyfriend of yours. With my blessing, now that it's too late to mean anything. Sorry I can't be there to give the bride away. I'd even pay for the honeymoon if I could get my hands on any cash, then pay *OK!* to do a big spread. *Love-struck gang boss's son says he's finally going straight. Ha ha.* Every fucking account frozen now, though. And the ones they couldn't find? Well, Stephanie was the only one who knew the codes, and they went up in smoke when she did.

Jesus, when they killed her, they really fucked things up.

Item one: kill those cunts.

Whoever they fucking are.

He sat up and swung his legs off the bed. He knew what was giving him the headaches. It was all this sitting and lying about. He was like Rooney, his old Ridgeback. Two good walks a day or he'd bite your fucking leg off. With him it was running. Davey and Pat fucking hated it. It meant they had to run, too, not just run but keep up, and they were carrying. *Ha*. It got them fit, anyway. They were supposed to be in tip-top condition, the amount of time they spent in the gym, but a good 5k run would have them heaving. Probably spent most of it looking at each other's pecs and checking their body mass index on their smartphones. It was Stephanie who suggested the treadmill. It's madness putting yourself at risk outside like that. And fuck Pat and Dave, they'd be too out of breath to do anything if someone had a pop at you. She was right, of course. It was only a matter of time. But he hated the fucking treadmill, all the same. I mean there's a reason they call them treadmills, right? Makes you think you're in the workhouse like poor old great-grandpa. Or a hamster in a cage.

Prison, that's what treadmills made you think of. Which was funny, because if there'd been a treadmill in this one, he'd have been the first one on it. Boring as shit, maybe, but better than going round the mulberry bush, as they say.

He went and stood at the door. Across the landing he could see through the open door of a cell. He needed someone in there. That line of sight. So he was covered whichever side they came at him from. In the cell next door, Parker could only pick them off if they came right past his nose. Easy enough to just come the other way down the landing and then when Parker heard them starting on him, and finally got off his arse, they just needed someone strolling along on his side to whack Parker on the back of the head when he stuck his nose out. Maybe he'd take a stroll over, introduce himself, if the geezer didn't already know who he was, suggest he might like to upgrade his accommodation. I'm sure the governor would oblige. Find him something with a view of the common. Wave your hanky out the window to your missus. Either that or he might have a nasty accident, walk head-first into the door of his cell, for instance. Or fall down the stairs on the way to chow.

He turned. Parker nodded. 'Mr Mason.'

Good. Doing his job. He had a funny look on his face, though. Nervous. Not the usual boss-eyed stare.

'What is it?'

Parker shuffled his feet. He was shorter than Mason by a good couple of inches. And slighter. Never seen the inside of a gym, that was for sure. Got plenty of exercise, though, beating the shit out of people. He scratched at the scar on his chin through the stubble.

'Just some things I've been hearing.'

'What things?'

'That kiddie-fiddler on A Wing. Screws must have been looking the other way for a moment. Someone got him with a screwdriver on the way to see the doc. He's in the infirmary. Might lose a kidney, they're saying. Not to mention his bollocks.'

Mason sucked his teeth. 'If you find out who did it, tell him there's a Christmas hamper packed with hooch and puff coming his way.'

Parker nodded, but didn't move.

'What else?'

'There's a rumour started up.'

'About what?'

Parker started shuffling again.

'For fuck's sake, spit it out.'

Parker looked down at his feet. 'It's about you, Mr Mason.'

Mason stood up straighter. 'Go on.'

'That you . . . you used to like girls. Little girls. When a shipment arrived, you'd be first in the lorry, looking for the young ones. Take them out if you found one you liked, before sending the rest on.'

Mason took a deep breath. His knuckles were going white where he was holding onto the rail. So that was how they were going to do it. No need to organize a hit. Just put out the word he was a nonce and see who wanted to try their luck.

If you were a lifer – and there were plenty of those – what did you have to lose? Fuck all. And what you got in return was respect. The only currency that really mattered.

Brilliant. Fucking brilliant.

He looked across at the opposite landing. The occupant of the cell he'd been looking at was now standing outside the open door, arms folded across his chest, his eyes fixed on Mason.

9

They'd warned him the turn-off was easy to miss, and if he hadn't made a previous visit, he probably would have. They'd used the words 'discreet' and 'private' a lot during the two phone conversations he'd had, after his personal assistant, an Oscar-worthy performance from Alex, had first contacted them to explain his situation. He made it very clear that discreet and private, not to mention confidential, was exactly what he was looking for and also made sure to throw into the mix the fact that money was no object.

The tone of the conversation, cool to icy to begin with, had changed after that. '*If you'd like to speak with one of the consultants, I'm sure that could be arranged.*' He got a bit icy himself at that point, telling them that, no, he didn't want to speak to '*one of the consultants*'. He wanted a meeting with the Director of Pathways, Dr Redwood, and if that wasn't possible, then he would take his problem – and his money – elsewhere.

He pulled up in front of the barrier and waited for the camera to clock his new number plate. The steel rods retracted smoothly, and he drove on. As he emerged from the wood and the buildings became visible, he couldn't help scanning the lawns in case she was there.

He wondered again if she'd seen him on his previous visit. She couldn't have seen his face properly, but would she have known, somehow, it was him? If she had, if she'd seen him, then she'd also have known he'd be back.

Was she waiting for him now? Had she been nervously counting the hours until his return?

Or had she scarpered? Put as much distance between them as she could so he'd never find her again?

Heads or tails?

And what, in the end, did he even know about her? None of what he thought he knew added up. How could the woman he'd saved from throwing herself in the Thames now be treating patients in some sort of high-end nut-house? And that was just for starters. That dead expression when she'd got in the car . . .

Just stop.

He closed his eyes, took a breath, then opened them again. The lawns were empty. No sign of the Mad Professor. Which made sense, of course. They'd be sure to keep the patients out of the way when there were visitors about.

Looking at their website had been a frustrating exercise in reading between the lines, and after employing his best 'soft interrogation' techniques on whoever it was who spoke to him on the phone (she wouldn't give her name or title), he still only had a very sketchy idea of what the Mayview Clinic actually did.

That it treated patients with mental health issues that mainstream private psychiatric clinics couldn't – or wouldn't – deal with was clear enough. But how it treated them was harder to get a handle on. He'd made notes, underlining the words 'ontological' and 'performative', which seemed to come up a lot, but reading them back, they still didn't make much sense to him and even Alex had eventually thrown in the towel, shaking her head.

Maybe Dr Redwood would translate it all into plain English once she saw the colour of his money.

He drove past the main entrance, as instructed, and parked in a discreet tarmacked area at the back of the building. There were no other cars. As he walked back, brushing down the lapels of his pinstripe suit and adjusting his tie, both courtesy of the walk-in closet in the penthouse's master bedroom, he noted the narrow smoked-glass windows on the second floor. If this was where the patients were housed, it certainly didn't look as if fresh air and sunlight were a big part of the cure.

A young woman dressed like an airline stewardess in first class met him at the door with a bright smile. 'Mr Markham?'

He instantly got into character, scowling at her and grunting something unintelligible.

'If you'd like to follow me.'

They walked through an empty reception area with low, Scandinavian-style chairs and down a dimly lit corridor. She knocked once on a pair of double doors and ushered Logan through.

Dr Redwood was standing with her back to him in front of a floor-to-ceiling window covering the entire length of the room, looking out onto more rolling lawns and a scattering of silver birches. She waited until the stewardess closed the doors behind her with a soft click before turning. She was wearing the same outfit as the night he'd first seen her, her blonde hair pulled back into a tight bun.

For a moment she just looked at him, a neutral expression on her face, as if she was examining a piece of abstract art to try and figure out what it was meant to be. Her eyes were grey, and with her pale lips and slightly waxy complexion, there was something of the showroom dummy about her. What was that movie? *The Stepford Wives*. Logan thought of the bit where one of the husbands stuck a fork into his wife's thigh and she didn't react, just kept on smiling.

Dr Redwood gestured to a pair of boxy grey armchairs. 'Please.'

The chairs were close together but angled so your gaze was drawn to the window and the view. Logan could see it was designed to give you an out if the conversation became too stressful.

Dr Redwood sat back in the armchair and finally smiled. 'So, Mr Markham, I suppose the first thing I should ask is how you heard about the clinic. It's not as if we advertise.'

Alex had bet him that would be the first question, and he was ready. 'I'm in the information business. Information is what I buy and sell. So I know how to find it when I need it.' It was vague – pure bluster – but Logan figured it would be more convincing than some long tale of a friend of a friend with no names attached.

Dr Redwood pursed her pale lips thoughtfully. 'So you'll know that what we do here is something rather different from mainstream therapeutic practice?'

He waved a hand at her impatiently. 'I don't care what you do, frankly. As long as it's not surgery – I don't want that.'

She looked shocked. 'I can assure you—'

'I know, I know, it's all *performative*.' He said the word as if he thought it was the purest bullshit.

'Yes, exactly,' she said. 'I sense you're a practical man, Mr Markham. The sort of person who doesn't care about the theory as long as it works in practice. Am I right?'

He gave a light shrug. 'Something like that.'

'Well, I'm afraid before your wife can be admitted to the Mayview, I am going to have to give you a little more insight into our methodology.'

He grunted. 'Of course.'

'In one way, it's all very straightforward. It's simply that the entire history and practice of psychiatry is based on a fundamental error.'

She paused to let that sink in.

'Don't tell me,' he said, shaking his head. '*People aren't really mad.* Well, if that's your theory, I've got news for you.'

She smiled indulgently. 'No, we don't say there is no such thing as mental disorder. Quite the opposite, in fact. What we do say is that the traditional diagnostic categories are meaningless. To paraphrase Tolstoy, all sane people are the same, but each mad person is mad in his or her own way. Not that we use that word, of course.'

'So you're saying that the doctors who've diagnosed my wife – and there are a few of them, I can tell you – have got it all wrong?'

She raised her hands, palms up, from the arms of her chair, and smiled sadly. 'Why else would you be here?'

He looked out of the window. It had started to rain. 'But you can cure her? You can cure my wife?'

'I sincerely hope so, Mr Markham. But going back to what I just said, until your wife is admitted, we can't assume anything. Whatever you've been told about her condition is simply not relevant. People don't suffer from mental diseases in the way they do from physical ones. If two people have malaria, the causes of the illness, the symptoms they display, the treatment – all are more or less identical. Because our bodies are more or less the same. But when your personality, your identity, suffers a breakdown, by definition your experience and its causes are unique. Because in the end, madness, if we are going to use the term, is a disease of the self.'

'Right. I see. You don't know what you're dealing with, so no guarantees.' He said it in a half-scornful, half-appreciative tone of voice that made it sound as if he thought the whole thing was a clever confidence trick.

'But while I can't share any of our patients' personal details,' she said quickly, trying to reel him back in, 'I can tell you that we significantly outperform conventional psychiatric treatments in terms of positive outcomes.'

'Really?' he said. 'Even though you only get the tough nuts?' He smiled wryly. 'To coin a phrase. I'd like to see the numbers. The data. But I'm sure that's confidential too.'

He cocked an eyebrow at her, but she held his gaze. 'I quite understand if you'd feel more comfortable if your wife took a different route to recovery.'

She looked completely relaxed. If she was desperate for his money, she wasn't showing it. *She'd be a good poker player*, he thought.

He sat up straighter in his chair, then leaned forward. 'I think we've run out of road, as far as that's concerned. This is the final stop for me. The last-chance saloon. It doesn't matter what I think about your methods. I don't have any choice.'

'There's always a choice, Mr Markham,' she said.

'Well, I've made mine. I just need to know a few things.'

Logan tried to recall the list he and Alex had made, questions about his 'wife's' treatment that would tell them more about what was going on here.

'Will she be restrained? Is she free to come and go?'

'All our patients must admit themselves voluntarily. But they must also sign a declaration committing themselves to a certain period of treatment. Within that period, they must remain here.'

'You mean you'll prevent them from leaving? Physically?'

'If necessary,' she said.

He nodded. 'What about drugs?'

'We don't use drugs,' she said firmly.

'Not even sleeping pills?'

She shook her head. 'Not even painkillers. And no alcohol.'

'And she'll have her own room?'

'Of course. With a view. They're really very nice.'

'What about mixing with the other patients?'

'You don't have to be concerned for her safety, Mr Markham. We have fully trained staff in attendance at all times.'

'That isn't an answer.'

'Sometimes social interactions can be beneficial,' she said. 'If they're strictly controlled, of course.'

He pretended to consider that. 'Fine. You know best. I just don't want her mixing with . . . I just don't want her to get upset.'

'Of course.'

'Right.' He hesitated, knowing this was the risky bit. 'One last thing. I've looked at the profiles of your . . . I don't know what to call them.'

'Our therapeutic team?'

'Yes. I'd like to talk to one of them.'

She nodded. 'I can see who's available.'

'There's one. One in particular. I thought she sounded . . . her background sounded as if it might be relevant to my wife's . . . preoccupations.'

She raised an eyebrow. 'Really? Who was that?'

'Lucy Summers. Dr Summers.'

There were six of them listed on the website: three men and three women. The Mad Professor had called her 'Lucy' when she came to talk him down from whatever delusions he was having. One of the 'therapeutic team'. It had to be her.

She looked at her watch. 'Dr Summers should have just finished a session. I'll see if she can spare us a few minutes.'

'Thank you.' He looked away as she tapped out a text, hoping she wouldn't be able to detect his elevated heart rate, the blood rushing to his head. He pretended to brush some invisible lint from the sleeve of his jacket.

'Can I get you anything while we wait?'

'No. Thank you.' He willed himself to remain in the chair, not to jump up and start pacing.

'Excuse me for a moment.' She got up and opened the door. He heard her heels clacking down the corridor. He turned his head away, watching the raindrops zig-zagging down the glass.

After a few minutes he heard footsteps returning and muffled voices. He forced himself to keep his gaze fixed on the window.

The voices stopped and he turned slowly.

Dr Redwood was standing next to a middle-aged Asian woman in a brown woollen skirt and a baggy jumper.

'Mr Markham? I'm Dr Summers.'

Logan looked at her. He couldn't think of anything to say.

Dr Summers threw Redwood a quizzical glance, then turned back to Logan.

'You wanted to ask me some questions about our treatment regime?'

Logan swallowed. 'Yes. Yes, that's right.'

He wracked his brain for an intelligible question. He could feel a sheen of sweat forming on his forehead.

'The . . . treatment. How long does it take? I mean, on average.'

Idiot, he thought.

'Well, if I had that figure – which I don't – it wouldn't be very meaningful. As I'm sure the director has explained, everything we do here is focused on the individual.'

He nodded. 'Sure, I get all that. I mean, what I suppose I'm asking is, what I'd be curious to know . . . I mean, for instance, what's the longest a patient has stayed here?'

Dr Summers glanced at Redwood again. Dr Redwood gave her an almost imperceptible nod.

'We have some patients who have been with us for extended periods. But that is rare, very rare.'

'What are we talking about? Months? Years?'

'In one case more than a year.'

He thought of the Mad Professor. A year. That didn't sound like treatment. More like incarceration. He wondered who was paying his bills.

Dr Summers looked at him with a sympathetic smile. 'I understand your concern, Mr Markham, but at this stage I'm afraid we can only talk in general terms. Once . . . your wife, I believe? Once she has – if you both choose to go forward with treatment, of course – once she has been assessed, then hopefully we can be more specific. We don't like to set targets, but we have expectations, and of course, we keep you constantly updated with progress reports.'

'Yes, I'm sure.' He stood up and looked at his watch. 'I have to go, I'm afraid. Thank you for . . .'

'That's quite all right.'

He nodded then turned to Dr Redwood. 'I'll be in touch.'

She walked with him back towards the entrance. Had he let the mask slip? He was sure she could sense his anxiety, the wild emotions churning inside him: she was a shrink, after all. Would she wonder why he'd lost it when Dr Summers appeared? Or would she just assume he was worried about his wife?

He made it to the car without screaming out loud, and drove slowly down the drive and through the trees, then out onto the road. He turned left, then drove for ten minutes in no particular direction, before pulling into a lay-by. He sat with his hands on the wheel, staring at nothing.

So, that was Lucy Summers. Dr Summers.

Unless . . .

Unless she *had* seen him, and they'd made a switch?

The real Lucy Summers was now long gone? Somewhere he wouldn't be able to find her.

He shook his head. Who was he trying to kid?

He replayed the scene with Lucy and the Mad Professor in his head. The Professor had been agitated. The voices in his head obviously giving him a hard time. Then Lucy had appeared. Calmed him down. She'd looked to be in control. So he'd assumed . . .

But now he realized there was another way of looking at the scene. The Professor hadn't been agitated, just impatient. As if he was waiting for someone.

Sometimes social interactions can be beneficial . . .

Christ.

Deep down, had he known the truth all along? Had he just been in denial?

Well, he couldn't deny it any longer. Lucy wasn't a doctor at the Mayview Clinic.

She was a patient.

10

'Are you all right?'

Logan looked up. Alex was looking at him, frowning.

'Sorry, I was miles away. What did you say?'

'Doesn't matter. Tell me what happened. I'm guessing it was nothing good.'

They were sitting on narrow benches either side of a scarred wooden table that looked as if it had been reclaimed from a skip and then half-heartedly sanded down. Two coffees were steaming in front of them in oversized cups. Through the window you could see down a cobbled street to the canal, but mostly what caught the eye were cranes cramming the skyline, like vultures jostling each other over a corpse.

The corpse of the city.

The corpse of the past.

'You know, I think I might have dossed down in this place, once upon a time. When it was just an abandoned warehouse. If you told me then that one day I'd be sitting here drinking a four-quid cup of coffee served by a pixie with pink hair and a ring through her tongue, I'd have thought you were mental.'

'Didn't you like it? I was thinking of getting one, actually.'

'It would look good on you.'

'Not sure Mrs Allenby would agree.'

'You never know. She's a dark one. She's probably got tattoos all over.'

Alex winced. 'Let's not go there.'

They picked up their cups and drank for a bit in silence.

Then Logan said, 'I'm sorry, it's difficult. It wasn't what I was expecting.'

Alex nodded, putting her cup down. 'OK.'

'You see, I'd got it into my head she must be a doctor there. Stupid.' He looked at her. 'You knew, didn't you? You'd figured it out.'

Alex didn't say anything.

Logan sighed. 'Anyway. I had the big meeting with Redwood. Got all the chat. I wasn't paying attention, to be honest. Didn't catch the half of it. I was just waiting so I could see . . . her. *Dr Lucy Summers.*' He shook his head. 'Fucking idiot.'

'So Dr Summers wasn't her.'

He paused. Took another sip of coffee. 'Course it fucking wasn't. She's not a doctor there, is she? She's a patient.' He closed his eyes for a moment. 'Sorry, Alex, this is doing my head in.'

Alex waited until he'd taken a couple of deep breaths.

'It's all right. I'm OK.'

The pixie walked past their table. 'Can I get you guys anything else? We've got some really nice almond croissants baked, like, a couple of minutes ago.'

'We're good, thanks.' Alex flashed her a smile. The pixie shrugged good-naturedly and walked back to the counter. Alex turned back to Logan. 'I was worried you were going to tell her you used to shit in the kitchen area.'

Logan managed a smile. 'There's still time.'

'OK, so what's the plan now?' Alex said.

'I was afraid you were going to ask me that.'

'Well, now I have, so what is it?'

'How do you fancy being my mad wife for the day?'

Alex sat back. 'I've had better offers.'

'I'll bet. And if you say no, that's fine, I understand.'

'For how long? My boyfriend gets jealous when I get married to other men.'

'You haven't got a boyfriend.'

'Imaginary boyfriend.'

'Now you're getting into the swing of it.'

'How mad do I have to be?'

'Not a big performance. You'll be under sedation – I mean, that's what I'll tell them. If you agree, that is. So, you just have to be a bit of a zombie, you know. Just say yes and no when they ask you questions. No frothing at the mouth or telling them aliens have stolen your brain.'

She nodded. 'Flattened affect, they call it.'

'Whatever.'

'So how long does this performance have to go on for? I know this might sound pathetic, but I really don't want to get locked up in some private loony bin if I can help it.' She put a hand to her mouth. 'Jesus. Sorry, that was insensitive.'

He shrugged it off. 'Won't happen, I promise. I just want them to give us the tour, you know, show us round. See how comfy your room is. The lovely views. All that. Then I say thank you very much, it all looks splendid, my wife needs to go home for a lie-down now, I'll be in touch.'

'But why? What's the point? I thought the idea was to find Lucy.'

'It is. And if we can see where the patients' rooms are, how many, get a sense of the layout, the security, then maybe we can think up a way of . . .'

He trailed off.

Alex's eyes widened. 'What? Getting her out?'

He sat back and folded his arms. 'Yes.'

'Bloody hell, Logan. Do you have any idea what you're getting yourself into? I mean, let's look at it logically. She tried to kill herself. She gave you a fake name. And then her psychiatrist came and took her back to the hospital, where she . . .'

'Belongs?'

Alex paused.

'Maybe. Yes, maybe. I mean, she's definitely not well.'

'But something's not right. I know it isn't. Something about that place. And those people – Redwood and her two goons. When they took her. It was like Lucy was a prisoner.'

Alex sighed. 'OK. Just so long as you've thought it through. If you take her away from there, you'll be responsible for her. She could be . . .'

'I just have to know, Alex. I just have to know. I have to talk to her, to hear her side of it. I can't just leave her there.'

'Even though she left you?' She winced. 'Sorry, that was below the belt.'

He shrugged. 'Maybe she didn't have any choice. I want to give her the choice.'

Alex shook her head, smiling. 'You're really mad about her, aren't you?'

'I suppose you could say that.'

'And I must be mad to go along with it. But I will. When are you planning our visit?'

'I'll call them today. See what they say. But I reckon it'll be soon. With a bit of luck I managed to give them the impression that money's no object when it comes to my darling wife, so they'll be keen.'

'You just want to have me locked up somewhere where I won't be an embarrassment to you with my ranting and raving at you,' she pouted. 'Just like Mrs Rochester in *Jane Eyre*.'

'Just shut up and take your meds,' Logan said.

Alex caught the pixie's eye and ordered two more coffees, plus one almond croissant.

'I'm starving,' she said, demolishing it in three bites, then wiping her mouth with the back of her hand.

She took a swallow of her coffee. 'And what about you, Logan? Are you sure you can cope with all this shit on top of the day job? We've got a contract killer to run to ground, remember?'

'Don't worry. I'm going to see a man about a dog, tomorrow.'

'Fine, but seriously, you're putting a lot of pressure on yourself.'

Logan picked up his cup and took a swallow. 'Look, I hear what you're saying. But this is the way I look at it. We've all got two lives, yeah? All of us in this business. We get up, go to work, do crazy shit, then come home and try to be a husband, a wife, a . . . father. It's hard. Marriages break up. People start drinking, using drugs. But I've only got one life now. The Blindeye life. The rest is a blank. I had Sarah and Joseph for a while, but not any more. I've got one thing, though . . . maybe. And that's Lucy. So maybe, I don't know, maybe I'll have a second life again. So I'm just doing what everybody does: I'm trying to juggle things. Because if there's one thing I've managed to get into my thick skull, it's that you need more than just the day job, if you're not going to go totally out of your fucking mind.'

'Right,' Alex said. 'Right. I get that. And I . . . approve. I think you've got the right idea. You deserve to have a life. It's just . . .'

'Yeah, I know,' Logan said. 'Maybe getting involved with someone like Lucy isn't the best way of going about it.'

'Maybe not,' Alex nodded, but she was smiling. 'A bit like juggling flaming torches with chainsaws.'

'Or hand grenades,' Logan said.

'Yeah. But I guess when it comes to love you don't get to choose.'

'No, you don't.'

They finished their coffee in silence.

'You know what, though?' Logan said at last. 'I think there's someone you should be worrying about more than me.'

'Christ, who could that be?' Alex said.

'Alan. I think he might be unravelling a bit. You know the last job really got to him. Thinking he was a target. That was a first. He's used to being the back-room boffin, not on the front line. And getting in Tenniel's face now, that just feels like tweaking the tiger's tail. He's scared shitless.'

'But if we don't find out who killed Claire, Craig and John Jennings, then he can never feel safe, can he? He's always going to be looking over his shoulder.'

'I think he'd rather go and hide under a rock.'

Alex considered that for a moment. 'Is this going to be a problem for us?'

'Depends on how far he unravels.'

She nodded thoughtfully. 'I've often wondered about that.'

'What?'

'Well, what happens to old intelligence officers when they start losing their marbles. You know, they can't remember their own names, they've forgotten they ever signed the Official Secrets Act, but there's still all this classified stuff rattling around in their heads that could pop out at any moment.'

'Yeah, but who are they going to tell? Those poor bloody minimum-wage care workers in the old folks' homes aren't going to be paying attention when the old codgers start babbling about the good old days, are they?'

'Maybe not. Unless they're plants, of course.'

'Fucking hell, Alex, what have you been reading?'

'Nothing. I was just thinking. And it doesn't have to be old codgers, either. What if you're someone like Alan, you just want out of it. But now you're walking around with all this information. You can't just press delete, can you? Can't put it all through a shredder.'

She laughed and shook herself.

'I don't know why I'm thinking about this morbid stuff.'

Logan downed the last of his coffee. He thought for a minute.

'I do.'

Alex cocked an eyebrow.

'It's the Mayview Clinic. Who knows what's really going on in there?'

Alex frowned. 'I don't get you.'

'Well, what if that's what they're doing? Deleting files. Wiping the slate clean.'

Alex looked at him. 'Sometimes I don't know when you're joking.'

He held her gaze, not saying anything.

'Jesus. Are you serious?'

'I . . . I don't know.'

'Come on, now you think Lucy's a spook? Some sort of intelligence operative who knows too much?'

He frowned. 'It doesn't have to be that. I mean, think about it, there are plenty of other reasons someone might want to wipe your memories. It doesn't have to be intelligence-related.'

Alex blew out a breath. 'I don't know. It's a fuck of an idea. There was nothing about this in the brochure?'

He didn't smile. 'It doesn't have to be all their patients. Maybe some of what they do is legit. You know, a front for the real stuff.'

'Well, when you sign me up, just remember to tick the box for normal treatment, yeah? No extras.'

'I promise.'

'Great. That makes me feel a lot better.'

'Anyway, it's not like you're going to be – I don't know – committed. We're just going to be visiting.'

Alex nodded, but she didn't look convinced. 'I have a funny feeling that's what they always say.'

11

The address Jockey had given him turned out to be only a couple of miles from the penthouse block. Logan probably would have been able to see it from his window if it hadn't been buried down a narrow alley under the railway bridge. But even on the ground, it wasn't easy to find. The mound of old tyres behind a chain-link fence suggested he was on the right track, but the potholed tarmac – which was bad enough – had given way to broken cobbles, making it an unlikely location for a garage, particularly if you had a problem with your suspension. A scrapyard, maybe, but hardly somewhere you'd bring your Lamborghini for a tune-up.

He crept round the corner, and the grinding sound under the bonnet started up again. Under the bridge were a series of alcoves, most with corrugated-iron shutters pulled down, but two of them were open and in one he could see a white Range Rover was up on a ramp. A gleaming maroon Jaguar XJ Sport waited its turn below. A man in jeans and a stained T-shirt was crouched under the Range Rover, while another in blue overalls and a flat cap was sorting through a pile of parts in the corner. Logan drove slowly past the bays until he got to a grey portacabin tucked into the next alcove. Above the window was a sign with the words *J. M. Molloy Motors* in a flowing yellow script.

Inside there was just enough room for a battered leather armchair and a narrow desk with a phone facing the window. There was no one behind it. To the left of the desk was a half-open door and Logan could hear low muttering and the squeak of a chair. He knocked, and pushed the door wider.

A fat man in an emerald-green shirt with dark curly hair and a pasty complexion was sitting behind a desk, half hidden by a stack of files and what looked like unopened boxes of parts. His stubby fingers were stabbing at an old-fashioned keyboard as he glared at a computer screen.

'You wouldn't happen to have an ABS sensor for a Jag about you, by any chance?' he said, not turning from the screen. It was a whisky-drinker's voice, low and raspy, with just a trace of a Dublin accent. 'I've been after the bastard thing all day.'

'Sorry,' Logan said.

The fat man grunted without looking up from his screen. His fingers continued their frenetic tapping. 'Never mind. I thought for a moment my prayers had been answered, but it would appear I am to be disappointed yet again.' He hit one final key decisively and swivelled round in his chair.

'Well, if you're not an angel from heaven come to solve my problems, I'm guessing you've a problem of your own.

Don't tell me it's a dodgy ABS sensor because you'll be out of luck.'

He waved a flabby hand at a grey plastic chair on the other side of the desk.

Logan sat down. 'No, nothing like that.'

'What's the problem, then? A tenner says it's the A/C. Always is on those things.' He jerked his head towards the alley. 'I'll even give you odds. Seven to one.'

'There's nothing wrong with the car.'

Molloy sat back and looked at him carefully. 'Nothing wrong with the car. You're after selling it, then?'

Logan shook his head. 'I only just bought it.'

Molloy put his hands down flat on the desk. 'And it runs like a wet dream, you'll be telling me. Well, I enjoy a good mystery as much as the next man, and I would normally be delighted to continue with this twenty questions malarky, but I am a little on the busy side. You don't want your car fixing and you don't want to sell it. What exactly is it you do want?'

'I need your help,' Logan said.

'But not a problem with your car, you say. You may have seen the sign outside with the word "motors" in it and a couple of fellas with spanners in their hands and engine oil in their arse cracks next door. I'm sure there are one or two other clues about the place if you look hard enough. Are you sure you've not taken a wrong turn somewhere?'

'I don't think so. Assuming you're Mr Molloy.'

'I'll admit to that. Unless you're from the Revenue, in

which case I suggest you speak to my wife. God rest her soul. So what is it you think I can help you with?'

'Perhaps we could shut the door?'

Molloy narrowed his eyes. 'You wouldn't be trying to rob me, would you?'

Logan got up and pushed the door closed.

Molloy stiffened. 'Now hold on a minute, there, fella.'

Logan sat down again and reached into his jacket. Molloy dropped a hand under the desk and started easing open a drawer. Logan pulled out a fat envelope, put it down on the desk in front of Molloy and pushed it towards him.

Molloy shut the drawer and put his hand back on the desk without touching the envelope.

'And what would that be?'

'Take a look.'

Molloy's expression darkened. 'Now look, Mr . . .'

'Bailey. Gavin Bailey.'

'Well, Mr Bailey, I think you are labouring under some sort of misapprehension. I run a garage. I fix cars. I over-charge occasionally, but only surly bastards who deserve it.'

'I heard you can help fix other things.'

Molloy paused, sucking his teeth. 'And what sort of things might they be?'

'People. When they become a problem. You make them go away. Or at least you know a man who does.'

Molloy heaved himself up and leaned forward, his knuckles whitening on the desk. 'I think it's time for you to go, Mr

Bailey, or whatever your real name is. And I'd suggest you don't come back any time soon.'

Logan stayed where he was.

'Do I need to get a couple of the boys to escort you off the premises?' Molloy growled.

Logan folded his arms. 'I'm impressed, Mr Molloy.'

'What?'

'If you'd taken the cash, I would have walked away. Jockey said you were serious, top end, but I wanted to be sure.'

Molloy slowly lowered his bulk back into the chair.

'Jockey sent you?'

Logan nodded.

'And what's your connection with him?'

Logan grinned. 'I buy the odd painting from him. A lot of money for a few squiggles, but I get my money's worth, if you know what I mean.'

Molloy nodded. 'And how long have you two been in the art business?'

Logan picked up the envelope and put it back in his pocket. 'Oh, me and Jockey go way back.'

Molloy scratched his chin thoughtfully. 'So if I was to give him a call?'

Logan shrugged. 'Feel free.'

'Oh, I will,' Molloy said. 'And if he says you're an upstanding fella and I should extend you every courtesy, and I decide to do what I can to help out . . . how urgent is this problem of yours? It's just the one, I take it.'

'Just the one,' Logan said. 'But I want it sorted. And I

want it all neat and tidy, if you know what I mean. I want the top man on the job. The best.'

'Oh yes, neat and tidy. It'll be that all right. You don't have to worry yourself on that score. You pay for the best, that's what you get.'

'So what's it going to cost me?' Logan said.

Molloy sucked his teeth, pushing himself back in his chair. 'Well, let's just say, Mr Bailey, that you might have to get yourself a bigger envelope.'

And some real money, Logan thought, *not just bits of newspaper*, relieved that his gamble had paid off.

'Now what about that car of yours?' Molloy said. 'I'll have to get one of the boys to take a look at it, just for appearance sake, if you get what I mean. What'll we say's the problem?'

Logan gave himself another pat on the back for having come prepared. 'Now you mention it, there's a horrible noise coming from somewhere round the front driver's side.'

'Is that a fact?' Molloy said. 'Well, not the electrics, then. That'll be another ten pounds lost to the terrible vice of gambling.'

'I thought you were giving me odds,' Logan said.

'So I was,' Molloy nodded, with a wink. 'But I'm thinking the race might have been fixed.'

Logan smiled, holding out the keys. 'I stuck a little bit of gravel between the brake disc and the protection plate or whatever you call it. Makes a hell of a racket. Shouldn't take your lads long to find it.'

Molloy took the keys. 'Very cute, Mr Bailey. Very cute.'

He leaned on the desk to push himself upright. 'Excuse me for a moment.' He manoeuvred his bulky frame through the doorway and Logan heard him call out, 'Lenny!' There was a muttered conversation and then the sound of Molloy's heavy tread as he re-entered the office.

'Right,' he said, settling himself down again in his chair. He reached under the desk, and Logan tensed for a moment. Molloy pulled out a bottle of whiskey and two tumblers. 'Not too early for you, is it?'

'Not at all,' Logan said. 'What are we drinking to?'

Molloy poured two generous measures and handed a glass to Logan before raising his own.

'To a problem shared,' Molloy said. 'Because, as they say, a problem shared is a problem halved.'

They clinked glasses. Logan took a sip while Molloy downed half of his glass in one gulp.

'I want it more than halved,' Logan said.

'Ah, it's just an expression,' Molloy said.

'I want it chopped up into little bits and put into a wood-chipper.' Logan grinned. 'Just so you understand.'

Molloy put his glass down carefully on the desk.

The two men looked at each other.

'I get your meaning right enough,' he said.

'So what now?' Logan asked.

'OK, so this is the way it works. You leave the motor with me. The boys'll have a poke around under the bonnet, and in a day or two I'll give you a bell, give you the bad news about what they found. You'd best be prepared, because it might be a bit worse than a couple of spark plugs and a new fan-belt, if you know what I mean.'

'I'll make sure I'm sitting down,' Logan said. 'What then?'

'We arrange a time for you to come in and collect the car. Early evening's best. Sadly I'm in the office late more often than not, catching up on all the damnable paperwork after the lads have gone off to unburden themselves of their wages at the nearest licensed premises.'

Logan nodded. 'Sounds sensible.'

'Just make sure you bring all the relevant details, you know, so I can add them into the mix when it comes to the invoice.'

Logan raised an eyebrow.

'The details of the problem. You know, name, address, a photograph's always handy, anything else you think might be relevant.'

'Like?'

'Timetables, schedules, *habits*. That sort of thing. Like, for instance, on the third Friday of every month, your man sets his alarm for four a.m., makes himself a thermos of tea, then drives himself to a lonely spot on the edge of Hampstead Heath and waits for the dawn, so he can catch a glimpse of some rare feathered visitor.'

'I don't think I can guarantee anything like that.'

'Of course you can't, Mr Bailey. Otherwise you could put a bird-caller and a tyre iron in the back of your car and do the job yourself. It tends to be a wee bit more complicated than that. Which is why you need some professional assistance.'

'I'll do what I can,' Logan said.

'Well, you've time to think about it. Go home, give the old piggybank a good rattle and I'll give you a bell when we've discovered what a pitiable state your motor's in.'

Logan shook his head wryly. 'Just like a real garage. And if I don't have a problem with the invoice, what then?'

'I'll be in touch about handing over the cash.'

'All of it? The whole lot upfront?'

'That's the way it works, Mr Bailey, I'm afraid.'

Logan scratched his chin. 'And what if I'm not happy with the repairs? What if the problem hasn't gone away?'

'Oh it will, Mr Bailey. You give us name, rank and serial number, and if it's doable – if it's not an actual member of the royal family, if they don't have round-the-clock protection from that gang of murderers, the SAS, then my man will do the rest. There's no one better. If in his expert opinion it can't be done, then I'll adjust the invoice accordingly, just a few quid to make things look kosher.' He leaned forward, making his chair squeak uncomfortably. 'You have to pay to play in this game, Mr Bailey. If you're not comfortable putting all your chips on the table, if the stakes make you feel a wee bit light-headed, then maybe it's not for you.'

'It's not the stakes I'm worried about, Mr Molloy. It's the odds.'

'Oh, you can rest easy on that score, Mr Bailey. With our man in the saddle, it's a dead cert.'

'OK, so our friend scopes out the target, assesses the level of difficulty and names his price,' Logan said. 'Then I come back here with the cash?'

Molloy waved a hand airily. 'Let's not get ahead of ourselves. Since this is our first waltz together, we'll take it a step at a time. Sufficient unto the day,' he added with a lopsided grin. 'Sufficient unto the day.'

12

'So where exactly is this garage?'

They were crowded round Ryan as he brought the details up on his laptop. Logan pointed. 'There. That's Molloy's office, and there are the two bays with the ramps.'

Mrs Allenby tapped her fountain pen on the screen. 'What about here? Looks like some sort of warehouse. Is it still in operation?'

Logan leaned closer, squinting. 'Not sure. Sorry.'

'Well, you're the experts, but I can't see anywhere that would serve as an observation point, where you wouldn't be exposed.'

'And anyway,' Alex said, 'it's all a bit of a rat-run. If you had to move fast, how long would it take you to exit?'

'Too long. We need two followers minimum if they're in a vehicle. We can't afford to have one of them stuck there,' Logan said.

'What if they're on foot?' Mrs Allenby asked.

'Worse,' Alex said. 'We just haven't got the bodies. We'd need a proper team if they're not going to make us.'

Logan stood up. 'With respect, I don't think our guy is going to risk making an appearance at the garage. Molloy's too cute for that. Jockey says he's been in this game a while. No one keeps their nose clean that long without being very, very careful. He looks like a slob and the garage is a dump, but I think he's neat and tidy where it counts – when it comes to his real business.'

'How do you think they'll make contact, then?' Mrs Allenby asked.

'If it was me?' Logan thought for a moment. 'Probably send a text message. Your car's due for a service or I've found that Jag you were after or something. Code for "I've got a job for you". The guy replies, something with a date in it, and that's when they'll meet.'

'And that's where Molloy will hand over the money,' Ryan said.

'Yeah, he's not going to do it at the garage.'

Mrs Allenby turned to Alan, who was still sitting down, looking pensive. 'What about his phone? Could we get access to his messages?'

'Assuming he's not using the landline . . . tricky. We'd have to get hold of his mobile, and then get it back again.'

'You couldn't do it remotely?'

Alan rubbed his chin. 'I'd still have to get close. In that location? I don't know . . .'

'And anyway, even if we could see all his messages, how do we identify the one we want? Like Logan said, it's going to sound routine, that's the point,' Ryan said.

'It's going to be right after Logan delivers the money, though, isn't it?' Alex said. 'I mean, why wait?'

Logan turned away from the screen and started pacing. 'We'd still be guessing. We need to be a hundred per cent sure it's our guy.'

'Or gal,' Alex said.

'You've been watching too many movies,' Logan said. 'It's not going to be some cute kid, either. It'll be a hairy-arsed ex-Army bloke with all the tattoos to prove it.'

'That's just unconscious bias,' Alex said. 'It'll trip you up one of these days if you're not careful.'

'If we could return to the task in hand,' Mrs Allenby said. 'You mentioned "the money", Mr Logan.' Logan stopped pacing. 'Would you care to expand on that?'

'Well, I got away with showing him an envelope stuffed with old newspaper the first time, but next time I'll need to deliver the real goods.'

'And how much do you think that might be?'

'Well, I'm guessing here. It depends on how easy we make the hit look. You know, if the target is some old geezer living alone in a bungalow, that's one thing, but if there's security involved . . .'

'I imagine if it's supposed to be to do with business and not personal, then there would very likely be security consid-erations,' said Mrs Allenby.

'And this . . . person,' Logan said. 'I don't think they do common or garden "bashing the wife on the head so you can run off with your secretary" type of jobs.'

'Listen to yourself!' Alex said, rolling her eyes.

'How much?' Mrs Allenby said firmly.

'Fifty grand? A bit more maybe,' Logan added sheepishly.

'And where were you thinking that was going to come from? There are some things I can produce, but a briefcase full of crisp twenty-pound notes is not one of them, I'm sad to say.'

'OK, fair enough. But maybe we can make a virtue of necessity,' Logan said.

Mrs Allenby sat down. 'I'm listening.'

'OK, let's say Molloy gives the green light. In an ideal world I stroll up to the garage with the money and Molloy tucks it away in the safe. But from that point on, we've got to be watching Molloy 24/7, ready to follow him wherever he goes in case he's meeting our guy, even though for all we know there's another cut-out – Molloy hands the package over to someone else and *he* delivers it to our man. And even if we get lucky, we then have to switch to our new target in mid-stream and *then* figure out a discreet way to remove him to a location where we can interrogate him. It all gets a bit complicated. Too many working parts.'

'Bit negative,' Alex said, frowning.

'I see your point,' Mrs Allenby said. 'Do you have an alternative suggestion? Something that doesn't involve large amounts of cash that we don't have?'

'I go to Molloy. I say, "I've got your money." He says, "Thank you very much, if you'd care to just hand it over." I say, "Well, you come highly recommended, but I don't feel comfortable just handing over such a sizeable sum seeing as we've never dealt with each other before. I want to know who I'm dealing with. I want to make sure my horse has got all four legs before I put my money on him. I want to examine his teeth and look him in the eye."'

'And if he says no?'

Logan shrugged. 'I say, "Oh well there goes your commission, you greedy fat bastard."'

'Nice,' Alex said.

'You could wear a wire,' Ryan said. 'Get him to incriminate himself.'

'Then play him back the tape,' Mrs Allenby suggested.

Logan chewed his lip. 'That could put people at risk.'

'You mean apart from us,' Alan said.

'Jockey,' Alex said.

Logan nodded. 'Yeah. If I turn out to be a wrong 'un, it's his reputation on the line.'

'I thought you said he was a major-league drug dealer,' Mrs Allenby said, pursing her lips. 'He's paid to have his competitors killed, you said. Wouldn't it be poetic justice if the tables were turned?'

'He's a friend,' Logan said, not quite sure if he meant it or in what way. '*Was* a friend. Whatever.' He shook his head. 'Anyway, I can't stitch him up like that.'

'Then we seem to have a problem,' said Mrs Allenby. 'We need to devise a way to intercept Mr Molloy's communications and then a practical plan of surveillance.'

'And kidnap,' Ryan added.

'It's not as if you haven't done it before,' said Mrs Allenby, looking at Logan.

'Let me think,' said Logan. He put on his cheeriest smile. 'Brew, anyone?'

'I could do with a cuppa,' said Alan, standing up slowly, as if in pain, and heading slowly over to the kitchen area.

'Is he all right?' Alex asked in an undertone.

'Arthritis, he says,' Ryan said. 'He's been popping pills all morning.'

Mrs Allenby looked over at Alan, filling the kettle. 'Keep an eye,' she said softly, looking around the table.

Logan went and joined Alan.

'You all right, mate?'

Alan gave him a baleful stare. 'Not really.'

Logan put an arm round his shoulder. 'Look, I know you're shit-scared. All your career you've been tinkering away in the back room. Now you're on the front line and you're—'

Alan frowned. 'That's not what I'm scared of.'

'What, then?'

Alan dropped teabags into a couple of mugs and filled them with boiling water. 'It's my mum. She's losing her marbles a bit. I can see a time when I'll have to be looking after her full time. I mean, there's no one else, and I'm not putting her in a home.'

'That's tough,' Logan said, trying to imagine having a parent you cared that much about.

'Yeah, well, that's life, isn't it? But you know the thing

that's eating away at me? I'd have to give this up. Yeah, it's not nice when you think someone might be out to push you under a train, but without all this, I'd . . . I don't know what I'd do.'

Logan grinned. 'You're just an adrenaline junkie underneath it all.'

Alan gave him a rueful half-smile in return. 'Yeah, something like that.'

Logan picked up his mug. 'Tell you what, let's get that fucker Tenniel and then we'll figure something out. There's always a way.' He steered Alan back to the table where Mrs Allenby was studying her notes, while Ryan tapped away at his laptop. Alex stopped chewing a nail and raised an eyebrow as Logan sat down and he gave her a brief wink.

'Something's been bothering me about this whole set-up. A couple of things, actually,' Ryan said hesitantly.

'Yes?' said Mrs Allenby.

'The price is going to vary depending on the target, right? The logistics. I mean, we're guessing how much, but it could be significant.'

'Yeah, we know that,' said Logan.

Ryan hesitated. 'So you need to give Molloy the details of the target before he tells you how much. And he's not going to want a text or an email. Not even a phone call. He's going to want a good old-fashioned bit of paper he can destroy. Maybe a photo. Hand-delivered for preference.'

'OK,' Logan said. 'Where are we going with this?'

'Well, it means you're going to have to make another visit to the garage to hand over the money.'

Logan started drumming his fingers on the table. 'And?'

Ryan looked to Alex for help.

'I . . . think what Ryan's getting at,' she said slowly, 'is that if Molloy's as security-conscious as we think, a third trip to the garage might be one too many. It might start to look a bit suspicious.'

'Also, is he going to want to be holding onto the cash?' Ryan said, more confidently. 'My guess is, once you've handed over the target details, he's going to suggest another location for the handover of the money.'

Logan thought about it, then nodded. 'Maybe.'

'In which case, there'd be no point in setting up an OP at the garage,' said Mrs Allenby.

Alan, who was gripping his mug tightly with both hands, visibly relaxed.

'So the chances are, we're going to be looking at a new location,' Alex said. 'And not much time to figure out how we're going to track the money once Molloy's got it.'

Alan stopped with his mug halfway to his mouth and looked around nervously.

'Which brings us back to the money,' said Mrs Allenby tersely.

'Actually there is another problem,' Ryan said, closing his laptop slowly. 'I've been thinking about the target. I mean, they've got to be real, haven't they? The hit-man, or . . .'

'Shall we just say "assassin",' said Mrs Allenby. 'Even

though it sounds rather old-fashioned. Perhaps "killer" would be better.'

Ryan nodded. 'Our killer's going to want to check everything out, all the details, aren't they?'

'He's not going to make any serious moves until he has the money,' Logan said. 'With a bit of luck, we'll have taken him off the streets before he starts making plans.'

'But what if Molloy passes on the info and the killer decides to do a bit of a feasibility study before the money changes hands? If you've put Mr S. Holmes at 221B Baker Street, he's going to know it's not kosher, isn't he?' said Ryan.

'Right,' said Logan. 'So it's got to be a real person. With the right address. All of that.'

'And it's got to be doable,' said Alex.

Logan shrugged. 'So pick someone out of the phone book. What's the problem?'

'The problem,' Mrs Allenby said, 'at least I think this is what Mr Oldfield is getting at, is what happens if we lose track of the money? What if we aren't able to stop the killer before he carries out the hit? An innocent person gets killed because we handed their details over. Because, not to put it too bluntly, *we* hired someone to kill them.'

'We just make sure we bloody well do get to them before that happens,' said Logan.

'Not good enough,' said Mrs Allenby, shaking her head. 'Do I need to remind you we're in the business of reducing the risks to innocent civilians, not creating new ones?'

'I'm sure I could think of a few people who wouldn't be

missed,' said Logan. 'I might even put a few quid in the kitty myself.'

'This is not a joke,' Mrs Allenby said sternly. She turned to Ryan. 'Since you identified the problem, I'm looking to you to find an appropriate solution.'

Ryan nodded solemnly. The rest of the faces around the table looked grim.

'But we're still going ahead?' Logan said, looking at Mrs Allenby.

She looked down at the table, tapping her gold pencil on her notepad for a few seconds before looking up.

'While we have no alternative, yes,' she said, with obvious reluctance. 'But I would sleep a lot easier in my bed if we had a Plan B.'

Alex glanced quickly at Logan before speaking. He had his arms folded and an expression on his face that she'd seen before: he was sick and tired of talking about the pros and cons, the what ifs and the maybes. He was itching to get out there and start doing something, whether it made sense or not.

'Well,' she said, 'I mean, what we want to find out is if Tenniel ordered the hits on Claire, Craig and John Jennings and why. So, who else might know, apart from the killer? And Tenniel, obviously. What about Terry Mason? Tenniel seems to have taken a lot of risks to put him in jail, and we think he may have had Mason's wife killed as well because she hired the hit-man. Maybe Mason knows what's behind it all.'

'And how would you propose finding out?' Mrs Allenby asked.

'Someone talks to him,' Alex said.

'And why would he talk to anyone?' Logan said, arms still crossed. 'Anyone he doesn't know.'

'Because . . . they've got evidence that would blow up the prosecution case.'

'Come on: how many counts was he convicted on?' Logan said.

'I don't know – planted evidence, illegal searches, fruit of the poisoned tree – something. It just has to be plausible enough to get his attention.'

Mrs Allenby tapped her pencil on the table. 'It's a big risk, putting yourself in that environment. And how are you going to persuade him to see you in the first place? We must assume his mail is being monitored, and visits will be severely restricted. You're going to have to come up with a better plan before I consider giving it the green light.'

Logan unfolded his arms and looked at Alex. 'I reckon you'd better come up with it quick, too.'

13

Logan felt a bit of a twat in the Range Rover, but while his own car was still at Molloy's garage, he didn't have much choice. There were three cars in the basement garage belonging to the man he was being paid to impersonate, the Range Rover and some sort of kit car without a marque that looked as if it went from nought to a hundred in the time it took you to think about it. It would have been fun to pull up in front of Jockey's gates in a speed machine like that, just to see the look on his face, but in the end it would have made his job more difficult. Plus, if you drove a car like that at anything under ninety on the open road, you'd look like even more of a twat than someone driving an off-roader through Belgravia without a splash of mud on it, and Logan wasn't going to risk getting pulled over by the plods, or worse, wrapping two hundred grand's worth of car round a tree. He wasn't supposed to use the cars at all, in fact – the whole point was to stay home, not tootle round the country-side – but he'd found the keys in a drawer, and one afternoon when he'd had nothing better to do, he'd gone down to the garage and figured out which overpriced status symbols they belonged to. Now, like any other self-respecting Range Rover owner, he was hoping to keep his car out of the muck so it wouldn't look out of place when it rejoined all its shiny friends in the city.

He parked up fifty yards from the gates, then strolled over and pushed the buzzer. He'd thought of dressing up a bit, too, just to keep Jockey off-balance, but again, he'd decided that looking like a successful hedge-fund manager might not work in his favour when he came to make his pitch.

Lisa appeared a bit quicker than the last time, which was nice, and she even had a cool quarter-smile on her face when she got to the gate.

'Mr Logan.'

'Lisa. Nice to see you. I don't have an appointment, on account of it slipping Mr Cameron's mind to give me his email or phone number. But I was in the neighbourhood, and I thought I'd pop round on the off-chance he was free for a bit of a chin-wag.'

The quarter-smile turned into a half-smile, she pressed a button on her walkie-talkie, and the gates started to swing open. So Jockey already knew he was here and had decided not to give him the brush-off. Well, that made things easier. He could forget all the bullshit he'd rehearsed on the drive down.

He walked through. 'After you,' he said, expecting her to lead him to the house, but she merely stepped to the side, without speaking, the hint of a smile gone. It seemed to

Logan that she was discreetly removing herself from the line of fire.

Maybe not such a warm welcome, then.

Logan heard the low hum of the gates closing behind him. Should he make a dash for it, while he still could?

Instead, he found himself standing still, looking expectantly at the front door at the end of the drive as it slowly opened, resisting the urge to turn his head and do a quick three-sixty threat assessment before getting Lisa in a headlock and putting a blade to her throat.

Why was he doing nothing?

Was it just that he was afraid of looking a twat in front of Lisa if it turned out he was over-reacting?

He knew plenty of people who'd died that way.

Come on, soldier. You can put away that gun. You're not afraid of a wee girl, are you?

Maybe he just didn't care enough.

Bring it on.

Then he saw an image of Lucy in her green trouser suit, talking to the Mad Professor, and touching his arm, and he felt himself jerk awake.

He *did* have something to live for: to find out why she was a patient at the Mayview Clinic.

To find out what they were doing to her.

He glanced behind him. The gates were closed. Lisa had her back to him. She was walking away, along a path that wound through the long grass towards the tennis courts. Not fast, but not slow either. He turned back to the house.

A man was walking towards him with a shotgun broken over his arm. It was Jockey, wearing a waxed jacket and a flat cap over his eyes. Logan waited, letting him come.

'Matty. I don't see nothing of you for ten years, and now twice in a week. Always a pleasure and all, but what the fuck?'

'You're not going to invite me in?' Logan asked in a neutral voice.

Jockey sucked in his cheeks. 'Not today. Stuff going on. But we can walk. I got woods. A lake even. With fish. You like fishing?'

Logan glanced at the shotgun. 'We usually use a rod where I come from. Lengthens the odds a bit.'

Jockey grinned. 'There's big pike in there. Fucking big monsters that'd take your hand off, if you let them. You need more than a fucking fishing rod for them bastards. I've seen them eat a fucking swan and they're tougher than they fucking look, believe me.'

'Sounds like a dangerous place, your woods,' Logan said.

Jockey laughed. 'Stick with me, you'll be all right.'

They walked past the tennis courts and round the back of the barn where Jockey had shown him the paintings. There was a field, bordered by thick hedges, with a gate at the other end. He didn't see any sign of Lisa or the other help. They crossed the field in silence. As Logan looked around him Jockey said: 'Don't worry, there ain't a bull or nothing.'

Logan nodded. 'Pike ate him, right?'

Jockey laughed, opening the gate and nudging Logan through. 'Into the woods,' he said.

Logan was impressed. As soon as they were among the trees it felt as if the world had been left behind. And it wasn't just the change in the light; these trees looked old, big oaks like in a fairy tale, with thick, gnarly branches and roots that squirmed across the path like snakes.

A good place to lose yourself in, he thought.

Or lose somebody else.

'Just follow me. I know where I'm going,' Jockey said, seeming to sense Logan's unease.

They followed the path down a hollow and up the other side, where the trees seemed less menacing, then along a ridge and down a gentle slope until they came to a stream. A black, slippery-looking log had fallen across it.

'Twenty says you fall off,' said Jockey.

'Fifty says I fucking push you off first,' Logan said.

'Says the man not holding a shotgun.' Jockey tutted, shaking his head.

They walked across the log together. On the other side the trees began to thin out until Logan could see light reflecting on water.

'Nice, innit?' Jockey said as they walked to the edge of the lake. It was bigger than Logan had expected, with woods coming right to the water's edge all around it. 'Deep, too.'

'You ever caught any of these monster pike, then?' Logan asked.

'Nah,' Jockey said. 'I leave 'em be.'

Logan snorted. 'You're scared they're going to pull you in and eat you. You're such a pussy.'

Jockey sat down on a weathered stump. 'What I want to catch them for? What they ever done to me?'

Logan shrugged. 'Why does anybody go fishing?'

'Beats me,' Jockey said. 'I just come here now and then for a bit of peace and quiet. Which is what I was enjoyin' until you turned up.' He pushed the peak of his cap up and looked at Logan. 'So what's the game?'

Logan decided to get straight to the point. 'I need some cash.'

'Ah, man.' Jockey shook his head sadly.

'A loan, that's all. I'll pay you the vig and all. Whatever you say.'

Jockey scowled at him. 'How much?'

Logan hesitated. 'I don't know.'

'You don't know? *You don't know?* What sort of a stick-up is this?'

'You'll get it back. With interest, like I said.'

'What you need this money for? Some sort of deal, right?'

'My business,' Logan said.

'Right, right, your business. But my money.' Jockey picked up a stone and tossed it into the lake. They listened to the splash and watched the widening ripples for a few moments.

'When?'

'I'll let you know. Soon. I just need to know you're good for it.'

Jockey spat. 'Let me get this straight. You want money,

but you don't know how much and you don't know when, and you won't tell me what you gonna do with it.'

'I always said you were quick,' Logan said with a grin.

Jockey gave him a hard look, running his fingers over the stock of the shotgun. 'Why the fuck would I do this? You think I still owe you?'

Logan shook his head. 'No, man, you gave me a name. That's it now. We're quits.'

Jockey continued to stare, like he was trying to figure it out. 'Wait a minute. Is this all connected? First you want this name and you don't say why. Now you want a chunk of cash but you don't know how much. You planning on having someone killed? Is that it?'

Of course, Logan had hoped that Jockey would just say 'yes' and leave it at that. But that was about as likely as a hand suddenly popping up out of the lake with a sword in it, inviting him to become the next king of England. He'd known he'd have to come up with a story, and with Alex's help, along with the six-pack of pretentious-sounding lagers she'd brought along, he'd come up with a few. But now, with Jockey giving him that look, he knew none of them would fly. Deep down, he'd always known he'd have to tell him the truth.

Or at least some of it.

'That's about the size of it, yeah.'

'Right. Now we getting somewhere. So now you tell me the rest.'

Logan pretended to wrestle with himself for a moment.

'OK. There's this fella. We had some business together. Long story short, he's welshed on me. Owes me some money.'

'OK. You tried threatening him, like any normal person?'

'He's not too smart. But thinks he is, you know what I mean? Thinks he can get away with it. Stubborn bastard, too. I'm at the end of my tether.'

'I feel your pain, man. So you gonna knock him off his perch, take what's owed you and pay me back out of the proceeds?'

'In a nutshell.'

Jockey got to his feet. 'What do you take me for? I don't want no dirty money from some gangster that's just had his head blown off. My accountant would fucking kill me.'

'I guarantee you'll get your stake back. I mean, the exact same notes. Down to the last fiver.'

'How you gonna do that?'

'Or else I'll run it through a legit business, so it's all nice and clean before it gets to you.'

'I'm beginning to wonder if you know any legit businesses.'

'Says the man holding the shotgun.'

'This is for shooting foxes.'

'Why would you shoot foxes?'

'Why does anyone?'

'Beats me.'

Jockey shook himself. 'Shit. This isn't getting us anywhere.'

He started trudging round the lakeside, the shotgun cradled over this arm, with Logan trotting at his heels. Logan couldn't think of anything else to say that would persuade him.

'*My boss wanted to throw you to the wolves because you're a no-good scumbag drug dealer, and I said no?*'

Instead, he said the first thing that came into his head. 'You know how this ends, right?'

Jockey gave him a sidelong glance. 'How what ends? This conversation we having?'

Logan shook his head. 'Nah, I mean this business you're in. How you're making your money.'

'Paintings, you mean.'

'Yeah, call it that if you want.' He paused as they stepped over a rotten log. 'My point is, you don't meet a lot of retired drug dealers. Not unless you're opening drawers at random in the morgue, you know what I mean? You don't meet them pottering about in the garden and playing with the grand-kids.'

Jockey spat a fat gob of phlegm into the lake. 'Fuck, who wants to end up like that?'

'Better than on a slab.'

'I dunno. Live fast, die young, all that.'

Logan chuckled. 'Now you're having me on. You're too crafty for that bullshit. You were smart enough to get into this game. Are you smart enough to get out, though?'

It was Jockey's turn to laugh. 'You giving me career advice, now?'

Logan shrugged. 'More like . . . what do they call it? Life coaching.'

'No offence, Logan, but the day I start taking advice from you on how to live my life, that's the day I slit my wrists.'

'Bit harsh,' Logan said.

'Sorry, didn't mean it like that. What I'm saying is, if we was talking on your yacht, cruising round some place, drinking champagne, then maybe I'm gonna listen to what you got to tell me. But right now . . .'

'You think I'm a fuck-up.'

'I don't know what you are. I think you're a killer, but I can't figure out who you killing and who's paying you to do it. You a fucking man of mystery.'

'No, you were right first time, Jockey. I am a fuck-up. I had a life once. But then it got taken away.'

'So what you saying? You giving me the benefit of your experience? "Don't let it all go to shit like I did"?'

Logan stopped. 'All I'm saying is, the next time I see you, I'd rather it wasn't slumped in the back of a car, full of holes.'

Jockey looked at him carefully. 'OK. That's very nice. I'm touched. So what are you telling me?'

Logan looked away. 'I don't have any advice. All I'm saying is, if things start to go, you know, tits-up, you can always give me a call.'

'Like old times,' Jockey said.

'Like old times,' Logan agreed.

They walked on in silence. After a couple of minutes, Jockey stopped and picked up a branch, then heaved it into the lake. He turned to Logan.

'OK – but I don't want no fucking monopoly money that you just made on a fancy photocopier, you hear me?'

Logan held his hand out with a smile. 'So is it a deal?'

14

Dr Khan took a deep breath and concentrated on keeping his heartbeat steady. He looked straight ahead through the windscreen, resisting the urge to turn his head and look once again at the black-painted door and the row of buzzers with their brass plaques. *Clearwater Security*. He mused on the irony. *Security*. Meaning, of course, the complete opposite. For the Faithful it meant insecurity, oppression and death. They had killed Masood and Hamza on the boat, rescuing that pathetic, drug-addled buffoon, the Foreign Secretary, in the process, and destroying months of careful planning in a few minutes of bloody, hand-to-hand combat.

In this, alas, the game he had been playing with such passionate intensity for so long was not like his other love, the game of chess. In chess it was your mind against the mind of your opponent, pitting your skill and intelligence against his. The pieces on the board, once you had decided your move, simply went where you put them and executed their functions with total predictability. But people were not chess pieces. You trained them as well as you could, but in the real world, in the life and death game as opposed to the one played on a board, sometimes they did not behave as they were supposed to. Sometimes one of the opponent's pawns would show unexpected abilities, taking your most important pieces when they had no right to.

Mr Davies, for instance. The man who, through an extraordinary coincidence, he had treated in hospital immediately after the debacle on the houseboat and the freeing of the Foreign Secretary. He had been involved in a particularly vicious carjacking, the police had said when they brought him in. Did they think he was a fool? The man had been shot and stabbed, but his other injuries showed that he had fought, too, no doubt viciously. Even in this barbaric country, carjacking did not usually involve such a fight to the death.

So, frail and bleeding, 'Mr Davies' had been literally put into his hands. It had seemed so obviously the work of fate, indeed the will of God himself, that the urge to instantly take revenge – to cut off his oxygen or give him a fatal morphine dose – was almost irresistible. But luckily he had managed to calm himself and consider more carefully. Could it really be the will of Allah that his plan to live-stream the beheading of the Foreign Secretary should be thwarted by this man, and then that he should be presented with the opportunity of taking his revenge? What would be the sense in that? Surely the lineaments of a divine plan could not be discerned in such a pointless tit-for-tat? Dr Khan would have lost two pawns. In turn he would have taken one of his opponent's. Perhaps more than one, if he had acted quickly. His ultimate game plan would not have been advanced. His opponent's king would have remained safe.

So, his plan to take a rook off the board had not worked. But perhaps it had only been a ruse. A feint. A more subtle – and ultimately more devastating attack – had lain behind it. It was simply that he, even as he had manipulated the pieces around the board, had not been aware of it. The workings of the Almighty are indeed not comprehensible to the mind of man. One must simply do one's best, and then when divine guidance pushes you in a different direction, you must obey without thinking and submit yourself to His will.

So, now he knew 'Mr Davies' was a spy. And the 'visitors' who watched over him were spies, too. There was an old man, thin and frail but with the unmistakeable bearing of command, who had come only once. Dr Khan was certain he was a very senior officer in the intelligence services, perhaps even the head of one of its departments. He would be a great prize indeed. But although he had followed him out of the hospital as quickly as he could while not drawing undue attention to himself, he had not been able to identify the number plate of his car before he had been driven away by his minder. The others he had identified over the next few days appeared to come and go by other means, or perhaps they were careful to park their vehicles away from the hospital and its cameras.

One of them was not so careful, however. The blonde whore who rode the motorbike. She was the one who came most often. Perhaps she and 'Mr Davies' were lovers. At any event, it was she who led him gently away when it came time to discharge him. But in the meantime, it had been easy for Dr Khan to memorize the number plate on her motorcycle, it had been parked there so regularly. Perhaps those were the real lovers, the woman and the machine, she seemed so attached to it. When she gripped it between her thighs and made the engine roar into life, he could tell that she gained an obscene pleasure from it.

Well, whatever else she had done – and he would find out every immoral act before he was finished with her – she would pay for that perversion. Indeed, she was already paying, because it was the motorcycle that had finally led Dr Khan to their secret base, to Clearwater Security.

And now he had them all.

Firstly there was 'Mr Davies'. Was it possible to recognize a killer simply from the way he walked? Or was that his imagination? Because he already knew what this man must have done. Unconscious bias they would call that, in the ridiculous way of the unbelievers, he supposed with a bitter smile.

Then the woman. Sometimes blonde, sometimes not. But more often than not walking like a man and dressed like one too, as if she was arrogantly rejecting the holy gift of woman-hood that God had bestowed on her.

Then an older woman. More conservatively dressed, to say the least. A harmless grandmother. It was hard to imagine her as a tool of the devil, though that was undoubtedly what she was. The Evil One's disguises should never be under-estimated. Perhaps she would, in fact, turn out to be the most dangerous of all.

Certainly more dangerous than the fat man with glasses, who shuffled nervously along the pavement before ringing the buzzer as if he expected to be struck down at any moment. Perhaps he had been granted a glimpse of the divine will and understood that he was on the path to hell. Or perhaps he was simply a coward and a fool. Dr Khan assumed he was not the kind of agent who operated in the field. A tech-nician of some sort, most likely.

And finally the man with long hair, who always walked as if he was deep in thought, his legs moving as if under their own volition. He had the look of a chess player, Dr Khan thought, and a good one. Perhaps *he* was the real danger.

Anyway, he knew he could not take them all. A bomb, of course, would do it. But that would take time and he would have to wait for resources to be gathered and for an expert in such tasks to be reassigned. Such people were becoming rarer; pieces that the spies had been methodically removing from the board, because their training and their expertise made them stand out. He was left with pawns, and pawns could only do so much.

But in any case, killing them all made no more sense than putting a lethal dose into 'Mr Davies's' vein when Dr Khan had him at his mercy. He did not think the Almighty had presented him with this opportunity in order for him to squander it like that.

No, it was information that Dr Khan wanted, and revenge would come later, as it always, inevitably, would. He was reminded of the phrase, 'If you wait long enough on the riverbank, the bodies of your enemies will come floating by.'

It also appeared to apply to a busy street in Pimlico.

That thought reminded him that he had been parked within sight of the Clearwater offices long enough to make himself potentially conspicuous. He had been patient: identifying the owner of a vehicle was not as easy as calling up a brother in the DVLA, unfortunately. A certain amount of what they called 'hacking' had been necessary. So he had had to wait. And when the information had finally come to him, he had to follow up himself. After what had happened to Masood and Hamza there was no one else he could trust. This was too big. Too important. And no one was better trained than himself. After all, he had managed to stay out of the infidels' clutches for so long only because he had always been so meticulous, so careful. He must not throw it away now.

He needed to think about his next move. Indeed, like all good chess players, he needed to think several moves ahead. And anticipate his opponent's at the same time. There was a park a few streets away, where a man on a bench lost in thought would not be conspicuous. He turned on the ignition and slowly drove away.

15

The young man, in his early twenties, clean-shaven and dressed in dark trousers and a parka with a Yankees baseball cap, walked down a street alive with the sound and smells of Turkish restaurants and shisha bars. His name was Mohammad, but at school the white boys had all called him Mo, or Little Mo, because he was so tall, and the name had stuck. Even at the mosque, his brothers had continued to call him Mo, despite his protests. After all, if people don't call you by your proper Islamic name – and the most revered, at that, the name of the Prophet – when you are among the Faithful, then when will they? And while at first he had been annoyed, after a time, after the imam had taken him under his wing and started to teach him about jihad, he had seen it as a blessing. Unbelievers would be less suspicious of a young man known as Mo. How could he be a so-called fanatic if he allowed his friends to call him by such a harmless name? Whereas the most corrupt and irreligious man you could imagine, a man who turned his back on God and cared only for money and women and alcohol, such a man, if his name was Mohammad, would instantly strike fear into the hearts of the Godless, imagining under his business suit a suicide bomber's vest and hidden in his briefcase a butcher's knife, ready to cause bloody mayhem on the streets.

So, Mo it would be. And he made sure that alongside his name, there was nothing else to encourage the spies to turn their attention on him. In particular he did not associate with the other young men whom the imam had chosen for special instruction. In times gone by they might have been actively encouraged to spend time together, to become a team, knowing that if they were called upon to sacrifice themselves, the strength they drew from each other when it came to the final moments would be important.

But those days were past. The spies, after all, for all their surveillance technology, the way they could track your every move online, the satellites that could see you from space, the databases they shared with other countries – for all that, they were not so smart. In the end what made them suspicious were your associations. It was as simple as that. If your brother or your cousin was a jihadi, then you could assume they would be suspicious about you, too. If your sister or your cousin married a jihadi, the same. To be part of a cell was to be asking for trouble.

Whereas if you avoided travelling to 'suspect' places – even back to Pakistan to visit family, even if that meant missing your cousin's wedding, for which Uncle Omar had never forgiven you – if you had never been to a camp and you did not associate with anyone who had been – well, why should they pay attention to you? And by the time they came and broke down the door to your flat and looked at what was on your laptop and on your cell phone, it would be too late. By that time you would be in paradise, and what the imam had told you to do would be done.

But, of course, if you wanted to do more than kill a few unbelievers with knives, you could not operate entirely on your own. Sometimes you had to rely on others for – what was the phrase? *Logistical support.* He checked his watch. Kerem had not specified a meeting place; he had simply told him to walk down a certain street at a certain time. Presumably he would be watching – watching to see if Mo was truly alone as he had said, or was being followed. Mo resisted the temptation to scan the faces of the early evening crowd. It was a pleasant evening and the street was busy with old women sorting through vegetables at the open-air stores or haggling for the best cuts of meat at the halal butcher's, while young men greeted each other or sat outside the shisha bars in groups of three or four, smoking and laughing. Kerem could easily be hiding among them while he decided whether it was safe to reveal himself.

As he neared the junction, Mo wondered whether he should simply carry on walking, or cross over and walk back down the street the other way. If he was being followed, that would go against everything he had learned, but with so many people on the street, would it really look out of place? Before he had to make a decision, he felt a touch on his arm.

'Salaam.'

Mo turned. The leather-jacketed man smiling at him through stained and crooked teeth was not Kerem.

'Salaam,' he replied hesitantly. In this part of London, tensions were high and strangers on the street would be quickly noticed. Which was why Kerem had suggested meeting here in the first place. Perhaps this man had simply registered that Mo looked out of place – had it been that obvious? – and had decided to interrogate him a little on his own initiative.

'Listen, brother, I'm here to meet with Kerem. You know him? He told me . . .'

Before he could finish, another man had appeared on his other side, taller even than Mo, like a basketball player, gripping his elbow firmly.

'Careful you do not slip, my brother. The shopkeepers here care for nothing, throwing their rotten vegetables onto the street so unwary people may break their necks.'

Without thinking, Mo checked his stride and looked down at his feet. As he did so, he felt the man in the leather jacket put his arm around his waist as if they were about to begin a dance and then pull him sharply to his left, while the giant gave him a hard shove on the other side. He felt himself stumbling into a narrow alleyway he hadn't seen.

'Hey!' he said, trying to keep the alarm out of his voice. 'What are you doing, brother? Where is Kerem?'

The man in the leather jacket was smiling and making clucking noises, the way you would try to calm an animal, as the two of them marched him deeper into the alley. The walls reached up to the sky on both sides and there were no lights. He almost tripped over something hard, but held by strong arms on both sides he was almost floating over the ground. He felt his breathing become ragged as his heart started racing. He tried to speak but no words would come out, just a low moaning that made him sound like a woman. He gritted his teeth and breathed in deeply through his nostrils, trying to summon the strength to take charge of the situation. As if sensing his intention, the giant leaned closer, saying, 'Kerem, yes, Kerem. We must go quick.'

For a moment, Mo felt his rising panic recede. It was OK. They were bringing him to Kerem. He almost laughed. What had he thought? That these men, smelling of cigarette smoke and body odour, were spies?

They were at the end of the alley now and it was almost pitch dark. Mo felt his heartbeat rising again, and then a door opened in the blackness and he felt the arms releasing him. He felt foolish as he almost lost his balance, and then he saw Kerem in the doorway, grinning.

'Mo!' he said, as if Mo suddenly appearing like this was the greatest surprise.

Mo straightened and took a breath. It was important he regain his dignity. They were equals, after all, weren't they? He took a step towards the doorway, so Kerem would have to look up.

Kerem held a hand out. 'Wait. One moment, please.'

Mo had been stabbed before. Once he'd bled so much he'd thought he was going to die. So he thought he knew what a blade felt like. But this . . . There was pain, but mainly his whole body felt cold, as if he'd been plunged into an ice bath, so he could only feel the place where the blade had gone in as a stinging in the numbness somewhere in his back. He wanted to ask Kerem what was happening, but when he took a step forward his legs gave way under him and he started falling and all he could see was a blurry Kerem stepping smartly back into the doorway as the concrete step came up and hit Mo hard in the face. He started to feel the pain then, pain everywhere, and he didn't know whether they were stabbing him some more or he was just beginning to feel where they'd stabbed him before and he wanted to tell them to stop, there was no need, because he was already dead.

The last thing he saw was an open door with the light spilling out into the alley and he wondered if that was paradise and if he would be admitted even though he had not died a martyr's death as he'd planned.

He just needed to get up and see if they would let him in.

And then the door closed.

16

Alex found Logan sitting on a bench in the park watching the ducks. He had a bulging black daysack between his knees.

'You all right? You know we've got a meeting in . . .' She looked at her watch. 'Five and a half minutes. We don't want to get detention.'

Logan imagined Mrs Allenby making him write 'I'm a cold-hearted killer' a hundred times on the whiteboard.

He shuffled along so she could sit down. 'Yeah. Just having a think about things.'

'What sort of things?'

'Lucy. Sarah. You know.'

'You getting cold feet?'

'No, it's not that. I'm committed. I'm just not sure what exactly I'm committed to.'

'Sounds like getting married,' Alex said with a wry smile.

Logan nodded. 'You have to pay to play, as someone recently told me. But what about you? I feel bad roping you into all this. We haven't even really talked about it.'

'Nothing to talk about. I'm committed too. And you know

me, I like all the dressing up, the acting. It's a good part, too, the mad wife. Could be my finest hour. I was a pretty good Blanche DuBois in college.'

Logan smiled. 'Whoever she was. Sorry you won't get an Oscar for it.'

Alex sighed theatrically. 'The sacrifices I make for my country.'

'You're still up for it, then? Tomorrow night?'

'You bet.'

They sat in silence for a minute while a young mum in a headscarf pushed a stroller past the pond.

'Something else,' Logan said. 'But maybe it's nothing.'

Alex cocked an eyebrow.

'That bench over there.' He nodded towards the trees at the other side of the park. 'A fella came and sat down. Middle-aged. Business suit. Grey hair. Neatly trimmed beard. We made eye contact for a moment, and . . . I don't know. I could swear he looked shocked. Scared even. Just for a moment. Like he'd seen a ghost. Took him a moment to calm himself down, then he scarpered.'

Alex was about to say something flippant, then thought better of it. '*Appointment in Samarra.*'

Logan looked at her quizzically. 'You what?'

'It's a story. By . . . can't remember. Anyway, this bloke's walking through the marketplace where he lives and comes face to face with Death. He's scared shitless and runs away as fast as he can. But Death looks a bit gobsmacked, too. So the bloke puts as much distance between him and the town as he can, ends up hundreds of miles away in some godforsaken place. Finally sits down for a rest by a fountain or something, looks up, and there's Death. "Blimey, when I saw you back in your hometown," Death says, "I wondered how you were going to get to our appointment in time."'

Logan nodded, smiling. 'Yeah, that's just how this guy on the bench looked. He couldn't get away from me fast enough. Thing is, I think I recognized him too. I just can't remember where from.'

Alex shrugged. 'Maybe you'll remember when you meet him again.'

A fox had emerged from the bushes and was sniffing around the bench where the mystery man had been sitting. As Logan and Alex watched, it bared its teeth in a snarl and started snapping at the air. Then it turned and looked straight at them.

'It looks like it's trying to tell you something,' Alex said. 'What is it with you and foxes, anyway?'

'I dunno. They like me, I guess.'

They sat in silence for a few moments, waiting for the fox to move on. Eventually a man walked past the bench with a black Lab on a lead and the fox slunk away.

'We used to keep one, me and Jockey, when we were on the streets.'

'You kept a fox? What, like a pet?'

'Sort of. It stayed with us, anyway. We found it by some bins, half-starved. It was too weak to run away. Something wrong with its foot as well. I remember, I took my coat off and sort of wrapped it up in it. Jockey thought it was going to bite me and I'd get rabies. He didn't fancy it at all. But I didn't care. We took it back to where we were sleeping and I gave it some food. You know, bits and scraps we found outside supermarkets after they closed up. I think we even gave it some milk with a bit of rum in it, or something. Anyway, it perked up after a bit, but it didn't run away. Must have reckoned it was better off sticking with us. It was a youngster, I reckon. Maybe it got confused, thought we were its mum and dad. We'd go out at night, looking for stuff, together, like a team, you know?'

'What happened to it?'

'Dunno. One night we heard this fucking awful noise, like somebody was being murdered. We legged it in the other direction in case the law was on its way, but Foxy wouldn't come. It was like he wanted to get involved.'

'It was other foxes, yeah?'

'Maybe it was his real mum and dad, having a bit of a to-do. Anyway, we never saw him again after that. It was sad. I never had a dog or a cat or anything. But a fox was better, I reckon. For a bit, anyway.'

Alex smiled. 'Makes sense.'

'What?'

'Why a fox might get confused and think you and him were the same species. You were a bit feral yourself at that time, by the sounds of things. A wild animal living outside its natural environment. No offence.'

'None taken.'

Alex stood up. 'Right, come on, before you start rummaging in that bin for scraps. I've seen you looking at it.'

In the office, Logan quickly dumped out the contents of the daysack on the conference table.

Ryan whistled. 'So that's what a hundred grand looks like.'

'Are you sure it's real?' Mrs Allenby asked, with a disapproving look.

Logan shrugged. 'Jockey's handy with a paintbrush, but I don't think he's up to this kind of detail.'

'And where did it come from?'

'I didn't ask,' Logan said. 'But he said it was cold. No one's looking for it. Anyway, it's just a loan.'

'And what if it . . . goes astray?' Mrs Allenby asked. 'How are we – how are *you* – going to pay him back?'

'Cross that bridge,' Logan said airily.

Alan picked up one of the bundles and pulled out a fifty-pound note, taking off his glasses and squinting at it as he held it up to the light.

'Nice work if it is funny, I must say.'

Logan grinned, putting his hand on Alan's shoulder. 'Not as good as you could do, though, mate.'

'And why this amount?' Mrs Allenby asked. 'Molloy hasn't given you his "invoice" yet.'

'I had a chat with Jockey. Gave him a few details about the target – just made-up stuff – and he said this was in the ballpark. If there's any left over, I'm buying the drinks.'

Mrs Allenby was still looking at the money with an expression of distaste. 'Well, let's put it in the safe for now. You mentioned the "target".' She turned to Ryan, as Logan began to neatly stack the bundles. 'Have we made any progress on that?'

'I think so.' He sat down and pulled his laptop towards him, then flipped it open. The rest of them sat down around the table as Logan zipped the daypack closed and put it on the floor.

'The thing is, the target has to be a real person, because the hit-man or assassin or whatever we want to call him is going to be checking them out. Secondly, they have to be a plausible target.' He nodded towards Logan. 'You posed as a businessman type, so it makes sense the target's going to be some sort of business rival. In which case he'll probably be reasonably well off. Big-ish house, Jag in the drive, that sort of thing. But not Fort Knox, armed guards patrolling the grounds, anything like that. It has to look feasible.'

'Shouldn't be problem finding someone like that,' Logan said.

'No,' Ryan agreed. 'The problem is the fact that we're going to be putting a target on their back. And just in case we lose track of the money and the hit-man, we've got no way of putting the genie back in the bottle.'

'Well, we just bloody well make sure we don't lose track of the bastard,' Logan said. 'It's what we bloody do for a living, isn't it?'

'Not good enough,' Mrs Allenby said sternly.

'What we want, then,' Alex said, rocking slightly in her chair, 'is a real live businessman who walks and talks and generally makes a spectacle of himself, and then five minutes later . . .' She spread her hands in a dramatic gesture. '*Disappears.*'

'But in a good way,' Ryan nodded. 'Exactly.'

'Sounds like a handy trick,' Logan said dubiously. 'How're you going to pull that off?'

'Well,' Ryan said, with a grin, 'the funny thing is, when you start looking at people who fit the profile – independent businessmen with a bit of money but not too much – it's surprising how many of them have got themselves into bother with the boys in blue. A bit of tax-dodging here, a bit of fraud there, some threatening behaviour – even the odd assault. It seems it's hard to do business these days without bending the rules a little.'

Mrs Allenby pushed up her glasses and looked down her nose at him. 'A pithy critique of the current state of British capitalism, Mr Oldfield, but what has that got to do with protecting our man?'

Ryan hit some keys on his laptop and started scrolling through a file. 'I started with the Fraud Squad. One or two likely lads, there. Then I moved on to Serious Crimes. And that's where I struck gold.'

'You hacked into their databases?' Mrs Allenby said in a tone half disapproving and half impressed.

Ryan nodded. He turned the laptop round so they could all see the screen. 'Meet Mr Green. Jeffrey Green. Managing director of Green Imports, which, needless to say, has nothing to do with solar panels or biodegradable coffee cups.'

They craned forward and the face of a jowly middle-aged man with an unconvincing fringe glared defiantly back.

'Mr Green is currently under investigation for importing and distributing unlicensed opioids and other illegal narcotics through his fleet of Green Trucking lorries.'

'He could be looking at eighteen months just for that weave,' Alex said.

'And I take it an arrest is imminent?' Mrs Allenby asked.

'They're waiting for the next shipment to arrive. They reckon the serious stuff goes straight to his McMansion in Loughton hidden in crates of champagne for a final quality check before being moved on.'

'And that's when?' Logan asked.

'A week from now.'

Mrs Allenby nodded. 'Just enough time to put together a dossier, deliver it to Mr Molloy, and let our man complete his due diligence before Mr Green magically disappears in a puff of blue smoke.'

'Exactly. Classic bait and switch.'

'And if the timing goes awry?'

'Then either our guy gets picked up by the Met surveillance team and has to explain the sniper's rifle in his boot, or . . .'

'Or he does the job and we're down one scumbag in a bad wig,' Logan said. 'Sounds like win–win.'

'I'd rather let due process take care of Mr Green, thank you,' said Mrs Allenby. 'But I think those odds are acceptable. Well done, Mr Oldfield. If you could just organize the requisite paperwork for Mr Logan, then we can get this thing moving.'

'I'm on it,' said Ryan.

Logan gave him a thumbs-up. 'Nice work, mate.'

'We just have to hope, if we can pull this off, that it turns out to be worth the effort,' Mrs Allenby said. 'We still have to apprehend our hit-man and then extract the relevant information from him, which he may or may not have – a long shot whichever way you look at it. We may end up no nearer to finding out what Tenniel's involved in than when we started.'

Everyone slouched lower in their chairs as an air of gloom settled over the table.

'Actually, on that note . . .' Ryan said.

Mrs Allenby looked up. 'Yes?'

'I've got a theory – well, an idea anyway. I need more data, and it's all a bit speculative, but . . .'

'Let's have it, Mr Oldfield.'

'OK, bear with me . . .' Ryan hit the keys on his laptop for a few moments. 'I was looking at MI5 files on terror suspects and cross-referencing them with news reports.'

'Because?' said Alex.

'Not sure, really,' Ryan said. 'Just a hunch. Anyway, I found a couple of things that might be of interest. A guy called Tarek Mahmoud. Aged twenty. Relatives in Libya. He'd been back and forth a few times. The usual thing. Then he pops up on a video, denouncing Britain for being in cahoots with Gaddafi, all a bit kooky, but it gets people's attention and the Service starts to take an interest, starts keeping tabs, and a pattern appears, travelling here, there and everywhere around the country – Manchester one day, Cardiff the next – even though he's got no known relatives or associates there. Anyway, none of it seems to come to anything, nothing to push him up the list, so he's just simmering away on a low light like so many of these kids.'

'So why are we interested in him?' asked Mrs Allenby.

'Because he's dead,' Ryan said. 'Beaten up and dropped in the Grand Union.'

Logan sat up straighter. 'So?'

'Then there's Mohammad Jamaya. Known as "Mo". Nothing special about him either, but the mosque he goes to has this radical imam Five are keeping tabs on, and Mo's spending lots of time studying with him, so maybe he's being groomed. And he's just the type they're looking for. Left school without any GCSEs. Hangs out with some bad boys. Zero prospects. An accident waiting to happen, basically.'

'Don't tell me – he's dead, too,' Logan said.

'Stabbed sixteen times and dumped in a council bin in Dalston.'

'Any more?' Logan asked.

'A couple,' Ryan said. 'One I'm not sure about.'

Mrs Allenby picked up her gold pencil and started tapping it gently on the table. 'And these deaths – at least one of them a murder, certainly. The victims were all on file with Five? Persons of interest?'

'Yes. Electronic intercepts. Physical surveillance, off and on. But nothing that warranted further action.'

'Except it looks like someone did take further action,' Logan said.

'But who? And what's this got to do with Tenniel?' Mrs Allenby asked.

Ryan tapped at his laptop then swivelled it round again.

Logan looked closer. 'OK, that's a map of London. What's the orange bit?'

'This is where Tenniel comes in. I think. Maybe. When Terry Mason got sent down and his wife was murdered, effectively his criminal operation was wound up. His previous sphere of influence, where other criminal gangs wouldn't dare to operate, was suddenly up for grabs. Nature abhors a vacuum, and another gang quickly moved in to take over his territory.'

'The orange bit,' Logan said.

Ryan nodded.

'That's quite a chunk of real estate. Not that you'd want to live in most of it. So who was it that moved in?'

'The Turks,' Ryan said. 'Durgan's crew. They've put their flag firmly on it. Cleared out all the old dealers or brought them onto the team. It's mostly drugs, but they control what's left of the loan-sharking and protection as well. You can't nick an apple off a stall without their say-so now.'

Mrs Allenby stopped tapping her pencil. 'Would I be right in saying that all the deaths you mentioned took place here?' She indicated the orange portion of the map. 'So Mr Durgan moves into Terry Mason's old territory and decides to clear out some of the young jihadis. I can see why he'd do that. They attract the attention of the police and the security services, and that's bad for business. How does this connect with Tenniel?'

'Someone's got to tell him who's on Five's watch list,' Ryan said.

'And you think that's Tenniel? He would certainly have access to that information. But why?'

'Let's go back to the beginning,' Ryan said, turning his laptop back around. 'Tenniel's gunning for Mason. We think he co-opted Claire, Craig and John Jennings to help him, but we don't know exactly what they were looking for or what they found. Mason is duly nicked, Tenniel gets to sit behind a bigger desk, and Durgan's gang inherits Mason's old territory.'

'"Inherits" makes it sound as if you think they were given it,' Mrs Allenby said.

Ryan nodded. 'I think they were.'

'So what's the quid pro quo?' Alex said.

Ryan shut his laptop. 'As I say, this is just a theory. But what if Tenniel allowed Durgan to fill the hole made by Terry Mason's demise in exchange for him taking terror suspects off the board.'

'You're kidding me,' Alex said. 'The head of the NCA in bed with a Turkish drug gang in the war on terror?'

Mrs Allenby sighed. 'There's a historical precedent. The CIA conspired with the Mafia after the war, in the fight against communism.'

Alan nodded vigorously. 'That's why they had to kill

Kennedy. He wouldn't play ball. Lucky Luciano was the main conduit, if I remember.'

'And now Durgan is the lucky one,' Logan said.

'It fits the data, that's all I can tell you,' Ryan said.

'But what about Craig, Claire and Jennings? Why did Tenniel murder them?' Alex asked.

'Maybe because whatever it was they were looking for, what they actually found was the link between Tenniel and Durgan. Some evidence of the deal.'

Logan got up and stood behind his chair. 'So Terry Mason knew about it, too.'

Mrs Allenby looked over at Alex. 'Perhaps I was wrong. Perhaps we should try and make contact with Terry Mason. You had a plan, as I recall?'

Alex nodded enthusiastically. 'I've thought a bit more about it. If we're going to get on his visitors' list, we have to go through his brief. Mason isn't going to OK anyone he doesn't know.'

'And why would his lawyer put you on the list?' Mrs Allenby said.

'Because I have information about the case. About the trial. I'll say I know one of the witnesses for the prosecution perjured themselves.'

Mrs Allenby looked unconvinced. 'Have you looked at the transcripts? It would need to be something that would undermine the entire prosecution case. Tenniel had enough evidence to put Mason away ten times over. One suspect witness isn't going to be enough.'

'Tenniel,' Logan said. 'It has to be Tenniel. You say Tenniel was involved in a criminal conspiracy. That would get you a mistrial, no problem.'

'But what's your evidence? How are you going to get his legal team to take you seriously?'

'I don't have to,' Alex said. 'That's the point. I just tell them it's about Tenniel, and what I've got to say is for Mason's ears only. I don't trust anyone else. They can huff and puff, but as long as they pass the message on, I think Mason will bite. If we're right, if Tenniel was involved in something big and Mason knows what it is, then he'll be curious.'

Mrs Allenby nodded. 'Well, at least it has the virtue of simplicity. As long as you can get an appointment with his solicitor, and convince him you're not a journalist, you don't need to provide any more details. And if Mason does agree to see you, what then?'

'Easy. I just tell him everything we think we know – that Tenniel's in league with the Turks – that we have reason to believe he had three intelligence officers killed, and—'

'Who's "we"?' Mrs Allenby interjected.

'I'll leave that to Mason's imagination,' Alex said. 'Met anti-corruption, Special Branch, Five, even. Take your pick. I don't think he'd expect me to tell him.'

Logan was nodding. 'Woman of mystery.'

'Less is more,' Mrs Allenby added. 'Now, let's see who it is you have to sweet talk.' She turned to Ryan.

He was already at work on his laptop. 'I'm on it.'

17

For the hundredth time, Terry Mason wondered who the fuck Danielle Hart was. Hopper had been no help, useless, greedy cunt. 'She wouldn't give any details.' Then fucking find out. Look her up in the phone book, and if that doesn't work, have her followed. 'I'm a solicitor, Terry, not a private eye. What do you want me to do, jump in a cab and say follow that blonde? You've been reading too much Raymond Chandler.'

Fucking cheek. He could have just said no, of course: fuck her, whoever she is. But then what did he have to lose? Maybe she did have something on Tenniel. Parker said no, of course. Too risky. What, she's going to cut me up with her visitor's pass? But he didn't mean that. They're not going to send some killer through your own brief, are they? Not unless Hopper's in on it, which I'm beginning to wonder about, frankly. But even then, they search the visitors more thoroughly than they do the bloody cons. And everyone knows why: they're hoping to score some pills or some puff the bastards can then sell back to you. That Gerretty, he's the worst. He should be in a bloody cell, not walking around as if he owns the place. I'd give him a taste of his own medicine all right.

Anyway, Parker didn't mean she was the risk. It was putting yourself out in the open. Where Parker couldn't keep an eye on him. That's what made him nervous. Well, it made him bloody nervous too. Even with two screws escorting you, one in front and one in back. What were they going to do if someone came at him with a shiv? Put their fat arses in the firing line? I don't bloody think so. No, they'd wait until Terry was on the landing, bleeding out, before they got their batons out, by which time matey would be on the floor himself, with his hands behind his head, while the shiv was still sticking in me guts. It's just along the landing, down the stairs, past the recreation area, through the refectory and down the corridor to the visitors' hall. How far is that? A hundred yards? Less?

Too bloody far, though. It would feel like a mile. He just had to hope most of the other cons were in lockdown. If they gave a shit, that's what they'd do: lock the place down. Or let Parker come with him. Why didn't Hopper think of that? He should have asked if she had a sister. For my mate, like. We could do the visit together. No, too complicated. The screws'd never go for it. They liked to keep things simple. Anyway, too late to back out now. He looked at his watch.

Five minutes.

Alex emptied her handbag into the tray provided and then put the bag in alongside.

'Do I need to take off my shoes?' she said.

A squat prison officer with rolled-up sleeves and meaty forearms was watching her. 'Not unless you got blades that come out the toes, like in that Bond film.'

She laughed, wondering how many times he'd used that one.

'Have you got your ID?'

'Oh. It's in my jacket. Can I . . . ?'

He waved her over to the table where her jacket and scarf were lying in a heap. She fished her driving licence out of the front pocket and handed it over. He held it at arm's length, like an unexploded firework and squinted back and forth between the licence and a list on his clipboard.

'Danielle Hart.'

'That's me,' she said.

Alan had been nervous about whether it would pass muster, given how little time he'd been given, but it looked pretty good to her. He'd even faded the photo a bit, so it looked like it had had some use.

The officer was still looking at it, though, as if he knew who lived at 27 Hurrydown Avenue and it wasn't her. Or maybe he just liked pissing people about. He took a breath, as if there was a problem – then handed it over.

'First time?' he said.

No, I blag my way into top-security prisons to chat with notorious gang bosses on a weekly basis.

She smiled nervously. 'Um, yeah, actually.'

'If you just wait over there.'

'Thank you,' she said.

She went and sat down on one of the grey plastic chairs and settled her hands primly in her lap. She could see he was still looking at her.

Fuck off, she thought.

Actually, she couldn't blame him. Anyone coming to see Terry Mason would be of interest, especially someone with no known connection to him. Not a lawyer, not a former associate – not even a former associate's wife or girlfriend. They'd all be on a Met database somewhere. But Danielle Hart wasn't. Like Logan said, she was a mystery woman. She just hoped they hadn't sent a couple of uniforms to poke around at 27 Hurrydown Avenue while she waited for Mason to show. They'd make sure he was late, she knew that. Partly to fuck her around, see how she reacted, if she got stressed, and partly because that was how prisons worked.

Yes, I have visited someone in prison before, she thought. *But it's none of your business.*

Behind a table a thin-faced female screw was going through the contents of her handbag. Alex had seen that look before, on the faces of the nuns at school. Any moment, she thought the woman was going to hold up a packet of condoms pinched between finger and thumb with an expression of triumphant disgust on her face.

Gotcha, you little hussy!

Alex shivered. She knew when the examination of her things was finished, the woman would be giving her a body search in the little room off the corridor.

She thought back to the last time she'd been in this situation. Christ, she'd been so nervous. Wanting him to appear and at the same time not wanting him to, scared of how he'd be, what he'd look like. When they had finally brought him into the dingy hall with its mouldy chairs and chipped Formica tables, she'd done a double take. *No, that's not my dad. There's been a mix-up.* But then she saw it was him, just different. It wasn't just that he looked older, and dead tired, like he hadn't slept for a week. Thinner, too, the sallow skin tight over his cheekbones. No, it was that the hope had been wrung out of him like a dishcloth that had been squeezed dry. The laughing, playful father with a twinkle in his eye was gone, and an old rag was all that remained.

He cried when he saw her.

'*Alex . . .*'

Even his voice sounded different. Like he was trying to put some emotion into it but had forgotten how. The tears were real enough, though.

And then he'd asked her how her mum was, and that's when she'd started crying.

'Miss Hart?'

Alex snapped out of her reverie, instinctively putting a hand to her cheek to wipe away tears that had dried twelve years earlier.

The woman was standing. 'If you would just come with me.'

Parker sat on the edge of his bunk and let out a long breath. He still didn't know what he was going to do. He looked at his watch again. *Four minutes. Jesus.* He felt as if time had speeded up and he was racing towards the edge of a cliff. Funny, normally in here it felt as if time had stopped. The end of your stretch felt as if it would never come. While outside people were rushing around like there was no tomorrow, clock hands whizzing round like in a speeded-up movie, in here everything was frozen, never getting anywhere, like in one of those dreams where you're trying to run away from something or someone and your legs won't work.

But not any more. Now everything felt as if it was in fast-forward and he couldn't handle it.

Bastards. If he could just get his fucking hands on them. You spend your whole life sticking to a set of rules, being stand-up, and then . . . *bam.* Now he'd be remembered as just another cunt. After everything he'd done. All the times he'd told them to fuck off, keep their money, their flash motors, their villas in Magaluf. He didn't give a monkey's for all that crap, anyway. A man's reputation, that's what counts. In the end. Because when you're dead, that's all you've got. He wished he was dead now. First time in his life he'd ever truly felt that. Even when that evil bastard Devlin had started on him with the pliers that time, he'd never quite given it up. He'd just been thinking about what he'd do to *him* when the time came. That's how they knew they couldn't break him. But now, if someone came and put a gun to his head and threatened to pull the trigger, he'd tell them to get on with it.

How had they found her? He'd tried hard enough – at

least for a few years. Then he'd given up. You do your best and that's all you can do. It wasn't to be. Not that he blamed her. She was better off without him, even if all he'd actually wanted to do was give her some money so she wouldn't have to sell drugs or go on the game. It's not like he wanted to play happy families. No illusions there. If she'd spat in his face it would have been no more than he deserved. But at least he'd tried, and however she'd turned out he'd take it on the chin.

Well, they'd done the job for him. Tracked her down to Rochdale. Fuck knows how she ended up there. Boyfriend, he supposed. Or running away from a sticky situation. It's not like you flick through a few brochures and choose these places. Anyway, they must have put some effort into it, even with their resources. And now here he was. He pulled the creased and torn photograph out of his pocket with trembling fingers and looked at it for the hundredth time. That was Tara all right. He wished she'd been smiling. At least then he could have told himself she was happy. Not sure how he'd have described her expression. Suspicious? He looked into her eyes and couldn't help the feeling that she was looking back into his.

'Fuck.'

But it wasn't Tara, in the end, who really got to him. It was the little one she was holding. He was a grandfather. He couldn't tell if it was a boy or a girl. Maybe it wasn't even hers. Maybe she was just looking after it. Babysitting. Nah, don't be stupid. Look at the way she's holding it. You can tell.

And so they had him.

Fucking Turkish cunts.

Three minutes.

Terry Mason stood up, straightening the collar of his shirt and sucking in his gut. 'Right. No more fucking about. Let's see what you've got to say for yourself, Danielle, my love. Who knows, maybe we can help each other out.' He'd had plenty of time to think about how he was going to play it. The main thing was to try and find out who the fuck she was, or more to the point, who had sent her. And why. So whatever this 'information' was she had, don't react. Don't give her anything in return. At least not the big thing. The thing that had got him into this fucking mess. Not until you've figured out the game. Maybe have another sit-down with Hopper. Feed it all into that devious little mind of his and see what comes out. He was a dab hand at figuring out the angles, even if he wasn't a world champion at playing them. Bit unfair, maybe. It would have taken something very fucking special up his sleeve to beat the hand Tenniel was holding. And give him credit, Hopper didn't sugar-coat it when he saw what they had on him. 'Trade up, if you want, Terry,' he'd said, 'but Johnny Cochrane couldn't get you out of this jam. You're better off saving your money to grease a few palms when you're inside, make things as comfortable as you can. You're looking at twenty years, by my reckoning.'

Jesus. Make things as comfortable as you can. You could tell he'd never been inside. What did he think he was going to do? Put up some nice curtains? Buy some comfy slippers? Order an extra helping of custard? This isn't *Porridge*, you stupid cunt. No, every last penny he had was going into staying alive. Not that Parker was expensive. Old school, that one. He'd have probably done it for an extra bit of snout. He didn't touch drugs. Didn't even drink. Didn't spend his money on anything as far as he could see. And there was no one outside to give it to. Had Parker been married? No, course not. There was a girl once, he remembered now. Little blonde. Parker had been head over heels. It was a bit embarrassing, to be honest. Made him look soft. He'd bring her to the club and sit there mooning at her like a little puppy instead of doing his job.

He was about to tell him to get rid of her before people started taking the piss, but she got there ahead of him. Packed up all the clothes and jewellery and shit he'd been lavishing on her in one big suitcase and scarpered. Didn't even leave a note. Christ, he'd taken it bad. Couldn't stand to be in the same room with him after that, blubbing like a fucking baby. She was pregnant, or that's what she'd told him. You're better off, then, he told him. Most blokes would be thanking their lucky stars they'd been let off the hook. Not him, though, dozy twat. He'd got over it, though, thank God. Twice as hard once he'd cooled down. Cut the heart right out of him, he supposed. Anyway, no more trouble with the ladies after that. Kept his mind on the job, even if he wasn't exactly a bundle of laughs. So all for the best, maybe. Pretty little thing, though. Had his eye on her himself, if truth be told.

Through the background clatter of the prison, the shouts and the groans, the faraway banging of doors being slammed closed, the rattle of keys and the scrape of batons against the bars, with some maniac laughing like a drain over on D Wing, his ears still somehow picked out the tread of their heavy boots on the metal stairs. He looked at his watch.

One minute.

They were early for once. Where the hell was Parker?

As the female prison officer was patting her down, Alex went through what they'd rehearsed in her head. Mason would be suspicious, obviously. Whatever yarn she spun him, he'd want to get it checked out before he committed himself, so it made sense to keep it vague: something he *couldn't* check out. Hint at a connection with the intelligence services, a Special Branch unit no one knew about, secrecy being the name of the game since their brief was to target the big fish, people like Tenniel. So he'd have no choice but to take her at her word. Or not, of course. Either way, it was a one-shot deal. Either he came through in the next forty minutes, or the whole thing was a bust. She'd have to give him something to make him sit up and take notice, though – tell him something that a scheming journalist or one of those fucked-up women who fixated on gangsters couldn't know. But what? They'd had a right ding-dong about that around the conference table: Mrs Allenby adamant that they couldn't divulge sensitive information about a senior police officer to a convicted criminal, even if said police officer was the one in their sights. 'Even if said police officer had had Craig and Claire killed?' Logan had countered bitterly. But we don't know that, she'd said. That's the whole point. And what if it gets back to Tenniel? What if Mason thinks he's got a bargaining chip and starts negotiating? Logan had got up and stalked off to the kitchen. Alex was with Logan. What did it bloody matter what they told Mason as long as it gave him the confidence to reciprocate and tell them what Tenniel's game was? But she knew Mrs Allenby wouldn't budge; not with a lifetime of service to the Director General of MI5 under her belt. She probably had the Official Secrets Act embroidered and hung up over her bed. So she came up with a compromise: we'll tell him we know Tenniel had his wife Stephanie killed. But we can't nail him for it. Unless Mason can give us something we don't have. Tell us how it all fits together.

And actually it made sense. After all, somebody did put a bomb under Stephanie Mason's car. They just had to hope Terry Mason was actually upset about it. So that's what Alex was going with. The trick would be to give him time to think through his options without seeming too eager. As soon as they sat down, the clock would be ticking. Actually the trick would be to convince herself that as soon as she sat down they weren't going to bring her father in through that door. Damn it. Alex felt herself beginning to sweat. She felt the female screw's fingers gliding down her arms and was sure the woman could smell her fear.

'Take off your shirt, please,' the woman said.

* * *

Parker methodically cracked the knuckles in each hand and then straightened the fingers, as much as he could, anyway, and surveyed the landscape of lumps, scars, and faded tattoos, thinking of all the things those hands had done. And what they were about to do. You've always got a choice, he thought. Even when you're backed into a corner with no way out, there's still a choice. What he'd like to do, of course, was to kill the bastard who'd threatened his daughter, and then find the bastard who'd sent him, and kill him, too. Unfortunately, that wasn't on the cards. But he still had two ways he could play the hand he'd been dealt. If he topped himself, well, they wouldn't be expecting that. But they'd leave the girl alone. No point in killing her just because they were pissed off. Both ways, if he was being realistic, ended up with him dead. If he did what they wanted, they said he'd be protected, but he knew what bollocks that was. They'd wait until he was out of solitary, give him a bit of time to let his guard down and then they'd come for him too. He'd be a loose end: who knows what he might do. He might even break the habit of a lifetime and blab. Couldn't be having that. So, he was headed for the morgue whatever he did. But he could decide how he was going to get there. As the crow flies or the scenic route. Not much of a choice, maybe, but when it came down to it, wasn't that as much choice as anyone ever had? Or had the appointed time been fixed on the day you were born?

He looked at his watch.

He just had to decide quickly. He reached behind him and

felt for the slit in his belt. His fingers found the edge of the blade and for the first time in his life he found they were trembling.

Alex was just buttoning up her shirt when the alarm bell went off. The female screw ran out without a word, like a scalded cat. Through the half-open door, Alex could see officers on walkie-talkies listening to squawked commands and heard the sound of boots thumping down a corridor. The short guy in shirtsleeves caught her eye as she looked out. He walked towards her and she could see he was sweating. The sour stench of fear came off him in waves.

'Sorry, love. There's been an incident. Visiting's been cancelled. You best go home.'

'Mr Mason . . . ?' she said.

He looked at her pityingly, shaking his head. 'Just go home,' he said.

18

'Back to Plan A, then,' Alex said. She had to bite down hard to stop her teeth from chattering, even though it wasn't cold.

'You OK?' Logan said, handing her a mug of tea. She wrapped her hands around it gratefully. 'You look like you've seen a ghost.'

'Maybe I did,' she said.

'What?'

'Never mind.' She put the tea down carefully on the desk so it didn't spill. 'Do we know what happened yet?'

Logan looked round. Ryan was on his mobile, pacing. Mrs Allenby sitting at the conference table with a dark cardigan around her shoulders, looking thoughtful.

Ryan turned, tucking the phone into the top pocket of his golf shirt. 'OK, nothing official yet. But there's plenty of chatter. Mason got stabbed.'

'Is he dead?' Logan said.

'By the time the two screws who were supposed to take him to the interview hall got there, there was blood dripping over the landing, apparently. Word is he bled out before they got him to the infirmary.'

Alex sipped her tea, a faraway look on her face.

'Who did it? Anyone we know?' Logan asked.

'That's the funny thing,' Ryan said. 'It was Alfie Parker.'

Logan shook his head. 'His minder? Bloody hell, he's been watching Terry Mason's back for twenty years.'

'Well, in the end he stabbed him in the back,' Ryan said with a wry look.

'Bad fucking timing,' Logan said. 'For us, anyway.' He turned to Alex. 'Jesus, they must have known Mason was meeting you. I wonder how they turned him.'

'Everyone has a price, I suppose,' Mrs Allenby said, looking grim.

Logan frowned. 'Well, whatever they offered him, he won't have much chance to spend it where he's going. He'll be in solitary for the rest of his stretch, I reckon.'

'You say "they" as if you know who "they" are,' Mrs Allenby said, wrapping her cardigan more tightly around her shoulders.

'Come on,' Logan snorted. 'We try to get to Mason so he can tell us what he's got on Tenniel, and the next minute he's lying in a pool of his own blood like a stuck pig. It's Tenniel – just like it's Tenniel who had Craig and Claire and John Jennings killed and then Stephanie Mason. And if he's hand in glove with Durgan, he's got eyes and ears everywhere. Mason wouldn't have been able to take a piss without Tenniel hearing about it.'

Alex finally spoke up. 'I might as well have stuck the knife in him myself, then. That's what you're saying.'

Logan shrugged. 'Tenniel would have got to him eventually. It was just a matter of time.'

'You did your best, my dear,' Mrs Allenby said, leaning forward and putting a hand on Alex's arm.

Ryan had stopped mid-stride and was pulling at his ponytail thoughtfully.

'What are you thinking?' Logan said.

'It's just . . .' Ryan began, trying not to make eye contact with Alex. 'If Tenniel did have Terry Mason killed so he wouldn't talk, then . . .'

'Go on,' Alex said.

'Well, he'd have checked Danielle Hart out and found out she doesn't exist.'

'So?' Logan said. 'The meeting never happened.'

'But he'll want to know why Mason decided to see a complete stranger with no possible connection to him. He'll want to know who Danielle Hart really is.'

Logan looked unimpressed. 'No chance. It's a dead end.'

'Yeah, maybe,' Ryan said. 'I mean, I suppose all he's got is the CCTV. And he's never had any contact with Alex, so . . . yeah, I'm just being paranoid.'

Logan looked at Alex, who seemed not to be listening. Clearly something had happened at the prison, and not just Terry Mason getting stabbed. Maybe she'd open up over a couple of beers later on. *Shit, no.* They were booked in for a visit to the Mayview Clinic. His phone beeped and he went over to the kitchen area to answer it.

A couple of minutes later he came back, a smile on his face.

'That was Molloy. He says the car's ready to be picked up. We're on.' He walked over to the coat rack and started putting on his jacket.

'Aren't you forgetting something?' Mrs Allenby said.

Logan looked blank.

'The target information.'

He grinned. 'Oh yeah.' He looked at Ryan.

Ryan lifted his chin, indicating Alan's desk. 'Alan's just making sure it all looks kosher. Not too professional.'

Logan nodded. 'Good stuff.' He hurried over to see if Alan was finished.

Back at the penthouse, Logan quickly changed into pressed Levi's and a striped shirt, then put on a fancy-looking black raincoat with a hood for the walk to Molloy's, but by the time he was out on the street, the rain had stopped and a brisk wind was chasing the remaining clouds across a blank sky. He carried a bag from a posh shoe shop he'd found in one of the walk-in closets.

When he got to the garage, Molloy seemed to have dressed up for the occasion in a tweedy three-piece suit with a checked shirt and spit-shined brogues. His hair was plastered to his scalp with pomade and Logan could smell aftershave. He wondered who Molloy was meeting.

'Here you go,' Molloy said, holding out the keys. 'I think you'll find everything's to your satisfaction.'

'I'm sure I will,' Logan said, taking the keys.

'Is there something you have for me?' Molloy asked.

Logan pulled an envelope from his bag and put it on the desk. Molloy swiftly put it in a drawer.

'Grand. My man will have a gander and then I'll be in touch.'

'With the bill,' Logan said.

Molloy nodded. 'Exactly so.'

'Payment in cash, of course.'

Molloy grinned, showing tobacco-stained teeth. 'That's the fella. The stuff that makes the world go round, Mr Bailey.'

Logan drove the car slowly back to the penthouse and parked it in the basement garage, next to the Merc. He'd thought the bloke he was impersonating having three cars was just him being a twat, but he was beginning to see how handy it could be. If you had the money, it was just like having more than one suit. Anything could seem normal, outrageous wealth or desperate poverty, once you got used to it.

Back in the flat he tidied up, made a cup of tea and texted Mrs Allenby:

Message delivered. Now we wait.

Then he called Alex.

19

The light was just beginning to fade as they turned down the track towards the clinic.

'You sure you're OK?' Logan said, glancing over at Alex.

'Stop asking me that. I'm trying to get into the part,' she said, pulling the fur collar of her coat up around her chin.

'You want to go through it again?'

She shook her head irritably, or pretend irritably – he wasn't sure.

'No more rehearsals. I don't want to get stale.'

'OK . . . Melissa.'

She pursed her lips and gave a little snort. '*Melissa Markham* . . . I still don't know if I like it. It doesn't really have a ring to it.'

'Talking of which.' He looked over again, and she held up her left hand. The thin gold band twinkled dully in the dashboard's glow.

'Yes, I hadn't forgotten. And before you ask, it was my mother's. She left it to me. Well, they gave it to me after she died, anyway.' She smiled. 'If she wants it back, she's going to have to come and ask me herself. It fits, too. Isn't that amazing?'

Logan nodded. 'Yeah, amazing.' For the first time he really felt what it must be like to be driving down a dark country lane knowing that the woman in the passenger seat was completely insane. He shivered, even though the heater was on full-blast. Perhaps it was something he'd need to get used to.

Anyway, there was no more talking to Alex, that was obvious. It was Melissa now.

'OK, here we are, darling,' he said in his best Markham voice.

She gave him a brilliant smile. 'Is this the Ritz? What a lovely surprise!'

The main building was almost completely dark, with just a wan light coming from a couple of windows on the second floor, so it almost seemed to merge with the surrounding gloom. Logan parked on the gravel out front and locked the car while Alex yawned and stretched herself, looking around. Her eyes glittered in the dark like a cat's.

The front door opened and a figure, silhouetted in the light, beckoned them forward.

'Mr and Mrs Markham. Please do come in.'

Dr Redwood led them through the empty reception area and down the corridor. In her office, standing by the big window, a woman turned to greet them with a smile. She was wearing jeans and expensive-looking trainers with a silk blouse and a loose-fitting black jacket. She had amber beads around her neck and a medium Afro. The main thing, though, was that she wasn't Dr Summers. Dr Redwood had obviously taken onboard Logan's confused reaction when they'd been introduced.

'Hello, Mr and Mrs Markham,' she said in a warm, sing-song voice. 'I'm Dr Angelou – but I'd much rather you called me Diana.' She smiled brightly at Alex. 'May I call you Melissa?'

Alex ignored her and started looking around the room like a prospective buyer checking out the fittings and fixtures. She wandered over to a niche in the wall where a small bronze bust of a young woman was illuminated by a hidden spotlight. She lightly ran her fingertips over the face.

'This looks like Ronnie,' she said in a voice Logan had never heard before. He felt another little shiver go through him.

Alex turned to Dr Redwood, who was still standing in the doorway. 'Do you know Ronnie?'

Logan stepped forward and took Alex gently by the elbow. 'Why don't we sit down?' She let herself be guided into one of the armchairs.

Logan made brief eye contact with Dr Redwood and Dr Angelou. 'We've not had the best of days.'

Logan sat down in the chair next to Alex and Dr Redwood sat down opposite them. There was another chair with its back to the window but Dr Angelou remained standing for a moment with her hands on the back of the chair.

'It's very dark outside,' Alex said. 'Why are there no lights?'

Dr Angelou smiled. 'I guess because we're out in the sticks.

I actually find it quite calming, the lack of artificial light. It's more natural, don't you think? Cities, where it never really gets dark, can be very stressful.'

Alex gave her a look, as if she thought she was insane.

She grabbed Logan's arm. 'Can we go home, please?'

Steady, he thought.

'We've only just got here, darling. Dr Redwood and . . . sorry, Mrs Redwood and . . . Diana wanted to meet you.'

'Why?' she said, sounding genuinely baffled.

Logan turned to Dr Redwood for help.

She nodded and smiled. 'Your husband – David – thought it might do you good to come and stay with us for a while.'

Alex looked as if she was considering this, then burst out into a peal of wild laughter. Logan flinched involuntarily, then mentally slapped himself. *You're supposed to be used to this shit*, he thought.

'I couldn't possibly leave David at home by himself,' Alex continued, still laughing. 'He doesn't know where anything *is*. And he can't cook.' She leaned forward, conspiratorially. 'If I let him, he'd eat all sorts of dreadful things.' She lowered her voice, as if Logan wouldn't be able to hear her even though he was sitting next to her. '*Roadkill*. Horrible. He made us stop on the way here, you know. We hit something. I don't know what it was. And he got out and put it in the boot. I hope it wasn't a *child*. Perhaps you ought to go and look.'

No one said anything for a few moments.

'Look, I'm sorry. I . . .' Logan began.

Dr Angelou shook her head, smiling. She sat down on the edge of the last chair, leaning towards Alex so her beads rattled. 'I'm sure if we made a list of meals, you know, easy things you can just heat up or put in the microwave, and David promised us he'd stick to the plan, then he'd be quite all right. Don't you think?'

Alex took some time to think about it. 'Maybe,' she said finally. 'I'm a vegan, of course,' she added.

'Good,' Dr Redwood said. 'So, would you like to come and have a look around? We have a really nice room where you could stay.'

Alex stood up abruptly. 'We'll have our usual suite, thank you.'

As they trooped down the corridor towards the stairs, she linked her arm in his. He wanted to kick her. She was supposed to be a drugged-up zombie. That was the plan. *Lack of affect*, and all that. Not some completely bonkers madwoman. He found himself tensing up, waiting to see what she was going to come out with next.

They made it to the first floor without incident. Dr Redwood and Dr Angelou seemed happy to accompany them in silence. To their right was another floor-to-ceiling window with no doubt stunning views in the daylight. They turned left and Dr Redwood brought them to a halt, waving a key card over a door handle. It clicked open and they walked through into a spacious room with a queen-sized bed. There was an antique desk against one wall, under a huge gilt-framed mirror, and a worn but elegant leather sofa against the other. A vase of bright flowers stood on a little mahogany table by the window. Above the bed was a painting, some kind of blurry landscape with a rainbow.

Alex stopped in the middle of the room, looked around approvingly, then flopped down onto the bed and lay there with her arms wide and her eyes closed.

'So good to be back,' she said, dreamily. 'You know, I think I might just have a swim before dinner, if the sea's not too cold. And then a glass of champagne.'

She sat up abruptly, as if she'd only just noticed the other people in the room. 'But first I'm going to have a little nap.' She looked pointedly at Dr Redwood and Dr Angelou. 'You can bring up the bags later.'

Logan looked at them helplessly.

Dr Redwood nodded. 'Of course, Mrs Markham. I'm sure you must be tired from the journey.' She indicated that Logan should go first, and the three of them left the room. She shut the door behind her.

Alex got up off the bed and put her ear to the door. She could hear voices, growing fainter, then stopping as they turned the corner and went down the stairs. So far so good. Now it was Logan's turn to do his bit. He was supposed to tell them that the drugs made her more animated at first, then she'd sleep, usually for twenty minutes, and after that she'd be fine, just a bit 'flat', but if she was woken up before then, she got upset. If they sent one of the goons up to stand guard by the door, then she was fucked, but hopefully they'd buy it. She had to say she thought her own performance had been pretty convincing. She smiled to herself. Even Logan had been taken in a bit, she could tell. Twenty minutes. Long enough to have a bit of a scout around and hopefully find out where the other patients were, assess the security and be back in bed by the time Alphonse came up with the champagne.

Here goes. She put her ear to the door again. Nothing. She took a deep breath, then slowly turned the handle and pulled the door open.

She gasped.

A woman was standing there. She was tall, with pale skin, long, dark hair and green eyes. She was wearing a pale-blue, knee-length dress and her feet were bare. The skin around her wrists looked bruised.

The woman cocked her head and looked at her the way you might look into a mirror, trying to decide if you liked the way your hair looked.

Alex stood very still and steadied her breathing, as if a wild animal had just stepped into her path and she didn't want to spook it.

The woman glanced to her left and then to her right, then darted past Alex and into the room. Alex closed the door. The woman did a little pirouette, checking every corner, then turned back to Alex. Alex wondered if she was going to speak.

'You must be Lucy,' Alex said.

The woman didn't say anything. Her hands were clenched

tightly, the skin of her knuckles bone-white. Alex could see her nails were bitten to the quick.

'I'm a friend of Logan's,' Alex said.

The woman relaxed a notch. 'He's come back. I knew he would.' She smiled the saddest smile Alex had ever seen. 'He shouldn't have.'

Alex took her hand and guided her to the edge of the bed. They sat down. Lucy closed her eyes. Alex squeezed her hand. 'Stay with me, Lucy.' Lucy opened her eyes again.

'We haven't got much time,' Alex said. 'Logan's keeping them busy, but they'll be back soon. You need to tell me everything.'

Lucy nodded. She took her hand away and laced her fingers together on her lap.

'Mr Herbert. He's very clever. Very good with locks. He opened my door.'

'Is he a patient?'

'Yes. There's only two of us. In this great big place. But they check every half hour, so I'll need to be back in my room.'

Alex nodded. 'OK. Go on.'

Lucy sighed. 'There's so much I don't know. I get so confused. I . . .'

'Tell me what you do know,' Alex said, trying to keep her voice calm.

'Right, yes,' Lucy said, pulling herself together. 'It started after the accident – you know, my husband and . . . Did Logan tell you about that?'

'Yes.'

'After that, it was such a . . . I couldn't cope, I suppose. I had some sort of breakdown. I lost my memory. I didn't know anything about my life, I didn't know I'd been married, or had a family. It was all gone.' She choked back a sob. 'But Ursula helped me. My sister. She got me help.'

'Here? At the clinic?'

'Yes. Dr Redwood. She was so good. I don't know how she did it, but she got my memories back. Of course it was awful at first, suddenly remembering, like, you know, when you wake up after something terrible's happened and at first you don't remember why you feel so sad and then it comes flooding back. It was like that.'

'And then?'

'Well, I could remember everything now, so I wanted to go home. To face everything. I felt I'd abandoned Brian and the kids by forgetting about them, can you understand that? I just wanted to be home, to be in the last place we'd all been together. I wanted to grieve properly, I suppose.'

'And did you?'

Lucy shook her head. 'Dr Redwood wouldn't let me. She said I wasn't completely recovered. – that I was a suicide risk. She kept talking about that, that if I went home I'd try and kill myself. I told her I was fine, I felt fine, I wanted to go. But she said I wouldn't be safe, and Ursula – my sister – had signed something that meant I couldn't leave unless Dr Redwood agreed.'

'So what happened?'

'I was getting desperate. In despair, really. I wanted to talk to Ursula, to tell her I was OK. But she'd gone away, that was what they said. Anyway, one night I woke up and the door to my room was open, and when I went out into the corridor the sensor things, they weren't blinking, so it looked like the whole security system wasn't working. I thought this was my chance. I went down the back stairs and out through the door to the kitchens and no one was there and no alarms went off – I couldn't believe it. I was so stupid, I didn't have any shoes, and I walked through the woods so they wouldn't see me, and then I thought how stupid that was, I should have gone on the road, because it took me so long and they'd realize I'd gone and come after me, but no one did, and eventually I got to the main road, my feet were bleeding, I could hardly walk, but eventually a car came and I flagged it down – I'm surprised they stopped, the state of me, soaked through, covered in blood, just wearing a nightie, but I just stood in the middle of the road so he had no choice. Anyway, this man agreed to take me home, I can't even remember what story I told him, but I was so frightened, I thought he'd take me back, like in the film, you know, with that awful Nazi dentist, but he didn't and I got home, and there was a key, under a flowerpot if you can believe that, and I let myself in, and then . . .'

She stopped as a huge sob wracked her.

'I'm sorry. It's just so . . .'

Alex put a hand on her shoulder. 'It's OK. I know this must be hard. You're doing brilliantly.'

Lucy smiled, nodding. 'I'm fine. Thank you. The thing is, I got into the house and there was nothing there. Everything had gone. I mean, my things were there but no photographs of the kids, our wedding photo, the kids' room had been turned into some sort of office. All of Brian's stuff had gone. The garden was completely different. I couldn't understand it. I called Ursula to see if she could explain, but she didn't pick up. I felt desperate. It wasn't how I thought things would be at all, and I just couldn't deal with it. So that was when I decided to kill myself. It seemed the only thing left for me to do, really.'

'And that's when you met Logan.'

Lucy nodded. 'He was so nice. He saved me. I thought, all right, maybe I'm not supposed to die. Not that way, anyway.'

Alex sneaked a look at her watch. 'What then?'

'I finally managed to get through to Ursula. I told her what had happened, about escaping from the clinic, and the shock of seeing the house the way it was, and Logan, and everything. We ended up having a big argument. She said I obviously wasn't well enough yet, I should go back to the Mayview. She meant well, I know, but that was the last thing I wanted to do.'

'But you did go back.'

'They came for me. After the last time I saw Logan. We'd sort of said goodbye. He said he had to go away, couldn't tell me where, or when he'd be back. I was so confused. I was in a daze, really. Then suddenly there they were, Dr Redwood and those two horrible security people. They made me get in the car. I was just too . . . I didn't have any fight left. They drugged me anyway, some sort of sedative.'

'And what's it been like since you've been back?'

Lucy put her fingers to her temples. 'I'm so frightened. I don't know what's happening any more. They won't let me speak to Ursula. And my memories, of Brian and the kids, they're . . . I can feel them fading. It's horrible, like I'm forgetting them all over again. Instead, I have nightmares – horrible, horrible. And Dr Redwood – I don't know what she's trying to do, but I don't feel I'm getting any better. I was better before, when I met Logan.' She turned to face Alex and grabbed her hand. 'It's the only thing that's kept me going – seeing him in the grounds when I did. I thought, he didn't leave, he did come back.'

Alex stroked her hand gently. 'Yes, he did. And we're going to get you out of here, I promise. But quickly, I need you to tell me some things. Is there anything else you can tell me about the security?'

'There's an alarm system, I know that. And I think there are sensors or something in the grounds. The foxes some-times set them off, which drives them mad. And they patrol at night, with dogs. That's all, I think.'

'And what about the staff? There's two security guys, you said.'

'Yes, and then Dr Redwood and Dr Angelou and Dr Summers. Oh, and Dr Quigley. There used to be more but since they brought me back it's only been them.'

'And just one other patient?'

'Yes, Mr Herbert. I felt so bad leaving him here, the first time. Do you think you could . . . ? It's probably too much to ask.'

'I promise we'll try,' Alex said, not wanting to commit herself to the impossible. They hadn't even figured out how they were going to spring Lucy yet.

Lucy sniffed. 'Thank you. Maybe you could talk to Ursula? I don't think she knows what's going on.' She took a crumpled ball of paper out of a pocket on her dress and held it out.

Alex took it. 'Sure. One last thing. Where's your room?'

'The end of this corridor. The last one on the left. And Mr Herbert, he's on the next floor, the second on the right.'

'OK.' Alex looked at her, trying to see what was behind those green, terrified eyes. 'You need to go now.'

Lucy stood. 'Yes.' She tiptoed to the door, then turned, with her fingers on the handle. 'I don't know your name.'

'Alex.'

'Thank you, Alex. And please tell Logan, tell him . . .'

A silent look passed between them.

'I will,' Alex said. 'Now go.'

After the door had closed, Alex went to listen. She couldn't hear any footsteps or sounds of a scuffle or anyone crying out. She quickly scanned the room to make sure Lucy hadn't left any trace of her presence, smoothed down the counterpane on the bed, then went and sat on the sofa, steadying her breathing and getting her head back into the role of the mad wife.

When the door opened a few minutes later, she half-expected Logan to be in restraints, with a security guard on each shoulder, because they'd seen through them, or the room was bugged and they'd heard everything. But he was just flanked by a smiling Dr Redwood and Dr Angelou.

'Hi, Melissa. You certainly look refreshed. How are you feeling?' Dr Angelou said brightly.

'Fine,' Alex said, without expression.

'I'm going to take you home now,' Logan said.

Alex stood up. 'All right.'

All the way to the car, Alex forced herself to drag her steps, even though all she wanted was to get the hell out of there as quickly as possible. She kept thinking they would try to fool her at the last minute by shouting out, 'Good luck, Alex,' or something, like that bit in the *Great Escape* with that bloke from *Upstairs, Downstairs*. She knew all she had to do was keep her mouth shut and say nothing, but her pulse was racing all the same. Poor Lucy. What must it have been like?

Pulling the passenger door shut at last as Logan turned on the ignition, she let out a long, deep breath.

'Where do you want to go?' Logan asked.

'Away from here,' Alex said.

He shrugged. 'OK. I thought you did good, even if you were enjoying yourself a bit too much at times.'

'Thank you.'

He glanced over at her. 'Are you OK?'

'I wish people would stop asking me that. Just keep driving.'

They passed the security barrier and then turned left on the main road. After a mile or so Alex began to feel herself again.

'They didn't turn you into a zombie or replace you with a clone or anything while I was having my nap?'

'I don't think so,' Logan said.

Alex nodded to herself. 'Good.'

Another mile went by.

'She's nice,' she said.

Logan turned. 'Sorry?'

'Lucy. And pretty.' Alex smiled. 'I can see why you fell for her.'

Logan wanted to know everything: how she'd looked, how she'd seemed, everything she said. But in the end they decided to wait until they got back to the penthouse. Logan ripped off his jacket and tie like Houdini getting out of a straitjacket. Alex kicked off her shoes and flopped down lengthways on one of the huge leather sofas.

'Drink?' he said.

'Fucking big gin and tonic, please. I think I deserve it, the day I've had. I think I'm going to have some funny dreams tonight.'

He made her drink in a large tumbler, threw in some ice and lemon, then got himself a beer from the fridge.

'Big enough for you?'

She took a gulp. 'We'll see.'

He sat down on a matching armchair facing her and she went over her meeting with Lucy, trying not to leave anything out.

He mulled it all over for a minute or two.

'I don't get it.'

'What do you mean?'

'What's their angle? Why did they practically kidnap her to bring her back? Why are they keeping her a prisoner?'

'Money?' Alex offered.

'The fees are exorbitant all right, but really? They'd do all that just for the monthly cheque?'

Alex shrugged. 'They only seem to have two patients. Maybe they're desperate.'

'I don't buy it. There's something else going on.'

They sat thinking about it. Logan drained half his beer in one go.

'I seem to have finished this drink,' Alex said.

Logan got up and made her another one.

She took a sip. 'Thanks. What about all that stuff about the house being cleaned out? That's odd.'

'I guess. Unless her sister thought, I don't know, it would be too upsetting for her when she came back.'

'Maybe. So what do we do now? Please don't tell me you've booked me into that lovely suite.'

He grinned. 'I don't think Mrs Allenby would be too pleased. You've got a day job too.'

'I should fucking say I have. And I don't think I'm up to being the mad Mrs Markham again.'

'What about the sister?' he said. 'Lucy obviously thinks she could get her out. Makes you wonder why she hasn't.'

'Maybe Redwood's keeping her in the dark. We should talk to her, anyway. See what she's got to say.'

Logan finished off his beer, wiping his mouth with his sleeve. 'What's the cover story?'

Alex took another sip of her gin. 'You can't say you've seen Lucy, obviously. But she told her sister about you. You can say something like, Lucy gave you her details and said to make contact if you didn't hear from her or something. Just say you're worried. Keep the lies to a minimum.'

He gave her a wry look. 'That'll make a change. It might even work.' He took the crumpled note from his pocket. 'Ursula Fitzroy. So Lucy is really Lucy Fitzroy?'

'Or Fitzroy could be her sister's married name.' Alex finished her drink, then lay back against a cushion and closed her eyes.

Logan squinted at the pencilled scrawl for a few moments. 'Where the hell's Morton Stanwick?'

Alex didn't answer. Logan looked up. The empty glass had slipped from her hand and fallen onto the carpet. She was fast asleep.

20

Morton Stanwick, it turned out, was a leafy village in East Sussex, not far from the site of the Battle of Hastings. The village pub was the Duke of Normandy and with its thatched roof and lopsided facade, it looked as if it had been standing since soon after the battle. Logan thought a pub in these parts would have more likely been called the King Harold, or at least they would have hedged their bets and called it the King's Arms, but maybe the people of Morton Stanwick liked winners. There were certainly plenty of big old houses, some of them behind nasty-looking thorn hedges, through which Logan glimpsed swimming pools and tennis courts and vintage cars – even the odd stable – so the current inhabitants certainly seemed to have come out on top.

The Fitzroys, on the other hand, judging from the state of the decaying pile at the end of a narrow lane where Lucy's sister lived, were on the way down and had been for some time. Tattered plastic sheeting on the roof didn't manage to cover all the missing tiles, one window on the first floor was boarded up, and the garden in the front was overgrown with brambles.

As he approached the front door, Logan wondered if anyone actually lived there or if Ursula had been mysteriously spirited away to a secure location just like her sister, leaving the house to rot, but he heard a chime somewhere inside when he pressed the bell, followed by the furious barking of at least two dogs, and then a woman shouting. 'Edmund! Edgar! Be quiet!'

A door slammed and the barking became muted, Logan heard brisk footsteps clicking on a wooden floor and then the front door opened. The woman was wearing faded jeans, a baggy green pullover and grey trainers that must have once been white.

For a long moment Logan just stood and stared, his mouth half open like an idiot.

The same green eyes, the same mouth, the same pale skin and long, dark hair. Even the half-sad, half-amused expression was the same. He started to say her name, then stopped, making himself seem even more like an idiot.

The woman's expression became less amused. 'Yes? I was expecting someone to come to fix the roof. That's not you, is it?'

'No,' Logan managed to say.

He couldn't stop looking at her.

She started to shut the door.

'Wait. I'm sorry. You're Ursula – Lucy's sister.'

She stopped halfway. 'And you are?'

'Logan. Matt Logan. She told you about me?'

Now it was her turn to stare. A wave of different emotions

Logan couldn't quite interpret passed over her features. Surprise, certainly. Or was it fear? Then something else, a momentary flash of something that looked like cold fury, but was immediately covered over by a weary smile.

'You'd better come in. You'll have to excuse the mess.'

She led him through a dark hallway, past the entrance to a large room with a huge fireplace. Glancing in, Logan saw furniture covered in sheets, a stepladder against a wall and several buckets.

'I'm afraid the kitchen's the only safe area at the moment.'

There was an oak table and four spindle-backed chairs. By the butler's sink under the window looking out onto a jungle-like garden was an Aga, with oak cupboards around the walls. As they walked in, the barking started up again, along with the scrape of paws against wood. 'Don't worry, they can't get out,' she said, pointing to a door to what Logan assumed was a utility room. 'Are you a dog person?'

'Not really.'

She filled the kettle. 'Me neither. Especially not those two. But if you live round here, they're de rigueur, I'm afraid. If you don't have at least two, people think you're odd. Tea? Coffee?'

'Tea would be fine. Er, white no sugar, thanks.'

'Good. I've only got the coffee from the shop in the village left, and I wouldn't wish that on anyone. Please, sit.'

As she made the tea, Logan tried not to watch her, her hands, the way she moved. He couldn't help seeing Lucy.

She brought over a pot and two mugs, with a little jug of

milk, then sat down on the other side of the table while it brewed.

'She didn't tell you, did she?' she said.

'Sorry?'

'That we were twins.'

'No. She didn't.'

'It must have been a shock. Seeing me. But I can assure you I'm not her, if that's what you were thinking.' Her mouth curled into that familiar half-smile and Logan's insides clenched. 'I'm her big sister, actually, that's what we always say. Born three minutes earlier.'

Logan raised his eyes from the table and she let him look at her.

'If she was here now, you'd see we're quite different. At least, I think so.'

She stirred the tea and poured, handing Logan one of the mugs. He could see it now, or thought he could. Something about her mouth. And her voice was harsher, more brittle.

'She told me all about you. Well, not all. She didn't seem to know very much, actually. But I know what you did – how you saved her life. She was quite smitten. When did you last see her?'

Despite the fact that he had now recovered from the initial surprise, Logan still felt in a weird way that he was talking to Lucy. His mouth felt dry and he took a sip of tea before answering.

'We met in Soho, at a diner. End of October? I didn't

hear anything from her after that. I was worried that she'd had a relapse.'

'A relapse,' Ursula said, as if she was unfamiliar with the word.

'Yeah, you know, that she'd do something stupid.'

Ursula put a spoonful of sugar into her tea and stirred it slowly, her eyes cast down.

'How much do you know about my sister?' she said, eventually.

'Well, I know she was a teacher. That she was married, with kids. And then, you know, the accident, the car crash.'

Ursula nodded to herself, stirring the spoon round and round.

'The car crash.'

'Yeah, the one where they died.'

'Her husband? And the children?'

Logan felt his gut tighten. 'Yeah,' he said.

Ursula let out a long sigh, laying the spoon carefully back on the tray.

'Lucy has never been married. And she doesn't have any children. Alive or dead.'

Logan felt a lurch in his chest.

'Then why . . . ?'

'Why did she try to kill herself?' Ursula let a bitter smile twitch at the corners of her mouth. 'Why has she tried four times? Because she's psychotic, Mr Logan. She's been in and out of hospital since she was a teenager.'

Logan opened his mouth, then shut it again, trying to process what he'd just heard.

'My goodness, that's two shocks you've had today. Are you sure you don't want any sugar in your tea?'

'No, I . . .'

He gave himself a little shake, as if that would help the pieces fall into place. First he'd seen Lucy's double, and now the Lucy he thought he knew had split into two people, and he couldn't decide which one was real: the woman he'd rescued, the woman he was in love with, or this other woman, this mad person who had told him all these lies.

'I'm sorry,' Ursula said. 'I didn't mean to be flippant. But after a few years you get hardened, I suppose. You develop a shell. From the outside, it can make you sound a bit unfeeling.'

'No, no, it's fine,' Logan said, recovering himself. 'So where is Lucy now?' he asked, trying to sound casual.

'Somewhere where she'll be safe,' Ursula said.

'A hospital?'

'A private clinic.'

'And before?'

'As I said, in and out, various places. Different treatments. And then they'd say she was well enough to be . . . to live on the outside again, and then the same thing would happen and back she'd go, to the same doctors or psychiatrists or whatever, the same treatment or a new one: drugs, cognitive therapy, group therapy, hypnosis, *diet* – can you believe that? Sometimes when she was having one of her better periods we'd try to look after her at home for a while, not here, the family home, when our father was still alive, but in the end it was always the same.'

'And the diagnosis?'

'Schizophrenia. With all the trimmings: voices, delusions, you name it. Though, to be quite honest, I'm not sure the word means all that much. I mean, if they knew what it was, they'd be able to find a cure, wouldn't they?'

She picked up her mug, brought it halfway to her mouth, then put it down again.

'Look, Mr Logan. I'm grateful for what you did for Lucy. Very grateful. But you weren't the first, and sadly I doubt you'll be the last. Sorry if that sounds brutal. I can tell you really cared about her. You obviously thought there really was something between you. But I'm afraid the truth is there wasn't. She just got you caught up in her fantasies.'

'I'd like to see her,' he said.

She frowned. 'That won't be possible. They don't allow visitors where she is now. Not even family. It's part of the treatment regime. I'm sorry. You're better off trying to forget about her.'

'Can you at least tell me where this place is?'

'I'd rather not.'

There was nothing more to say. Part of him wanted to get the hell out of there, to get away from this woman who was and was not Lucy and find a place where he could be alone with the desperate thoughts whirling through his brain. But part of him wanted to stay, to be close to her, to keep looking into those eyes, those eyes that had once looked into his with . . .

She stood up, perhaps sensing that he might be about to do something rash.

'Perhaps you ought to go.'

He followed her mutely to the door. She held it open for him, then at the last moment seemed to relent, holding out her hand.

'Thank you again, Mr Logan. For what you did.'

He looked at the long, pale, ringless fingers and felt an overwhelming desire to touch her. When he lightly gripped her hand, he seemed to feel an electric shock shoot up his arm.

She pulled her hand away, as if she'd felt something too.

'Goodbye,' she said, and quickly shut the door.

The drive back to London was a blur and his hands shook all the way. Alex called twice but he didn't pick up. He didn't want her to hear the panic and hurt in his voice. And anyway, he couldn't imagine what he was going to say. He parked the car in the underground garage and took the lift up to the penthouse. He got dressed in his running gear, took the back stairs down again, and then out into the wind and the rain. He headed for the river, thinking about nothing but his breathing and putting one foot in front of the other. On the towpath a group of youths on a bench, huddled against the cold, shouted out, but he ignored them and ran on, welcoming the freezing rain as it soaked through his T-shirt and ran down his face, numbing him.

He got wetter and colder and then gradually warmer as he quickened his stride, his feet pounding the tarmac until his knee joints screamed. He pushed harder, his lungs on fire, embracing the pain, wanting more of it, so it filled him up and pushed everything else out. Past, present, future: everything. He was just an animal, running for its life, oblivious.

He carried on, driving himself to the limit, until his left knee buckled and he sprawled on the ground, skinning his elbow on a paving stone and banging his head. He couldn't go any further. He heaved himself up on all fours, then got to his feet, sucking in great lungfuls of cold air as the blood ran into his eye. He turned round and started back, a pathetic weekend jogger's shuffle all he could manage, and by the time he reached home, his whole body was shaking with the cold.

He stood under a scalding shower until he could feel his extremities again, then limped into the bedroom and got dressed in a fresh pair of jeans and a white cotton shirt. He scarfed down an energy bar, made himself a mint tea and sat down at the breakfast bar, looking out at the clouds and the rain. He felt nothing.

When he'd finished his tea he sent Alex a text, trying for a breezy tone.

> Can you come over? I've had the butler restock the liquor cabinet for you.

She texted back straightaway.

How was the sister???

He thought of ignoring it, then texted:

Just come.

21

In the Clearwater Security office the next day, they were discussing the logistics of the snatch. The atmosphere was tense.

'My word, we really are flying by the seat of our pants here,' said Mrs Allenby with a tight-lipped frown.

'Improvisation,' Logan said. 'That's the name of the game.'

Alex didn't like his manic look. He'd been calm and rational the night before, when he'd told her about his meeting with Lucy's sister, but she worried that in some fundamental way it had unhinged him.

'You improvise,' said Mrs Allenby, 'when your plan starts unravelling. We don't have a plan.'

Logan shrugged. 'I hand the money over to Molloy. We follow him. He leads us to our mystery man . . .'

'Or woman,' Alex put in.

Logan ignored her. 'After the handover we leave Molloy and pick up our guy, and then somewhere along the way we take him.'

'And then?' Mrs Allenby said.

'There's nowhere secure we can take him, and anyway, we

don't want to be babysitting him for any length of time – too risky – so we do it hard and fast – sling him in the back of a van.'

'One that comes equipped with appropriate instruments of torture, I suppose,' said Mrs Allenby.

'We won't need any of that,' Logan said. 'A gun to the head should do the trick. He's a pro, he'll quickly see where his best interests lie.'

Mrs Allenby looked unconvinced.

Alan had been making notes. He looked up at Logan. 'So you'll be in the car. Alex following on the bike. She stays with Molloy after the handover, hopefully to a meet with the target, she then stays with the target. Meanwhile you've transferred to the van – who's driving that?'

'You or Ryan. Doesn't matter,' Logan said. 'Actually I want to stay in the car. The van's going to be no use in a chase if he starts playing silly buggers. Me and Alex box him in, secure him, and you get there quick as you can and we transfer to the van. Then we get him to spill the beans.'

'Where's all this going to happen?' said Mrs Allenby.

'No way of knowing ahead of time,' Logan said. 'That's where the improvisation comes in.'

Mrs Allenby turned to Alan. 'And communication?'

'I've been working on a modified version of the old A4 gear. Smaller, easier to carry. I haven't tested it yet.'

'You'd better do that, then. We don't know how fast our target works, but he's had Mr Green's details for twenty-four hours now. He might not have a plan yet, but he'll know whether it's feasible and what it's going to cost. Molloy could call to set up the meet at any time.'

'Where are you going to get the van?' Alex asked.

'Nicking one would be best. And then torch it after.'

'I'll pretend I didn't hear that,' Mrs Allenby said.

'If you need a bit of tech support, I've got a handy little gizmo to help with the alarm,' Alan said.

Logan nodded. 'Sweet.' He looked around the table, rubbing his hands together. 'It's been a while since we've done a snatch. This could be fun.'

Alex shook her head. 'It's been a while since we had proper logistical support, you mean. This'll be like walking a tight-rope a hundred feet up with no net.'

'Exactly.' He grinned.

Alex looked at him. Kidnapping as therapy. *I wouldn't want to be in this hit-man's shoes if Logan decides to take all his frustrations out on him*, she thought. Still, it would be good to be on the bike again, with a target to follow. Make a change from pretending to be mad, at any rate.

The call came at 4 p.m.

Logan took it at his desk and they all gathered round the conference table. He didn't look happy.

'He wants to do it at a hotel.'

Mrs Allenby looked bemused. 'A hotel?'

Logan shrugged. 'Maybe he's going to make a weekend of it.'

'What's the deal?' Alex said.

'I bring the money in a suitcase or a travel bag or whatever. I ask for a room, using the name John Windsor. They won't ask for ID. I get the key, go up to the room, leave the bag there, and walk out, leaving the key at reception.'

'And then what?'

'I presume they have someone on the street, watching to make sure I fuck off. Then when the coast is clear, Molloy goes to the room, checks the money's all there, and then, I don't know, puts it in the back of his Jag and he's away off to meet his man.'

'Or,' Ryan said. 'Molloy could stay out of it. Our target waits until the coast is clear, walks into the hotel – or he's already there, in a different room – picks up the money and walks out.'

'Just like any other punter.' Logan was nodding his head. He was beginning to see it. 'So Molloy and the target never meet.'

'Which means we can't identify him,' Alex said. 'We won't know who to follow.'

'Fucking brilliant,' Logan said.

'It is, actually, isn't it?' Mrs Allenby said.

'Alan, what about a tracking device?' Ryan said.

Alan took his glasses off, then put them back on. 'Tricky. He'll switch bags, so it would have to be hidden somehow in the money itself. It depends how thoroughly he checks it, I suppose.'

'If they're being this careful, then pretty thoroughly, I would think,' Mrs Allenby said.

'We need eyes on the inside,' Logan said.

'Don't even think about it,' Alex said quickly. 'I had a summer job making the beds in a seedy hotel in Bournemouth once. Yuck.'

'Not enough time, anyway,' said Mrs Allenby.

'Unless someone else checks in before you?' Ryan said.

'And then what?' Logan said. 'It won't be the sort of place you can sit in the bar or read a paper in the lobby, watching people come and go. You'd stick out like a sore thumb.'

'And even if you knew which room the money was in, how would you watch it, unless you're in the room opposite?' Alex added.

'Anyone got any brilliant ideas?' Mrs Allenby said.

'We use our noses,' Logan said. 'We put eyes on the place and someone comes out who smells wrong – with a bag the right size – we go with them.'

Mrs Allenby looked sceptical.

'Look,' Logan continued. 'Maybe Molloy's not as clever as we think. I'm supposed to check in at 10 p.m. So our guy's going to walk out some time after that, carrying a bag, like he's just checked out.'

'Right . . .' she said.

'Who checks out of a hotel after ten o'clock at night? No one – unless the roaches are seriously getting on their nerves. And anyone staying there who's just going out for a drink or meal and then coming back, they're not going to be carrying a travel bag, are they?'

Mrs Allenby thought for a moment, then nodded.

'All right. But we're going to be putting an awful lot of faith in your gut feelings.'

'Don't worry,' Logan said, with a funny expression. 'When it comes to judging people, I'm never wrong.'

Mrs Allenby left just after three, looking for all the world as if she was off to John Lewis to spend a therapeutic hour or two in the haberdashery department. Alex was hunched over Alan's desk, getting him to talk her through the upgrade to the A4 communications equipment.

As usual, Ryan was scrolling through some files on his laptop.

'Can I interrupt?' Logan said.

Ryan looked up. 'Sure, I was just seeing if any more jihadis had disappeared off the watch list.'

Logan walked round the conference table. 'It's not such a bad little scheme. Maybe we should just leave Tenniel to get on with it.'

Ryan smiled. 'The thing about keeping a cat to catch mice is you don't know what else the cat is going to catch.'

Logan sat down in the chair next to him. 'Right.'

'Anyway, it might not even be happening. I could just be, you know, connecting random dots. We need more data to be sure.'

Logan nodded. 'So that's what you're doing now.'

Ryan leaned back, put his hands behind his neck and stretched. 'Like I said, could be a waste of time.'

'Can I ask you to connect a few dots for me, then?' Logan said.

Ryan straightened, instantly intrigued. 'Sure. When you say "for me", you mean . . . ?'

'Something personal. Between you and me. If that's all right.'

Ryan grinned. 'Always a pleasure. What do you want me to find out?'

'Everything you can about a woman called Ursula Fitzroy. Lives in a village called Morton Stanwick. She's got a sister called Lucy, not sure of her last name, could be the same.'

'That's it? What do you want to know?'

Logan looked sheepish. 'I don't really know. I mean, I'll know it when you find it. Just anything that's . . . off.'

Ryan pulled at his ponytail. 'Deep background. Got it.'

'You sure you're OK with that?'

Ryan didn't reply, his fingers already dancing over the keyboard.

Two hours later Logan's phone buzzed. He'd gone for a walk along the river, too antsy to sit around in the office trying not to peer over Ryan's shoulder, then decided to go back to the penthouse.

Got as much as I can. Want me to download? R

He turned round and headed back to the office, resisting the urge to run. Alan had gone but Alex was still there, trying on earpieces.

'What do you think – the pink or the blue?' she said when he walked in, closing the office door behind him.

'The whole point is they're supposed to be invisible,' he said with a frown.

'Ooh, in that case I might go for the purple,' Alex said, ignoring his tone.

Ryan was still sitting at the conference table. An empty coffee mug sat beside his laptop.

'Tell me what you've got,' Logan said, making his way over.

Ryan raised his eyebrows, nodding towards Alex.

'It's fine. Alex is in the loop.'

'I'm glad someone is,' Ryan said wryly. Logan started to speak, but Ryan held up a hand. 'Only kidding. You want to tell me what this is all about, fine. If you don't, also fine. I'm just curious, that's all.'

Alex came and joined them around the table. 'We're just trying to stop something bad happening. It's what we do, isn't it?'

'Good enough for me,' Ryan said. He looked down at some notes he'd scribbled on an A4 pad. 'OK, so, the Fitzroys. Interesting family.'

'Interesting, how?' said Logan.

'Well, it's all a bit *King Lear*. With a bit of Agatha Christie thrown in.'

'O-kay,' Logan said, looking bewildered.

'Try and keep the literary references to a minimum if you can,' Alex said, reaching over and patting Ryan's arm.

'Sorry,' Ryan said. 'Right, well, Ursula Fitzroy, the one who lives in Morton Stanwick, she's the eldest. Technically, anyway.' He caught Logan's look of bewilderment. 'Eldest of three sisters. Ursula, Lucy – they're the twins – and then Deborah. Actually they're triplets, but Ursula and Lucy are also twins, identicals, if that makes sense.'

'Three of them . . .' Logan seemed to be having difficulty digesting this new information. 'So, all born at the same time – well, one after the other – but two of them are identical.'

'That's it,' Ryan said. 'Seems like they were sort of local celebs in the village. Lots of snaps in the local paper growing up, winning trophies at the pony club and that kind of thing. Deborah died young, I think she was eleven. An accident. No mention of their mother, so I assume divorce, some sort of scandal, or she died, too, somewhere along the way.'

'Right, so three daughters,' Alex said. 'And what about their father?'

'George Fitzroy. Intriguing character, actually. Brilliant chemical engineer. Invented some process, or it might have been a new substance – some kind of polymer; it's very hard to find out the details because instead of going public, it looks like he sold it to the government. I guess it must have had some sort of military application. Anyway, he clearly made a ton of money out of it and then retired to his laboratory, and then he was never really seen or heard of again. The odd rumour, that he was cooking up something funny away from prying eyes, but that's village gossip for you. If someone hides themselves away, they must be up to no good, you know. Probably nothing in it.'

'So the villagers didn't all turn up with pitchforks and torches one night?' Alex said.

Ryan smiled. 'Well, if they did, he was already gone.'

'Disappeared?' Logan said. 'Or dead?'

'Ah, that's the sixty-four-thousand-dollar question,' Ryan said. 'Actually, rather a bit more than sixty-four thousand. More like three or four million.'

'You've lost me,' Logan said.

'Sorry. The thing is, George Fitzroy is still officially a missing person.'

'Because they haven't found a body,' Alex said.

'Exactly. One day he's there, the next he's gone.'

'And he didn't leave a note saying he couldn't bear to see his invention being used for evil purposes and he was doing away with himself?' Alex said.

'Nope. Nada. Complete mystery.'

'Who saw him last?' Logan asked.

'They all had a cosy family dinner, apparently, him and the two surviving daughters, the night before.'

'And he was acting normally?' Alex said.

'That's what they told the police.'

'And you got all this from where?' Logan asked.

Ryan looked almost sheepish. 'It wasn't hard. Most of it's in the local papers. They followed the investigation and all the court proceedings pretty closely, as you can imagine.'

Alex raised an eyebrow. 'Court proceedings?'

'That's where it gets interesting,' Ryan said. 'Ursula tried to get their father declared dead. As far as she was concerned, he wouldn't have just gone off without telling anyone, so he must have been murdered.'

'By who?' Alex said.

'She said she'd seen a mysterious car lurking about near the property with two men in it. And her father had complained someone had put a dead crow through the letter box, apparently.'

'That does sound like something out of Agatha Christie,' Alex said, shaking her head.

'Quite. And the coroner didn't buy it either. But Ursula wouldn't let it go. She's got a whole team of lawyers on it. You should see their bills.'

Logan chewed his lip. 'When I met her, she didn't look like she was exactly swimming in cash. So why's she doing it?'

Alex looked at Ryan, narrowing her eyes. 'You saw a bit more than just their invoices, didn't you?'

He nodded. 'Their cyber-security was pretty shit, actually. There's a ton of correspondence, of course. You know what lawyers are like – send you a letter telling you they're going to send you a letter, and then send you another letter charging you a hundred quid. I didn't plough through it all, to be honest, once I'd got the gist. But I did find something a bit more interesting: old George's will.'

'And that's how you know he left four million quid to his daughters,' Logan said. 'Sorry, I was being a bit slow. Ursula wants him declared dead so she can get her hands on the money.'

'Not quite,' Ryan said.

Logan and Alex looked at him.

'Ursula doesn't get a penny. It all goes to Lucy. Ursula must have really done something to piss the old man off.'

'I don't get it,' Logan said, scratching at the stubble on his chin. 'Why would Ursula be spending money she hasn't got to have her father declared dead so her sister can inherit all his money? It doesn't make sense.' He thought for a moment. 'Hold on. What can you tell me about . . . Lucy?' Alex could see the pain of having to say her name.

Ryan flicked though his notes. 'Not much, to be honest. Most of what I've managed to dig up has been through the lawyers, and she hasn't been involved in that. She doesn't appear to have taken an interest. And the local papers stopped writing stories about her once she grew up and stopped riding ponies.'

Logan took a deep breath. 'Do you know if she got married, had kids? That would still make the local rag, wouldn't it?'

'Yeah, you'd think,' said Ryan. 'But there was no mention that I could find.'

'And what about . . . mental problems. Getting sectioned, anything like that. Ursula said Lucy had a history.'

'Well, if she did, the local paper chose to draw a veil over it. I don't know, maybe the family still has some influence in the village.'

Logan sighed. 'Listen, thanks, Ryan. I owe you.'

Ryan tilted his head to one side, working a crick out of his neck. 'Any time. Like I say, it wasn't difficult. And to be honest, it doesn't sound to me like I've helped you with your problem, whatever it is.'

Logan and Alex exchanged a look.

'No, Ryan,' Logan said. 'I think you've told us exactly what we needed to know.'

22

Lucy woke up with a start. For a split second her mind was blank.

She didn't know it, but that would be the best part of her day.

A moment later she remembered the dream. That was when she screamed. It seemed to be pulling her back into sleep, into the dark, where the terror was. Her breath coming in ragged gasps, she fought against it.

'I'm awake, I'm awake, I'm awake.'

She repeated the mantra, her eyes wide, trying to drink in the physical details of the room – the bed, the chair, the curtains – to prove to herself that she was no longer asleep.

The dream receded, like a dark tide, leaving a handful of ghastly images behind: teeth, a claw, blood pumping.

She lay back, her nightie soaked with sweat, and started to cry.

She wanted to be away from this place. She wanted to be home. But most of all, she wanted to know where home was.

After a few minutes she had no more tears. She peeled off her nightie and went into the bathroom. She wanted a bath. A proper soak. She hadn't had one in so long. But baths made you think of people who slit their wrists in the hot, numbing water. So, as usual, she stepped into the shower cubicle instead.

She turned the dial to cold and the first blast of icy water almost made her convulse, hunching over like an old lady. But it also banished the last wisps of the dream. Gasping in shock, she felt the reality of her body return as she hugged herself.

I'm real, she thought. *I can feel my skin, my bones, my hair. I can feel my pain.*

She dialled the temperature up to lukewarm and washed herself with a bar of soap. There was shampoo in an unmarked plastic bottle, but she used the soap instead, unable to shake off the absurd idea that the shampoo would somehow be poisoned. She was mixing up her fairy tales in a ridiculous way, she knew – *Rapunzel* somehow morphing into *Snow White* – but she didn't have much else beyond fairy tales to guide her any more. She knew she couldn't trust what anyone said, what anyone told her, so she relied on the tried and trusted wisdom of *Hansel and Gretel* and *Little Red Riding Hood*.

Look out for jealous queens or ravenous wolves posing as harmless old ladies. If it smells nice and looks nice, don't touch it. Following the rules was sometimes hard – especially with food. She'd tried refusing to eat anything that didn't come in a sealed packet, surviving the first few days on the little sachets of biscuits in her room, but they soon got wise to that and the biscuits stopped appearing. In the end she'd got so hungry she'd given up, telling herself that she needed to stay strong if she was going to fight them; if she was somehow going to get out of there. She also reasoned that the effects of the drugs they were giving her would probably be worse on an empty stomach, but for all she knew, the opposite was true. It wasn't as if she knew how these things worked.

Thinking about food suddenly made her realize how hungry she was. Every morning it was the same, that exhausted, emptied out feeling, making her fingers tremble when she held her hands out, as if it had taken every bit of energy she possessed to fight off the dream. It was another reason for trying to keep her strength up, worrying that if she went to bed hungry, the dream would seize on her weakness and drag her under at last.

She dressed quickly in a clean pair of jeans and a white shirt, then slipped her trainers on. It was 7 a.m. and she knew the door would have been magically unlocked. She let her hand rest on the handle for a moment, summoning her courage for the day, before pushing it down. The door clicked open.

The corridor was empty, as usual. Not just the emptiness of no one there, but the deeper emptiness of no one ever there, as if the place had been long abandoned. She wondered for a moment whether she was the last person at the clinic, if Dr Redwood and the others had gone in the night, like concentration camp guards fleeing the advancing Allies, leaving her to wander through the grounds, bewildered and disoriented, until help arrived. Or perhaps the gates would be open and she could just walk out, like before.

As she descended the stairs, her fingers lightly tracing the bannisters, she heard the sound of muffled conversation from somewhere on the ground floor and the fantasy evaporated. The breakfast room, however, was empty. As usual, there were a dozen tables, each covered in crisp linen and with a little vase containing a single flower, even though no one aside from herself and Mr Herbert ever appeared. She supposed it was possible that there were other patients locked away somewhere in the complex of buildings (it wasn't as if she had explored very much of it), too ill or dangerous to be let out into the common areas, but she had come to the conclusion (she had become a connoisseur of emptiness) that if there ever had been, they were now gone. It was just her and Mr Herbert.

She sighed, seeing that he wasn't there at his usual table. Could he have already had his breakfast and gone back to his room or out into the grounds? Surely it was still too early; he wouldn't have had time. And besides, if he didn't come down first, he always waited for her, smiling and nodding across the room as if they were a couple of retirees in a Torquay guesthouse.

She felt a spark of panic. Had he gone? Or had they done something with him: what he always feared they would do? How awful to be the last person in this place, the last patient; all the doctors and the rest of the staff here just for her, as if the place itself had been built for the single purpose of containing her, so they could . . .

So they could what?

That was the question. That was always the question. Why was she here and what were they trying to do to her? Because if the idea was to make her feel better – calm, clear-headed, *sane* – well, it wasn't working. Whatever was wrong with her, every day she spent at the clinic made it worse.

And yet, day after horrible day, night after horrifying night, the treatment continued.

She went to the sideboard where a thermos of coffee and a jug of milk stood by a basket of fruit and a tray of still-warm croissants. She poured herself a milky coffee then picked up a pear from the top of the pile, quickly sniffed it, and put it back, easing another one out from underneath and putting it on her plate. There were four croissants. She reached for the nearest one, then stopped, her hand in mid-air, considered the other three, hovered over one of them. And then decisively snatched the first one.

She felt acutely the madness of what she was doing. But she hadn't always been like this, had she? She'd had a normal life once, she was sure of it. It was this place, this place and the dreadful people in it, who had made her this way for their own perverted and incomprehensible reasons.

She sat down and ate her breakfast and drank her coffee, knowing that as soon as she had taken her last bite, they would come for her. Today, she thought, it will be Tweedledee.

And it was.

Tweedledee was the clean-shaven one, slightly chunkier, with the meaty forearms. Or it could be that they were in fact identical, and he simply chose to wear shirts that were slightly too small for him to emphasize his physique. Otherwise, they might as well have been identical, with the same brutal haircuts, shiny, wolf-like smiles and stunted conversational skills. Thugs, basically. They'd never hurt her, nothing beyond a firm, pincer-like grip on her biceps that had left a livid bruise the day after, but she could tell they'd be more than happy should the necessity arise. Dr Redwood just needed to say the word. Or perhaps she could just whistle.

She wiped her mouth with a napkin and walked towards the door without acknowledging him. He pirouetted neatly in the doorway as she passed, like a matador with a bull, and followed her down the corridor towards the consulting rooms. She could feel his grin on the back of her neck. She stopped outside Dr Redwood's office and he leaned past her to give the door a brisk double-tap, his breath, smelling of bacon and cigarettes, hot on her cheek. She willed herself not to flinch and walked in.

She went and sat in her usual chair, keeping her eyes on the big window, and the view onto the sunlit lawns with their scattered trees. She folded her hands in her lap.

'Good morning, Lucy,' said Dr Redwood, following her eyes. 'It *is* a lovely day, isn't it? The forecast was clouds and rain, but we woke up to this. So much for experts, eh? Perhaps after our session this morning we could go for a walk in the grounds. Would you like that?'

Yes? No? Did it matter what she said?

'Yes,' said Lucy.

Dr Redwood was wearing a shapeless beige linen dress. Underneath it, Lucy thought that she was putting on weight. Her blonde hair was pulled back in a tight ponytail and her blood-red lipstick matched her fingernails. As ever, her skin seemed to shine.

'You look bright this morning, Lucy. Did you have a better night?'

'No,' Lucy said.

Dr Redwood made a little frown of concern. Lucy thought it was the most insincere thing she had ever seen.

'The nightmare again? The same one?'

Lucy nodded and went back to staring out the window.

'Can you tell me about it?'

'I don't want to. Anyway, you've heard it all before. What's the point?'

'We've discussed this, Lucy, haven't we? The point is to bring it into the light, to look at it – together – so we can understand it and not be afraid.'

'But that just makes it worse. Every time you make me describe it, it gets worse. The next night is worse. It's getting worse all the time, and I wake up more frightened.' She turned her head and looked at Dr Redwood properly for the first time. 'I don't want to understand it: I want it to stop. I want to dream about something else – actually, no, I don't want to dream about anything.'

Dr Redwood smiled. 'That's not how the mind works, I'm

afraid, Lucy. We can't make things we don't like go away by just ignoring them. That just makes them bigger, more powerful.'

'*This* is making it bigger!' Lucy cried, ashamed of the pleading tone in her voice. 'What we're doing – what you're making me do – is making it worse.'

She put a hand over her eyes, trying not to sob.

Dr Redwood didn't say anything. She didn't have to say anything. Lucy knew perfectly well that if she refused to talk about her dream, then Dr Redwood would summon Tweedledee or Tweedledum and they'd give her a shot of something that would sap her will and then it would be even worse because in her drugged-up state she wouldn't be able to tell whether she was asleep or awake and the dream would seem even more real and she might as well go back to bed and have the damned thing properly.

Lucy breathed in deeply, then took her hand from her eyes and opened them.

'There is something I want to talk about, though.'

Dr Redwood looked at her neutrally.

'Please.'

'And what's that, Lucy?'

Lucy shifted in her seat. 'It's my . . . memories.'

'Your memory?'

'No, just certain parts of my memory. Certain things.'

'Like what?'

Lucy felt a lump forming in her throat. 'My family. Brian and the children.'

Dr Redwood uncrossed her legs and rested her hands on her lap. 'What about them, exactly?'

Lucy closed her eyes, trying to find the right words. 'Sometimes I think about them and I . . .'

'Go on.'

'I can't see them. I can't see their faces. They're just blank. And then yesterday . . .' She stopped. It was too upsetting. And Dr Redwood was the last person in the world she wanted to tell these things. But she could be the only person who could help. Maybe it was the drugs. If they changed the dosage, or maybe even stopped giving them to her, then maybe the fuzziness would clear and everything would come back.

'What happened yesterday?'

Lucy looked up at Dr Redwood. She had that self-satisfied half-smile all psychiatrists or psychoanalysts or whatever they were seemed to have, as if everything, however painful and distressing, was all unfolding according to some plan that only they knew about. Or it could be they just didn't care. Right now, Dr Redwood didn't look as if she cared about Lucy losing her memories. If anything, she looked pleased.

Lucy wished she'd never opened her mouth, wished she could take it back.

'It doesn't matter.'

'Tell me,' said Dr Redwood.

No, fuck off, Lucy thought, even as she felt the words rushing out of their own accord:

'I couldn't remember their names. *My children!*' she almost wailed. 'It was like the dream, only worse. I couldn't even remember if they were a boy and a girl, or . . .' She sniffed. 'I concentrated really hard until it came back – until *they* came back. Timmy and Marie. I wrote their names down on a piece of paper.' Her hand made an involuntary movement towards the front pocket of her jeans. 'But I'm so afraid. What happens if one day I look at the piece of paper and I don't know who they are? It's like I lost them once, and now I'm losing them all over again.'

She looked up at Dr Redwood, her eyes brimming, expecting a glimmer of sympathy, but all she got was that dead look. There was a box of tissues on a little round table. Dr Redwood leaned across and handed it to Lucy.

'How distressing for you,' she said, and at that moment Lucy knew that if she wanted one thing more than to escape from this place, it was to find the secret room where Dr Redwood had hidden her black and evil heart and plunge a dagger right through it.

23

DCI Tenniel got up from his desk and walked to the window. A fly was buzzing against the bomb-proof glass, desperate to escape into London's grey drizzle.

What was the old nursery rhyme? *There was an old lady who swallowed a fly*, something, something, *perhaps she'll die.* Then she swallowed a spider to catch the fly. Then – what was it? – a bird? Yes, a bird to catch the spider. Then a cat to catch the bird, and a dog to catch the cat. Then what? What would you send after a dog? What eats dogs? Or was that the end?

Whatever it was, at this moment he was feeling very much like that old lady, and it didn't seem as if he was anywhere near to the end of his troubles. He waited until the fly had settled for a moment, then slowly moved his hand until it was hovering over it, closer and closer – then slammed it against the glass. He went back to his desk, opened a drawer and took out a box of tissues. He wiped off the remains of the fly, screwed the tissue into a tight ball and dropped it into the waste basket, before returning to the window and the rain.

If only it could be that easy.

With Mason dead, it should all be over. He'd finally closed the loop. Except that the loop was never closed. After the spider, the bird. After the bird, the cat, and the dog. On and on. What was that line from *Macbeth*?

> *I am in blood*
> *Stepped in so far, that, should I wade no more,*
> *Returning were as tedious as go o'er.*

He still remembered that from school. Bored out of his mind, but some things just stuck, as if somehow he knew: 'That'll be me one day.' He shook his head. First nursery rhymes, now Shakespeare. Elizabeth would have been proud of him.

He turned away from the window and sat down at his desk again. There were two phones, an open laptop, a fountain pen and a yellow legal pad with nothing written on it.

There was also an A4 print-out of a photograph showing a woman's face in three-quarter profile. He picked it up, turning it this way and that in a vain attempt to make the grainy image come into sharper focus. She was blonde, with her hair in a neat ponytail. Pale lips, almost a cupid's bow, but not quite. No make-up, unless it was very subtle. The natural look. But the no-nonsense navy skirt and jacket were all-business. If he had to guess, what would he say? Lawyer? PR? Maybe something in sales?

'Who are you?' he said aloud.

Not Danielle Hart, that's for sure. Danielle Hart, as far as he'd been able to ascertain, did not exist. Or, rather, the various Danielle Harts he had been able to track down didn't look anything like this young woman.

He just needed a name to go with that pretty face, a face that had so far drawn a blank on all the visual databases, so whoever she was, she didn't have a record. Not that he was a hundred per cent sold on the technology. Call him old school, but the smartest computer programme still couldn't match the human ability to recognize faces. If this had been a regular investigation, he would have had a few dozen copies made and sent some of the boys and girls out into the pubs and clubs, to see if anyone had a light-bulb moment. There was nothing special about any of her features, but there was definitely something about her. Once you'd seen her close up, you wouldn't forget.

But this wasn't a regular investigation, which meant his available resources were limited. He could go to Durgan, he supposed, ask him to put the word out on the street. But that would entail its own risks. Another spider scuttling down the old woman's gullet that might need to be dealt with in its turn. If Tenniel had known who the hell she was and why Terry Mason had taken his life in his hands to talk to her, that would have been one thing. But that was what he needed to know. And if Durgan got his hands on her and extracted the information first, that would give him another card to play, another bit of leverage, and he couldn't afford that.

There was another option, of course. The smart play, perhaps.

Do nothing. Let it go.

After all, Danielle Hart never got her meet with Terry Mason, so he couldn't have passed on what he knew, if that's what he'd been planning to do. It had been a close-run bloody thing, but in the end Durgan had got it done. Parker was still there, of course, and until that particular loose end had been tied up, he couldn't be a hundred per cent sure the genie would stay in the bottle, but Parker must know he's a dead man walking. In fact, he was old school, one of the last of that generation, so he'd probably do the job himself before too long.

She swallowed a spider to kill the fly . . .

So if Danielle Hart was none the wiser, why not leave her be? Why put himself at risk by trying to track her down, and then it would be one more body to add to the count, one more death that would need to be accounted for, tidied up, erased from the record.

She swallowed a bird to catch the spider . . .

The answer, of course, was because he had to know. He had to know what she knew, or thought she knew, and who was pulling her strings. And if it turned out she had even the vaguest inkling of what Terry Mason had to tell, then she would have to be taken off the board. The fact that she was sniffing around was enough.

Sometimes doing nothing was sensible; but doing nothing wasn't in his nature. If you see a problem, fix it; and if by fixing it you give yourself another problem, fix that. And the next one. You had to keep moving, like a shark; that had always been his motto.

A knock on the door made him snap out of his reverie. 'Come.'

Bolton came in, closing the door behind him and stood to attention. He'd taken Tenniel's advice and got himself a decent suit. Be seen out and about in a shitty off-the-peg outfit that made you look like a trainee estate agent, and the crims would instantly think you were bribe-able. You needed to look as if you went to the same tailor as they did, even if the effort cost you half your wages.

'Have a seat.'

'Sir.'

Tenniel suppressed a smile. Even sitting down, Bolton looked as if he was standing to attention. He had the obedient but eager look of a good hunting dog, like a taut bow waiting to be released.

She swallowed a dog . . .

'They keeping you busy downstairs?'

'Not as busy as I'd like, sir.'

Good answer.

'I might have something for you to do.'

Bolton sat up even straighter. If he'd had a tail he would have wagged it.

Tenniel held up the picture of Danielle Hart. 'This is the woman who was waiting to see Terry Mason before he was murdered.'

Bolton took the print-out and scanned it.

'Except that it isn't. She booked herself in with fake ID.'

'Did Mason know who she was?' Bolton asked.

'Good question.'

'If he didn't, why see her?'

'Another good question.'

'Was she bringing something in, do you think?'

'Unlikely. She underwent a standard body search and she must have known they'd be monitoring her contact with Mason pretty closely.'

'She was bringing information, then? You think there was a plan to spring him?'

'Either that or he still had some assets somewhere we didn't know about. Maybe he was going to give her an account number or a passcode.'

Bolton nodded. 'Makes sense.'

'In which case, we'd like to find those assets before they become irretrievable. Which means finding Ms Hart.'

'And the sooner the better, I'd imagine.'

'Exactly.'

Tenniel watched Bolton's face. His expression didn't change, but his eyes gave it away as the penny dropped. *Why me?* he was thinking.

'I don't want Serious Crimes involved in this,' Tenniel said. He looked Bolton in the eye, letting the implication sink in. 'I need someone who reports solely to me.'

Bolton nodded, maintaining eye contact.

Good, thought Tenniel. *He thinks this is all about money.* He allowed himself a weary smile. *If only.*

Bolton leaned forward, proffering the print-out.

'Keep it,' Tenniel said. 'I want you to get to know that

face so it's as familiar as your own mother's. And I'll send you the footage. It won't help much, but at least you can see the way she carries herself.'

Bolton nodded, folding the print-out carefully and tucking it away in the inside pocket of his jacket.

Tenniel waited for him to ask more questions, but he was sharp enough to know that if Tenniel had anything else to tell him, he would have done it.

'Needle in a haystack, I know,' Tenniel said, spreading his hands apologetically.

For the first time Tenniel could remember, Bolton smiled.

'Don't worry, sir,' Bolton said. 'If she's out there, I'll find her.'

24

The slim blond-haired boy stood near the touchline, just inside the opposition's half, with his hands on his hips. He watched the ball pinging around the centre circle as if it was in a pinball machine, neither team's midfield able to hold on to it for more than a couple of seconds, and sighed theatrically. He was just reaching up to readjust his Alice band, when the ball unexpectedly ricocheted off an opposition knee as one of his teammates tried to hoof it towards the goal. It spun invitingly in his direction. As all eyes turned towards him, he deliberately didn't change his stance in anticipation, and at first it looked as if the ball was going to sail over his head and out for a throw-in. Then at the last moment, he spun and neatly trapped it on the touchline. Having looked a moment earlier as if he had no interest in the game, he suddenly came alive, accelerating into a fluid sprint along the touchline with the ball seemingly glued to his right foot.

Bunched together in the middle of the pitch, for a few moments the other players seemed frozen in place, as if they couldn't understand how the ball had escaped. Then a short, wiry boy with a stiff black quiff sprang into life, his face set in an outraged snarl as he locked onto the lanky winger. At first it looked as if he had no chance of catching him, but as the blond boy continued to hug the touchline with his eyes on the ball dancing at his feet in front of him like an excited puppy, it began to look as if he'd got his angles right. Legs pumping, jaw set, with every stride the dark-haired boy got closer, and the little knot of spectators on the other side of the pitch seemed to draw in a collective breath as they waited for the inevitable collision.

The blond-haired boy seemed oblivious, one of those fancy-dan players who only focused on themselves, as if a football match was just a stage for showing off their skills. If anything, he seemed to slow down fractionally as the dark-haired boy put on an extra spurt, ready to catch him around the eighteen-yard line. One of the spectators, a woman in a white Puffa jacket with wraparound sunglasses, put her hand to her mouth as the dark-haired boy gathered himself, then launched into a two-footed, studs-up lunge. Even as this human missile entered his peripheral vision, the blond-haired boy didn't look up. Instead, socks around his ankles, advertising what at that moment seemed like a fatal disdain for shin pads, he seemed to simply freeze in mid-stride, like a movie suddenly paused, the ball magically sucked out of the path of the impending tackle, then dipped his shoulder to the left and moved off towards the goal, while the dark-haired boy flew past, skidding over the grass, studs, knees and elbows connecting furiously with empty air.

'Go, Rory!' the woman in the sunglasses squealed, doing a little dance on the touchline.

The man standing next to her was smoking a short cigar. As the would-be tackler picked himself up on the other side of the pitch, the man dropped the cigar on the grass and ground it under his foot. The boy looked over. The man and the boy locked eyes for a moment, then the boy put his head down and set off towards the penalty area.

By this time the blond winger had evaded two more tackles, his lazy, fluid grace seeming to give him the ability to slow time down or speed it up at will. The ball stopped dead, vanished, came back again. If it had suddenly turned into a rabbit or a bunch of flowers, the opposition defenders couldn't have looked more baffled. With only the keeper to beat, he finally looked up, seeming to be aware of his surroundings for the first time. He stopped, put his foot on the ball, and smiled. Two defenders who'd been busting a gut to catch up to him, suddenly slowed, as if they wanted to avoid being made monkeys of and ending up on their arses. The blond boy jinked left, then right, all the time keeping his foot on the ball, trying to body-fake the keeper into diving prematurely, so he could roll the ball into an empty net.

He waited another half-second before deciding where to put the ball.

It was a half-second too long.

The dark-haired boy had learned his lesson. He didn't launch himself, two-footed, this time. Instead he grabbed a fistful of blond hair, jerked the winger back, and stamped down on the back of his ankle. There was a snap like a rifle-shot, a shriek of pain, and the boy went down. As the winger's teammates crowded round, faces pale with shock, the dark-haired boy calmly took the ball and booted it to safety, then stood, hands on hips, with no expression on his face, waiting for the referee.

The woman in sunglasses screamed, then tried to run onto the pitch. A man in a camel-hair coat pulled her back. 'Let the first-aid chap deal with it, Moira,' he said, as a man in an orange vest clutching a red first-aid bag hurried past.

Once he got to the goalmouth the first-aider bent over the boy and the referee shooed the other players back. He then turned to the dark-haired boy. As soon as he saw the ref's hand move to his pocket, the dark-haired boy spat on the grass and started walking. He didn't look back.

On his way to the changing rooms he passed the specta-tors. The man who'd been smoking the cigar nodded to him, and the boy nodded back, trying not to grin.

'Is that your son?' the woman with the sunglasses said.

The man turned and looked at her.

'I want to know his name. That was assault,' she said furiously.

He shrugged. 'It's football,' he said. 'It's a tough game. Maybe your boy should try netball instead.'

The man in the camel-hair coat opened his mouth as if he was about to say something, but the other man looked at him and he closed it again.

'Come along, Moira,' he said, ushering the woman away. 'There's no point talking to people like that.'

The man took a cigar from his pocket and lit it. A tall man in a long raincoat joined him.

'You've obviously never been to a netball match,' he said.

'Stupid bitch,' the shorter man said, blowing out a stream of smoke. 'Her twat of a son made Carl look like a cunt.'

The tall man shrugged. 'He got him in the end.'

'Only after he'd been made to look a cunt. I tell him, don't just jump in, feet first. Think what you're fucking well doing.'

'He'll learn.'

'He fucking better.'

'Anyway, very entertaining game. Glad I came.'

'You being funny?'

The tall man shrugged.

'Fancy a cigar?'

'Only if we've got something to celebrate.' He paused. 'Do we have something to celebrate?'

O'Dwyer stepped away from the touchline so they were out of earshot of the other spectators. 'Seems like we're both in the clear. No comeback after Stephanie Mason.'

Hansen didn't say anything.

'The Old Bill probably think Durgan did it.'

Hansen let out a breath. 'You made me come all the way out here to tell me that? We're keeping our heads down, remember? No meets unless it's absolutely necessary. Or did you feel I really needed to see what a talented footballer your son's turned out to be?'

Something flashed in O'Dwyer's eyes for a second, then dimmed.

'All right, all right.'

'What, then?'

'It's Molloy.'

Hansen made a clucking noise. 'What's that fat cunt want?'

'He's got a job.'

Hansen made another noise. 'He's always got a job. You said lay low for twelve months. Keep our noses clean. Let any investigations rot on the vine. Why didn't you tell him to fuck off?'

'I did tell him to fuck off.'

'And he didn't take the hint? He tried to twist your arm?'

O'Dwyer snorted. 'He wouldn't fucking dare. No, it's just good money, that's all.'

Hansen nodded to himself. 'Ah. Dory's maxed out all her credit cards – is that it? Or have you been having some bad luck on the horses?'

'I don't gamble.'

It was Hansen's turn to snort. 'You gamble all the time.'

An ambulance was slowly making its way over the grass towards the goalmouth, followed by the woman in the sunglasses and the man in the camel-hair coat at a trot. O'Dwyer took another long puff of his cigar. 'Maybe it's just about keeping your hand in. Staying in the game. You turn too many jobs down, the jobs'll stop coming. They'll find someone else.'

'There is no one else. Not like us. Maybe it's just you enjoy the work.'

'And you don't?'

'Beats being in the Army, I suppose. At least this way the other fella doesn't shoot back.'

'There you go,' O'Dwyer said.

The paramedics had got a stretcher out of the back of the ambulance. They put it down on the grass while they took a look at the boy with the busted ankle. O'Dwyer and Hansen could hear him moaning softly. A couple of his teammates were crouched beside him, but most of the players had started to drift to the sidelines, rummaging in their bags for sports drinks or just to look at their phones. The referee was leaning on a goalpost, writing in a little notebook.

'That's the end of Carl's season, I reckon,' O'Dwyer said.

'You'll have to find another reason to get out of the house, then,' Hansen said.

O'Dwyer frowned. 'Do you want to know about this job?'

Hansen didn't answer.

'Because if you don't, that's fine. Not a problem. I'll do it myself.'

'If you reckoned you could do it yourself, we wouldn't be standing here,' Hansen said. 'There's got to be a bloody good reason if you're willing to split the money. No offence,' he added.

The referee had put his book away and was now talking to the woman in the sunglasses, while the man in the camel-hair coat stood with his arm round her shoulder. Every now and then she looked in their direction.

'So?' O'Dwyer said.

'How much?' Hansen said.

'A round hundred. Split down the middle.'

Hansen considered that. 'When?'

'Soon as. It just needs a little bit of thinking about. The ins and outs. There might be some electronics involved.'

'Ah.'

There was an orange supermarket bag between O'Dwyer's feet. He nudged it with his foot. 'It's all in there.'

He stood back, tapping the ash from his cigar onto the grass.

Hansen reached down and picked up the bag. 'Let me look at it, first, before I say yes or no.'

'Fair enough.'

'Then I'll be in touch.'

As they turned and started to walk towards the car park they heard a shout from the next pitch. One of the players was down in the goalmouth, clutching his face. A player from the other team was leaning over him, jabbing a finger, before aiming a gob of spit at his face. As he stood back up, one of the injured player's teammates swung a fist and connected with his jaw, and then it was difficult to see what was happening because everybody had piled in.

O'Dwyer and Hansen watched for a few moments, before moving on.

'I'll choose the location next time, if it's all right with you,' Hansen said. 'Somewhere everyone isn't trying to kill each other.'

25

Logan turned away from the window. The penthouse room was dominated by the big, L-shaped leather sofa, which allowed you to look at the view through the floor-to-ceiling window (today: high-rises just visible through driving clouds and rain) or at the long fireplace with the giant plasma TV screen mounted on the wall above it.

Instead, Logan was looking at the single spindle-backed wooden chair, which was strangely at odds with the rest of the furniture. Maybe it had sentimental value for the hedge-fund owner he was impersonating, he thought. Maybe it was a relic of a different time: the kitchen chair his mother used to sit in, or maybe something he bought with his girlfriend at a flea market to furnish their first flat together. Wherever it had come from, Logan had decided it was the most likely place for Sarah to materialize. Which was why he fixated on it, as if staring at it might conjure her into appearing, like those optical illusions where you could trick your brain into making the image of a face or an animal suddenly appear out of the background if you let everything go slightly out of focus.

So far it wasn't working.

Which meant either she no longer wanted to communicate with him, or she never had in the first place: it had all been in his head.

He wasn't sure which was worse.

He just wanted to know they were all right, wherever they were.

Well, at least I tried, he thought.

He went and sat down in the chair. He didn't feel any warm fuzzy feelings from the previous owner, just the hard spindles against his back.

Fuck it. He wanted to get out, go for a long run in the rain until everything hurt. But he needed to show his face around the flat, show the watchers he was earning his keep as a decoy or whatever it was. Plus, he was expecting a call from Molloy, confirming when he was supposed to check into the hotel and hand over the cash.

So he had to keep moving. Keep acting like a bored, super-rich hedge-fund arsehole.

In the kitchen there was a half-eaten tin of tuna on the black marble island. He found a fork and shovelled the last of it into his mouth, chewing slowly.

He wondered what Lucy was doing. Alex had told her they'd come for her. Which meant Alex was going to have to check in as Melissa Markham. But when? They had a hit-man to kidnap and interrogate first. And would Alex still be up for it? Terry Mason's murder seemed to have hit a nerve: since her abortive prison visit she'd seemed anxious, antsy, not her normal who-gives-a-fuck self. Or was it the clinic? Was she genuinely scared that she'd get stuck there, like Lucy, unable to convince anyone she was sane enough to leave?

No, Alex was all right. She'd come good when he needed her to. She always had in the past.

But what about Lucy?

His brain was still reeling from what her sister, Ursula, had told him, and then all the stuff about her father and his will that Ryan had uncovered. It was like a jigsaw puzzle with too many pieces, or where the pieces were the wrong shape. It just didn't fit together.

In the end, though, it came down to one thing.

Was she really crazy?

Or was someone trying to make her crazy?

All the stuff about inheriting her father's money pointed to the second option. Let's say she's depressed after her father dies. If he left it all to her, they must have been close. Her sister persuades her to get treatment at the Mayview Clinic. Then Dr Redwood gets her hooks into her. Puts her on drugs, hypnotizes her, therapy, whatever you want to call it. The long and the short of it being she puts the idea in her head that she's got a husband and kids and they've just been killed in a car crash. Tells her she can't leave the clinic because she's a suicide risk. Tells her enough times, the idea starts to seem real. Until one day, they leave the door of her cage open and she flies home. Finds no trace of the family she thinks she's lost. It's the final straw. The trigger. She finds the nearest bridge and jumps off. All the money then goes to Ursula as next of kin. Minus Dr Redwood's cut. What would you charge for that kind of service? Half a mil? Plenty left over for Ursula, anyhow. Once she's managed to get the old man declared dead.

Except that wasn't the way it panned out. Yours truly just happened to be in the wrong place at the right time and screwed up all their plans.

But for that kind of money, you don't just give up. Try, try, try again. Redwood and her goons pick her up off the street and take her back to the clinic.

What then? Go through the whole procedure all over again? Or is there a Plan B? Something foolproof – the fool being him – this time. Stronger medicine.

In which case he needed to get her out of there, get the drugs and whatever else they put into her out of her system, before it was too late.

He went and put the empty tin in the sink.

Or . . .

Everything Ursula told him was true.

And everything Lucy had told Alex was a fantasy.

Heads or tails?

Was he willing to take a gamble?

And what if it was tails? What if Lucy was mad? Did that mean his feelings for her were different? Could he just wave goodbye and leave her to Ursula and Dr Redwood?

She thinks I'm coming to save her. What if I don't?

'I need some help here,' he said out loud, looking accusingly at the chair.

He turned back to the kitchen. Maybe he'd take his life in his hands and finally give the coffee machine a go.

He stopped.

There was a third sister, wasn't there?

Deborah. She'd died, aged . . . eleven, was it?

Maybe that was the missing piece of the jigsaw.

His phone was in his pocket. Ryan picked up after the first ring.

'What is it, mate?'

'You got your laptop handy? Not a bad moment, is it?'

'Yes,' Ryan said. 'And no. What do you need?'

'The third Fitzroy sister. Deborah. The one that died. Can you . . . ?'

'Do a bit of digging? Metaphorically speaking.'

'Now?'

'I'll call you back.'

Logan went back to his pacing. He was too wired to deal with the coffee machine now. He was likely to take a hammer to it if it started screwing with him. He couldn't go out for a run, but maybe he could use the gym, lift a few weights, crash out 10K on the bike. Somehow he knew he couldn't. He went and washed up the empty tin in the sink and tidied up the rest of the kitchen, then picked his dirty clothes up off the floor in the bedroom and put them in the laundry basket. He was so wired he was considering doing some ironing when his phone buzzed.

'Fell off a roof and broke her neck,' Ryan said without preamble.

'Where was that?' Logan asked.

'The family home. Big pile out in the sticks.'

'Was she alone?'

'At the inquest Ursula said she couldn't find her. In the end she found the door to the roof was open. Apparently it was out of bounds. All the stonework dated back to the sixteenth century and was crumbling away. She went up and had a look and there was one of Deborah's toys. A teddy bear, I think. She must have gone to the edge and slipped off.'

Logan breathed in slowly. In his head, he heard the sound of the little girl's body hitting the flagstones. And then a jigsaw piece clicking into place.

'You still there, mate?'

'Sorry, yes. That's very helpful. Thanks. Again.'

'No worries.' Ryan cut the connection.

Logan put the phone down and nodded to himself. Now he could see the whole picture. Ursula was the real psycho. Always had been. She'd pushed Deborah off the roof. Made it look like an accident. Lots of tears, no doubt. *I tried to save her* – all that. But Daddy knew the truth. Or suspected it. Maybe he'd always seen it in her. Which is why he'd cut her out of his will in the end and given everything to Lucy. What he hadn't realized was that by doing that he was putting Lucy's life in danger. Because Ursula was now trying to take care of *her*.

He breathed a sigh of relief. He could believe in Lucy again. He felt a sudden tightness in his chest.

I'm coming for you, Lucy.

And I'm coming for you too, Ursula, you fucking psycho bitch.

He thought back to the moment when he'd left the house and their hands had touched and it was like he was touching Lucy.

Jesus. He shook himself. He wanted to just get in the car and drive to the clinic, grab her and go, shoot his way out if he had to.

His phone buzzed again.

He picked it up.

Molloy.

26

Logan found a parking spot one street over from the hotel and made the approach on foot. If Molloy had someone watching, he didn't want them to see the car, just in case they decided to slash the tyres or immobilize it in some other way so he couldn't follow the target after he'd made the drop. When Molloy had first told him the location was going to be a hotel, Logan had envisaged a building with multiple entrances and exits, service lifts to a basement, maybe an underground garage, a real nightmare if you were trying to keep control of a target – especially one you couldn't even ID before you started tracking them. But the Palace Hotel, despite its fancy name, was surprisingly simple and straightforward. Three storeys high, with a faded stucco front, it was located two thirds of the way along a dingy Edwardian terrace harbouring a cluster of similar establishments. A rung or two up from actual flophouses or hot-sheet establishments, they looked the sort of cheap hotels you might rest up in for a night if you were a tourist just arrived at Paddington, finding the better-known places either full or too expensive, and you were too tired to look further afield. Logan doubted it had more than twenty rooms. Maybe fewer. No on-site parking. No basement. And just an alley running along the back where they kept the bins.

With Alex covering the front in another car, her bike handily parked in the next bay, and Ryan parked down a side street that intersected the alley, with Alan two streets further away in the van, it looked as if they had the location locked up tight, which was something. At least they had the target in their sights, which almost – but not quite – made up for the fact that they wouldn't know who the target was until they saw him – and even then, they couldn't be sure. Logan walked up the steps to the front door with a gnawing worry that they were about to grab someone off the street, throw them in the back of the van and discover that the bag they were hefting was full of dirty underwear. Because they only had one shot. Get it wrong first time, and the real target would slip through their fingers. Logan wondered if that explained the relatively simple layout. Was Molloy going to use a decoy to throw them off the scent before the real target waltzed out a few minutes later? Or was that over-thinking it? Maybe Molloy wasn't that cute. Either way, a lot was riding on Logan making the right call. He'd acted super-confident when they'd made the plan, knowing it was the only way to convince Mrs Allenby the thing was doable, but now it was coming down to the wire, his gut – the thing everything depended on – was churning uncomfortably.

He walked in and dropped his bag by the narrow reception desk. A hundred grand made a satisfying thump as it hit the floor. The thin man in a white shirt and glasses behind the desk looked up from his phone.

'Evening, sir.'

'I'd like a room. A single. Just for the night,' Logan said.

The receptionist nodded, turning to the rack of pigeon-holes behind him and selecting a key.

'Number twelve, on the second floor.'

'Perfect. How much?'

'Seventy-five – that's with the continental breakfast. In advance. Will that be cash or card?'

Fucking thieves, Logan thought. He was about to dump a hundred grand in crisp fifties on the bed and they were stiffing him on the room rate. *Continental breakfast, my arse.* He resisted the temptation to argue the point and reached into his jacket for his wallet, pulling out four twenties and putting them on the desk. The receptionist scooped them up, put them in a drawer, and handed Logan a fiver, along with his key.

'The lift's out of order, I'm afraid. But the stairs are dead ahead. Number twelve's right at the end of the corridor.'

'OK.' Logan nodded and picked up his bag.

Once he'd rounded the corner at the top of the stairs, he paused, scanning the corridor and listening out for footsteps. There was always a chance Molloy had a different plan entirely, and he was about to feel a cosh on the back of the head. After all, if a hundred grand was the price of a man's life, then in theory it was worth just taking the money and getting rid of him, instead of Mr Green. Cut out the middleman. Literally. Molloy could have made sure there were no other guests at the hotel tonight, and then they'd have all the time in the world to cut him up into manageable pieces and dispose of him, knowing it was unlikely that he'd put the appointment at the hotel in his diary.

He took in a slow breath. No creaking floorboards. No TV sounds. But he stayed alert as he walked down the corridor, waiting for the click of a door opening behind him. He stopped in front of room twelve and put the old-fashioned key into the lock.

Inside it was less dingy than he'd expected. The counterpane on the queen-sized bed was a dull purple, matching the thick velvet curtains that had been drawn over the single window. There was a narrow blond-wood desk, with a scattering of glossy tourist magazines and a single uncomfortable-looking armchair. He put his head round the door into the bathroom, pulling aside the shower curtain, then looked in the closet with its row of coat hangers and an ironing board with a frayed cover. He walked over to the curtains and pulled them back just enough to see the alley below. It was empty.

He went back to the door and stood listening for a minute. Nothing.

Everything seemed to be kosher. There was nothing else to do but leave the bag on the bed, walk back down to reception, deposit his key, and leave.

So what was holding him back?

Was it just the thought of leaving a hundred grand behind with no guarantee they'd ever see it again?

Or just the feeling that there was something he hadn't thought of. That Molloy had somehow outsmarted him.

No. That was just paranoia. They had all the bases covered. If anyone left the hotel with the money, they'd know. It was after that things might get a bit hairy.

Logan put the bag on the bed and unzipped it. Yep, the cash was still there. He zipped it up again and went to the door, then went back and crouched down to look under the bed.

OK, enough.

He put his ear to the door briefly then opened it. The corridor was empty. He locked the door behind him and walked briskly to the stairs, then down to reception. The receptionist looked up.

'Off out, sir?' he said.

Was that the hint of a smirk? Logan couldn't tell.

'Yeah.' Logan held out the key and the receptionist took it, returning it to its pigeonhole.

'The front door's locked at twelve,' he said.

Logan nodded. 'Right.'

He walked out.

At the bottom of the steps, he paused for a moment, as if he was taking in a lungful of night air, then carried on down the street. Alex knew that was the sign for job done, no surprises. He made himself walk at a leisurely pace and turned right at the end of the street. Fifty yards further on was his car. Once inside, he activated the discreet communications device that Alan had provided.

'Alex, I'm back at the car. Anything?'

'No one came out of the hotel. No other bodies on the street. Doesn't look like they have eyes on you.'

He should have been relieved, but somehow Logan would have felt happier if they'd put someone on him, to check he'd left the vicinity before someone else exited with the money. Maybe Molloy was over-confident. Maybe he'd done this plenty of times and nothing had ever gone wrong. Or maybe he was just short-handed.

'Cool. Ryan – anything going on at the back?'

'Not as far as I can see. Unless you count foxes nosing around the bins.'

'Alan? All good at your end?'

Alan had nothing to do but wait with the van. A circus could go past, complete with performing unicorns, and all he had to do was sit tight. But even so, Logan couldn't help worrying.

'Yes, fine. No problems.'

'OK, now we wait.'

Logan sat back. He was guessing twenty minutes. Time to be sure the coast was clear, but keeping the time they were babysitting a hundred grand to a minimum.

After that, the big worry was that they'd use a cut-out: someone other than the hit-man would exit with the money and hand it over at another location. If it was a woman, they still might have a chance. Despite Alex's *Nikita* fantasies, Logan was sure the hit-man was going to be just that, a man. In which case they could follow the woman to the drop-off and then make their move. But if they had to keep their distance all the way and make sure they didn't spook her, that would increase their chances of losing control. More moving parts. More things that could go wrong.

He had to hope he'd judged Molloy right and he'd keep things simple: Logan delivers; the target picks up. Job done.

Fifteen minutes.

'Alex. Anything?'

'Fuck's sake, Logan.'

'Sorry.'

He sat back, annoyed with himself for being so twitchy. *Too much bloody going on*, he thought. He closed his eyes and tried not to think about what might or might not happen. They had a plan: now just let things play out. He tried to make his mind a blank.

He saw Lucy, in the grounds of the clinic, talking to the Mad Professor, putting her hand on his arm. Then he was standing in front of Ursula's house. She put her hand out, and—

He jerked awake.

Ten minutes.

A light rain had started to fall. He sat up.

'How are those foxes doing, Ryan?'

'They've just walked past with a black holdall in their snouts. Maybe they don't know you can't eat money. Should I follow?'

'Very funny.'

Logan watched the rain coming down harder. Was that

going to make things easier or trickier? Easier at first, probably: fewer people on the street. Then harder when they
were on the road, with restricted visibility. *Whatever.* They
had to have a target to follow first. Then they could worry
about losing them.

He stopped himself from pinging Alex to make sure the
comms were still working.

He put the wipers on but he still couldn't see much. Even
if someone walked from the hotel to the junction, he'd
probably miss them, unless they were wearing something
very light, or reflective, and what were the chances of that?

Suddenly there was a voice in his ear.

'Got a possible. Stand by.'

He sat up straighter. 'Description?'

'Male. Six-foot. Dark raincoat, dark trousers, some kind
of waterproof hat. Clean-shaven, but face mostly obscured.'

'Carrying?'

'Backpack.'

'Colour?'

'Black. He's heading your way.'

'OK, get on the bike. I'll pick him up and follow on foot.
Then if he gets in a vehicle, be ready to go.'

'Roger that.'

Logan zipped up his jacket and got out of the car, pulling
on a baseball cap to keep the rain out of his eyes.

At the end of the street he looked left and right, as if he
was going to cross. There were no cars approaching in either
direction, but he remained on the pavement for as long as

he could without seeming conspicuous. Then he saw him between two parked cars on the other side, walking purposefully, shoulders hunched, hat pulled down low.

'I have control.'

The man in the raincoat turned left. Logan crossed. The man kept going, head down, like he was on autopilot. He certainly wasn't checking if he had a tail. It was a busy road, all double yellows. If he was heading for a vehicle, Logan guessed it would be next left. On the corner was an off-licence. The man turned. Logan had guessed right. *No.* He was going into the off-licence.

What?

'Target has entered off-licence.'

Maybe he was checking for a tail. With no parked vehicles there was no cover. Either Logan had to follow into the off-licence or keep going, with the risk of losing him. Fuck it. He pushed the door and entered the off-licence. The man was standing by the counter with his back to him. Logan headed down an aisle as if he was in search of a bottle of wine. He risked a look. The man seemed to be chatting to the Asian guy on the checkout, who was pulling bottles up from somewhere and putting them on the counter. It looked like vodka or gin. Half a dozen bottles. The man put his rucksack on the counter and unzipped it. Then the checkout guy pinged the barcode on one of the bottles, did something at the till, and the man in the raincoat started filling the rucksack.

Shit. It was empty. Definitely no room for a hundred grand

and half a dozen bottles of Smirnoff. This wasn't their man. Logan turned to go and got a glimpse of a quarter-profile as the man swivelled to look at the mixers.

It was the skinny bloke on reception.

He'd just made a quick dash to the corner offie to restock the bar.

Logan exited onto the street and headed back towards the car, walking fast.

'It's not him. Alex, have you got eyes on the hotel?'

'Affirmative.'

'Anyone else exited?'

'No. Nothing happening.'

'Shit. Ryan?'

'All quiet this side.'

Had they somehow missed him? Or was he still inside? But if so, why would he wait that long?

Logan suddenly had a thought.

'Alex. Any movement from the other hotels adjacent?'

'You mean . . . hold on. Yeah, the one two doors along, the Topham. A minute ago, maybe. Fits the profile. And yes he had a bag.'

'Where is he now? Have you got eyes?'

'He's headed west, away from you. OK, he's stopped. He's getting in a vehicle. Black BMW.'

'OK, when he moves, stay with him. I'm almost at the car and I'll follow. Alan, pick Ryan up in the van and stay tuned.'

There was a moment's silence on the other end. 'Are you sure?' Ryan said.

'Oh yeah.'

'But he came out of a different hotel.'

'That's how they did it,' Logan said. Ryan heard the sound of a car door opening, then closing. 'I knew that slippery bastard would have something up his sleeve. The hotels must be connected through the cellars. Maybe all the coal got delivered through one chute back in the day, I don't know. But you can walk in one and walk out the other.'

'He's on the move,' Alex said. 'Heading west.'

Logan turned the ignition. 'OK, whatever you do, don't lose him.'

If Alex answered, it was lost in the roar of the bike.

27

'Talk to me, Alex.'

Alan had spent the last couple of days tinkering with the audio balance in Alex's helmet device, so it picked up her voice and screened out the noise of the bike and surrounding traffic, but it was never going to be perfect. Which was why Alan had also put a tracking device on the bike, linked to a screen on the dash of the van, so he and Ryan could keep tabs on Alex's location and communicate with Logan, leaving Alex to focus on staying with the target.

Logan could feel the adrenaline beginning to pump through his veins. The chase was on. But for now, he had to take it easy. Traffic was light, but he couldn't afford to put his foot down in the middle of Paddington. He'd have to stay under the limit and hope their target was taking it easy too, at least for now. Hopefully, with a hundred grand sitting on the back seat, he wouldn't want to get pulled over. The big question was whether he now thought he was home free, no need for precautions, or whether he was on the lookout for a tail, and was going to start being tricky, stop-starting, going back on himself, to see if he could spot it. If he did, it was vital that Logan caught up as quickly as possible, so Alex could drop off and he could take over for a while, to make sure the target didn't have the same vehicle in his rear-view for too long at a stretch.

'Still . . . west on . . .' The rest of Alex's message was lost in a spurt of acceleration.

Logan slowed as the lights ahead turned red.

'Ryan?'

'Got her. OK, she's turning right off Star Street, a block ahead of you . . . and right again.'

'He's doubling back.'

'Maybe. Or he could be heading for the flyover.'

Was that why they had picked the location? Quick access to the Westway and then out of London? Logan tried to work out if that was good or bad. One thing was for sure: they couldn't do a snatch on the motorway. On the other hand, if he was heading for the sticks, some nice little B-road in the dark might do the trick. Mrs Allenby was right: they were flying by the seat of their pants.

The lights turned green and Logan crossed the intersection, keeping his foot light on the gas.

'Take the next right and right again, and you might pick the target up ahead of Alex.'

'Worth a try,' Logan said.

He made the turn and then a white Prius pulled up in front of him to let out a fare, boxing him in.

'Shit.'

'OK, she's passed you, but make the turn anyway.'

'Where do you reckon he's headed?'

'He's got to take a left on Norfolk Place. If he takes a right on St Michael's Street, my bet is he's heading out of town. Let's just hope we can run him to ground before he reaches the M25.'

Maybe he's heading for Heathrow, Logan thought wryly, with sunglasses, flip-flops and a hundred grand in his carry-on.

Logan made the turn and gave it a little gas. Alex knew what she was doing, but he wasn't going to feel comfortable until he had eyes on the target.

'OK, Alex is on the Edgware Road,' Ryan said. 'My money's still on the A40 out of town.'

Three minutes later he was proved right. Logan took the slip road onto the flyover and settled into the flow of traffic heading west.

'How close am I?' he asked.

'About a hundred yards, maybe a bit more.'

'OK, I'm going to try and close in. Alex, do you have the reg?'

He didn't hear anything for almost a minute. Then: '. . . Oscar Oscar . . .' something.

He wasn't going to waste too much time worrying about it. He'd be willing to bet the whole hundred grand the plates would be fake. After all the hoops he'd gone through, the guy wasn't going to make it that easy for them.

He moved over into the outside lane and picked up speed.

'Alex is dropping back. I think she's letting you take over.'

'Roger that.'

He accelerated past a stream of cars in the middle lane, watching out for a black BMW. He spotted Alex and gave her a quick flash.

He switched his eyes back to the middle lane and there he was, three cars ahead. He checked his rear-view and pulled into a gap. There was now one vehicle between him and the target.

Perfect.

'Ryan, where's the van?'

'On the A40, about half a mile back.'

'OK. Keep your position. I'll let you know if you need to move.'

'What's the plan?'

'We stay on him. Even if he takes us onto the motorway, unless he's onto us, sooner or later he's going to have to pull off again. And then . . .'

He let the rest of the sentence hang in the air.

'Roger that.'

'Alex, I'll take it as far as Hangar Lane, then he's yours.'

He heard a burst of static. Then: 'Roger that.'

Got you, he thought.

Two minutes later, at the junction, the BMW stayed in the middle lane, indicating he was going to cross straight over as if he was aiming for the M40. Then it could be anywhere: onto the M25 or carry on towards Birmingham. The lights turned and Alex passed Logan, giving him an airy wave.

As he pulled away from the lights, Logan started to go through the next stage of the plan in his head. The big question was: would the target be carrying? Surely it was an unnecessary risk to have a weapon if you weren't planning on using it, but then again, if you were also carrying a hundred grand in cash, you wouldn't want to make yourself an easy target. It might seem counter-intuitive, but Logan reckoned if this guy was the pro they thought he was, he'd stayed lucky by never being caught in possession. Explaining away a hundred grand in the back of your motor was one thing: a silenced Ruger in the glovebox would be a whole different ball game.

They'd argued it back and forth, whether he and Alex should also be tooled up just in case, but in the end it was Mrs Allenby who'd settled it. If it turns into a shooting match, then the plan has already gone tits-up. Not that she used those exact words. But the key to success was speed: it all had to be done so quickly he didn't know what was happening. What they used to call a 'hard stop' back in A4.

Now it was all a question of where. The problem was, since they didn't know where the target was going, Logan would only know the right place for the stop when they got there, and he'd just have to hope all three vehicles were in position and everyone was alert enough to go straight to action mode.

He looked at the clock on the dash. He'd give it another couple of minutes before switching with Alex again.

'Ryan, what's your position now?'

'Two hundred yards.'

'OK, maintain that. Hope everybody's got a full tank. Our boy seems to be flying.'

Logan heard something unintelligible on the other end, as if Ryan and Alan were having a conversation. He waited.

'Ryan?'

There was a pause.

'Alan says there's a problem with the tracking . . .'

More unintelligible noise.

'Sorry, there *may* be a problem. The signal's a bit erratic. She's faded out a couple of times. Just for a second or two.'

'OK, let me know if it gets worse. I might have to take the lead and Alex can follow.'

Not ideal. Not ideal at all. If Alex went completely off the radar he might have to rethink the whole bloody thing.

He waited another minute.

'Alex, I'm going to take control.'

He heard her gunning her engine. 'You got it.'

He pulled out into the fast lane and put his foot down. Half a mile later he saw Alex peeling off and he had the BMW in his sights again.

Logan drummed his fingers on the steering wheel. They'd soon be on the M40, and then the junction with the M25. If there was a problem with tracking Alex's bike, they needed the target to get off the motorway in the next five minutes and into an environment where they could stop him without causing a fifteen-car pile-up, not to mention away from the traffic surveillance cameras.

'Come on, you fucker.'

Still the BMW sat there, cruising along at a steady 75mph, showing no signs of going anywhere except dead ahead. They passed the turn-off to Uxbridge and now they were on the motorway. The junction with the M25 was up ahead.

Logan was willing the BMW's indicators to start flashing. If anything, the car just picked up a bit of speed. Logan began to wonder if the target was onto them. What would he do? Take them onto the M25 and pull in at the first service station? Then what? Stick or twist? Ideally he'd want Alex to stay with the target while he and Ryan kept going; then see where they were when the target got on the move again. But what if Alex went off the radar? All the target would have to do was get off the motorway again and make a box turn, and she'd have nowhere to hide. If he was tooled up, he could take her out and be on his way and that would be the last they'd see of him.

Now Logan was gripping the steering wheel tightly, praying the target didn't hit the indicators.

The turn-off for the M25 was coming up. No signal yet.

Of course, he'd leave it to the last second.

Logan held his breath.

The junction flashed past.

They were through.

Now what?

The BMW slowed a fraction, waiting for a gap to open up in the inside lane, and slotted neatly into the line of slower traffic.

OK, *now* he's turning.

'Alex, he's going to exit at the next junction. I'm going to have to fall back. Can you take control?'

'Got it.'

A few seconds later he saw the bike passing cars on the inside lane, then indicating left, Alex tucking herself neatly behind the BMW.

OK, if he was ever going to make you, he's made you now, Logan thought.

'Ryan, take the next exit.'

'Roger that.'

'You still got Alex?'

'We got her.'

'OK, let's do this.'

Logan swung hard into the inside lane, almost clipping a grey SUV which flashed him angrily, before taking the exit.

'Fuck you too, mate.'

The exit curved round to a junction with a straight road that crossed over the motorway. He saw the BMW stop at the junction, indicating right, with Alex right on his tail.

'Alex? Can you ease off a little bit when he turns?'

He didn't get an answer.

Fair enough. He wouldn't want anyone back-seat driving at this stage in the game, either.

He slowed as he approached the junction, and a red Audi rocketed past him, almost losing its back end as it swept after Alex and the BMW without indicating or even slowing down.

Fuck was that?

Logan made the turn. Up ahead the Audi had already caught up with the other vehicles. Alex was now boxed in. Logan passed a church, then a pub. He started to wonder if the target had made Alex before they'd even left London and had then called in backup. A sign indicated the road forked up ahead.

OK, maybe now we'll see.

Heads or tails?

He waited, keeping a hundred yards between himself and the Audi. No point giving the whole game away.

Three sets of tail-lights went right.

Bollocks.

The target could be close to home now. They couldn't afford to wait much longer or he'd be pulling up into his drive. It would definitely be better not to try and grab him with his missus watching from the kitchen window. There were woods on his left and fields on his right. It was starting to look doable.

But they couldn't do anything with the Audi in the mix. They needed it to either turn off or overtake. Maybe he didn't have room to get past the BMW *and* Alex's bike. He just needed the BMW to make it easy for him, but he had a feeling the target wasn't the type to take his foot off the accelerator if some annoying twat started nudging his bumper. More likely he'd put his foot down. Or would he play it safe, given that he was surely minutes away from being able to stow the cash under his mattress?

Bollocks, bollocks, bollocks.

A turn in the road took the vehicles ahead out of sight for a few seconds.

'Ryan, where are you?'

'Just got off the motorway, turning right at the junction.'

'OK, the environment's looking good but we've got a complication. A red Audi's sticking to Alex. We need to get rid before we can move.'

'Tag-team?'

'Dunno.'

'How many in the vehicle?'

'Just the driver. I *think*.'

'What do you want to do?'

'I'll give it another minute, see if he overtakes or peels off. If he doesn't, I'll have to tell Alex to take evasive action. Right now she's the meat in the sandwich.'

'Roger that. Don't take any chances.'

Logan didn't know what to say to that.

He made the turn. The road ahead was clear.

What the fuck?

He saw the turn-off on the right just in time. Is this where they'd gone?

Heads or tails?

He almost lost the back end as he steered into it, braking hard, then put his foot down, fighting the wheel to straighten himself out.

He was relieved to see brake-lights dead ahead.

Was it the Audi?

He put some speed on, trying to close the distance.

Yep, definitely the Audi.

Shit.

He lost them for a moment over a shallow rise. Wheels barely keeping contact with the tarmac, he flew over it, the suspension groaning as the road flattened out again.

He could see the Audi a hundred yards ahead and put on another burst of speed.

The distance between them suddenly receded.

It had stopped at the side of the road. The driver's door and front passenger door were open. In his headlights Logan could see Alex's bike in the ditch. There was a barbed-wire fence, and Alex was crumpled against it, her helmet tilted to one side. Two men were crouched down beside her. Logan saw the glint of a syringe as one of the men took hold of Alex's arm.

Logan screeched to a stop ten yards from the Audi and leaped out of the car. The two men looked up, blinded by his headlights. One of them pulled the other to his feet and shoved him towards the Audi.

Logan crouched down beside Alex. 'Alex, can you hear me!' he shouted. He put his hand on her neck, feeling for a pulse. He heard a gasp, so she was breathing. Then she seemed to shake herself awake.

'They . . . ran me off the road.'

'OK, don't talk. Just take it easy.'

He heard the Audi's doors slam shut and the driver gunning the engine.

'Fuck that, Logan!' she said, grabbing his arm. 'Don't let them get away!'

The Audi was struggling to right itself as its wheels spun in the dirt.

Logan hesitated for a split second, then sprinted back to the car and jumped in behind the wheel.

The Audi's engine was screaming as the driver frantically tried to get some purchase, then its front wheels grabbed onto the tarmac and it roared away into the dark.

By the time Logan was moving, it was fifty yards ahead.

Logan slammed through the gears, his foot furiously pumping the accelerator.

'Ryan . . . Alex is down. She needs help. I'm after the Audi.'

He didn't wait for an answer.

He had the Audi's tail-lights in his sights. A blur of trees went by in the beam of his headlights. Up ahead he could see streetlights.

The Audi slowed, and Logan could hear the screech of tyres as it made a left. Seconds later he followed. There were houses, shops, a pub, then the village petered out and the streetlights ended. Up ahead the Audi fishtailed noisily as it turned right, with Logan seconds behind.

The road ahead stretched out into the darkness as the Audi pulled away.

He wondered if the Audi driver knew where he was going. If he'd just been tailing Alex, maybe he knew where the fuck he was as much as Logan did. *He's got me beat on the straight*,

Logan thought. *But let's see how good you are when things get twisty.*

The Audi's lights started to recede.

Logan hoped to God things got twisty soon.

The Audi disappeared round a bend. A sign warning of dangerous curves flashed by as Logan followed, gripping the wheel hard, barely keeping his wheels on the road. If anything came the other way he'd be fucked.

He thought he saw the eyes of a startled deer pinpricked in his headlight beams as they swept past.

The curve unspooled and he locked onto the Audi again. He saw the chevrons indicating the next curve up ahead. He dropped a gear but increased the revs, the engine whining furiously, hoping to spook the Audi into taking the turn too fast.

The Audi shot round, Logan right on his tail.

The tarmac rose as they went over an old stone bridge.

The Audi kept accelerating and Logan saw its wheels losing traction as it tried to stay on the tarmac. The back end hit the bridge. The driver tried to wrestle the car back into the middle of the road but overcompensated and crunched into the other side of the bridge, then the car seemed to be flung sideways out of the turn and off the road. Logan heard the impact as it slammed into a tree and he had to wrench the wheel hard to the left to avoid going the same way. He felt his wheels leave the road and time seemed to stop as the car floated in mid-air. He let go of the wheel, bracing himself for impact.

Nothing happened.

The car had stopped.

He was facing back the way he'd come, on the wrong side of the road.

He could see the remains of the Audi in his headlights.

He stumbled out of the car, suddenly weightless, and fell to his knees on the tarmac.

He closed his eyes, and breathed in. He waited for the weightless feeling to pass, then stood up.

The Audi had hit the tree at a forty-five-degree angle. The front on the driver's side was crumpled like a concertina and Logan could see the driver had gone through the windscreen and straight into the tree. He looked as if he'd broken his neck. The passenger was slumped forward on the dash and there was blood coming from a wound on the side of his head. Logan walked round and pulled open the passenger door. He put his fingers on the guy's neck. Nothing.

On the back seat, Logan could see a black bag. He thought for a moment, then pulled a pair of latex gloves from his back pocket and slipped them on. He tried to open the rear passenger door but it wouldn't budge, so he reached in through the shattered driver's side window. He grabbed hold of the bag and pulled it out. Inside were rolls of duct tape, bandages, zip ties, two syringes and some ampoules of yellow liquid. He put the bag back in the car and went round to the front. He lifted the driver's head and tilted it towards him. One side of his face was gone, stoved in by the impact. Logan took a good look at the rest, then let it go. The driver seemed to be looking at him with his one remaining eye.

Logan felt his mind coming back to itself. Time was speeding up again, and he knew he didn't have much. He reached under the driver's torso, and felt around, his fingers lighting on what felt like a wallet. He pulled it out and shoved it into his back pocket without looking at it, then walked back to his car, ripping off the gloves as he went. He got in and started the engine, hoping he hadn't fucked up anything too badly. He pulled out slowly, the sensation of movement briefly making him feel dizzy. He blinked it away and started back the way he'd come.

Soon he saw the van up ahead. He parked on the same side of the road and got out. Ryan and Alan were hoisting Alex's bike out of the ditch.

'Where's Alex?' Logan said.

Ryan looked up. 'She's in the van. She's OK. Just a few bumps and bruises. And a bit shook up.'

Logan nodded. 'Let me give you a hand with that.'

They wheeled the bike round to the back of the van. Alan opened the doors and together they lifted it up and inside. Alan got in and Ryan slammed the doors.

'We'd better get the fuck out of here,' Logan said.

'What about the Audi?' Ryan said.

'Had an accident. Lost control and went into a tree.'

'The driver?'

'Dead. There were two of them. I'm pretty sure the other one's dead too. Hold on a minute. Have you got your phone?'

Ryan handed it over.

Logan went back to the ditch and turned on the phone torch, sweeping methodically from side to side. Then he bent down and picked something up. He went back to Ryan and gave him back his phone.

'Looks like he dropped this,' he said, holding up a syringe, still half full of yellow liquid.

'Fuck,' Ryan said. 'Be careful with that, yeah? I've got a cooler in the van you can put it in.'

Logan nodded.

They got into the van and Ryan started the engine. They could hear a siren in the distance.

'Let's go,' Logan said.

28

The next morning, the mood around the conference table at Clearwater Security was sombre.

'Well, you're OK, that's the main thing,' Mrs Allenby said.

Alex was wrapped in a thick fleece, her hair in a loose ponytail. She was nursing a cup of coffee.

'I'm fine. Bit of a stiff neck, that's all.'

'You need someone to look you over,' Logan said.

'I told you,' Alex said. 'I'm fine. My pride's the only thing that's hurting right now.'

Mrs Allenby gave her a quizzical look.

'Letting them run me off the road like that. I wasn't paying attention.'

'You were focused on the target,' Logan said.

Alex shrugged.

'As soon as I saw the Audi was after you, I should have warned you,' Logan added.

The cooler from the van was in the middle of the table. Mrs Allenby nodded at it. 'Can we see that?'

Logan opened it up and held out the syringe, holding it gingerly between index finger and thumb.

'We need to get that analysed,' Mrs Allenby said.

'I've got a tame lab technician can do it, no questions asked,' Ryan said. 'Unless it turns out to be anthrax, of course.'

'Not worth the bother,' Logan said. 'They didn't intend to kill her. Otherwise, why bring the restraints and the other bits and pieces? It'll just be something to knock her out. Doesn't really matter what.'

'Agreed,' said Mrs Allenby. 'It's the "why" that interests me. And the "who".'

Logan put the wallet down on the table. 'I've got some news on that score. I didn't check the passenger for ID. Sorry, my head was a bit scrambled and I was pressed for time. But I found this on the driver.'

'And?' said Mrs Allenby.

Logan fished a plastic card out of the wallet. It was attached to a lanyard.

'Dr Ismael Khan.'

Mrs Allenby raised her eyebrows. 'A doctor?'

'Good to know I was in the hands of a professional, I suppose,' Alex said.

Logan nodded to Ryan. 'I asked Ryan to do a bit of digging.'

'He's got a background in biochemistry and clinical psychology, specializes in addiction,' Ryan said. 'He runs a clinic in Harley Street. Or he did, I should say. He's attached to various hospitals in the south-east, but one name struck a chord. The Royal Buckingham.'

'Why does that ring a bell?' Mrs Allenby asked.

'It's where they took me after the thing with the Foreign Secretary,' Logan said.

'By "the thing", you mean when they attempted to live-stream his decapitation?'

Logan nodded. 'I recognized him. He was the doctor who treated me.'

Mrs Allenby put her hand down on the table. 'I don't understand. Why should the doctor who treated you in hospital try to abduct Miss Short?'

Logan shrugged. 'Beats me. But I've seen him another time as well. Recently.' He jerked his head. 'Just around the corner. And I had the feeling that when he saw me, he was properly spooked.'

'But why should he be? Presumably he'd tracked you here somehow.'

'I don't think so. It was Alex. Or more specifically, Alex's bike. Alan can explain.'

Alan held up two small metallic objects the shape of a matchbox, one black, the other metallic. 'When we were following the target last night, I was tracking Alex's location with this.' He held out the black object. 'But I started to get interference in the signal. It was only when we examined her bike after she came off the road, that I discovered why.' He held out the silver object. 'A second tracking device. This is the one Dr Khan must have been using. It's how the Audi was able to follow her.'

'So what about the "why"?'

'Well, it must have started at the hospital. Khan clocks Alex visiting me. He takes down the registration of her bike and gets a name and an address. Then he follows her here.'

'And decides to abduct her.'

'Yes.'

'That still doesn't tell us why.' Mrs Allenby looked thoughtful for a moment. 'What concerns me is whether Blindeye's security has been breached. We need to do some more work on Dr Khan's background.'

Ryan nodded.

'Fair enough,' Logan said. 'But my guess is this whole thing didn't go any further than him and his pal – and they're in paradise now. Plus, there was obviously a lot he *didn't* know.'

'What do you mean?' Mrs Allenby asked.

'I think he tried to abduct Alex so he could interrogate her. The other phials I saw in his bag – I'll bet they were psycho-actives of some sort. Truth drugs, if you like. He didn't know who she was or what she was involved in. He wanted to find out.'

'I hope you're right,' Mrs Allenby said, sounding unconvinced. 'Anyway, we're agreed that Dr Khan wasn't connected to our target. Which means the target wasn't aware that we were pursuing him. I suppose that's good news,' she added, 'although now that he's slipped through our fingers, it doesn't really matter, does it?'

'If it hadn't been for Dr Khan getting in the mix, we would have had him,' Alex said bitterly.

'I'm not blaming anyone,' said Mrs Allenby, although from her tone of voice it sounded as if she very much was. She didn't need to add that she'd never liked the plan in the first place. 'However, the fact is that we are back to square one. Terry Mason is dead, so that avenue is closed to us. And our hit-man is God knows where.'

No one said anything. In particular, no one mentioned the hundred grand.

'Mr Oldfield?' Mrs Allenby said. Ryan looked up. 'We'll need to keep tabs on Mr Green. I'd rather he didn't get his head blown off unnecessarily.'

'Yeah, of course.'

Silence settled round the table again.

'I don't think we need to worry about Mr Green,' Logan said after a time.

Everyone looked at him.

'What do you mean?' Mrs Allenby said.

'I didn't give Molloy his details.'

Mrs Allenby sat up straighter in her chair. 'Whyever not?'

'Well, just in case our kidnap scheme didn't pan out, for one thing.'

'Even though it was your plan?' she said, sounding sceptical.

'You must have given him someone's,' Alex said.

'Yeah, obviously.'

Mrs Allenby leaned forward. 'Come on, Mr Logan. Don't

play games. If you didn't give Molloy Mr Green's details, as agreed, then whose did you give him?'

He looked at the expectant faces around the table.

'I gave him mine,' he said.

29

Everyone seemed to be talking at once. Even Alan was shaking his head and muttering to himself. Eventually Mrs Allenby held up her hand for silence.

'Please! Can we all just calm down a minute.'

She stared at Logan. She didn't look calm. In fact there was a fire in her eyes Logan hadn't seen before. He steeled himself for the onslaught.

'Mr Logan, you're going to need to explain yourself.'

Logan leaned back in his chair and folded his arms. *Fuck you all*, he thought.

'It was a backup, that's all. In case we didn't manage to secure the target. We had a good plan. It almost worked. But we all know from experience that something you never saw coming can fuck everything up. Like Dr Khan popping up out of nowhere. So I made sure there was a Plan B, that's all.'

'Without consulting the rest of the team,' Mrs Allenby said. She quickly looked around the table. 'Assuming you didn't.'

Alex, Ryan and Alan all looked back at her blankly.

'I didn't tell anyone,' Logan said.

'And why was that?' Mrs Allenby said, acid in her voice.

Logan shrugged. 'They would have said I was crazy: the level of risk was unacceptable.'

'It *is*,' she hissed, slapping her hand on the table.

'Would you rather we were back at square one?' he said.

'I would rather we had a plan we all agreed on,' she shot back.

'We did,' Logan said. 'It went tits-up.'

Mrs Allenby took a deep breath, trying to control her anger. Logan could see her chest rising and falling. He hoped she wasn't about to have a heart attack.

'Look, maybe I should have told you what I was thinking, OK? But I was pretty sure you'd have said no.'

Mrs Allenby pursed her lips. 'Without question.'

'So I knew if I was going to do it, I'd just have to . . . do it.'

'And now you have.'

Logan thought he detected a note of acceptance in her tone.

'It does have its advantages. As a plan.'

He waited, seeing if she'd bite.

'Which are?' she said finally.

'He's playing on our turf now. So we control the environment. Which means we can predict what he's going to do more easily. And unlike our Mr Green, we'll be ready and waiting for him.'

'We set the terms of the problem, so we can predict the available solutions,' Ryan said, nodding.

Mrs Allenby gave Ryan a sharp look. 'You make it sound very easy.'

'Think of it like a mousetrap,' Logan said.

She frowned. 'And you're the piece of cheese.'

'A piece of cheese with a Glock 17,' he said with a grin.

Mrs Allenby looked thoughtful. 'What about photographs? If you provided Mr Molloy with a photograph of yourself, then he'd know it was a set-up.'

'I'm betting Molloy wouldn't have looked at the dossier before handing it over. Best not to know who the target is, so if the coppers come round asking what he knows about the bloke that's just been offed, he can put his hand on his heart and say, "Never heard of the fella".'

Mrs Allenby sighed. 'Well, I suppose it's a *fait accompli*. Whatever I may think of the way you engineered the situation, this is where we are. Our hit-man now has his money. We'll have to assume he hasn't been spooked by our attempts to apprehend him, not to mention Dr Khan's unfortunate intervention. The clock is ticking. We have to move forward.'

Logan tried hard to wipe the smile off his face, nodding soberly.

'What's the layout of your place, then?' Ryan asked.

'It's a penthouse apartment. Docklands. I'll give you the address, then maybe you can dig up the building plans? Obviously I've had a few thoughts, but I need everybody's input. We need to look at it through our hit-man's eyes, figure out how we'd do the job if we were him. Reduce his options, so he has no choice but to go where we want him. Funnelling – isn't that what it's called?'

'I'll leave you to it, then,' Mrs Allenby said, pushing her chair back. 'Let me know when you have a plan I can see.' She looked hard at Logan. 'And I do mean that.'

He nodded. 'Of course.'

Mrs Allenby sighed as she took her raincoat from the hatstand, put it under her arm and walked out.

'You're a devious bastard,' Alex said when she'd gone.

'Thank you,' Logan said. 'You're not so bad yourself.'

'Shall I make a brew, before we get down to it?' Alan said. For the first time in a while, he had a twinkle in his eye. Logan supposed he was looking forward to getting stuck into the building plans. Maybe some electronics to play around with.

'Let's have that address then,' Ryan said. 'Like the boss said, the clock is ticking.'

Twenty minutes later they were looking at print-outs of the architectural plans spread out over the conference table. Ryan and Alan were sitting next to each other. Logan and Alex were standing, looking over their shoulders.

'Of course, there's no guarantee these correspond exactly to the actual building,' Ryan said, 'but let's assume for the moment. Can you just walk us through the main features?'

Logan nodded. Alan shifted over and Logan picked up a pencil so he could point to what he was talking about.

'Nice gaff by the way,' Ryan said, a questioning look on his face.

Logan frowned. 'Long story. OK, first you've got the lobby. Three security guys on alternating shifts 24/7 with a CCTV monitor on the desk. Two lifts: one lift goes down to the garage and up to each floor. Each floor has two apartments.'

'So you could access either apartment from the lift?'

Logan nodded. 'Then there's the maintenance lift which goes down to the basement and up to the roof.'

'Any other access to the basement?'

'Only the emergency stairs, connecting all the floors. The main lift also goes to the penthouse, of course, but exits in an external corridor, like the other floors.'

'Maybe it was originally planned to be two apartments,' Ryan said.

'Or it could be a security thing,' Logan suggested. 'Like an air-lock.'

'Presumably the lift doesn't go anywhere unless you've got a key card or something,' Alan said.

'Yep. Reprogrammed every week.'

'What about the door to the penthouse?' Ryan asked.

'Same key card plus thumbprint ID.'

'And that's the only way in?'

Logan nodded. 'It's all air-conditioned. The windows don't open. Not that getting in that way would be very practical, unless he's planning on being winched down from a chopper.'

'I was hoping we could rule that out,' said Alan.

'Let's forget tunnelling into the basement, as well,' Logan said.

Alan followed a line of the diagram. 'It would be good

to know where the electronics hub is. There must be a central control point connecting everything. Basement, I expect.'

Ryan opened up a legal pad and began to write. 'OK, let's start with the basics. What are the potential execution locations? Then let's look at each one in detail, and see how they'd work.'

'The first one is obviously outside the building,' Alex said. 'If it was me, I'd shove you in the river when you went for a run. Easy-peasy.'

Logan smiled. 'I thought of that. I put in the brief that I never leave the penthouse on foot, always take one of the motors.'

'That's the next location, then,' Ryan said. 'Basement garage. You come out of the lift and *bang*.'

'Or, talking of "bang", a bomb under the car,' Alan said. 'He's got previous on that score, hasn't he?'

'Could even be he's got a bit of jelly left he needs to use up before it goes off,' Alex suggested.

'All right, next?' Logan said.

'In the lift,' Ryan said. 'You're on your way down, it stops at another floor, he gets in. When it gets to the bottom, only he gets out.'

Alan chewed a pencil. 'Are there cameras in the lifts?'

'I think the residents voted to have them turned off,' Logan said. 'Didn't want to get caught picking their noses or something.'

'OK, that's a weak point.'

'Next one's the entrance to the apartment. He rings the buzzer, you open up, and . . .'

'You're not going to open the door to someone you don't know though, are you?' Alex said.

'Delivery guy,' Ryan said.

Logan shook his head. 'The guy on reception would call first, ask me if I'm expecting something.'

'Birthday surprise?' Alex offered.

'Maybe.'

'OK, last but not least: in the apartment,' Ryan said. 'For whatever reason you let him in, and then he can take his time, and most importantly, not worry about being seen.'

Logan noticed Alex was frowning.

'Alex?'

'It's just . . . I know you get upset when I mention this, but you all keep saying "he" all the time, and I think you might be missing something.'

'Are we back to this female assassin thing?' Logan said.

'I didn't say that. It's just that if you're a bit paranoid about security, you're less likely to open the door to a man, even if he is dressed up as a UPS guy. Whereas a woman, especially if she's cute, and let's say she's delivering flowers, the security guy is much more likely to send her up without checking first, and you're more likely to open the door to her.'

'So we are talking a female hit-person, or whatever you want to call it?'

'Not necessarily. I mean, why are we assuming there's only going to be one of them? Why not a team?'

'And one of them's a woman?'

Alex shrugged. 'Why not?'

'Worth thinking about,' Ryan said. 'OK, let's go back to our four options: basement car park, lift, outside the apartment, inside the apartment. Number one, first question: access to the basement?'

'Forget from inside the building,' Logan said. 'Unless we reckon our female accomplice is going to give the security guard a private lap dance while the guy swipes a spare key card.'

He looked at Alex and she rolled her eyes.

'It's got to be through the exit. The security gate goes up as a resident drives out, our guy slips in.'

'Then what?' Ryan said. 'Where does he hide himself? He could have a long wait. And he's got to be able to keep the lift under constant observation, so he doesn't miss you coming out. And then what? How does he exit?'

'Easy. He takes the keys and my security pass and drives out in my car. Or one of them.'

'And easy enough to get into another car that gives him the sight line he wants when he enters, then just sit tight,' Alan said. 'The only problem he's got is the cameras. I'm assuming there's cameras in the basement with all them fancy motors around. He's got to find a workaround for them.'

'Why don't you have a think about that?' Logan said.

'Right you are,' Alan said, turning over one of the printouts. 'He'll need to get into the main system somewhere.'

'OK, the advantage of the garage is he doesn't need to

come through the lobby. He doesn't need to deal with the guy on the desk. Every other scenario involves somehow getting past that choke point.'

'Which means it's got to be a delivery guy,' Logan said. He glanced at Alex. 'Or girl.'

'And it has to be something where the guy on the desk isn't just going to say, "Leave it with me and I'll make sure Mr So-and-so gets it."'

'So we're back to birthday surprises,' Logan said.

'You know one thing I like about that?' Alex said. 'Flip it round and look at it from our point of view. Where do we want *him*? Outside the door to the penthouse is perfect. He's boxed in. And we can come at him from two directions: from the apartment and from the lift.'

'So long as we remember to disable the camera on that floor,' Alan said.

'I still like the garage,' Ryan said. 'He doesn't leave a trail coming in, assuming he's circumvented the cameras somehow, so nobody misses him when we take him out in one of the vehicles. Nice and clean.'

'Assuming no surprise guests pop up. Remember, it's a lot harder for us to control that space,' Logan said.

Ryan grunted. 'Sure, we need to keep the variables to a minimum.'

'That's always been my motto,' Alex said. 'Along with "kill like a girl", of course.'

'Right. Let's keep moving,' Logan said. 'We've got two probable scenarios, agreed?'

'Sounds about right,' Ryan said.

'So let's drill down into the detail. Play them both out in real time. See if there are any possible glitches we haven't thought of, levels of risk he might not fancy. I'm sure he doesn't like variables either. See what we're left with. Whatever it is, that's what we plan for.'

Alan was wiping his glasses. He didn't exactly look happy. He nodded at the plans. 'If this is all we've got, it might take a while. I don't even know if we—'

Logan cut him off. 'Then work fast. He's got a head start on us. I reckon we need to be in place with all our ducks in a row tonight.'

30

Two men sat at table outside a Turkish restaurant with two tiny cups of bitter, black coffee in front of them. One was heavy-set, his belly straining under his grey flannel shirt, with a thick neck and short, iron-grey hair. He wore a cheap-looking leather jacket, and in the dim streetlight, his close-set eyes looked almost black. The other man, wearing an open-necked blue shirt and a close-fitting sports jacket, was slimmer and neater in appearance. He was clean-shaven, had thick, raven-black hair and grey eyes. Alongside the coffees, three phones lay on the table.

'It bothers me,' the man with grey eyes said.

The other man shrugged. He took a sip of his coffee and wiped his mouth with the back of his hand.

'Why? It is better for us that Mason is dead.'

The man with grey eyes sucked his teeth. 'I am not so sure.'

The big man shook his head dismissively. 'He had to die. Sooner or later.'

'Sooner or later,' the man with grey eyes repeated. 'But this was very soon. A few months from now, a year even, no one would have cared. That is how I would have done it, if it had been up to me. No one would have connected it with us. But now . . . we are in the spotlight. Who else could it be but us? It will put pressure on Tenniel to act, to show he's doing something. I am waiting for him to tell me he needs to arrest some people.'

The heavy-set man drained the rest of his coffee in one gulp and smacked his lips. His phone beeped and he snatched it up, scowled at the message and put it down again.

'Well, Tenniel said Mason must die and we had no choice but to do it. Now it is done. Maybe the police will be busy for a little while. Maybe they will cause some trouble. But with Mason gone, things will also be easier out here, on the streets. If any of his people thought he could still be a powerful man and make things hard for us . . .' He chuckled. 'Now they know he cannot.'

The man with grey eyes tapped his forehead, frowning. 'Think, *think*! Was Tenniel so keen to have Mason dead to make life good for us? Always he is thinking of us?'

The other man laced his fingers together, making a tight fist. 'We are bound together now. What is good for us is good for him.'

The man with grey eyes shook his head. 'No. This was good for him only.'

'So?'

'I want to know why. Why did he need him dead? Why did he risk what we have by asking us to do it? He is not a rash man, I think. The rewards for him must have outweighed the risks.'

The heavy-set man scratched his armpit, then leaned over and spat onto the pavement.

'Or perhaps it was Mason remaining alive that was the risk,' the man with grey eyes continued. 'Perhaps that outweighed everything for him.'

A young man wearing a crisp white shirt and black trousers came out of the restaurant with a tray. The man with grey eyes nodded, and the young man cleared away the cups.

'More coffee, Mr Durgan?'

The heavy-set man waved him away.

'All right, I am not stupid,' he said when the young man was gone. 'I see where your thinking is going with this.'

'And where is that?'

'Mason knew something. Something that could be a big problem for Tenniel. Something that could maybe destroy him. He had to move fast before Mason found a way of using that information – before he could find someone to trade with. Perhaps the woman who was going to meet with him was connected with that someone. A messenger.'

The man with grey eyes nodded. 'Yes. That is exactly what I think.'

'OK. Fine. So, now the man is dead and Tenniel is safe. Why do we concern ourselves with this?'

'I want to know what he knew. I would like to have such a bargaining chip. When the bear is on the loose, the wolf and the fox must fight him together. But there comes a time when the wolf and the fox will no longer be friends.'

'When the bear is dead.'

One of the phones beeped. The man with grey eyes picked it up, scanned the message and tapped out a reply. He put the phone down and looked at the heavy-set man. The heavy-set man shook his head. 'What . . . ?'

The grey eyes narrowed.

'Ah,' the heavy-set man said, beginning to understand. 'You want me to find out this thing. You want to have this bargaining chip in your pocket in case Tenniel breaks his bargain.'

'He may find he can no longer protect us, without exposing himself. He cannot be the only smart one among these policemen. He must prove he is serious. He will say it is just a few arrests, no one important. We will pretend to plan something, and he will come down hard in front of the cameras. He will say after this that things will go back to normal. But he will be lying.'

'But if he tries to sacrifice us, he knows we will bring him down too.'

The man with grey eyes shrugged. 'Perhaps he believes he has been clever enough, he has brushed away his footprints.'

The heavy-set man ran his fingers over his stubble. 'Where to begin?'

The man with grey eyes smiled.

'Ah, you have thought of that. Of course.' He held a hand up. 'No, don't tell me.' He frowned with concentration. 'Tenniel and Mason: follow the threads back to the beginning and see where they join. Where were their destinies first linked together?'

The man with grey eyes smiled for the first time. 'Yes. Back to the beginning. I am certain the secret Mason knew will be there.'

31

'Another tea?'

Alex shook her head. 'Any more and I'll be in the loo when the guy finally makes an appearance.'

Logan shrugged. 'Best place, maybe. We could have turned it into a safe room.'

'It's big enough,' Alex said.

'Don't tell me: you could fit your whole flat into the master bathroom,' Logan said.

'Have I mentioned that?'

'Once or twice.'

Logan was taking items out of a large cardboard box on the kitchen island: rolls of duct tape, pliers, a hood made out of some kind of black material.

'You really planning on using that?'

'Nah. It's just for show. So he gets the idea, you know.'

'What about that?' She pointed to a long roll of clear plastic sheeting propped up against the fridge.

'Best bit,' Logan said. 'We unroll a bit of this on the bathroom floor and he'll start pissing himself as soon as he figures out what it's for.'

'Good thing you'll have the plastic sheeting down, then, I suppose.'

Logan started hacking at the tape holding the roll of sheeting together with an evil-looking knife. It was matt black with a wide blade and a ring on the handle like an oversized bottle opener.

'And what the fuck is that?' Alex said.

Logan grinned. 'This? It's a Raven. Very handy blade, I can tell you.'

He held it out. Alex recoiled in mock horror.

'But also fucking scary. I think I might be about to piss myself, and I'm on your side.'

Logan grinned. 'Exactly.' He went back to cutting the plastic sheeting loose.

'Do you want a hand with that?'

'You take the stuff in the box and I'll take the sheeting.'

They hefted everything into the main bathroom and Alex helped Logan unroll the sheeting on the floor.

'What about this stuff?' Alex said, indicating the box.

'I don't know, arrange it artistically, maybe? For maximum psychological effect?'

Alex started taking things out of the box and putting them on the floor. She stood back. 'I'm sure I saw something like this at Tate Modern one time. What it was worth was scary, if nothing else.'

They went back to the main living space.

Logan picked his automatic up from the coffee table and

ejected the magazine, then slammed it back with the heel of his palm.

'How many times you going to do that?' Alex said, settling back on the sofa.

Logan gave her a scowl.

'And please don't start sharpening that knife.'

'No need, it's got a—'

'I don't care what it's fucking got. Just fucking stop doing stuff before you drive me nuts. You're like an old woman. I'm telling you, at this rate some bloke in a balaclava turning up and shooting me in the back of the head's going to come as a blessed relief.'

Logan sat down in an armchair. 'Sorry.'

'What's the latest betting, then?' Alex said, after a moment.

'Garage. Definitely. That's how I'd do it. Shove the victim in the boot of his own car and drive away. Gotta love that. Anyone can rock up and put a bullet in someone. It's what you do next that makes all the difference.'

Alex nodded. 'Hmmm.'

'What do you reckon?'

'I'm still going with delivery. That's the ideal killing space, out there.' She jerked a thumb towards the apartment door and the corridor beyond. 'You don't have to worry about being interrupted.'

'A fiver?' Logan said, reaching out his hand.

Alex leaned forward and gave him a brief fist bump. 'Done.'

'You want to go through it one more time?' Logan said.

'Why not. OK, so Ryan's parked up with eyes on the garage exit. If he sees a walk-in when a car comes out, he texts you. We give it twenty minutes for the target to get comfy and in position. I go down in the lift and get in one of the cars. A couple of minutes later you come down, with the shades and the baseball cap. He steps out from wherever he's been waiting, but can't positively ID you so he says, "Mr Barrington?" Next thing he knows, I'm standing behind him with a silenced Luger pressed against his skull, and you introduce yourself.'

'OK. We're trusting he really is a pro and doesn't have an itchy trigger finger, but even if he does, I'll have the Kevlar on by this point, so things should be all right.'

'Assuming he goes for centre mass,' Alex said.

'Centre mass to take me down, then the headshot. Gotta be.'

'Fine. Then we haul him back up here and introduce him to the bathroom of horrors, or, if we have unexpected company, we put him in the motor and take him out that way.'

Logan nodded. 'Right. And if he goes for the delivery option, there are two scenarios: if I get a call from security to OK the delivery, I say fine, send them up, then go out and wait at the top of the emergency stairs. He, she or they press the buzzer, you open the door but stay behind it so they can't see you, they hesitate, I pop up from the stairs and you come out from behind the door. Bingo.'

'Who was wearing the vest in that scenario?' Alex said. 'I can't remember what we decided.'

'We were going to flip a coin.'

'Oh, right. And if there's no prior call from security, the buzzer goes, I open the door but stay out of sight, you call out for them to come into the apartment, then I approach from behind and you take them from the front.'

'I think that covers it.'

'Unless they decide to do something completely different we haven't thought of.'

Logan made a face. 'Like what?'

'I don't know. That's the point. We haven't thought of it.'

Logan shrugged. 'If the lights all go out and we see gas coming in under the door, then blokes start coming through the ceiling with submachine guns, then fair play to him.'

'We could always lock ourselves in the bathroom,' Alex said.

Instead, they waited.

After a while, Alex relented and made a pot of strong coffee. She stood by the window with a mug in her hand, looking out.

'Window cleaner?' she said.

Logan snorted. 'Behave. You'd have to hire a crane or a cradle or whatever it is they use for buildings like this.'

'I wasn't being serious,' Alex said, sounding miffed. 'You sure he's coming at all?'

'I'm not sure of anything,' Logan said.

'You don't think him and Molloy just hopped on a plane

to Cancún and now they're sipping pina coladas and rubbing suntan lotion into each other?'

'Jesus, that's an image I didn't want to have in my head. Thanks a lot.'

She came and sat back on the sofa. 'You know the one thing that's missing from this apartment?'

Logan was perched on the edge of a stool. He thought for a moment. 'Swimming pool? Tennis court? Bowling alley?'

'Books. Reading matter. There isn't even a magazine.'

'There was an old copy of *Rich Bastard Monthly* in the bathroom, but I put it in the recycling. Sorry.'

Alex got up and started walking around the room, trailing her fingers over the furniture.

'I don't think I could concentrate now anyway.'

'You don't say,' Logan said. 'I don't think I've ever seen you so nervous. And you're not even the one he's trying to kill.'

She paused, leaning on the back of the sofa. 'It's funny. I've always been OK with surveillance. I went twelve hours straight once. Didn't even go for a pee. No problem staying alert. You know what it's like; you just get into a kind of zone where you're totally relaxed but if anything happens you snap back and you're right on it, you know?'

Logan nodded. 'Sure. It's like battery-saving mode. Don't expend wasted energy, but you can just power up when you need to.'

'But this is different. I guess it's because we're the targets.'

'It's not too different from being on manoeuvres in the Army. You're trying to capture the flagpole or get to the top of the ridge or whatever, but there's a hundred bastards out there waiting for you to make a move so they can pop you.'

'So what's the secret?'

Logan thought for a moment. 'You just say, "Fuck it, what's the worst that could happen?" and get on with it.'

'And what was the worst that could happen?'

'Someone slots you after ten minutes and you look like a twat.'

'Right.' Alex nodded to herself. 'This is a bit different then. You've deliberately invited a top professional hit-man to your lovely home to kill you, so I suppose if he succeeds you will look like a twat. Especially since you paid him a hundred grand to do it. But you'll also be dead.'

'If you're getting cold feet, you can always go and wait with Ryan,' Logan said.

'Are you kidding? We've got a fiver resting on this. If I'm not here to watch, how do I know you're not going to cheat?' After a moment she added: 'You didn't seriously think I was . . .'

'Don't be daft.'

'OK. You know what, I might do a bit of yoga.'

'Knock yourself out.'

Alex went over to the window and settled into a lotus position.

'Just don't go into some, you know, higher state of consciousness or anything,' Logan said.

'Don't worry. I'm not very good at the meditation side. Although it would be just my luck to attain Buddhahood just when the shooting starts.'

'If you start levitating, I'll give you a kick up the backside,' Logan said.

'Cheers.'

Alex closed her eyes.

Twenty minutes later Logan's phone buzzed on the coffee table. He picked it up and squinted at the number, then put it to his ear.

'Yeah?'

Alex watched his face.

'Stupid cunts,' Logan said, tossing the phone onto the couch.

'Who was it?'

'*We've heard you were recently in an accident . . .* one of those.'

'Maybe they're just getting a bit ahead of themselves,' Alex said.

Logan made a face. 'Thanks for the vote of confidence.'

'You're welcome,' Alex said, closing her eyes again.

The rest of the morning passed slowly. Alex got up for a pee, then went back to doing her yoga routine in front of the window. Logan pottered around the apartment, checking things he'd already checked. He called down to the security desk using the intercom by the door and asked if there had been any packages for him.

'We'd have let you know straightaway, Mr Barrington,' the security guy said. 'Are you expecting something?'

Oh yes, Logan thought. *I just don't know what.*

'It's fine. Don't worry about it.'

Just after midday, Logan's phone buzzed again. He was in the kitchen area making a sandwich.

'Yeah?'

It was Ryan.

'A guy's pulled up in a van and he's looking at the roll-up door to the garage. Could be legit. Just thought I'd give you a heads-up.'

'OK, thanks. Let me know if the guy enters the garage. I'll check with security, see what the guy downstairs says.'

He put the phone down and walked over to the door. He pressed the intercom.

'Hello? This is Mr Barrington in the penthouse . . .'

Nothing.

'Hello?'

Logan leaned back against the wall.

Alex got up from where she'd been stretching.

'What is it?'

'Nobody's answering.'

'Maybe he's gone for a whizz.'

'They're not supposed to leave the desk.'

Alex shrugged. 'Give it a couple of minutes.'

Logan nodded. 'Fuck it, we should have had eyes on the front.'

They waited.

Logan buzzed down again.

'Hello? Is there anyone there? Hello?'

Alex raised her eyebrows. Logan shook his head.

'What do we do now?' Alex said.

'One of us needs to go down there. See what's going on.'

Alex bit her lip. 'It should be me.'

'Why?'

'If it's a set-up, it's you they're targeting, remember?'

'OK.'

The intercom buzzed.

'Yes,' Logan said.

'Mr Barrington? Sorry if you were trying to get through to the desk. We just had a little situation here to deal with. Nothing serious. Is there something I can help you with?'

'Er . . . yeah. There's some guy looking at the garage exit. I just wanted to check, is there a problem? Can I still drive out?'

'Oh, sure, just some routine maintenance. You can use all the facilities as normal, Mr Barrington.'

'OK, thanks.'

Logan turned to Alex.

'Did you get all that?'

'Yeah.'

Logan was looking thoughtful.

'What? You still reckon there's a problem?'

'I'm calling from inside the apartment. He knows I haven't

left the building. He didn't ask how I knew there was someone looking at the garage door.'

'Why would he? He's not going to question one of the residents. It's all "Yes sir, no sir", isn't it?'

'I suppose.'

'You still want to check?'

'I think so. Yes. Sorry.'

'It's OK, I'll go.'

Logan nodded. He went to the spyhole in the door.

Alex walked through the living area and into the guest bedroom. She re-emerged a few moments later zipping up a yellow tracksuit top over a nylon shoulder rig.

Logan turned. 'I was going to say. Don't go down there naked.'

Alex tapped the left side of her chest. 'Bodyguard three-eighty. I know you think it's a girly weapon, but I like it. You don't have to wear a trench coat over it.'

'Just remember to take the safety off. It's that little button . . .'

'Fuck off. I even remembered to put some of those cute little bullet thingies in. Is the coast clear?'

Logan stood back from the door. 'I think so. This gizmo is supposed to give you a total field of vision but I'm not sure I trust it.'

'I'll take my chances.' She patted her pocket. 'Buzz me if anything happens.'

He nodded. 'Likewise.'

Logan opened the door and Alex walked out into the

empty corridor. He watched her open the door to the emergency stairs and slip inside. He waited a few seconds and then reluctantly closed the door.

Something didn't feel right. Why did he have the feeling he'd just closed the lid on his own coffin?

He went back into the living area and scanned the room. He knew it was irrational, but he found himself checking the main bedroom, the bathroom, guest bedroom. He even opened the closets and flicked through the rows of suits.

'There's no one here, you stupid prick,' he said aloud.

He could hear the edge of anxiety in his voice.

He looked at his watch, trying to calculate how long it would take Alex to get to the ground floor. He should have told her to keep her phone on so he could hear what was going on. He went back to the door and looked through the spyhole again, then went back to the living area and stood in the middle of the floor, his arms crossed, his eyes on the door.

He'd give her two minutes. Three. Then if she didn't give him the all-clear, he'd call.

He waited, not moving.

He went back to the kitchen area and retrieved his Glock, then took up position again in the middle of the apartment, holding the pistol loosely at his side. He glanced back at the window, then went to a bank of discreet buttons flush with the wall. A grey fabric blind slowly descended with an almost imperceptible hum, cutting off the view, as the lights went on. He didn't really believe in the watchers any more, but if something was about to go down, best they didn't see it.

He looked at his watch. She'd been gone three and a half minutes. That was too long. He pulled his phone out of his pocket and hit the speed dial, then listened as it went straight to voicemail.

'Bollocks.'

What now?

Stay or go?

He stood for moment, frozen in indecision.

The door buzzed. He walked over to the intercom and pressed the button.

Nothing.

'Yeah?'

Suddenly he heard Alex's voice.

'Sorry, darling, I've forgotten the code again. Can you let me in?'

He reached for the door handle, then stopped. No. This wasn't right. She said 'darling'. She never called him darling. Was she just pissing about? Or was that a signal something was wrong? Either way, he couldn't just let her stand there out in the corridor. He knew he had about five seconds to think up a plan.

He slid the Glock down the back of his jeans, pulled open the door and stepped back.

There was a blur of movement as Alex stumbled past him into the apartment. Behind her was a tall man with dark hair, dressed in the uniform of a security guard: dark trousers, short-sleeved white shirt and tie. He had one arm across Alex's throat and the other held an automatic pistol pressed to her temple.

He made eye contact with Logan. 'Get back!' he yelled.

Logan put his hands out in a placatory gesture. 'What the hell's going on?'

The tall man kicked Alex's legs from under her and she landed on her tailbone with a thump. He knelt behind her, forearm still against her throat, but with his pistol now pointed at Logan.

'Are you Jason Barrington?'

'What the fuck is this? What are you—'

'Just answer the fucking question or I'll blow your girl-friend's head off!'

Logan took a step backwards. The man must have seen the photograph. He must know who he was looking at. But maybe that was the protocol: you had to ask. Then when you went back to whoever ordered the hit, you could say, 'Yes, the target confirmed his identity before I pulled the trigger.' Seems there were rules for everything. Or maybe it was to guard against killing an identical twin by mistake. He thought of Lucy and Ursula for a split second.

He knew if he said 'yes' the next thing he'd feel would be a bullet exiting the back of his skull.

'Look, I think there's been some—' He reached behind him and snatched the Glock from his jeans. At the same moment, Alex grabbed hold of her assailant's forearm with both hands, tucked her chin to her chest and pivoted to her left. It was a classic chokehold escape move, and if she'd been standing, it might have worked, leaning back into her attacker, then dropping forward and pulling him down and around with her bodyweight until he lost balance. On her knees, she just didn't have the leverage.

The man grunted and pulled her back.

But his attention had been diverted for a split second.

Long enough for Logan to take a half-step to the side to give himself a better angle and put two quick rounds into the man's exposed shoulder. The first one tore through his shirt, leaving a bloody trail, but only grazed him. As he flinched back, the other round took off the top of his humerus, sending a chunk of blood and sinew slamming into the wall behind him. His grip around Alex's neck loosened as he let out a strangled scream and she managed to wriggle out from under him. Logan stepped forward and stamped down hard on the man's wrist. There was a loud crack, his fingers spasmed, and the gun slipped from his grasp. Logan kicked it to the side.

'Watch out! He's got my—'

Logan saw the man suddenly had Alex's compact pistol in his left hand.

He raised the Glock again, but time seemed to slow and his hand felt too heavy to move, like in a dream.

He waited for everything to go black.

He felt the shot go past his ear as Alex kicked the man's gun arm high and wide.

Logan suddenly had him in his sights again.

He went for centre mass.

Once. Twice.

Then, as the man flew back against the wall, he took two quick steps forward, put the muzzle of the gun to the man's mouth and fired another two shots that exited the back of his head, painting the wall with his brains.

They both stood back, breathing hard, the smell of blood and cordite heavy in the air.

Alex picked up her gun. Her hand was shaking.

'It's OK. He's dead,' Logan said.

Alex didn't say anything.

After a minute she said, 'Yes. I think he is.'

'You're OK?'

'Yeah. I had a stiff neck after coming off the bike. I think he might have wrenched it back the right way.'

Logan grinned. 'Always a silver lining.'

'He's made a mess of your wall, though. I don't think you're going to get your deposit back.'

'Yeah, we don't really want anyone seeing this.' He turned to shut the door.

There was a short, stocky man wearing a Puffa jacket just outside in the corridor in a pistol-shooter's stance, pointing what looked like a silenced Ruger at Logan's chest. He jerked his chin at the pistol in Logan's hand as he stepped forward.

'Drop that.'

Logan considered his options.

The man was here to kill him.

If he dropped the gun, he'd be shot.

If he tried to get a shot of his own off, just for the hell of it?

Same difference.

He kept his arm at his side, gripping the stock of the pistol. That seemed like a reasonable halfway house, even if it only bought him a few more seconds of life. He thought about Lucy, waiting for him to come and rescue her. She'd think he'd abandoned her. A wave of anger welled up, threatening to overpower him.

Fuck it.

He started to raise the pistol.

Instantly he heard a shot.

The short man twisted to the side, dropping the Ruger and falling to his knees, then slowly toppled sideways onto the carpet. He lay there, his eyes open, an expression of surprise on his face.

Logan bent down and picked up the Ruger. He turned to Alex, who was still pointing the little Smith & Wesson at the man on the floor.

'Thanks,' he said. It came out more as a croak.

'Are there any more of them, do you think?' Alex said.

Logan stepped past the man on the floor and shut the door with a satisfying *thunk*. He breathed out, his heart rate steadying.

'I fucking hope not. Wait here.'

He went into the living area and turned left, towards the main bathroom. He came back, holding the knife.

'What are you planning on doing with that?' Alex said.

Logan knelt down beside the body of the stocky man.

'I'm going to take a trophy. Which ear do you fancy?'

He held the blade in front of the short man's face.

Alex was wide-eyed, her mouth open in shock. 'Have you gone completely—'

The short man suddenly convulsed, twisting his head away from the knife.

'I didn't think he was dead,' Logan said, turning to Alex with a grin.

He ripped the Puffa jacket open.

'He was wearing a vest. At this range a nine-mil might have done for him, but not that little pea-shooter you've got.'

Alex blew out her cheeks. 'Fucking hell, Logan. I thought you'd gone mental for a minute. Hold on, how comes he's wearing a vest and you're . . .'

Logan shrugged. 'Forgot. Never liked wearing them anyway. It's like shin pads when you're playing football. You've got to show you're not afraid. Like Jack Grealish, you know?'

'Christ, you have gone mental. This bloke didn't come here to rake his studs down your shins.' She shook her head, lost for words.

'Come on fella,' Logan said, standing over the short man. 'Game's up.'

The let out a breath, then clutched his side, gritting his teeth and grunting in pain.

'Hurts like a bastard, I bet,' Logan said amiably. 'Probably bust a rib or two.' He waved the knife in the air. 'Tell you what, though – that's nothing compared to what's in store for you. Now, do you think you can walk?'

The man looked up at Logan as if he was trying to gauge how mad he really was. He pushed himself up on one hand, then fell back.

'That's OK,' Logan said. 'Crawling's fine.' He pointed behind him with the knife. 'After you.'

In the end they half-dragged and half-carried the short man into the bathroom. He was breathing hard, in short, sharp gasps, his face pale and waxy looking, but once they'd sat him down on the plastic sheeting, propped up against the wall next to the sink, he seemed to revive a little. Logan pulled his jacket off him and undid the straps of the Kevlar vest, while Alex kept the Smith & Wesson levelled at him in a double-handed grip.

'Heavy fuckers, aren't they?' Logan said, tossing the vest aside. 'I bet that feels better.'

Logan secured the man's wrists and ankles with cable ties, then stood back, looking at him.

The man opened his eyes and returned his gaze.

'Right. This is the way it's going to be. I'm going to ask you some questions. You're going to answer them. If you don't, or I think you're fucking around with me, I'm going to cut something off. With this.' He jiggled the knife. 'If you really act like a cunt, I'll let you bleed out, here on the floor, but not before I've introduced you to a world of pain you never thought could exist. If you think I'm all talk, I'll give you a little taster to show you I mean business.'

The man shook his head vigorously.

Logan nodded. 'One more thing before we begin. I have a feeling you might have been a squaddie once, maybe even a proper soldier. Regiment, even. Although your commanding officer wouldn't have been very impressed by today's shit-show. But maybe you had a bit of interrogation training yourself. Maybe you think you know all about counter-interrogation techniques? Well, you don't know as much as me. If you lie to me, I'll know. If I think you're not being a hundred per cent straight with me, I'm going to hurt you. So don't kid a kidder, right?'

The man nodded.

'Good. Next thing. I know what's going through your head right now. You're thinking, however the next bit goes, at the end of the day I'm a dead man, so the best strategy is string it out, play for time, and hope the mad fucker with the knife gets sloppy at some point.'

'Don't forget the mad fucker with the gun,' Alex said.

Logan nodded to her. He turned back to the man on the floor.

'The only way you get out of here in one piece – and I mean that literally – is to tell us everything we want to know. That's the only strategy that's going to work. Forget everything else.'

He waited to let all that sink in.

The short man didn't say anything. Beads of sweat ran into his eyes and he blinked them away.

'Right,' Logan said. 'To kick off, I'm going to mention

some names. Say "yes" if you know who they are. I might accept a nod.'

The short man looked at him.

'Claire Maxwell.'

The man visibly blanched. Logan could almost see his brain working, furiously trying to work out what this meant.

Logan waited.

'Yes.'

'Craig McKinley.'

A shorter pause this time.

'Yes.'

'John Jennings.'

'Yes.'

Logan felt his heart racing. 'One more. John Tenniel. DCI John Tenniel, I should say.'

The man's eyes flicked from Logan to Alex, then back again.

'Yes.'

Logan breathed out. 'Good.' He sat down on the edge of the whirlpool bath. 'That's a good start. But are you trying to pull the wool over my eyes? The next one's a bit trickier, so have a proper think first.'

He paused.

'How did they die?'

When he finally spoke, his voice was higher-pitched than Logan expected. But maybe that was just down to the stress of the situation.

'The woman was driving. She . . . had an accident,' he

said. 'McKinley's heart gave out halfway up a mountain. The other bloke fell under a train.'

'The *woman's* name was Claire,' Alex said, in a tone of barely suppressed fury. 'She had a little daughter.'

'And she didn't have an accident, did she?' Logan said. 'You killed her. You and your mate out there. You killed all of them.'

The man on the floor did his best to shrug. 'Seems like you already know that.'

'We knew someone did,' Logan said. 'Now we know it was you. And while we're taking down names, what's yours? We'll find out but it would save time if you just told us.'

'O'Dwyer. Liam O'Dwyer,' he said. 'What now, then?' O'Dwyer added, almost aggressively.

'We want to know why.'

'We were paid. That's how it works,' he said. After the initial shock, Logan could see he was gradually getting his nerve back. Maybe he thought he had nothing to lose. Logan couldn't help admiring his pluck.

'Why did someone want them killed?' Logan asked in an even tone, deliberately not rising to the bait. 'Was it Tenniel?'

O'Dwyer took his time, thinking about it. 'Terry Mason's wife, she was the contact. If someone else was behind it, I don't know who they were.'

'But you said you knew Tenniel.'

'I know who he is. That's all.'

Logan looked hard into O'Dwyer's eyes. O'Dwyer didn't blink.

'So who killed Stephanie Mason?' Logan said.

'Not Tenniel, if that's what you're thinking,' O'Dwyer said, as if Logan was stupid.

'OK.' Logan nodded. 'So you did that off your own bat?'

'We thought we were going to be next. You know, getting rid of the evidence. So we took pre-emptive action.'

Logan thought it all through. 'Well it looks like you did Tenniel a favour. Saved him the trouble. You see, we think Tenniel was pulling Stephanie Mason's strings. He used all three victims to bring down Terry Mason. My theory is they found out something they weren't meant to, something that threatened him. Any ideas on that? Stephanie Mason didn't drop any hints?'

'Not that one. You could call her a lot of things, but stupid wasn't one of them.'

Logan considered that for a moment. He tapped the blade of the knife against the edge of the bath.

'Any theories? You must have been curious.'

'I don't know – Mason had paid him off, back in the day? Maybe Tenniel was protecting him before he . . . wasn't.'

Logan nodded. 'Makes sense. But somehow . . . you'd think a man like Tenniel would have thought ahead, made sure he'd covered his tracks for when the relationship went sour.'

'Maybe,' O'Dwyer conceded.

'No other theories, then?' Logan asked.

O'Dwyer shook his head. 'Nah.'

'He's fucking with us,' Alex said.

'One way to find out,' Logan said, pushing himself off the edge of the bath. He knelt down. 'We could start with those ribs.'

'Less mess to clear up afterwards,' Alex said, nodding.

Logan used the knife to rip a hole in O'Dwyer's shirt, then started to feel around inside with his fingers.

'Jesus fuck!' O'Dwyer went white. Sweat started pouring off him. 'OK, there is something.'

Logan eased the pressure on O'Dwyer's chest. 'Yeah?'

'Stephanie Mason wanted someone to search their premises, the people she . . .'

'Did you do that?'

'No, the idea was to do it while the job was being done. She wanted a real pro, someone who wouldn't leave any evidence they'd been there if the police had a poke around later on. It just so happened we knew someone.'

'A professional burglar?'

'Yeah.'

'So Tenniel must have thought that whatever Craig, Claire and Jennings had found, they still had it.'

'Makes sense,' the man said. 'If your theory's right,' he added.

'And did they find anything, this burglar?' Alex said.

'I wouldn't know. I gave Stephanie Mason a name, that's all.'

'We need that name,' Logan said. 'We need to talk to them.'

'Charlie Stones. I've got a number.'

Logan stood back up. He put the knife down on the edge of the bath.

'All right. Here's the deal,' he said, pulling his phone out of his pocket. 'You're probably wondering who the fuck we are and what sort of fucked-up mess you've walked into. Well, you can keep wondering. All you need to know is that you've been fucking with the wrong people. And if you're smart, you'll do whatever we tell you from now on. But just in case you decide not to be smart, I'm going to record a little interview. A confession, if you like. To three murders. And you're going to put in lots of detail that only the killer would know.' He smiled. 'Will it stand up in court? Will it fuck. But it'll be enough for the police to get their teeth into you and they won't let go until you're in a cell.'

'Fair enough,' O'Dwyer said, wincing. 'It's not like I have any choice, do I?'

'That's the spirit,' Logan said. 'Now, I would quite like to kill you.' He nodded to Alex. 'I know my friend would like to as well. Generally speaking if someone tries to kill me, I like to return the favour. But I'm going to make an exception in your case. One, because we need you to clear up the mess you've made. You're going to remove your pal and then, well, do what you like with him. But I presume you'll want to put him somewhere no one's going to find him. We'll help of course. There's plenty of plastic sheeting, and if you think it would be easier to cut him up, we've got the tools for that, too. Secondly, if this Charlie Stones character turns out to be a bust – or a figment of your imagination – we need to know you're still around for a little chat to straighten things out. Make sense?'

'Sure,' O'Dwyer said.

'Oh, of course, I was forgetting. Last but not least, I need my money back. Don't tell me you've spent it already or bunged it in an ISA, or I'll have to go back to Plan A and cut your balls off.'

'You're a real joker, aren't you?' O'Dwyer said.

'I find it helps relieve the tension,' Logan said.

'So were you Regiment, then?' O'Dwyer asked. 'Or maybe you still are.'

Logan smiled. 'Man of mystery, that's me.'

'But you kill people for a living.' It wasn't a question.

'You trying to say we're both the same?' Logan said.

'If you kill people for money, it doesn't really matter who pays, does it?'

'Maybe not,' Logan said. 'But it matters who you kill.'

32

Lucy knew it was a dream. But she also knew it was real. Which is the way it is in dreams, sometimes. She also knew that she'd had the dream before, more times than she could count, and so was well aware of what was going to happen. The details changed a little sometimes: what people in the dream were wearing or what they ate; but what happened was always the same. Nevertheless, being a dream, Lucy was terrified.

Her father was at the head of the table, as always. And wearing his usual spotted bow-tie. This time his shirt was pink, though, and he was wearing a velvet smoking jacket. Lucy had never seen a smoking jacket and wouldn't have known what, if anything, distinguished it from any other jacket, but in the dream she knew what it was.

On his left, looking sad, was Deborah. She was sad, Lucy knew, because she was dead and would never grow up. She wondered where Deborah was when she wasn't in the dream. Some gloomy hell full of other wandering, unhappy spirits? Or just another part of the house, locked in her room with all her old dolls and toys? Lucy suddenly felt guilty that they'd given them all away to a charity shop in a nearby town, somewhere nobody would know where they came from.

She wanted to say sorry, but try as she might, she couldn't speak. Her lips had been sewn together.

How did she eat, then? That was never explained. She looked down at her plate. Someone had made a sad face out of two pieces of orange and a slice of melon.

They didn't have a maid, but she came and took the plate away anyway.

On the other side of her father was Ursula. She had brushed her hair until it shone, a glossy waterfall streaming down either side of her face. Her face was very pale and beautiful. Lucy thought that because they were identical twins, Ursula must also know that this was a dream. Something about that didn't quite make sense, but she couldn't say what. She tried to make eye contact, but Ursula looked past and through her, making her wonder if she was really there at all.

Of course I'm not: it's a dream, she thought.

The next part of the dream was the worst bit, until the end, which was even worse. Without wanting to, Lucy looked to her left. A man with collar-length dark hair and a neatly trimmed beard was sitting smiling at her. She could tell he was very much in love with her.

On one side of him was a little girl with pigtails in a pretty blue dress; on the other, a little boy with a dark fringe. They kept their eyes down, nervously.

'Aren't you going to introduce us?' her father boomed from the end of the table, as she knew he would. 'Your husband, and your beautiful children, my grandchildren.'

'Yes,' she said. 'Of course.'

She looked at the man and his smile got even warmer, more loving.

'Tell your father who we are,' he said.

'My mouth . . .' Lucy said. She put her hands to her lips. They felt numb, but there was no trace of the stitches.

'There's nothing wrong with your mouth,' Ursula said.

'What are their names?' her father said. He was still smiling, but a note of impatience had crept into his voice.

'They've come all this way,' Ursula added.

'Tell Grandpa our names,' said the children, in unison.

'Come on, darling,' said her husband.

'Shall we go through the alphabet?' said Ursula with a cruel smile.

'No, please, I can . . .' Lucy said.

'A,' said Ursula.

She raised an eyebrow.

'No? B, then. C.'

'Please don't,' said Lucy. 'Please stop.'

'D, E, F, G,' Ursula continued. 'H, I, J, K . . .'

Lucy hung her head and tears dropped onto her lap.

Ursula was relentless.

'L, M, N, O, P . . .'

The children looked at her pleadingly.

'Lucy, come on,' said her father, looking stern now.

'Q, R, S, T, U, V,' Ursula said, not bothering to pause between letters now.

'Shall I serve the soup?' said the maid who wasn't there.

'Please, please, please, just stop,' said Lucy, looking up through her tears.

'W, X, Y . . .'

Ursula paused dramatically. Everybody looked at Lucy's husband and her children.

'Z,' she said, and the three of them instantly disappeared.

'Oh dear,' said Dr Redwood, standing by the door in her bright lipstick and a camel-hair coat.

'Lucy . . .' said Lucy's father, shaking his head.

Lucy put her hand to her mouth again. She couldn't move her lips. The stitches were back. She tried to say, 'You see!' but no words came out, just a throaty gargle, like a bad ventriloquist's dummy.

Now for the next part.

'Well, let's now have our just desserts!' said her father brightly. It was the joke he used to make when they were little.

Lucy looked across the table.

'May I be excused?' Ursula said.

The bad part – the worst part – was about to happen.

'No,' her father said.

Deborah looked up at him. 'I want to go and play.'

Dr Redwood shook her head. 'That won't be possible.'

Lucy looked back at where Ursula had been. Her place was empty.

She waited for the sound, knowing what was coming next.

Perhaps this time it wouldn't happen.

But then again, she always thought that.

First it was a scuffling, then there was a panting, then the sound of something being knocked over in the hall and a precious heirloom smashing on the floor.

'Please excuse me,' Ursula said, from somewhere Lucy couldn't see.

Dr Redwood opened the door wide and the panting turned into a roaring as a huge black bear reared up on its hind legs and drunk-walked into the room, its head bobbing from side to side, drool flying from its mouth, black lips pulled back over its savage-looking teeth, black eyes gleaming. It tottered for a moment as if it was going to fall over, then lunged for Lucy's father. One huge claw raked his face, instantly turning it into a bloody mask. He slumped forward onto the table and the bear buried its teeth in his neck. There was a terrible snapping and grinding sound as the bear reared backwards, finally tearing her father's head from his shoulders with a savage *pop*. His torso bobbed back up like a toy, blood spouting from his neck and spraying the tablecloth.

Dr Redwood leaned over her. 'That didn't happen,' she said.

Lucy opened her mouth and screamed.

She found she was standing in the middle of her room.

The bedsheets were tangled on the floor.

Tears were running down her face and her whole body was shaking.

'Logan,' she said in a hoarse whisper. 'Please, please, come and get me.'

33

Logan was still wondering what to do with the bullet lodged in the wall, not to mention the blood heat-blasted into the plaster, but getting rid of O'Dwyer's pal had been surprisingly easy. First they'd wrapped the body in the plastic sheeting, tossing in as much of his brains and skull fragments as they could scoop up. Then Logan had driven O'Dwyer to where his car was parked up. They switched to O'Dwyer's car, drove back and re-entered the garage using Logan's key card. It was all a bit like the puzzle about crossing the river with a bag of grain and a fox and a chicken along for the ride, with the corpse as the bag of grain, Logan thought. Then they'd gone back to the penthouse, hefted the body between them, and carried it down the emergency stairs. O'Dwyer was breathing hard from his busted rib, but if he felt any emotion handling his dead partner's corpse, he didn't show it. Alex had gone down to the garage first, opened the boot and texted when the garage was empty. They quickly hefted the body in and got in the car just as a fat man in a bright pink shirt came out of the lift, waggling his car keys. They drove back to where Logan had left his car and parked up behind it.

O'Dwyer was in the front passenger seat, next to Logan, with Alex in the back. The fourth member of the party was wedged into the boot. It felt hard to believe that less than two hours earlier, they'd been trying to kill each other.

Logan felt like he ought to say something, but any final threat or warning seemed superfluous. He wanted to know what O'Dwyer was going to do with the body, but there was no reason for O'Dwyer to tell him. And it wasn't really any of his business.

Logan and Alex got out and O'Dwyer walked round to the driver's side and got in. Logan and O'Dwyer exchanged a look and then O'Dwyer pulled out and drove off.

'Fucking hell, I thought you were going to give him a hug,' Alex said as they got into Logan's car. 'Did you two bond over your favourite handguns or something while my back was turned?'

'He didn't seem such a bad bloke,' Logan said as he put the car in gear and pulled away.

Alex shook her head. 'Jesus,' she said. 'Men.'

Logan dropped Alex back at the Clearwater offices for a debrief. 'Mrs Allenby's going to love this,' she said with a sigh as she got out.

'Maybe don't mention all the shooting,' Logan said.

Back in traffic, he looked at the clock on the dash. O'Dwyer had told him how to set up a meet with Charlie Stones, but Logan didn't want to wait. He put the address of an internet cafe in the City into the satnav. ETA twenty minutes.

It took him almost that long to find a parking spot, and then he still had a ten-minute walk back to the cafe. Walking in, it seemed an unlikely hang-out for a burglar. Customers sat at tiny tables just big enough for a laptop and the obligatory cup of coffee, separated by wooden partitions. He counted thirty tables, about half of them occupied by twenty-something hipsters. None of them looked up when Logan walked in and made his way to the counter. *Funny place to do business*, he thought. Then he got it: everyone in the cafe was engrossed in their laptops, with buds jammed in their ears. They'd tuned the outside world out. You could have a lively discussion about how you were going to break into Buckingham Palace and kidnap Charles and Camilla and no one would bat an eyelid.

He felt a wave of nausea pass through him. He steadied himself, then ordered the nearest thing he could find on the menu to an ordinary cup of tea with ordinary cow's milk, then took it to the back of the cafe, by the toilets.

O'Dwyer had told him Charlie Stones always sat in the same booth, more or less day and night, wedged into the corner. Logan looked. The woman in the booth could have been anything between twenty-five and thirty, with big, red-framed glasses that matched the colour of her lipstick and a short black bob.

Shit.

He thought about what he would do to O'Dwyer, the next time he saw him.

She glanced up and caught him looking at her. He decided he might as well ask the question, even if he ended up looking like a twat.

'Charlie Stones?'

She looked him up and down.

'Depends on who wants to know. Identity can be a very fluid thing these days,' she added, confusingly.

'I got your name from Liam O'Dwyer,' Logan said.

She took her time with that. Logan could almost see the cogs whirring round in her brain.

'I suppose you'd better sit down then.'

Logan squeezed into the booth. There wasn't room to put his tea down, so he held the cardboard cup on his lap. He looked at the woman sitting in front of him. She certainly wasn't his idea of a professional burglar. She looked more like a librarian, or, given the setting, a digital marketing consultant.

'People usually message me if they need some consultancy work,' she said.

'I'm in a bit of a hurry,' Logan said.

'Everybody's in a hurry,' she said, taking a sip of her coffee. 'That's the digital world for you.'

Logan still wasn't sure this was the right Charlie Stones.

'O'Dwyer said he introduced you to a new client.'

She didn't say anything.

'They asked you to do three jobs.'

She put her coffee down carefully, then snapped her laptop shut.

'I think you've got your wires crossed somewhere.'

She unhooked a rucksack from the back of her chair and slipped the laptop inside.

'I'm afraid I must be going.'

Logan put a hand on her arm.

'You know O'Dwyer kills people, don't you?'

She tried to shrug his hand off.

'You know what?' he went on. 'He tried to kill me today, and all. But he didn't succeed. You probably think he's a scary bastard, but wait till you get to know me.'

'I have no intention of getting to know you,' she said, but her voice had a quaver in it.

'I'm afraid it's too late for that,' Logan said. 'If I were you I'd sit down and talk to me.'

He guided her back into her chair. She didn't resist.

'So how did you get into this lark?' he said. 'I have to admit, I was expecting someone a bit different.'

She picked up her cup and took a sip. Despite her blank expression, her hands were shaking.

'What? Bloke with a stripey shirt and a mask, with a bag marked "swag"?'

He smiled. 'Something like that.'

'I used to work for a company that sold security systems, on the IT side. When I got bored, I used to try and figure out ways to beat the system. Just for fun. Then I thought, maybe I could make some money out of it.'

'Gamekeeper turned poacher,' Logan said.

'If you like. And I found it was a bit more exciting than sitting at a desk. I used to do freeclimbing till I hurt my shoulder.'

Logan nodded. 'The buzz. The risk. I get it.'

'I found I was good at it, too,' she said, a note of defiance creeping back into her voice.

'And you meet such interesting people,' Logan said. 'Easy to get addicted, I'd say. Until one day you find you're in over your head.'

'What do you mean?'

'Who paid you? Who set up the jobs?'

She shrugged. 'It was a woman. Funnily enough she didn't give me her name.'

'And you were looking for something specific, weren't you? Did you find it?'

'I can't discuss—'

Logan leaned forward. 'Listen, Charlie. I've had a really stressful day. Don't make me get nasty with you.'

She thought for a moment, measuring Logan's tone.

'No, I didn't find anything,' she said.

'What were you looking for?'

'A disk, or a memory stick. Anything like that. It wasn't specific. But it would be hidden. That's how I'd know it was the thing I was looking for.'

'And if you found it – who were you supposed to report back to? This woman?'

'No. Someone else. I was given a number.'

'Was there a name attached?'

She shook her head. 'No.'

'But it was a man.'

'Yes.'

'I don't suppose he told you what was on this memory stick?'

She shook her head. 'But he told me if I looked, he'd know. And he'd know if I told the woman anything.'

'And you believed him?'

She was thinking back to the conversation. Logan could tell the memory frightened her. 'Yes, I believed him.'

'And you really didn't find anything?'

'I told you.'

'How did he take it?'

'He wasn't pleased, if that's what you mean. But he didn't throw a fit, either. I still got paid,' she added proudly.

'Good for you,' Logan said. He took a gulp of his tea. It was lukewarm and tasted of something he couldn't identify.

'So what can I do for you?' she said. Some of her confidence seemed to have come back.

'I want you to get in contact with this man again. You still have the number, yeah?'

She nodded warily.

'I need you to tell him that when you said you hadn't found anything, you were lying. You did find a memory stick. And what's more, you took a look at what was on it. And now, if he really wants you to hand it over, he's going to have to pay.'

She put her cup down, almost missing the saucer.

'You are fucking kidding. I may be an adrenaline junkie, but I don't have a bloody death wish. Why the hell would I do something completely insane like that?'

Logan smiled. 'Because if you don't, I'll tell him you've got it anyway.'

She stared at him, her face pale.

'You don't know who he is.'

'I'm willing to bet I do.'

'Bastard.'

'You don't know the half of it,' Logan said.

She took a deep breath. 'Then what?'

'He'll suggest a meet. Somewhere out of the way. Where you can do the exchange.'

'But I won't have anything to exchange.'

'That doesn't matter.'

'He'll kill me.'

'No he won't. I'll be there to protect you. With some friends of mine.'

She sat back, shaking her head at the madness of it. 'So what's the point of all this? What is it you want?'

'I want to know what it is he's been looking for.'

'Why?'

'The people whose houses you burgled: this man had them killed. Did you know that?'

Charlie didn't say anything.

'Two of them were friends of mine.'

He let that sink in.

'You might think you're smart, Charlie; you can handle people like Liam O'Dwyer. But this guy's in a different league. Sooner or later he'll decide he can't risk having you around, just in case you were telling him porkies. My friends were smart. Smarter than you. But he killed them. The only way you can be safe is if you help me bring him down, so he hasn't got the power to hurt anybody any more.'

Logan looked at her. She was trying to keep her cool, but her eyes glittered with desperation. *Welcome to the big leagues*, he thought. She had the look of a wild animal caught in a trap, with no means of escape. He thought about topping things off with another threat, to seal the deal, then thought better of it.

He leaned over and touched her arm.

'I know it might not feel like it right now, Charlie, but actually this is your lucky day.'

34

When Logan had called the clinic to tell them he wanted to admit his wife that evening, Dr Redwood had sounded cautious, perhaps even suspicious. Why the rush?

At first he didn't get it. It's not like they didn't have the room. Then he realized what she was worried about. Had Melissa's condition suddenly deteriorated? Had she become unmanageable? Was he just trying to offload her before she became violent?

'If you're wondering why it can't wait until the weekend, it's her: she wants to come. She won't let up about it, to be honest. Driving me nuts, to coin a phrase. I'm worried if I don't bring her now, she'll go the other way.'

'I understand,' Dr Redwood said, sounding happier. 'It can be like surfing a wave, sometimes.'

'Exactly,' he said, thinking: *Well, this wave's going to wipe you out.* 'Seven o'clock, then?'

'That will be fine,' Dr Redwood said. 'I'll personally make sure we have everything ready.'

Logan shuddered to think what that meant.

In the car on the way to the clinic, it was Alex's turn to worry.

'It does seem a bit quick.'

'You not ready?'

'It's not that. I mean, what could go wrong? It's not like it's the first time I've ever kidnapped a patient from a private psychiatric clinic.'

'We're not kidnapping her. We're rescuing her.'

'Right. But that's not the bit I'm worried about. It's after, when we get her back to your apartment. I mean, what sort of a state is she going to be in?'

Logan frowned. The woods were fading into the dusk as they sped past. 'If we leave her any longer, she'll be a whole lot worse. That's all I know. Every day that Redwood has her hooks in her, she's closer to . . .'

He didn't finish the sentence.

'And I don't know how much time we have, anyway.'

'You mean before Tenniel takes the bait and sets up the meet?'

He nodded. 'I don't think he'll waste any time. This is the only window we have.'

'Fair enough,' Alex said.

They were getting close to the turn-off into the woods. Alex pulled her scarf tighter around her throat and checked her make-up in the mirror.

She nodded approvingly. 'Bonkers but elegant. Perfect.'

When they arrived, Dr Redwood, wearing a black cocktail dress and a string of pearls, as if she was welcoming a minor royal instead of a psychiatric patient, met them out front and led them to her office, all smiles. Alex had decided not to be too manic, mainly because she knew it unsettled Logan, but also because she thought it suited the circumstances: she was happy but calm, looking forward to being pampered by the lovely staff at her favourite hotel on the Côte d'Azur. Logan was carrying a small cream-coloured suitcase to complete the picture.

'Could we have a moment alone, you know, just to say goodbye?' Logan asked, when he'd finished filling out all the paperwork.

'Of course.' Dr Redwood rose and went to the door. 'I'll be right outside.'

As the door clicked shut behind her, Logan quickly looked around. There was a bookshelf behind Dr Redwood's desk. What looked like rows of academic journals jostled with heavy diagnostic tomes. A bonfire waiting to happen. Perfect.

Alex pulled at his arm and gave him a wide-eyed look. *Shit.* A camera nestling in the cornice and pointed right at Dr Redwood's desk. How had he never noticed that before? What the fuck was he going to do now? Could he take the risk that it was just for show or only turned on for patient therapy sessions?

'Give me a hug, darling,' Alex said.

She pulled him in tight, and then as she pulled away, he felt her hand inside his jacket pocket. She palmed something expertly and then stood back, adjusting her scarf.

'You must get back to your precious work,' she said.

He looked at her, trying to find a way of saying *No! Don't do this!* with his eyes. But she just smiled back.

'I'll be fine,' she said.

There was a smart knock on the door and Dr Redwood was standing in the doorway.

'Mrs Markham?' she said, smiling.

Alex walked towards her. Logan clenched his fists. There was nothing he could do.

Dr Redwood and Alex walked out of the office and down the corridor. One of the security guys, the one with the meaty forearms, suddenly appeared, pointing to the suitcase.

'Let me take that for you, Mr Markham.'

'Sure,' Logan said, walking past him and turning back towards the entrance.

See you later, pal, he thought.

In the car, he thought about aborting the whole thing. Surely he couldn't let Alex take this much of a risk. It was his fault: he hadn't thought it through and didn't have a backup option. Perhaps he had been too hasty, jumping in with two feet, fuelled by concern for Lucy and anger at that bitch Redwood. Rookie error: just wanting to get the thing done instead of planning properly.

He drove out through the woods, then turned left, drove for another half-mile, and parked the car where they'd planned. By now he knew he had no option but to go ahead. He knew what Alex was going to do. From the look on her face, her mind was made up. And anyway, he had no means of communicating with her. There was no way of stopping her.

He just had to hope it worked.

He realized he hadn't slept for seventy-two hours, not properly anyway. He'd been running on pure adrenaline, and it was finally catching up with him. Lying back in the driver's seat, his whole body felt as if it was made of lead. If he didn't shut his eyes . . . He snapped awake, just long enough to set the alarm on his phone, then pushed the seat back. The last thing he heard before he fell into darkness was the bark of a fox.

In his dream, he rescued the wrong twin. With the connivance of Dr Redwood, Ursula had taken Lucy's place and was waiting for him when he busted open the door of her room. She reached out her hand and when he touched it, a jolt of electricity ran up his arm and his whole body tingled.

'You took your time,' she said. She looked over his shoulder. '*Edgar! Edmund!*' she screeched.

Logan turned. He tensed as he saw the two security guys were standing in the doorway.

They turned into a pair of grey dogs and bounded into the room, almost knocking him over in their eagerness to greet their mistress. Ursula knelt down, letting them nuzzle her.

'My naughty, naughty boys,' she cooed.

She looked up at Logan.

'Could you help me pack?'

'We need to get out of here before . . .'

Before *what*?

'I'm not leaving without my money,' she said firmly. She

pulled a cream-coloured suitcase out from under the bed. Banknotes were scattered over the floor and she started snatching them up and stuffing them into the case. A window was open and some of the banknotes flew up in the sudden breeze, so Logan had to bat them away from his face. The dogs started jumping up excitedly, snapping at them like flies.

'Where's Lucy?' he said.

'Lucy doesn't exist. She's a figment of your imagination,' Ursula said, not looking up from her furious work. 'Give me that, please.'

Logan looked down and saw he was standing on a bright pink fifty-pound note. He bent down to pick it up.

'You see,' Dr Redwood said from the doorway, 'because you are unable to admit to your violent feelings towards your wife, your unconscious has created a doppelgänger, a "good twin" who you can truly love.'

'I'm not . . .' He tried to say something but his tongue wouldn't work.

'Don't worry,' Dr Redwood said, smiling. Her teeth shone like pearls. 'We can help you. In a week or two you won't see Lucy any more. Eventually you'll forget you ever thought she existed.'

'There!' Ursula tried to slam the case shut, but it was too full.

An alarm went off somewhere.

'We have to go!' he said to Ursula.

'Not until I've got all my money!' she said. She sat on the case and pushed down.

The alarm got louder.

'We have to—'

He jerked awake, the alarm on his phone beeping.

'Shit.' He fumbled with the phone until he found the stop button, then sat for a few seconds with his eyes closed, waiting for his heart to stop banging against his ribs. Then he got out of the car and started jogging along the road.

When he got to the turn-off to the clinic he stayed on the tarmac road. In the thin moonlight, he didn't think the cameras mounted alongside the barrier would pick him up, unless they had infrared as well, of course, but would they really want to sit up all night watching badgers and deer scuttling across their monitors? In any case, making his way through the woods in this kind of visibility simply wasn't practical.

When the Mayview Clinic buildings came into view, a jumble of squat shapes just visible against the darker sky, Logan slowed his pace. There was a single light above the main entrance, but otherwise no signs of life. Logan wondered about Alex, waiting in her room.

He found it too unsettling to think about Lucy.

The grounds were swallowed up in darkness, but that didn't mean there weren't dogs on the loose out there, or even the goons patrolling. Not for the first time, he wondered about all the security and whether it was primarily to keep the patients in or curious interlopers like him out. Either way, he couldn't help thinking it was overkill. Certainly as far as Lucy was concerned.

So was it all for the benefit of the Mad Professor, then, Mr Herbert? Lucy had said he was good with locks. Maybe he was good with other things, too. Logan looked forward to sitting down with him and having a proper chat, just to find out who he was and what he knew that made it so important to keep him shut away from the world.

He looked at his watch. Almost 2 a.m. Any minute now.

'Silly bitch, Alex,' he said under his breath, but he couldn't help admiring her. 'You've got balls, I'll give you that.'

A few minutes later he saw it: a faint flickering behind half-drawn curtains in an upstairs window on the left side of the main building.

He found he was holding his breath.

The flicker became a glow.

Come on.

Did he see a figure moving?

She must be trying to open a window but everything was still locked down.

Come on!

The curtain had been pulled back all the way now and he could see actual flames. The figure seemed to have left the window. Maybe she was now trying the door. He imagined her banging hard with her fists, screaming at the top of her lungs. He thought about charging the entrance, furiously trying to get their attention, but he knew that would mess up everything.

There was nothing he could do but wait.

Finally he heard it.

The *whoop-whoop* of an alarm.

Thank fuck.

He sucked in a lungful of cool air.

There were shouts now, too, just audible beneath the shriek of the alarm. A light went on on the first floor, then more on the ground floor.

He breathed easier.

But he could see that Alex's room was properly ablaze now. If she was still locked in, she'd have minutes before she was overcome by the smoke and heat.

If the alarm was working, then the doors would simultaneously be automatically unlocked. That was the theory, anyway.

He saw movement at the entrance. The door swung open. One of the security guys came out, wearing a T-shirt and trackies, then stood, holding the door. A man in a towelling dressing gown followed.

The Mad Professor.

Then more figures spilled out onto the gravel drive: Dr Redwood, another woman Logan didn't recognize, then – there she was – Alex, in jeans and a grey hoodie, looking nothing like the elegant lady-out-to-lunch who had arrived a few hours earlier. The security guy with the goatee was trying to hustle her away from the building but she shook him off, looking back at the entrance. She was thinking the same thing as Logan.

Where was Lucy?

A short woman – Dr Summers, Logan guessed – came

out, and then the second security guy, the bodybuilder, looking agitated. He went straight for Dr Redwood. She followed him back into the building. The first security guy tried to herd the little group further away from the building, onto the grass. The Mad Professor seemed to take the hint, marching off towards the trees, and the security guy had to jog after him and haul him back. He spoke to Dr Summers, obviously trying to get her to take charge.

Dr Redwood came out again, followed by the bodybuilder, who had Lucy by the arm.

Logan found he was grinning like an idiot.

But would she know what to do?

The Mad Professor seemed to have the right idea though. Sow a bit of confusion. Make things difficult for the bastards. Hopefully she'd take her cue from him.

Logan looked up. There were livid flames at several windows now. Christ, it had moved quickly. Didn't they have a sprinkler system? It must have been overwhelmed. The group was huddled in a tight knot now, with Redwood and the two other doctors hanging onto the patients and the two security guys ushering the whole bunch forward, like a pair of sheepdogs.

Logan stepped onto the grass and made his way towards them. He needed them another twenty or thirty yards further into the dark, away from the building which was now emitting an orange glow which would soon be visible from miles away. If Redwood hadn't already called 999, somebody else would before long. Logan didn't know how much time he had before the fire engines arrived, but it was probably only minutes.

Logan stopped, close to a single elm, knowing he'd be invisible to the little group ahead of him so long as he stayed where he was. Now he needed someone else to make a move. Would Lucy have figured out what was going on? Surely as soon as she saw Alex, she'd know he was there too. In the confusion, Alex might even have been able to convey some hurried instructions. And what about the Mad Professor? Had Lucy told him something like this might happen and what he needed to do?

Logan could see that one of the security guards had Lucy by the arm. Dr Redwood and Dr Summers were standing side by side, looking back at the burning building, their faces lit by the flames. The other goon, the one with the goatee, was standing alongside the Mad Professor, his hands loose at his sides, obviously ready for him to try and make a break for it, while keeping a watchful eye on Alex. Logan saw Alex glance round at him. Then she turned back towards the fire and screamed.

'My dogs! My little babies! I must save them!'

For a second, Logan double took, wondering what the hell she was talking about, it was such a convincing performance.

She made a dash for the entrance to the main building. The goon keeping an eye on the Mad Professor hesitated for a split second, then lurched after her across the grass. Dr Redwood held her arms out to stop her, but Alex brushed past her. Dr Redwood shouted something at goatee guy, pointing back towards the Mad Professor, who had taken off like a hare and was now sprinting towards the trees. Goatee guy spun round and raced after him. The bodybuilder let go of Lucy as Alex went past, putting a meaty arm around her waist.

'Go!' Alex shouted.

Lucy seemed frozen to the spot. Logan resisted the urge to shout at her to move. Then she seemed to get a hold of herself and started running. Dr Redwood saw what was happening and darted after her. She quickly caught up with Lucy and grabbed her by the sleeve. Lucy gave a little yelp of surprise and Logan thought she was going to cry. But instead she pulled her other arm back and swung a wild haymaker which connected with Dr Redwood's cheekbone. She slumped to the ground with a shriek. Lucy looked at her for a moment and Logan wondered whether she was going to give her a kick for good measure, then she spun on her heel and started running again.

When he saw what was happening, the security guard who had been grappling with Alex let go. He stooped over Dr Redwood and she screamed something at him, pointing after Lucy. He started running.

Logan stepped out from behind the tree. There was a rumbling crash as something collapsed inside the building.

'Lucy!'

She stopped and looked at him, wide-eyed, her body tensed. For a moment he thought she was going to run in the opposite direction, but then she seemed to relax.

The bodybuilder was now almost on top of her.

'Run!' Logan shouted, breaking into a sprint.

The bodybuilder saw him just as he was about to grab hold of Lucy. He turned and set himself in a crouch. Logan kept going, snapping out a sharp kick to the guy's left knee, then, as he faltered, coming in for a leg sweep. Lucy had her hand to her mouth. Logan risked a glance back towards the clinic. Alex had detached herself from the group watching the fire. She ran towards them, past Dr Redwood, who was still on the ground, a hand to her cheek.

'Go with Alex!' Logan said.

Alex grabbed Lucy's arm as she flew past and the two of them stumbled towards the trees.

Logan turned back towards the bodybuilder just in time to receive a crashing blow to the temple. He staggered back, unable to focus for a second, then collapsed sideways as a boot slammed into his ribs. His fingers clawed the grass as he tried to get enough purchase to push himself out of the way of the next blow but he was too slow and the next one doubled him up as he took a kick in the stomach and all the air was forced out of his lungs. He slumped back onto the spongy ground, trying to get some part of his body to work. He managed to get one forearm across his head, thinking that would be the next target.

He heard a wet crunch and a sharp cry. He twisted his neck around and opened an eye. The Mad Professor was standing over the bodybuilder, holding a thick branch in one hand. Logan took a noisy breath.

'Take your time, young man,' the Mad Professor said, putting a hand on his shoulder.

'We don't . . . have any time,' Logan wheezed. He pulled himself upright. 'Where's the other . . .'

'I lost him in the woods,' the Mad Professor said. He grinned. 'It wasn't hard. They're really not terribly intelligent, the pair of them. I saw Miss Fitzroy, and another lady,' he added.

'Yes, we're going to join them,' Logan said.

'Very good,' said the Mad Professor, dropping the branch on the grass.

Logan grabbed the sleeve of his dressing gown. 'Come on.'

The Mad Professor nodded and smiled, and then suddenly his whole body jerked like a puppet as something seemed to slap him hard on the shoulder. As he started falling to the ground, Logan heard the crack of a rifle.

'Oh dear,' the Mad Professor said as blood bubbled over his lips and down his chin, spattering the front of his dressing gown. He gripped Logan's arm fiercely. 'Mozart . . . number three . . . adagio.'

Logan put his arms under him, trying to sit him up. 'Do you think you can . . .'

The Mad Professor shook his head, blood seeping through gritted teeth. 'You . . . go.' He fell back. Logan heard the crack of another round, and the air around him seemed to vibrate.

He scrambled to his feet and started running for the trees, back the way he'd come.

He heard a siren, faint but unmistakeable. Had Alex and Lucy made it to the car? He hit the tarmacked road and kept running, arms pumping and lungs burning. He didn't hear the sound of an engine in pursuit. They must have heard the sirens, too. Or maybe all they cared about was the Mad Professor. He got to the main road and swerved left. He slowed to a jog, breathing in hard, shallow gasps. He saw the headlights of a car accelerating out of the darkness towards him. He threw himself into the ditch as the car screeched to a stop and the passenger door flung open.

'Get in!' Alex shouted.

He got to his knees, then to his feet and fell into the car, pulling the door shut after him as Alex accelerated away. Lucy turned to him from the front passenger seat. Wild strands of hair half-covered her face. She pushed them away.

'Where's Mr Herbert?'

Logan closed his eyes and took a breath.

'I'm sorry,' he said.

'What happened? Are you OK?' Alex said over her shoulder.

'I got in a scrap with one of the goons,' Logan said. 'I was down and out, to be honest. The Mad Prof . . . Mr Herbert, turned up and whacked him. He'd lost his marker and doubled back. If it hadn't been for him . . .'

There were tears coursing down Lucy's cheeks. 'I'm so . . . glad you're . . . safe,' she said between sobs. 'But how did he . . . ?'

'They shot him,' Logan said simply.

She put her hand to her mouth. 'Oh my God.'

'Whatever it was he knew, I guess they couldn't afford for it to get out. I'm sorry,' Logan said again.

They drove on. Alex eased her foot off the accelerator a little, now it was clear they weren't being followed.

'We got you out,' Alex said, glancing over at Lucy. 'That's what matters. But we need to find out what the hell was going on in there.'

Logan twisted painfully in his seat to look out of the rear window. He saw a cluster of flashing lights winking out as they turned off the main road towards the clinic.

'Going to be hard to find out now,' he grunted.

'What do you mean?' Alex said.

'I don't reckon there'll be much left by the time they get the fire out. If there was a paper trail, it'll be up in smoke by now.'

Lucy reached her hand between the seats and Logan took it. He could feel her whole body shaking. He wrapped her hand in both of his.

'It's all right,' he said. 'It's all right. You're safe now.'

35

Lucy had briefly fallen asleep in the car, but after a few minutes she'd shaken herself awake with a cry, and spent the rest of the journey staring fixedly through the windscreen. She was still groggy as they took her up to the penthouse. Logan had covered up the damage as best he could, but he needn't have bothered: Lucy was in no state to notice. There was so much he needed to explain, and he still wasn't sure how to do it, or even how to begin. He got a blanket from the airing cupboard and settled her on the sofa while Alex made some tea.

'Do you want to sleep?' Logan asked.

'No,' she said, quickly shaking her head. 'If I go to sleep I'll have the dream – the nightmare.'

'We'll be here,' Logan said.

Alex put three mugs down on the coffee table and sat down in the armchair opposite.

Lucy shook her head again. 'No. Thank you. I'll be all right.'

'Are you OK to talk?' Logan said. Her face was like porcelain, marred only by the dark circles under her eyes.

'Yes. I want to talk.' She picked up one of the mugs, cradling it in both hands. 'I haven't been able to talk, really talk, for a long time. Not to someone who wasn't trying to . . . who I could trust. There was Mr Herbert, of course. You know, at first I thought he was a fake – a plant. That he'd get me talking and I'd tell him things – I don't even know what, or why they'd bother, but . . .' She shook her head. 'The things you end up thinking . . . Anyway, he wasn't, of course. He was like me, someone who'd been put in there – they were doing something to him, trying to do something. He was a very sweet man, I think.' She screwed her eyes shut, fighting off tears. 'Do you think he's dead?'

'I can't be certain, but yes, I think so,' Logan said. 'I'm sorry.' He didn't add that they'd probably dragged him into the trees before the fire engines arrived. Then they'd bury him there.

'No, no, you did everything you could,' Lucy said. 'You almost got yourself killed. If it wasn't for you, both of you . . .' She trailed off. 'They're monsters. *Monsters*. Dr Summers, she sometimes seemed, I don't know, uncomfortable with it all. Perhaps she had a conscience after all. Quigley always looked nervous, too. But Dr Redwood . . . I didn't used to know what the word meant, but she's evil.'

'You gave her a good whack, anyway,' Alex said. 'Put her right on her arse.'

Lucy looked astonished. 'Did I? I don't think I've ever hit anybody.'

She suddenly looked very tired.

'Are you sure you don't want to rest?' Logan asked.

'No,' she said firmly, putting her mug down and sitting up straighter. 'I want to talk. I've done enough sleeping. They always gave me something to make me sleep after the sessions – the therapy, or whatever they called it. I think that's how they put their ideas, their . . . I don't know . . . in my head.'

Logan nodded. 'That's what we need to talk about. What's real and what isn't.'

'Yes,' she said. But Logan could sense the fear lurking beneath the simple word. She knew the truth might be as frightening as the delusions. He felt suddenly way out of his depth, as if he was about to attempt an amputation with a kitchen knife and no anaesthetic, and no real idea what he was doing. He glanced over at Alex and she gave him an almost imperceptible nod. He turned back to Lucy. She was very pale, but her eyes were shining.

I hope you're strong enough for this, he thought.

'We think we might know why you were kept in there – in the clinic. What they were doing,' he said.

Lucy clutched at her dressing gown, pulling it tighter round her chest. 'Go on.'

Logan hesitated.

'Your father,' Alex said.

Lucy put a hand to her mouth. 'Has he been found? Is he all right? They didn't harm him?'

'We think your father's dead,' Logan said.

'Oh,' she said. The brightness in her eyes dimmed.

'We think that's how this whole thing started,' Alex said.

'I don't understand.'

'Do you know what's in your father's will?' Logan said.

'No. I mean, I assume he left everything equally to me and Ursula.'

'No. He didn't,' Logan said. 'He left everything to you.'

She looked shocked. 'How do you know that?'

'It wasn't hard,' Logan said, simply. Lucy looked at him as if she knew this was just the tip of a huge, dangerous iceberg: everything Logan hadn't told her about his life.

'But what's that got to do with what happened to me?' she said.

'It was Ursula,' Alex said.

Lucy flinched, but didn't say anything.

Logan felt as if he was about to plunge a knife into an open wound, but he knew they had no choice. He just hoped Lucy would be able to handle the pain.

'Do you remember what happened when your sister Deborah died?' Alex said.

'Of course, I do,' Lucy said, a hint of anger as well as confusion in her voice now. 'First you say it all started with my father, then Ursula – and now you're talking about Deborah. You're not making any sense.'

Logan reached out and took her hand. 'There's no easy way to say this. But this is what we think happened. Deborah's death wasn't an accident. Or not completely. Maybe Ursula planned it – maybe she just saw an opportunity and took it. But she pushed Deborah off that roof.'

Lucy gasped and pulled her hand away. 'No!'

Logan ploughed on. 'Your father knew – or at least suspected. Which is why he cut Ursula out of his will. She must have found out somehow.'

Alex sensed him hesitate and took up the baton. 'So then she needed to find a way of making sure the money went to her and not you.'

They waited, watching Lucy process it all.

'But my father was just missing. Nobody was getting any money.'

'Ursula was pressuring the courts to have him declared dead.'

'And then . . . what? She had me put in a private loony bin? But that was because of what happened to . . . because of the accident. I had a breakdown.'

'What do you remember before Ursula had you admitted to the Mayview? About your breakdown.'

Lucy frowned. 'It's . . . foggy. I don't remember anything, really. Look, what's this got to do with Ursula getting the money?'

'When you got out of the clinic – when you suddenly found all the doors were unlocked and nobody was there. You got back to your house and you found all traces of your family were gone. That's what you told me, right?' Alex said.

Lucy nodded, her face ashen.

'And then you tried to kill yourself.'

'Yes.' A whisper.

'Ursula didn't just need you out of the way,' Logan said,

knowing he was about to plunge the knife right to the bone. 'She needed you dead.'

'The family you remembered having, the accident, it was all a fantasy,' Alex said. 'Pargeter was your married name, wasn't it? But there's no record of a Lucy Jane Pargeter ever existing. That's why there was nothing at the house. There never had been. Dr Redwood implanted the false memories into your brain, then let you go back home, knowing what you'd find. She kept telling you that you were a suicide risk. She was putting that idea in your head, too. That's why the memories are fading. They're not real.'

Lucy leaned forward to pick up her mug. Her hand was shaking. She took two big gulps and put it down again.

'You're telling me that my sister paid Dr Redwood to drive me insane? To make me kill myself? So she'd get everything. *Ursula. My twin.*'

She gave Logan a hard look, a look he'd never seen before.

'I'm sorry,' she said, her expression softening. 'It feels like a lot of people have been messing with my head for a long time. Trying to make me believe things that aren't true. You saved my life. And you rescued me from that place. But all this about Ursula, it's just another . . . I don't believe it.'

Logan exchanged a glance with Alex. He didn't know what to do. How do you convince someone that their identical twin, the person who felt the most like themselves, their carbon copy, had deliberately sent them mad and tried to kill them? And in the end, what evidence of all that craziness did they actually have?

He got up and walked slowly to the window. The pain from the kicks to his ribs suddenly flared up and his whole body felt as if it might seize up. Maybe they should leave it for now. Lucy would crash soon, and they could start again in the morning. Maybe in the cold light of day it would all seem clearer.

Something changed in Lucy's expression. She opened her mouth, then closed it again.

'The dream,' she said.

Logan turned away from the window. Alex got up from the chair and went and sat down on the couch. She put a hand lightly on Lucy's forearm.

'What about the dream?'

Lucy took a deep breath. 'We're sitting down to dinner, in the old house. The whole family. Me, Ursula, Deborah and our father. Sometimes Dr Redwood's there, but not always. The main thing is the family.'

'And what happens?'

Lucy started to speak but her words got caught in her throat. 'I'm . . . sorry.'

'It's OK,' Alex said. 'I know this must be terrible for you. But maybe talking about it will help.'

Lucy looked at her as if she'd heard that sort of thing before.

'There are two parts. In the first part, my . . .' She choked out a sob, then recovered herself. 'My family – my *made-up* family – are there, and my father asks me to introduce them, and I can't because I don't remember their names.' She let out a brittle laugh. 'I can't remember them now, either. And then because I can't remember their names they disappear, as if my memory was the only thing that made them exist. Which I suppose, when you think about it, was true. Isn't that funny?'

'And what about the second part?' Alex said. She held on to Lucy's arm a little more tightly, as if she was afraid she might break into pieces at any moment.

'It sounds silly, when you say it. But believe me, it doesn't feel silly. It feels terrifying. My father is attacked by a bear. Oh, Ursula always asks to be excused first, and my father says no, and *then* this huge bear comes into the room and just . . . It's horrible.'

Figuring out the meaning of dreams was definitely above Logan's pay grade. But Alex was nodding, as if it all made perfect sense. He just hoped she knew what she was doing.

'Did you do Latin at school?' Alex said.

What? Now Logan really was confused.

But Lucy seemed to think it was a perfectly normal question. 'I did, yes. Daddy insisted. Good training for the mind and all that. I didn't much like it, though.'

'But you remember it, don't you?'

'What do you mean?'

'*Ursus*,' Alex said.

Logan saw something change in Lucy's expression.

'It's Latin for bear, isn't it?'

Alex nodded. 'Like Ursa Major, the constellation. That's what made me think of it.'

'And like Ursula.'

'Yes.'

'So you think in my dream, the bear is Ursula. It's really Ursula who kills my father.'

'Yes. I think you knew it all along, but you couldn't admit it to yourself. It would have been too painful. You couldn't face the thought that your twin sister had done such an awful thing. So you disguised the truth in a dream.'

'My God.'

'I think there's more.'

'Christ – isn't that enough?'

'Before the bear appears, you said Ursula asks to be excused, and your father says no.'

'That's right.'

'I think she's asking to be forgiven. For murdering Deborah. So your father won't cut her out of his will. But he says no.'

'And so she kills him.'

'Yes.'

'What a story,' Lucy said, shaking her head.

'One you've been telling yourself every night since you first put the pieces together.'

'And I knew about Deborah, too, then? All these years and I never thought . . .'

'You must have at least suspected. But again, the truth was too painful.'

'Well.' Lucy pulled a tissue out of the pocket of her dressing gown and blew her nose, then dabbed at her eyes. 'I feel I've lost two families now. My husband and children who never existed, and my sister – my lovely, caring, kind sister – who turns out to be a beast.'

'I'm sorry,' Alex said.

'You know, I do suddenly feel very tired. I'd like to go to sleep.'

'I don't think you'll have the dream again,' Alex said.

'No. I don't think I will. But maybe the reality's worse.'

She got up and pulled Alex in for a hug.

'Thank you.'

'I'll show you the bedroom,' Logan said. 'If you do wake up, Alex and me will be here.'

'That's good,' she said, reaching up to touch his cheek.

She settled in the middle of the bed, pulled the duvet around her and closed her eyes with a long sigh. Logan watched her as her breathing got deeper and she slowly curled into a foetal position.

The last thing she said before she went to sleep was: 'I'm glad you're here, Logan. I don't want to wake up and find you were a dream, too.'

He didn't know what to say to that, so he just leaned over her, kissed her lightly on the forehead and walked out.

Alex was sitting at the kitchen island with two open bottles of beer in front of her. Logan came and sat down on the other side. They picked up their beers and drank.

'Nice black eye you're going to have,' she said, gesturing with the bottle.

Logan touched his cheekbone. 'Yeah. I messed up there.'

Alex shrugged. 'We got Lucy out. The Mad Professor would have been a bonus.'

'You took a bloody risk setting fire to your room with the door locked,' Logan said.

'I was pissing myself, if you want to know,' Alex said.

'Those fucking people,' Logan said. 'I should have barricaded them inside and then set fire to the place.'

Alex took another drink. 'She OK in there?'

'Sleeping like a baby,' Logan said. 'For now, anyway.'

'I think she'll be OK,' Alex said. 'Now Redwood can't do anything to her.'

'How can you be so sure?' Logan said. 'Redwood was still giving her "therapy". Christ knows what crap she was putting into her mind. I mean, you did a cracking job with that dream interpretation stuff, but I reckon she needs professional help.'

'Right now she needs rest and a bit of TLC,' Alex said. 'She needs you.'

Logan took another slug of his beer. He wiped his mouth with the back of his hand.

'But I can't be with her 24/7. We've got the meet with Tenniel.'

'He hasn't set that up yet.'

'Which means we don't know where, we don't know when . . . we don't know anything. We haven't figured out yet how we're going to nail him.'

'We will. And Lucy will be safe here.'

'She's not going to feel very safe when she discovers the blood on the carpet and the bullet holes in the wall.'

'I think so long as nobody's trying to brainwash her, she'll be fine.'

Alex drained the last of the bottle.

'You look fucked. Go and get some kip. If Lucy wakes up, I'll give you a shake.'

'Just a quick nap. Twenty minutes.'

'Sure.' Alex went over to the fridge. 'I'm going to have another beer.'

Logan went and lay down on the sofa. By the time Alex turned round with a bottle in her hand, he was asleep.

36

Tenniel sat in an unmarked car and watched the rain coming down in the halo of the streetlights. Normally rain, at night, calmed him. But not tonight. Tonight he could feel his heart in his chest, could hear his breath, quick and shallow. He was glad he was alone in the car.

It was a risk, of course. He'd taken a gamble. But his career was built on gambles and so far they'd all paid off. The trouble was, the higher up you got, the bigger the gambles you had to take, and the more damaging the consequences if they didn't pay off. If this one turned sour, he thought he'd probably survive, but it definitely wouldn't look good. He could forget about a commendation, anyway, let alone a promotion. He'd have to re-group, think again. Two steps forward, one step back. But he was impatient: if he had a fault, he knew that was it. He wanted it all now. Though it could be a virtue too: while others hung back, he'd be pushing to the front, where he'd be in the spotlight.

He was in the spotlight now. Or, at least, he would be in the morning, when the operation was finished, win or bust, and the reports were all on the Chief Super's desk. He imagined standing in front of that desk, loosely at attention, eyes front, chin thrust forward, while the Chief Super turned the last page, preparing himself for what was to come: either, 'John, take a seat,' and the bottle of single malt coming out of the bottom drawer, along with a pair of Waterford crystal glasses, or the more formal, 'Detective Inspective Tenniel,' and an invitation to explain exactly how the events of the previous night had unfolded.

He thought about the other teams, all in position, waiting for Terry Mason's trucks to reach their final destinations. He'd pushed hard for the maximum manpower, and the Chief Super had reluctantly agreed, muttering darkly about budgets and cutbacks, even though he knew that was just for show.

Mason was a risk-taker too, by definition, but conservative with it. If he couldn't fix the odds, he preferred not to put too many chips on the table. No doubt he thought he'd fixed the odds tonight, and the big show Tenniel intended to put on for him, with plenty of uniforms and blue lights flashing, was intended to make him think he'd scooped the table as a result.

But the real winner would be decided here, in this narrow alley facing a row of dingy lock-ups. At least that's what Tenniel was gambling on. And he'd gone all in. He looked at his watch. 2 a.m. There was no knowing when each of Mason's trucks would arrive at their destinations, to be greeted by a surprise welcoming party dressed in blue. There had been six of them on the ferry, and they'd joined the M25 in a loose convoy around midnight, gradually peeling off at successive junctions. Surely the first one would arrive soon. Tenniel glanced down at the two-way radio on the passenger seat, waiting for the signal that the curtain had gone up. The voice on the other end would be controlled, professional, but with *that unmistakeable undercurrent of excitement. Then, a few minutes later, would come a second message – less excited, more downbeat, the voice now trying to conceal the speaker's frustration and disappointment.*

'*Nothing, Guv. Just what's on the manifest.*'

'*You're sure?*'

'*We've turned it inside out.*'

'*Well, good job anyway. Let's see what's in the other trucks.*'

But the other trucks would be the same. No huddled, tearful girls, dizzy with cold and thirst and fear, in among the legitimate cargo of building supplies and machine parts. Not even a crate or two of contraband cigarettes. Nothing illegal at all, in fact. Everything exactly as stated on the paperwork.

Which told you that the trucks, every single one, were a decoy. They were too squeaky clean not to be. Mason knew his operation had been targeted by Serious Crimes, and he walked into the trap with open eyes and a big happy grin on his face. 'People trafficking? Me? Someone's been giving you duff information, Detective Inspector. I'll bet it was that bastard Nicky Cross. He's been trying to put me out of business for years. Better luck next time, eh – oh, and you can expect a call from my lawyer. This is harassment, plain and simple.'

Mason would enjoy that. But Tenniel was betting it wouldn't be enough. The fake busts didn't just represent a bullet dodged: they were an opportunity. And Mason would be a fool if he didn't take it. Because while all eyes were on the trucks, no one would be looking while he brought something else in through the back door.

And that was what Tenniel was banking on.

At 2.23 a.m. news of the first truck's arrival came in over the radio. Commiserations all round. Then ten minutes later another one. Same story. Tenniel found it hard to maintain his air of stoic acceptance as he kept watch on the end of the alley and his anticipation mounted. He was tempted to turn the damn thing off, telling himself that it might give him away, but he knew he had to keep up the charade to the end. It was a small price to pay, after all.

If it all worked out as planned. If he'd correctly predicted how Terry Mason's mind worked.

At 2.37 a.m. he reached into his pocket for a pack of cigarettes that hadn't been there for eighteen months, then, frowning, unwrapped a stick of chewing gum from the packet on the passenger seat instead. As he started to chew, he heard the low growl of a diesel engine and then headlights swept across the end of the alley. He stopped chewing, staying motionless in his seat. A dark van passed slowly in front of him. He waited. The engine stopped and he heard a door open, then a voice, urgent but hushed. He turned the key in the ignition, flicked his headlights onto full beam and put his foot down. He shot out of the end of the alley then braked sharply, flung open the door and jumped out, pulling out his Glock from its holster as he did so. To his left, the van was now blocked into the little courtyard. Two men were at the back door. They turned towards Tenniel, shielding their eyes from the glare of his headlights. He pointed the Glock at them, holding his warrant card up in his other hand.

'Stop! Armed police!' he shouted.

One of the men froze, his hand on the door. The other bolted, dodging past Tenniel's car and swerving into the alley. Tenniel let him go, advancing slowly towards the van.

'Open it!' he barked.

The man opened one door and then the other.

'On the ground! Now!' Tenniel shouted.

The man got to his knees, then put his hands on the tarmac and lay down with his head twisted to the side and his arms splayed out. Tenniel put his warrant card in his pocket, crouched down and checked him over for weapons with his free hand.

'Stay there!'

Keeping his weapon pointed at the man on the ground, he looked into the van. He saw the reflections of a dozen pairs of eyes staring back.

'It's OK. I'm a police officer. You're safe now,' he said.

He reached into the car for the radio.

'Echo Delta One Nine, request backup. Constance Towers Estate, the lock-ups at the end of Fuller Close. One suspect and between ten and twenty trafficked females. Affirmative: transport, medical, the lot.'

He listened for a moment, then put the radio back on the seat, keeping his eyes on the van.

ETA two minutes.

He took a step nearer to the van. He could see them more clearly now, more of them than he'd first thought, sitting or lying together on what looked like a layer of sacking on the floor of the van.

'Does anyone speak English?'

There was a quick exchange of words in a language he didn't recognize.

'Yes,' came a hesitant voice. It sounded like a young girl.

'Does anyone require medical treatment? Is anyone hurt?'

Another flurry of urgent whispers.

'We are OK,' the girl said.

'Good. I need you to stay where you are just for one minute. More policemen are coming. And paramedics. They will look after you.'

He heard a shuffling from inside the van as one of the girls rose to her feet and moved forward.

'Just stay where you are,' he said again, holding his hand up like a traffic policeman.

He heard engines now and headlights suddenly raked the row of lock-ups. He lowered his hand and turned towards the sound. There was a flash of movement in his peripheral vision. Then he saw the man on the ground scramble to his feet. Tenniel slipped his gun back into his shoulder rig, grabbed the man by the front of his hoodie and swept his feet out from under him, spinning him onto his front, then kneeling on his back as he got hold of a wrist and twisted the man's arm behind him.

He heard voices and the crunch of boots.

'We've got him, sir.'

He let go of the man's wrist and stood up. Uniforms were helping the girls out of the van and leading them towards the alley where two police minibuses were parked nose to tail. Beyond them, Tenniel could see two squad cars and an ambulance.

He leaned against the car. The two-way was squawking, but he ignored it. He pulled his phone out of his pocket and hit a number on his speed dial.

'Sir? DI Tenniel. I think we've hit the jackpot.'

He explained what had just happened, then stood for a few moments, nodding and listening.

'Thank you, sir. Yes, well, I suppose it was a gamble, but it seems to have paid off. Yes, sir, nine o'clock. And to you, sir. Good night.'

He put the phone back in his pocket.

The minivans had gone, along with the ambulance and one of the squad cars.

A uniformed sergeant came up to him. 'Do you need anything, sir?'

'No, thank you, Sergeant. I'm fine.'

The sergeant nodded. 'Crime scene boys are on the way, sir. I'll secure the van until they get here.'

Tenniel nodded. 'I'll head off, then. Good night's work, by the way.'

He turned and got into the car. He took his gun out of its holster and put it in the glove compartment, then switched off the two-way. Again, he felt how good it would be to have a smoke. In the old days, the boss would have broken out the cigars, along with the Scotch, once the team was back together in the squad room, but he knew by tomorrow the craving would have passed. And in any case, this was a private moment: his own little celebration. He'd done this alone. If they'd come up empty-handed, he would have carried the can. But now that his plan seemed to have worked, he could take all the credit.

He did a three-point turn and headed slowly back down the alley. As he eased past the squad car, he touched a finger to his forehead in salute.

Back on the main road, he seemed to have the city to himself, in that window between the last Uber call-outs and the first appearance of the big rigs heading for the ports. He drove for a while, enjoying the emptiness, finally letting go of the tension and letting his mind wander.

He stopped at a set of lights and glanced in his rear-view.

A pair of dark eyes under a ragged fringe looked back.

The lights changed and a car hooted at him as it accelerated past on the inside lane.

He turned to look at her properly. Her eyes were very dark, almost black, but there was a light in them which glittered in the dim light. Her face was wide, with prominent cheekbones, and a pointed chin. Her mouth was small and she seemed to be pressing her lips together, which accentuated the effect.

He guessed she was about fifteen, but her voice when she spoke sounded older.

'I need you to help me,' she said.

37

Logan was watching Lucy sleep when the call from Charlie Stones came in. As his phone buzzed on the arm of the chair, he knew he had to take it, but it was a wrench to leave Lucy's side. He'd been enjoying just looking at her face and listening to her rhythmical breathing and detecting no sign behind her pale eyelids of any bad dreams. Maybe, he thought, just maybe, things would be all right.

He took the phone into the kitchen.

'Logan.'

'He got back to me.'

'OK.'

'He says he has the money.'

'That's good. What else did he say?'

'He seemed calm. You know – not flipping out. Like he was pleased I'd found what he wanted, even though I was trying to take him for more money. I don't think the money matters to him.'

Logan thought that was probably because he had no intention of actually giving her any: the logical thing would be to throw her in the boot of his car, torture her until he could be sure she hadn't made any copies, and kill her. He kept the thought to himself.

'Where does he want to meet?'

'He gave me a time, that's all. Half past midnight. He'll call again an hour before the meeting. He said that'll give me plenty of time to get there.'

Smart, Logan thought. No time to plan.

'OK. You call me as soon as he's given you the location. I'll pick you up and we'll take it from there. If I don't like the look of it, we'll walk away. I'm not going to put you in danger.'

'OK.'

She didn't sound convinced.

'Look, he'll think it's just you, and he won't want witnesses, so he'll come alone. But you'll have a team behind you. Do you understand?'

'Yes. OK.'

He ended the call and put the phone in his pocket.

Alex was leaning against the kitchen island with her arms folded. 'You reckon she believed you?'

Logan shrugged. 'I don't know.'

'We need to report back to Mrs Allenby.'

Logan chewed his lip. 'She'll want a meeting. Go through the options. One of which will be: don't accept his terms. Negotiate. Find a location that we can properly secure and get Charlie to tell him it has to be there or the deal's off.'

'Maybe,' Alex said. 'But you can persuade her. Just tell

her the most important thing is that he feels he's in control. His plan. His territory. Then he might relax and get careless.'

'I can't risk it.'

'What do you mean?'

'Leaving Lucy.'

'She'll be safe here.'

'That's not what I mean. What if she, I don't know – has a breakdown. I don't want her to be alone.'

'We're going to have to leave her tonight.'

'I know. But I want to stay with her for as long as possible. I want to make sure she's OK.'

'And if she isn't? I'll be honest: I don't fancy going up against Tenniel on my own.'

'Don't be daft. This is what we've been working towards for so long. The bastard has given us a window. We have to take it.'

'Even if you don't feel Lucy's . . . in a good enough state?'

Logan shook his head. 'Fuck. I don't know.'

'Look, we'll see how today goes. In the meantime, try and come up with some options of our own to deal with Tenniel.'

'And Mrs Allenby?'

'Assuming Tenniel calls Charlie at 11.30 to confirm the meet, we tell Mrs Allenby that's the first contact. Before that, we didn't know anything. She'll have no choice but to let us get on with it, play it as it lays.'

'OK.'

They heard a noise from the bedroom.

Logan quickly turned.

'Lucy?'

38

She hadn't said anything more on the drive back to Tenniel's house. But every time he looked in the mirror, she met his glance and spoke to him with her eyes.

Help me.

He drove in a daze, not thinking, not even knowing where he was going until he found himself pulling up in the drive. He got out and opened her door and after a moment she climbed out, stumbling a little before finding her balance. She was wearing jeans and tracksuit top over a tank top and in the faint glow of the streetlights she looked gaunt. He wondered when she'd last eaten.

Tenniel looked around. There were no lights on in the houses on either side. He got out his key and opened the door.

He knew as soon as she was inside, he was lost.

He led her to the kitchen, turning on lights as he went.

He got a pint glass out of the cupboard over the sink and filled it from the tap.

'You must be thirsty,' he said, holding it out to her. They were the first words he had spoken.

She smiled, as if there was something funny or odd in his voice, then took the glass and drank. She put the glass down on the counter.

'Do you want anything to eat? I could make you a sandwich,' he said.

'No. Thank you,' she said. Tenniel saw she had a little gap between her front teeth. She looked around her and her eyes alighted on a photograph in a silver frame on the windowsill.

She walked over and leaned down to look closely without touching it.

'This is your daughter?'

Tenniel found he couldn't speak.

He nodded.

'She is very pretty,' she said, standing back.

Like you, he almost said.

She turned and looked at him, and he suddenly had the absurd idea that she knew everything about him. All his secrets.

'I must sleep now,' she said.

'Yes,' he said.

39

'You're like a parent with their first baby!' Alex said. 'Not that I'd know,' she added quickly. 'But you know what I mean: every little sniffle and you rush upstairs to make sure they're still breathing.'

She grinned. Lucy, sitting on the sofa, wrapped in a dressing gown, was smiling too, and Logan, sitting opposite, was trying not to. Alex had never seen him like this. She suddenly thought how lucky Lucy was, despite all the terrible things she'd gone through, to have someone love her that much, and felt tears welling up. She pulled a tissue out of her pocket and noisily blew her nose.

'No dreams, then?' Logan said.

Lucy shook her head. 'First time in . . . I don't even know. I can't remember. Anyway, it was lovely.'

She was holding a glass paperweight in her hand. It was round with a small blue flower inside it. Since she'd found it on one of the bedside tables when she'd woken up, she hadn't let go of it. When she wasn't clutching it tightly in her hand, she was holding it up to her face, squinting at the little flower encased in its protective glass.

She took a sip of peppermint tea and put her mug down on the coffee table. She brushed her hair away from her face.

'What's going to happen to Ursula?'

Logan winced.

'It's OK,' Lucy said, catching his expression. 'Talking about her isn't going to send me doolally.'

From the other end of the sofa, Alex gave her an encouraging smile.

'It's up to you,' Logan said. 'I mean, you could go to the police. Tell them everything. How she killed Deborah, and then your father cut her out of the will. Then she killed him, and put you in the Mayview, so you'd . . .'

'So I'd kill myself and then she'd inherit.'

'Yeah, that about sums it up.'

Lucy thought for a moment. 'You know, I think if I turned up at a police station and told them all that, they'd probably think I was mad. They'd send me straight back to the Mayview. Well, OK, you burned it down, but somewhere else; the nearest available loony bin.'

'It's a lot to swallow in one go,' Logan admitted. 'But once they start investigating . . .'

'But what are they going to find? My father's still officially a missing person. Unless they have a . . . body, what can they do? And Deborah was so long ago. I've been thinking about it: if you look at it from the police's point of view, I'm not exactly the most reliable of witnesses, am I? And what actual evidence do I have? *A dream*. A dream about a sodding bear.'

'You're right,' Alex said. 'Unless you're lucky enough to find a copper who buys into it all from the get-go, it could get pretty unpleasant. Especially when the lawyers get involved.'

'Plus,' Lucy said, glancing at them both, 'I could hardly tell them the whole story without getting you two mixed up in it, could I? And I have a feeling you'd rather I didn't do that.'

They didn't have anything to say to that.

'We can't just let her get away with it,' Logan said finally.

Lucy took another sip of tea. 'I'm not sure I really care. Anyway, she hasn't, has she? I mean, they'll have to declare my father dead at some point, and then I inherit everything. Not that I want a penny of it. But she'll have lost. Everything she's done – it'll all have been for nothing.' She gave a little shrug. 'Maybe that's the best revenge.'

Logan looked uneasy. 'You're forgetting: she's the mad one, not you. I don't think you're safe while she's still around. We know what she's capable of. She might do anything.'

Lucy frowned. 'I'm more worried about that . . . Dr Redwood.'

'She can't do anything to you now,' Logan said.

'No, but I mean: what could she do to other people? What if she sets up somewhere else? I'm glad that place burned to the ground, really I am, but if there was evidence of what was going on there – well, it's all gone, hasn't it?'

'There's you,' Alex said.

'But as we've already established,' Lucy said, 'I'm not a

very reliable witness. I hallucinated a whole family that doesn't exist. Why believe anything I said about Dr Redwood?'

She closed her eyes and put her palms against her temples as if she was trying to stop her head from splitting open.

'Dr Redwood's—' Logan began.

Alex shot him a warning look.

'Let's not talk about her any more,' she said.

'This sounds ridiculous,' Lucy said, not taking her hands from her face, 'but I think I might have to go back to bed.'

40

*Her name was Katya, and she said she was afraid they were going
to kill her. He asked why she thought the police couldn't protect
her – even though it was too late for that now – and she looked
at him as if he was stupid, just the way his daughter used to, on
the rare occasions they had an actual conversation. It was clear
that where she came from, in Bulgaria, the dividing line between
the police and the gangs was blurred, to say the least. So he told
her what she wanted to hear: that she could stay and he would
protect her, and instead of bursting into grateful tears she had
nodded in a business-like way and said that it would be good for
both of them. 'Because you are lonely, I think,' she had said, fixing
him with those dark eyes again. And so she had stayed. She had
become his secret. And it was true, he did feel less lonely with her
there. For the first time in his career he would find himself watching
the clock as the afternoon wore on. He would still wait an hour,
sometimes longer if he could bear to, until the true nine-to-fivers
had all gone and even the young and hungry ones were beginning
to thin out, reckoning they'd put in enough conspicuous desk-time
to attract the notice of the boss. And then he would leave, trying
his best to look unhurried, as if he had an unavoidable appointment*

he wasn't looking forward to. But as soon as he was in the car, his heart would be hammering in his chest. And then he would pull up at the house and pause for a few moments before getting out, wondering what the hell he was doing and how it was all going to end. And then he would open the door and walk past the kitchen and into the living room where she would be sitting on the sofa with her legs curled under her liked a cat, watching TV with the curtains closed. And then she would look at him, and it would be like the first time, in the car, and it would all begin again.

When he'd found the phone, three weeks later, and seen what was on it, it was almost a relief.

41

Lucy woke up again in the late afternoon, but it wasn't like the morning. She seemed groggy, disoriented, and when Logan asked her how she was feeling, she looked at him oddly, almost as if she didn't recognize him, before things clicked into place and she said, 'Fine. Better. Just hungry.'

Logan thought that was a good sign.

'I'll make you some breakfast. Lunch. Whatever you want.'

He knew he was rambling.

She followed him into the kitchen and started opening cupboards.

'Do you ever do any actual cooking?' she asked.

'Not really,' he said. 'I could go out and get something. What do you fancy?'

'I don't want you going out,' she said. She had a tin of something in her hand. 'Soup. Perfect. Bread? Even you must have a loaf of bread.'

'Somewhere,' he said. 'It's either in the fridge or—'

'The bread bin? This thing?'

'Worth a try,' he said.

He felt sick. When the call came – if it came: if Tenniel

389

didn't have some other plan up his sleeve; if he wasn't already tracking Charlie down to her home address and getting ready to kill her there – then he'd have to decide. Stay or go. There were still a few hours left. If Lucy was feeling good – food would do her good, wouldn't it? – when he told her he had to go, then maybe it would be OK. He'd thought about leaving Alex and going on his own, but he needed Alex to keep Charlie onside: he'd told her there was a team – she needed to see at least one body apart from himself, and then she might even believe in the others, waiting in the shadows. And could he actually handle Tenniel on his own anyway? That depended on whether Tenniel had his own backup. Logan had told Charlie that wasn't likely but did he really believe it himself?

Fuck. Fuck. Fuck.

Lucy had found a tin-opener and a saucepan and was stirring the soup on the stove. He'd been too busy panicking to help.

'Where's Alex?' she said. 'Do you think she wants anything? What about you?'

'I'm fine.' He was hungry but he was feeling too nauseous to keep anything down. 'She's doing some sort of workout. Body-something. I think she ate earlier.'

'This place,' Lucy said, smiling. 'I mean, it's amazing, but how come you're living here? It's not yours, is it?' She stopped stirring. 'Sorry – am I allowed to ask that?'

'Yeah, yeah, that's fine,' he said. 'I'm just looking after it while the owner's away. Kind of like dog-sitting.'

'But with no dog.'

'Exactly.' He decided not to tell her about the other part of the deal: that he was supposed to be impersonating the owner so somebody would think he was still living there – somebody, he guessed, who wasn't exactly a friend.

She sat down at the kitchen island and poured soup into a bowl.

'You OK watching me eat?'

He smiled. 'I've done it before.'

She smiled back. 'Yes, you have.'

They were both thinking about the past. Suddenly it felt like what they'd had wasn't entirely lost. Maybe there *was* hope for them.

She ate in silence and he watched her.

'That's better,' she said, wiping up the last of the soup with a hunk of bread. She took the bowl and put it in the sink. 'You know what I haven't done for the longest time? Watched TV. Could we do that?'

'Sure,' he said happily. 'If I can figure out how to turn it on.'

They went into the main living area and he found the remote and pressed a few buttons and suddenly there was a programme about a couple trying to find the perfect house somewhere in the country, and they settled down on the sofa to watch. She picked up the paperweight, holding it tightly in her hand, then put her head on his shoulder and they watched the couple as they looked around inside the different houses without really listening to what they were saying about any of it and he thought: *Is this what people really do with their lives?* And then he felt bad, because watching it was what Lucy needed, and as he sat there, feeling her body's warmth as she pressed against him, he felt the beginnings of something that might have been what happiness felt like – it had been so long he wasn't sure – and he suddenly felt a rush of warmth for the couple on the programme and hoped they'd find the perfect house they were looking for and would be happy there.

He felt Lucy stirring beside him. She sat upright and gripped his hand harder.

He looked at her. Her face had gone white. Her eyes were staring.

'What is it?'

'There's some . . . something wrong,' she stammered. 'Something wrong with the houses.'

He looked at the screen. The couple were in a spacious living room with oak beams and a huge open fireplace. They were smiling, taking it all in.

'What? It's just a house.'

'They're all the same – don't you see? Can't you see it? Please, turn it off.' She covered her face with her hands.

He pressed the remote and the screen went blank.

She'd curled herself into a ball with her arms over her head. He felt helpless, confused. What was it that had spooked her? He thought about what they had seen.

Then it hit him.

In each house, whatever room they were in, there were no photographs. The personal stuff had been removed before the TV cameras arrived. So it looked like all traces of the family who lived there had been deliberately erased.

Just like Lucy's house when she had come home from the clinic.

He put his arms around her and held her tight while she sobbed.

'Is she sleeping?' Alex was waiting for Logan just outside the bedroom as he pulled the door almost closed.

'Yeah. I told her.'

'OK. How did she take it?'

'All right, I think. She said she'll be asleep so it doesn't matter. She says the nightmares have gone.'

Alex nodded. 'Look, maybe Tenniel won't call, or he'll change the meeting – who knows.'

Logan nodded. He didn't believe it, but there was no point in arguing about it.

At 11.34 Charlie called and gave them the address. Alex brought it up on her phone.

'We'll pick you up at Canning Town at 12.15, outside the station,' Logan said.

Then he called Mrs Allenby.

'Tenniel's just called back. He wants to meet at 12.30 . . . No – tonight . . . It's a construction site. Docklands . . . No, there isn't time.'

He listened for a while and then said, 'OK . . . Yes, I will . . . OK,' before ending the call.

Alex looked at him. 'What did she say?'

'Good luck,' Logan said. 'More or less.'

When they left, Lucy was still sleeping. In the car, Logan said, 'We should have given her something so she sleeps through.'

'She's had enough drugs,' Alex said.

Charlie was waiting for them, dressed in combats and a black hoodie with no make-up. She looked younger, too young to be doing what she was doing. Alex got in the back with her and introduced herself.

'We're both armed and we know what we're doing. And there's backup on the way. You've no need to worry.'

Charlie looked at her. Alex was wearing jeans and a bike jacket and her hair was tucked under a black beanie.

'OK.' She nodded.

They parked two streets away and walked through a wasteland of derelict warehouses and abandoned terraces waiting patiently for the wrecking ball, until they came to a high, chain-link fence surrounding the site. It looked like they'd managed four storeys so far, bare concrete platforms standing on four wide pillars at each corner. The top level was hidden in swathes of plastic sheeting that rippled faintly in the night air. The distant hum of traffic was the only sound.

'How do we get to the top?' Charlie asked.

'There'll be a way,' Logan said, kneeling down and feeling along the bottom edge of the fence. 'I'll go first, and Alex will cover us.'

Alex put her hand on Charlie's shoulder. 'In half an hour all your troubles will be over.'

'Foxes,' Logan said, beginning to peel a section of the fence away from a shallow trench that had been scraped out beneath it. When the gap was wide enough, Alex and Charlie squeezed through and he followed. They picked their way through a maze of breeze blocks, scaffolding poles and piles of steel rods for reinforcing concrete. At the bottom of one of the structure's concrete legs was a ladder. They began climbing.

One way up, one way down, Logan thought, not liking it. *Two ways down*, he corrected himself, liking it even less.

They paused on the first broad concrete platform. Aside from a few puddles and an explosion of feathers where a pigeon had been, it was empty. They began climbing again. The narrow steel ladder made Logan feel faintly nauseous, but he could tell from the rhythm of Charlie's steps behind him, almost nipping his heels, that the act of climbing was restoring her confidence.

When he got to the top storey Logan made Alex and Charlie wait on the ladder. He pulled the Glock from his shoulder rig and slid the safety off in a crouch, then slowly straightened, sweeping his weapon in a wide arc. He could feel the wind now, pulling at his tracksuit top. There were piles of building materials and in the middle of the platform was a jumble of large crates, half-covered by a tarpaulin. He turned and motioned the others to come up.

He walked towards the crates, the Glock held out in front of him.

A man stepped out from behind them. He was wearing a dark raincoat and his face was in shadow.

'Drop the gun.' He nodded towards Alex. 'And your friend.'

Logan kept the gun trained on him. He took a step forward.

'I said drop it,' the man said again. He didn't seem concerned that Logan was pointing a gun at him.

Logan could see his face now.

'Tenniel,' he said.

For the first time, the man seemed taken aback.

'Sorry – DCI Tenniel,' Logan said.

Tenniel smiled. 'Well,' he said. 'You've just bought yourself a few more seconds of life. Seems we need to have a conversation.' He looked over Logan's shoulder. 'Charlie, come over here.'

Charlie walked past Logan and went and stood next to Tenniel.

'Good girl,' he said.

'You're making a mistake, Charlie,' Logan said.

'Charlie's a smart girl,' Tenniel said. 'She told me all about you and your cock-and-bull story about a memory stick. You see, I know she doesn't have it. She doesn't have the balls to pull off a stunt like that.' He turned to Charlie. 'No offence.'

'Don't trust him,' Alex said.

Charlie's eyes flicked to Alex, then to Tenniel. Tenniel pulled her closer. 'Hey,' she said, putting a hand out to push him away. Then there was the muffled crack of a small-calibre round and she dropped her hand, then fell to one knee and toppled slowly onto her face. Tenniel stepped back from her body, putting his hand back in his pocket.

Logan started forward.

He heard the sound of several rounds being chambered at once and stopped.

There were four men pointing machine pistols at him, spaced in a wide semicircle at twenty-yard intervals.

'Now put the fucking guns on the floor,' Tenniel said.

Logan crouched down and laid his Glock on the concrete. He heard Alex doing the same behind him.

Tenniel walked towards them. 'On your knees, hands behind your head.'

Logan knelt and quickly felt hands patting him down. Alex knelt beside him.

'Well, well,' Tenniel said, peering at Alex. 'The elusive Danielle Hart. The plot thickens. We really are going to have to have a little chat before lights out.' He turned to Logan. 'And what about you? Mr Hart? Or do you have a real name?'

Logan tried to think up some bullshit that would buy them some time, but nothing came. All he could think of was how he'd fucked everything up and Lucy would wake up in the penthouse alone.

'Logan,' he said.

'A woman who isn't Danielle Hart and a man with no first name. It's a start, I suppose. And we have got all night, after all.' He went back to the pile of crates, pulled one free and brought it over so he could sit down. 'Right, your starter for ten: Terry Mason.'

Logan felt his mind clearing. 'Tell you what. We'll tell you everything you need to know about Terry Mason, but we want to know something first.'

Tenniel smiled. 'What?'

'What's on that memory stick that's worth killing so many people for?'

'Ah,' Tenniel said. 'So you don't know?'

'No.'

'Then why the fuck should I tell you?'

'Might help to get it off your chest.' It sounded lame, even to Logan.

Tenniel laughed. 'You know, you might have something there. My wife, God rest the silly bitch, she used to read a lot of crime novels, and then she used to bore the arse off me telling me about them. All bollocks, of course, if you've seen the real thing, but you know the bit that always used to take the fucking biscuit? Where the villain tells the cop why he did everything, just before he bites the bullet. Fucking lazy-arse writers, I thought: can't they think of any other way of doing it? But you know, the truth is, I've seen it, even with the hardcases, the career criminals, when they get in the interview room. Behind all the bravado, all they really want to do is confess.'

He stretched one of his legs out and started massaging his knee.

'All right. I'm going to tell you a story. And as it's the last one you two will ever hear, I'll try and make it a good one.'

He paused and looked past Logan and Alex, out into the

darkness. Logan thought he sounded tired – not physically tired, but tired of the story, as if all he really wanted was for it to end.

'It all began with an op to intercept Mason's fleet of trucks . . .'

Tenniel told the story simply and honestly, without emotion, as if he was talking about someone else. Up to now Tenniel had just been a name to Logan: now he began to take shape as a man – ruthless, ambitious, cunning; but with a fatal weakness at his core.

'They must have got to her somehow,' Tenniel was saying, his voice almost a whisper. 'Maybe she left the house during the day when I didn't know, and someone spotted her, then they told her to go back and pretend nothing had happened. Or maybe she'd been planning it all along. Either way, she started taking pictures, videos – some of them just her in different rooms, posing, but so you could tell where she was. And then others, of me when I was asleep . . . of the two of us together.'

'And she was sending them to Terry Mason.'

Tenniel looked up. 'That's right. The cunning little bitch.'

'So the trafficking case against Mason never made it to court.'

'Evidence goes missing. Turns out correct procedure wasn't followed. The CPS start to get cold feet. You know how it is.'

'And Terry Mason was bulletproof from then on.'

'He thought so. And he was for a while. But in the end

all he really did was sign his own death warrant. I mean, you can't let something like that stand, can you?'

'I suppose not,' Logan said.

'Right,' said Tenniel, getting to his feet with a grimace. He reached his hand into the pocket of his coat.

'Don't you want to know who we are?' Logan said.

'I've lost interest, to be honest,' Tenniel said. 'As soon as you asked me what was on the memory stick, I realized you were just fishing. You know fuck all. Mason's dead, along with that stupid girl, and you two are next. If that doesn't wrap things up, then . . . I don't know.'

'And the three A4 operatives?'

For the first time Tenniel looked genuinely surprised. 'You know about them? Maybe I've underestimated you. Mason had a lot of fancy security around his communications. For an old-fashioned East End bone-breaker, he did have some smarts. Or Stephanie did.' He smirked. 'I'm assuming you know who she is. Anyway, we couldn't break it, not a peep. So one day I had an idea and brought in a few of the heavy mob. They soon had his phone chirping like a budgie. Trouble was, they were downloading Katya's happy snaps along with everything else. I destroyed it all, obviously. And when we took Mason down, I sifted through everything we took from his place with a fine-toothed fucking comb to make sure there weren't any copies. But one thing I've learned is you can't trust those spooks. I was convinced they'd taken out insurance. And you know what? Here's the funny thing: I don't think they did. They were playing it strictly by the book. I don't think there was ever a memory stick at all.'

'So all those people needn't have died,' Logan said.

Tenniel shrugged. 'You can never be too careful, can you? It was easy enough to sic Stephanie onto them. And then get her to hire the lovely Charlie.'

He was holding the gun loosely at his side now.

'So here we are. No happy endings, I'm afraid,' he said. 'At least not for you.'

He stepped round behind them.

'Close your eyes, or not. Up to you. Who wants to go first? No takers?'

Logan had decided what he was going to do. By the time he'd got to his feet and turned towards Tenniel, Tenniel would have shot him, maybe more than once. But Alex might then have a chance of getting the gun off him and maybe if she put it to his head, the Turks with the machine pistols would back off, give her enough time to . . . she couldn't drag Tenniel with her down the ladder, she'd have to leave him . . . but if she made a dash for it . . .

He heard a shot and instantly looked round at Alex. She was white as a ghost but still kneeling, hands still on her head. Then he heard a noise from behind him like a sack of cement had just been dumped on the ground.

Somebody in the shadows shouted something in a language he didn't understand. There was more shouting. Then he heard footsteps on the concrete. Logan lowered his hands and looked round. O'Dwyer was advancing towards them, his hands held out to his sides to show he didn't have a weapon.

'Pick those up,' he said, pointing to their guns. 'But don't point them at anybody.' His voice had a parade-ground bark.

Logan picked up his Glock, keeping a wary eye on the men with the machine pistols. Reluctantly, he slid it back into his shoulder rig, knowing O'Dwyer was right. They were outgunned. Their only hope was that Durgan's men, seeing that Tenniel was dead, would see no profit in killing them. Whatever deal they had with him was now null and void.

For long seconds it seemed as if everyone was frozen in place.

Then a handful of guttural syllables shattered the silence. *Do it now* or *Let's go home*? Logan wondered.

One man lowered his weapon. Then another. Someone leaned forward and spat in Tenniel's direction. There was a laugh.

Then they were gone.

'Come on,' O'Dwyer said.

They stepped over Tenniel's body and followed O'Dwyer down the ladder. Logan's hands were slippery with sweat. Alex slipped on the last few rungs as her knees gave way and she fell in a heap. O'Dwyer hoisted her up.

'Sorry,' she said.

'Most people crap their pants,' O'Dwyer said. 'I thought you did well.'

Logan had so many questions, he couldn't work out what to ask first.

'How the fuck did you . . . where did . . . ?'

O'Dwyer grinned. 'You're not the only one who knows how to follow people.'

'But . . . why?'

'We're quits now, wouldn't you say?'

'Yes,' Logan said.

'That stuff you recorded on your phone?'

'I'll delete it.'

O'Dwyer nodded. 'You OK to drive?'

'We'll manage,' Logan said.

'Right, then.' O'Dwyer turned and walked off into the dark.

Logan and Alex started jogging towards the fence.

42

When they got back to the penthouse, Lucy was gone.

They checked every room, the closets, even under the beds. When Logan started going through the rooms for a second time, Alex grabbed his arm. 'She's not here. We have to think about where she'd go.'

Logan leaned against the wall and closed his eyes.

'Her old house, maybe. Or her sister's place.'

'Why would she go there?'

'I don't know – to confront her?'

'Her house more likely,' Alex said, her hand still on his arm.

'I should never have left her,' Logan said, shaking his head.

Alex gripped him harder. 'Focus on what we have to do now.'

Logan opened his eyes. 'OK. You go to the house.' He pulled out his phone. 'I'll text you the address.'

'OK. Are you going to stay here in case she comes back?'

Logan shook his head. 'No.'

He went to the front door and opened it.

'Where are you going?' Alex said.

He didn't answer.

He made it to the bridge in twenty minutes, abandoning the car on a double yellow. As he sprinted across the road a car swerved out of his way, blasting its horn. When he got to the spot, he couldn't see anyone. He felt a mixture of relief and terror. Had he got there before her? Or was he too late? He pulled out his phone. Alex hadn't called. Lucy wasn't at the house.

He leaned over the parapet and looked into the water, ready to dive in. All he could see was the reflection of the lights on the bridge, shimmering in oily pools. Part of him wanted to dive in anyway, in case she was there somewhere, just under the surface, but he knew it was madness. But he couldn't just stand there, staring into the darkness either. He had to do something.

He stood up straighter and took a breath of the cool air, smelling the water.

Think.

Where else would she go? What hadn't he thought of? Should they just have searched the streets around the penthouse? Maybe she was huddled in a doorway somewhere fifty feet away. The idea gnawed at him, causing him almost physical pain.

'*Lucy!*' he shouted, spinning around.

That was when he saw it.

On the stone flags, tucked in at the bottom of the railing:

the paperweight with the flower. He bent to pick it up and a piece of paper was caught by the breeze. He snatched it before it could blow away.

Dear Logan,

I'm sorry. You did your best. No one else could have done what you did for me. And I've never wanted anything as much as I want to be with you, to try and start again, to be myself again. But in the end I realized it was just a dream, a lovely dream. It could never come true. I don't know who I am any more. She put too much bad stuff in my head. And it's still there. I can feel it. It's like I'm carrying a bomb around inside me. One day, I know, something will trigger it and it'll go off. I couldn't bear that, starting a life together and knowing that was going to happen someday, when we were happy. So I have to do it now. Can you understand that? I'm so sorry. I love you.

Lucy

After a time, he read it again. Then he turned and looked down into the water. He stayed there, looking, for a long time.

Some time later, he wasn't sure when, but it was light, he found himself back in the car, one of the back wheels still on the pavement and the bonnet sticking out into the road. He was sitting in the driver's seat, holding the paperweight in his hand. Alex was there. He could feel her holding onto him. She was speaking, or trying to, her voice breaking, but he couldn't make out any of the words. He wondered why he had left the bridge, why he hadn't just let himself slip down into the blackness to be with her. There must have been something he had to do first. He tried to think and the image of a woman's face came into his mind and he realized what it was. He pulled out his phone without letting go of the paperweight and pressed a number.

'O'Dwyer.'

'It's Logan.'

'Do you know what time it is?'

'No.'

Logan's voice sounded as if it was coming from somewhere very far away.

'Is everything OK?'

'I need you to do something for me.'

'I thought we were quits.'

'We are.'

'Look . . .' O'Dwyer began. Then he stopped.

He listened to the silence on the other end of the phone.

'OK,' he said. 'Tell me the name.'

Acknowledgements

I would like to thank, Luigi, Wayne, Alex and Bill for all their hard work and patience. I know this isn't an easy or traditional process for you all!

My continued thanks and appreciation go out to my former department at Thames House. I will never break my oath to you.

Seller Vigilat